ALL THE STARS IN THE DAYLIGHT SKY

MAYA MACGREGOR

ASTRA YOUNG READERS
AN IMPRINT OF ASTRA BOOKS FOR YOUNG READERS
New York

Astra Young Readers
An imprint of Astra Books for Young Readers, a division of Astra Publishing House
astrapublishinghouse.com
Printed in the United States of America

ISBN: 978-1-6626-2098-0 (hc)
ISBN: 978-1-6626-2097-3 (eBook)

Library of Congress Control Number: 2024932086

First edition

10 9 8 7 6 5 4 3 2 1

Design by Anahid Hamparian
The text is set in Minion Pro Regular.
The titles are set in Belda.

Dham dhachaigh is dham choimhearsnachd Ghàidhlig, airson a' ghaoil a thug sibh dhomh agus airson nam freumhan a chuir mi nur measg. Cuimhnichibh cò leis a tha sibh.

Agus dham phàrantan uile. Gaol oirbh.

To my home and my Gaelic community, for the love you've all given me and for the roots I've planted in your midst. Remember where you came from.

And for all my parents. I love you.

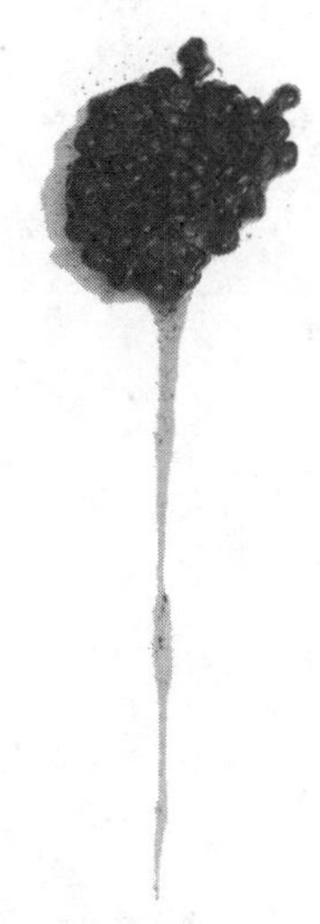

ONE

I don't think my mums will actually kill me, but from the look on Mam's face—and Mum beside her, nearly apoplectic and splotchy red—they haven't entirely decided against it.

"Lily Cameron Smith," Mam says. Her Glaswegian accent always comes out stronger when she's raging and, considering she's usually the calm one, she's *raging*. "If you walk out that door—"

"What, you'll make me walk through it again but with all my luggage?" The words, for once, snap past my lips faster than I expect. "Low blow, Mam, with the full name. Want to tell me I'm the selfish one again while you're at it?"

"Cam." The warning in Mum's own voice is all too clear, but I am so far past caring at this point.

In the midst of the barbs flinging back and forth through the air, Granaidh is in the kitchen, humming a Gaelic set of puirt-a-beul as she makes a bannock from her wheelchair, pointedly ignoring the other two generations inhabiting her house and polluting her living room with yet another row.

I can feel my words slipping away from me, and I push past both my mums and through the kitchen.

“Duilich, a seanmhair.” I apologise to Granaidh, and she just waves one hand at me.

Between my crap Gaelic and my rapidly receding verbal abilities in general, I can’t say much more than that, and though I can hear Mam spluttering behind me, I shove my feet into the only shoes by the back door—a pair of wellies one size too big—and throw the door open.

“Let her go,” Mum mutters behind me, loud enough for me to hear. “You both need to cool off.”

For some reason, that makes me angrier.

Without looking back, I fumble with the glass door and shut both it and the wooden one behind me, careful not to slam them even though I am desperate to do *something* loud.

I do let out a sound somewhere between an *ugh* and a yell as I march away from the house. The air is cool with a steady breeze, and though it’s late, it’s not anywhere near dark yet, not at nine at night in the Scottish Highlands. The sun’s still up for now, though the second I hit the old track into the woods, the warmth leaches from the air, embracing me with the cool, mossy damp of the forest.

Dad would never let me get away with walking out in the middle of a row, but Dad also lives in Texas, where one teen kid perceived as a girl runs a lot higher risk of danger at night. The thought sours me even more, since the entire reason I’m in Ballinacollie and not Austin is because of pure, American daylight violence.

I stomp one foot in a puddle as if it will help.

My mums’ words still bounce around inside my head. I shouldn’t have had to remind them that they *promised* no more moves. They promised last year when we moved to Ballinacollie to stay with Granaidh that we wouldn’t move again. Not again.

The path is muddy beneath my wellies, but I don’t care. I’ve never walked out of the house in the middle of a row before, and a week after my eighteenth birthday seems like a fine time to start. The days are shortening but still long, still stretching into that perpetual summer gloaming that holds the sun close into the late hours of night this time of year in the Gàidhealtachd, but thankfully the midgies don’t like the breeze.

Another hundred yards, and I still feel like I might explode. Anger is one feeling I recognise when I feel it without the help of the feelings wheel my therapist, Lindy, gave me. That said, usually I don't feel so lightheaded I'm afraid of actually passing out.

My blood pressure feels like it's about to send me into cardiac arrest.

It's just—another move. Another move. My *seventh* new school since nursery, the others spread all over Scotland and the southern United States because when joint custody makes you a human ping-pong ball with the Atlantic Ocean as the net, that's what happens when exactly zero of your three parents can manage to sit still for twelve months together. And now the mums are talking about uprooting me again before the school year has even started?

It's actually a miracle I haven't been at Oban's schools before now, since kids come all the way from the south half of the Isle of Mull and beyond, and I feel like that casts a wide enough shadow to cover some of our bouncing around Scotland.

I didn't mean it when I told my mums I'd rather die than move again. At least I don't think I did. This is my last year. I should be ready to cram for my Highers and going to parties and trying to get into uni, but as ever, all I'm really going to manage is to be the proverbial sore thumb of Oban High School—or wherever, if we really do move again. I'm a year older than literally all my peers since all the moves thoroughly confused my progression through any and all curricula. I don't act like my peers, I don't sound like my peers, and considering the reason ping-pong-ball me got swatted back to the east side of the Atlantic one final time, I'm pretty sure that I'm the only one who's had to watch a friend die.

I aim a weak kick at a thistle that doesn't deserve it. The path I'm on is an easy loop, back to a small waterfall in the river that gives the village to the north its name. Inverinan, an easy jump from Ballinacollie on the west shores of Loch Awe.

I'm still getting to know the place, despite visiting Granaidh often enough throughout my life. The forest is quiet, only a few birds I can't identify breaking the silence any more than the light wind. Whenever I come home from Texas, I'm always struck by the purity of the Scottish *green*. Even in the dimming evening light with the sun out of view behind the hill, the green is lush and alive. Moss covers everything—rocks, fallen logs, living trees, everything. Ferns and bracken grow where they can, and before too long, the trail stops being muddy and becomes grassy.

I keep walking, feet slipping in the too-large wellies.

Slowly, as if the mere presence of that living colour has healing powers, my heartbeat returns to normal, and the throbbing in my head and tightness in my chest release their grip.

I inhale deeply through my nose, pushing my lungs to capacity. It makes me feel like I could float away, up the hill and through the canopy of oak and alder and ash, into that sky above where only a few clouds are visible through the leaves.

The only thing I don't like about a Scottish summer is that I so seldom can see stars.

The tension in my body slowly releases. It feels like that first sip of cool water when you're feverish, the release of removing a restrictive piece of clothing.

Droplets of dew or drizzle still linger on the ferns around me, and they seem otherworldly, pale and silent where they lie.

Just looking around seems to chase some of the haze of rage from my mind.

Part of me wonders why this row is what did it. It's not like the mums and I never fight—we fight heaps. My autism diagnosis last year came as a shock to Mum (but not to Mam), and even though they know now why I don't answer sometimes when I'm upset and why I get so distressed when they interrupt me, they're still learning.

And part of me also is starting to understand that maybe some of it is guilt. Guilt that they have forced me through so many changes, guilt at hearing I have complex trauma, guilt that the changes only amplified said trauma.

My breath explodes out of me, and I stop walking for a second, eyes fixed on a ring of enormous, red-brown mushrooms without really seeing them.

My brain is still processing the row. I can hear Mam saying "We need to talk" all over again. I can feel myself shutting down all over again. I can see Mum's face, weary and resigned, all over again.

Belatedly, it hits me that maybe this was them trying to prepare me for a possibility rather than a certainty of another move. Maybe this was them *trying*, full stop.

Shaking myself, I march onward again, avoiding the mushrooms.

I walk for a long time. I don't have my mobile, and my Fitbit is charging, so I've no idea what time it is or how long I've been moving. Though the evening is still and the forest serene, I've got a gale worthy of midwinter raging in my skull.

The burble of water in the burn reaches my ears after a while. I'm deep in the forest now, and I know this track meets up with a trail near Inverinan, but I thought I would see it by now. My skin still feels buzzy from the adrenaline of the row—I hate confrontation. I probably missed the junction.

Strangely, the path under my feet is mostly flat stones instead of packed dirt. I glance back the way I came. I don't think I'm lost.

It's sort of impossible to be *really* lost here. If I go downhill, eventually I'll hit Loch Awe or, if I've managed to somehow get prodigiously turned around, the other loch, Loch Avich.

I stop moving again, disconcerted.

The forest feels different here, as if it's cut off from the twenty-first century. I think of those famous books where the main character falls back in time, and I snort. No, thank you. I'd be burned at the stake.

The path curves around a steeper section of the hill, and after a moment of hesitation, I follow.

The trees seem like they have grown taller. Mum's a horticulturist and is always talking about indigenous trees, how the ruling class planted Sitka spruce and other non-native species that eclipsed the old trees both passively and violently when the landowners uprooted trees and Gaels alike in favour of more profitable sheep.

No, thank you indeed—I do not want to go back in time.

People forget the Gàidhealtachd used to be widely settled when they talk about "rewilding" our highlands and islands. Mum and Granaidh both have feelings about that.

But I'm still in the twenty-first century, and there are no Sitkas here. No sheep, either. Oak and sycamore, birch and ash and hazel, a rowan here and there—all trees that belong, so I can't tell why I feel so suddenly unsettled among them.

The path is not at all how I remember it, not at all what it was even at the beginning of my walk. The stones seem almost deliberate, the moss growing on either side of the path almost like a vibrant kerb. Purposeful. Cultivated.

As I continue on, something strikes me that chases away the last of my anger.

I know I don't belong anywhere. I know I won't belong at Oban High School when we start up. But *here* here, this place? It feels like home.

It feels like mine.

I relax into that feeling, basking in it. My fingers unfurl from the tight claws I've been holding this whole time, and my hands give a happy, unstifled flap. It feels good to let my body do what it wants. I bounce lightly on my toes, bending my knees, feeling the breeze trickle through my outstretched fingers.

It's not just that I don't want to move again. It's that I don't want to *leave*.

Maybe it's the way this forest smells, the thick, heady scent of peaty loam beneath my feet or the damp bark of trees that make me shrink into insignificance. I stop walking again and reach out a hand to touch the trunk of an enormous oak. Darach, in Gaelic.

Sometimes when Granaidh sings, I think I should understand her. I've been in and out of Gaelic medium whenever I've been in Scottish schools, but I'm far from fluent, and Granaidh's Gaelic was learnt at her own mother's knee. Even our village's name, Ballinacollie, is Gaelic. Baile na Coille—village of the forest.

I am suddenly rooted to my spot like the oak under my palm, its bark rough and moist, covered in moss and lichens.

I don't want to leave.

The thought hits me with such force this time that my chest heaves with a sob, and I make a helpless sound that bursts out from my lips, inelegant and raw in the gloaming.

My therapist says some autistic people have crying meltdowns. Some autistics melt down explosively with yelling and striking arms; others of us implode. I'm the latter.

I'm teetering on the edge of this event horizon, the row, the confusion of this homesickness for the very place I'm standing, the smell of Granaidh's bannock-making, the echo of her puirt. All of it has poured into me with no outlet, and it's still here, pushing at my edges even as it paradoxically sucks me into it like a black hole.

Sometimes it helps me to turn my meltdowns explosive, to punch a pillow or my leg as hard as I can like a pressure valve releasing the force of steam. But there is nothing here that deserves my violence, not even me.

This is also something I'm learning from my therapist.

The sky is growing at once darker and lighter in that strange, sunset way. The deep blue of the day gives way to a word that makes most sense to me in Gaelic, liath, a colour that describes its desaturation just as much as its hue. Even as the light fades to night, it hovers like a mist across the blue, turning it pale and hovering between jade and agate and smoke.

I should go home.

But I'm not ready to leave this newfound truth yet. It frightens me to feel like this is where I am supposed to be.

It's because of that I take a few more steps forward, winding through the trees on this path.

In the gathering shadows, I'm almost upon it before I see the door.

TWO

It is a door, here in the middle of the forest.

It appears from one zigzag in the winding path to the next, looking like it was not carved but instead grown.

It has a hole in the centre of it where a window might be if it were on someone's house, but I am in the middle of the woods.

The door stands between two trees. Yews, I think. The path leads directly under it.

I remember a meme circulating that resurfaces every year or so of someone's gay uncles who made a fairy door and charmed the entirety of the internet both for that and the fact that they wear matching clothes every day. This looks kind of like that.

On impulse, I walk up to it. I want to poke my arm through it, and since I'm alone in the woods in the middle of nowhere, I do exactly that.

If I'm expecting something to happen, I'm disappointed straight away when nothing does. It's a bit silly. I stand here for a long moment, one hand through the bizarre forest door, amusement at myself chasing away some of the heaviness of the night so far.

I see movement through the hole a split second before something grasps my hand, shakes firmly once, and I jerk my arm back so fast I go stumbling backward, windmilling to keep my balance as my startled yelp echoes through the trees. Electricity zings from my palm to my shoulder, leaving me buzzing even through the movement of air my arms create with my precarious flailing.

"Bugger, sorry," a voice calls out. "I thought you were—never mind."

The person who opens the door and pokes their head around the edge of it looks every inch as mortified as I feel. They close the door behind them, and though it makes no sound, every vertebra along my spine seems to fall in line at once.

My mouth is moving—I can feel it—but I can't seem to get words out around the feeling of my heart suddenly hogging all the space in my chest.

When I still don't manage to make any words a moment later, they come closer, hands in the air as if to try and communicate they're not a threat, and I can see them more clearly.

"Ezra. Again, sorry. Erm . . . my pronouns are they/them." They peer at me as if bracing for impact. Their introduction has a flavour of practiced recitation, like they need to get it out of the way as soon as possible.

I clear my throat and let out a shaky breath, adjusting my shoulders where I think my sudden movement might have pulled something.

"I'm Cam," I say, finding my words at last. "She/her?"

I wait for the inevitable "you don't sound [insert locality or nation here]" or the comment on my name, which is the other usual option.

But neither comes.

"Is that a question?" Ezra asks, nonplussed.

I crack a smile. "I honestly don't know at this point. Can't be bothered to care about my own pronouns, but the rest of it . . ."

I give a waggle of my right hand, vaguely indicating the world around us.

"Guess I'm not used to strangers leading with their pronouns," I say after a beat. "But then again, I did just move back here from Texas."

Ezra raises an eyebrow at that, but they don't ask why I don't sound Texan. To my surprise, a certain amount of relief paints their face, though they look around me as if expecting someone else to pop out from behind a tree. They open their mouth to say something, then frown and shut it again. It's a nice mouth, which is a thought I'm not prepared to deal with.

Ezra is nice looking in general. Tall and looks more like they'd be found climbing rocks than under the bright lights of a Texan football stadium. I think their hair is dark, but with the sun down now, everything looks darker. Their hair is shortish and wavy, falling a little into their face.

"Were you waiting for someone?" I ask when the silence drags out. I am not usually the chattier one.

"What?" Ezra's hand falls to their side. "Oh. I thought I was, but it seems I was wrong."

I don't know what to say to that.

"Sorry I grabbed your hand." In the space of a heartbeat, their demeanour has shifted, and I see a flash of teeth as they grin. "What are you doing out in the woods?"

"It's okay. And I was fleeing parental drama," I say slowly. "You?"

"Fleeing political drama," Ezra says with another grin.

"You hear they want to have the Royal National Mòd in Oban again or something?" I ask dryly, and then at their blank look, explain hastily. "Annual Gaelic music thing. My gran's the Gaelic reader for the choir in . . . ah. Never mind."

I thought most people around here knew what a mòd was, but maybe not.

This might be the most awkward conversation I've ever fallen into, but if I had to have it with someone, another non-binary person in the literal wild is a good choice.

"A bheil Gàidhlig agad?" Ezra asks then—do I speak Gaelic—and I jump.

"Erm . . . beagan." I feel my cheeks flame into a blush. "My gran's a native speaker, but Mum never really learned to fluency, and I've moved around a lot, so I can understand it better than I speak it, but—"

I'm babbling now, but thankfully, they cut me off.

"Na gabh dragh." Ezra tells me not to worry with a smile I think might be meant to reassure me.

But just as my anxiety tries to relax, Ezra glances over their shoulder, back toward the door. I don't see anything there, but when they turn to look back at me, their face has changed again, so quickly I'm thrown off my guard all over again.

"You should go now," Ezra says quietly, and there is urgency in their voice that immediately makes my anxiety come flooding back with a tinny taste in my mouth.

I can't find the words to ask why. There's a light in their hand suddenly—the torch on their mobile maybe. It glints off their hair with an iridescent shimmer like a raven's wing in sunlight, and for a moment I can't move, transfixed by the sudden flash of colour and the intensity in Ezra's gaze.

"Cam," Ezra insists, voice gentle. "It was very nice to meet you. But you need to go. Now."

Fear flares for no reason, and scrambling backward, I turn and run.

I don't know how long I have been running. We have a treadmill, and I run on it every day, but I'm not used to running in the woods and definitely not used to running in wellies.

When I stop, it's because the rubber boots feel like they're sucking my feet into them with every step, and the combination of the feeling of it and the hollowed-out tyre sound has my teeth vibrating in my jaw. I skid to a panting halt in the falling dark.

Did I hit my head or something? The bizarre conversation with Ezra feels like a dream, just like reaching my hand through that hole in the door felt like a dream. I can't see Loch Awe through the trees, but that's not much of a surprise. I'm still on the path. I should just keep following it.

I feel like I've lost time again.

That happened a lot in the pandemic, but it got worse for me in the years after it. More moves, more schools, and then the last one. My therapist says grief and trauma can do that. Our brain forgets things to protect itself. She tells me that it's a defence mechanism. Right now I can't tell if I really lost time or what just happened. I don't even know if Ezra was real.

I also don't know where I am.

The path by my house is muddy, dirt packed with gravel, used mostly by local sheep when my family's not walking on it. The sheep usually cut downhill away from the thickest parts of the forest to graze. This path is nothing like that. Nothing here looks familiar.

It's getting dark and very quiet.

I am starting to wish I hadn't left my phone in the house.

With the encroaching darkness, I can't tell if anything even looks familiar. A few stars dot the sky, the brighter ones that can compete with the summer night, shimmering and flickering. At least if I am stuck out here till dawn, it won't be horribly long—it starts getting light again around four. The mums will still be *furious*.

A flash of guilt accompanies that knowledge. As much as we bicker, we are pretty close for the most part. It's been worse since I came back this time, but I don't think that's really about . . . us. I think it's more about Paul.

I don't want to think about Paul. Not when I'm lost and alone in the woods in the dark. It doesn't matter that this scenario is about as far away from a burning Texan summer afternoon as you can get—if I think about him, I will not be able to function to get home.

I walk long enough that my feet are starting to form blisters inside my wellies, especially since the boots are too big. I walk long enough that dread starts to pool in my stomach because I should have gotten out of the woods by now.

At least it's not raining.

The night's chill creeps up on me, though. Granaidh always says there's no such thing as bad weather, only the wrong clothes. I think she's probably right, and I'm wearing the wrong clothes. The weather is, by all accounts, fantastic for the west coast of Scotland.

There's a large boulder not far from me, sitting with the trunk of a dead snag leaning over it, the roots half-exposed where moss has already crept into the hole left behind.

I have to jump a little to sit on the rock, and the moment my weight is off my legs, I let out a sigh of extreme relief. My calves are tight and burning from running, and I think one of the blisters on my foot has already burst if the sting on top of my big toe knuckle is any indication. It's colder the second I stop moving, too. My perspiration evaporates quickly, leaving me shivering. I try to ignore it, instead flexing my feet to stretch my calves and pointing my toes as far as the wellies will allow. I desperately want to take off the rubber boots, but if I do, I'm never going to want to put them back on.

So this is maybe not my best teenage rebellion. In my defence, it's my first big one. I'm a compulsive rule follower and anxious perfectionist. Control issues, I guess. Something-something controlling what you can when everything else is out of control.

The thought is a good reminder. I maybe can't go back in time and not storm out of the house in a rage, but I can sit on this rock and get my bearings.

The worst thing in these woods is probably a surprised badger or angry deer, and I doubt the chances of running into either are very good. I'm not quite as brave as I sound, though. I like the dark in my room fine at night with my weighted blanket and eye mask with white noise (rain or waves). I'm less convinced sitting in the woods in the dark all alone.

My feet are throbbing in time with my pulse. I can already feel them growing hot, which is going to become unbearable really fast.

When a tinkling laugh breaks the silence a moment later, though, I *wish* for the aloneness again, feet momentarily forgotten.

I wonder if I'm just hearing things. An owl, maybe. Seagull? We get those here since the sea's just the other side of the hills.

But when the laughter comes again, joined by a second voice this time, the futile hope for a more fowlesque explanation is crushed. Neither of the voices sounds like Ezra's, not that I heard them laugh. Ezra's intensity when they told me to go still feels heavy, pressing at me. Maybe they were expecting a jealous partner. Who knows what people do around these parts when they want to hook up?

The voices sound young, playful. Not younger-than-me young, but peers. Curiosity pulls me onward. Maybe it's that I don't know how to get home. Maybe it's that indulging a second whim seems better than my arse getting cold on a damp rock. Maybe I'm hoping to see Ezra again. It doesn't matter if it's one or all of the above.

My sore feet take me up the hill, through the bracken, toward the west where the last smudge of the sunset lingers on the horizon.

As I pick my way up the hill, the sounds of talking and light laughter grow stronger, mellifluous and compelling. My dad used to take me hunting, and without thinking about it, I fall into the careful rhythm of rolling footsteps, even in wellies able to muffle my sounds. The hill isn't very tall. When I crest it, I find myself peering into a cleft of a clearing almost too small to be called a gully. Far too small to be a glen. There's a small burn running down the middle of it, which I note—I can follow that down to the loch if I need to.

The clearing is full of rowans. I recognise them immediately because when we were staying in Bearsden a few years ago, before my last, ill-fated stint with Dad, a rowan's roots were in the way of Mum's planned geranium patch, but she refused to remove the tree. They don't grow that tall usually, not like an oak or a sycamore, but they're noticeable mostly for their leaves, easily identifiable by the way they branch off their twigs on either side, two lines of parallel, jagged-edged leaves that fan out in a frond, interspersed with clusters of white flowers that turn into berries that ripen into deep, shining crimson in late summer as it turns to autumn. The ones around Granaidh's house all have clusters of red hanging heavily, and the birds have been feasting.

These are only just flowered, which is bizarre.

There is a soft, golden glow emanating from the clearing, and fireflies wink amid the rowan leaves.

Except we don't have fireflies in Scotland.

The two people in the clearing laugh again, and another voice calls out quietly from not far away. A third person strolls toward them out of the denser forest beyond.

"Any sign?" the newcomer asks.

"Ah, there she is," says one of the others, glancing in the young woman's direction. "We were wondering when you'd turn up. Or if."

Despite the light, I can only barely make them out. Their voices are melodious, clear enough to hear without straining my ears, but though I can guess that the strangers are dark-haired like Ezra—not at all uncommon in Scotland—I can't make out their features. It's like looking at them through mist or water.

"You didn't answer my question," says the new girl.

"No sign," says the one who's been silent till now. The third voice is deeper, a little gruff. "But Ealasaid said you were the one keeping track."

Despite the haze over the trio, from the way New Girl and Ealasaid turn their heads sharply to look at each other, I don't think either of them are happy with this statement.

"It takes three, and we've got three," says New Girl. "If there's no sign, we've got time."

More voices sound through the clearing, and the new girl falls silent.

"Smiles, everyone," says Ealasaid, and the three of them break apart just as another four people move into the clearing.

They walk so smoothly, it's like they're gliding. I edge closer to the crest of the hill as if the six inches or so will make my eyes able to make sense of what I'm seeing.

A hand claps over my mouth, and before I can so much as gasp, I'm jerked backward into the bracken and know nothing.

THREE

The first thing I hear is voices arguing. Neither are familiar—they're not the voices I heard in the clearing. Despite the fog in my head, I can't help but wonder just how many people are swarming over the hills of Loch Awe in the middle of the night.

"I have no idea who she is. She was spying on Ealasaid and the others, and that was reason enough to get her out of there before she ended up flayed."

It takes me a moment to realise this speaker is talking about me.

"Daibhidh. She's *mortal*."

There is a silence.

I must have hit my head. Maybe when I stormed out of the house, I fell down the hill and bonked my skull on a tree. That would explain the fireflies and the random beautiful stranger grabbing my hand through a hole in a door in the middle of the woods—and the glowing people with no faces.

But not the waking up from getting knocked unconscious by actual human beings.

The silence stretches on for another moment before I hear a heaving sigh and a "you've got to be kidding me" from the guy I presume is Daibhidh.

"She's also awake and listening to us now," says the other speaker flatly. "So we need to figure out what to do."

"There's nothing for *us* to figure out, a ghràidh," Daibhidh says, and his voice has taken on a tinge of sadness.

"You can open your eyes," says the other speaker. To me, I presume. "I'm Deirdre."

I open my eyes. From the throbbing in my blistered feet, I'm not actually dreaming. The sky is as full dark as it's going to get, which means it has to be around two in the morning by now. The mums are going to flay me themselves if these people don't.

They don't say anything while I push myself slowly to a sitting position, my heart strangely quiet in my chest.

Stars are bright white and brilliant across the sky, and there is little other light, only a soft glow around Daibhidh and this other person that I can't pinpoint.

I can at least see these people more clearly. Daibhidh is short and sort of stocky, dense in the way some men get where they look like they'd sink if you dropped them in water. His dark hair is long, though, pulled back from his face as if he couldn't be arsed to do anything else with it, and one piece keeps falling down over his forehead where he doggedly keeps pushing it back behind his ear. Deirdre is . . . impressive. She's got a head's height over Daibhidh, and my first thought is that I'd put my money on her if the two of them were to fistfight, despite Daibhidh being built like a brick. Deirdre's got to be six feet tall, though I can't really be sure from where I'm sitting on the ground.

Deirdre watches me with pursed lips. Her own hair is also dark, perfect waves parted right down the middle. She's wearing tweed trousers with leather boots that come up to her knees and a white shirt tucked in under a matching tweed waistcoat that she clearly had tailored to fit her curved, muscled body. When I just keep staring at her, she raises one hand and twitches a finger upward sharply.

I scramble to my feet. My head doesn't hurt. Nothing really hurts except for the bits that did before I passed out. I'm not even sure why I lost consciousness at all.

Part of my mind is screeching in the background that I am being denser than Daibhidh looks, just bedrock straight through my perfectly smooth brain, because there is clearly something not normal going on here.

"I'm Cam," I make myself say. "I didn't mean to . . . spy."

"Huh," says Deirdre. "She's telling the truth."

"That is actually a relief," Daibhidh mutters. "Though it doesn't change anything."

"You can talk *to* me, you know," I say bluntly, though the moment it's out of my mouth, I doubt my own wisdom.

"Very well," Deirdre says, interlacing her fingers in front of her. "If you didn't mean to spy, why were you eavesdropping?"

"I was trying to get home," I tell her. "I went for a walk and got lost, I guess. Then I heard voices and followed them."

"Also the truth." Deirdre watches me thoughtfully, chewing on the right side of one full lip.

I can't tell where the light is coming from. I don't see a lantern or a fire or phone or anything; I can just *see* somehow.

"You keep saying that like you can tell the difference," I say, unnerved.

"I can," the young woman answers blithely.

I say young, but I can't put an age to Deirdre or Daibhidh—he could be twenty or fifty, and so could she. Their faces are unlined, one moment full of the blush of youth, the next pensive and wearier, wiser.

I swallow. The skin on the sides of my neck is tingling the way ASMR feels but not. *That* usually starts at the top of my head. This just hovers.

After a moment, Daibhidh sighs. "Curiosity killed the cat."

"But satisfaction brought it back," I blurt out before I can process that all signs point to me being the dead curious cat.

Deirdre cracks a smile. "I like her."

Now that I am standing, I am certain she is over six feet tall, and I think I will choose to be relieved that the giant woman likes me rather than wanting to crush me to death, because I think she could.

"Can I go now?" I ask when neither of them says anything else. The mums are going to be shitting bricks.

But this time, it's Deirdre who sighs. "I'm afraid not, pet."

A flood of adrenaline washes over me. Moments like this are familiar—not the exact circumstances, but my reaction to stress. I can be calm, sanguine, fine. Right up until the moment I'm not.

All at once, the strangeness hits me. Lights in the forest. A door to nowhere. People that glow, faces swimming in secrecy. Walking in circles and unable to find the path home. Something is very wrong—my calibration of wrongness has been off since the pandemic and worse since the lake. Granaidh used to talk about the sionnachain, the will-o'-the-wisps, but I never thought *I* would see them. Hear them. Whichever sense fits.

When I don't say anything—because I can't—Deirdre gives me a sympathetic look.

"You've frightened her," Daibhidh mutters.

"Yes," the tall woman agrees. She sighs again, then goes on. "I can't tell you I won't hurt you, Cam. I don't make promises I can't be certain I'll keep, which is to say I don't make promises."

I want to ask why I can't leave, but my mouth won't make words.

"You're sensitive," Deirdre says, as if explaining despite my failure to voice the question. "You shouldn't have been able to see what you saw—the people you were spying on took measures to avoid just that."

"What are the odds?" Daibhidh says under his breath.

I have no idea what they're talking about.

"Slim to none but not zero," Deirdre answers, though I think Daibhidh's question was rhetorical. "Nevertheless, here we are. You're fortunate we're the ones who found you spying."

I wasn't spying. I can't make the sounds come out of my mouth, but I want to insist.

"Intentional or not," Deirdre goes on, again as if she heard me anyway. "You're fortunate. If it had been the others"—she breaks off when Daibhidh snorts as if something is funny—"you would already be dead."

She looks . . . sad. I think. I'm not always good at telling what someone is feeling from their face.

"You've a choice to make, kid," Daibhidh says. He looks at Deirdre as if she's going too slow for his liking. "It's not a good choice, but it's yours."

I can hear the sound of my heartbeat. The breeze has died at some point in the night, and there is nothing but the stillness and the starry expanse above us, broken by the dark silhouettes of trees.

They are both quiet, waiting.

"What choice?" I ask finally, my voice harsh.

I swallow, but my throat is dry. It doesn't help, just makes me feel claustrophobic. Sticky. My feet are hot, too hot, and like the rest of me, they are reaching the tipping point between *fine* and *not fine*.

Deirdre's face softens, and in a heartbeat, she's at my side, guiding me to sit on something I didn't see before. I don't see it now, just feel it supporting me. At least it's not damp. She kneels on one knee, her hands hovering by one of my feet.

"May I?" she asks.

I give a helpless nod, and she deftly removes one boot, then the other, dropping them at my feet.

The socks follow with a slight ripping sting as the damp fabric pulls away from burst blisters it fused to with drying lymph.

But the relief is immediate. Cool air bathes my skin, and I release a big breath with the sensory overload that, a moment ago, was about to topple me.

When Deirdre is satisfied I'm not about to pass out or melt down, she gives me a perfunctory nod and stands again, looking at Daibhidh, who motions her onward and mutters, "Siuthad, ma-tà."

The Gaelic is such a surprise that I just stare at him for a long moment, but he's just told Deirdre to go on, then, and she does.

"I've found in these rare cases it is best to be blunt," Deirdre says to me, standing just far enough away that she doesn't loom over me. "Magic is real, the Sìthichean are real, you've stumbled upon us, and mortals who stumble upon the Sìthichean cannot live. We have exactly two laws—"

Daibhidh snorts at this. "One, really."

For a moment I think she might kill him instead of me, but she rolls her eyes, and again I am unnerved by my inability to put an age to her. From her expression to the air of pure exasperation, she wouldn't be out of place in a high school classroom.

"He's wrong, but for all intents and purposes this evening, aye. One law that matters to you right now." Deirdre interlaces her fingers in front of her again. "That law is that mortals who find out about us have to die."

"So you're going to kill me," I say. My head feels light, like I might float away.

The thought is ludicrous. I shouldn't believe it. I'm sitting barefoot on a hill in the forest in the middle of the night with two people who say they're going to kill me in spite of so far being nothing but nice.

"That bit is up to you," Deirdre says. "That's the choice. Your choice. Perhaps you've heard we like to make bargains."

I look at her, helpless. Of course I've heard that.

I've also heard about all the hapless fools who try to escape those bargains. This Deirdre is named for a woman who lived precisely that sort of tragedy.

"If I want to live, what do I have to do?" My voice is monotone in that way it gets when there is too much emotion and not enough of my brain's bandwidth available to wrestle it into a mask.

Deirdre looks down at me, and now I can tell where the light is coming from. It's coming from her—and Daibhidh. It clings to them, growing stronger as I watch. Her eyes, so dark they're almost black against the night, take on a golden light like embers smouldering in the peat. She could no longer blend in anywhere on this planet.

"Very simply," she says, "you have to become one of us."

FOUR

"I don't know what that means," I blurt out.

It's the stupidest thing I could possibly say, because of course I don't.

There is a flutter and a rush of air before I know what's happening, and Daibhidh is gone, leaving Deirdre simply glancing off to her left for a moment before returning her gaze to me.

"Of course," she murmurs. I don't know if she's responding to me or remarking on Daibhidh's disappearance.

This time the silence is dreadful. It makes me itch until I can no longer just sit down with my feet in the cool moss.

I get to my feet, though my legs shake—actually shake—and I wobble before righting myself.

"The latter," Deirdre says. "He has no stomach for death. I'm afraid I don't either, but he has left me no choice, pending your own."

"If you don't want to kill me, why would you?" I don't expect the question to change my reality, but I have to ask. "You just . . . offer this choice to every mortal who finds out about you? Even by accident?"

Her fingers still interlaced in front of her, unmoving, Deirdre shifts her weight. "We abide by the bargains and promises we make, and we are bound by them. This one in particular is one we cannot break. As for the second question, usually the mortals are dead before there's any choice to be had. Were it not for Daibhidh plucking you out of the hornet's nest, that would have been your fate."

My words, having deserted me for much of the night, now pour past my lips in a flurry.

"What does becoming one of you mean for me?" The rest of what she said is irrelevant right now, and I don't like that she has changed the subject. "How does that even work? What would happen? Does it hurt?"

"It means you will be bound by our bargains and benefit from our many boons, but the price is higher than some wish to pay." Deirdre doesn't look at me so much as through me. "Mortals dream of immortality without considering the cost. As for how it works, that question is above my pay grade. You make your choice, and the bargain is struck. You either drop dead or join us."

Die and never see my mums again. Or live and . . . never see my mums again.

"Don't be maudlin," Deirdre says. "You're only half right."

"Will you stop reading my mind?" I burst out, but then my mind processes what she said. "Which half?"

"If you die, you'll never see your mums again. If you live, you can still see them." For the first time in a while, her lips quirk in a smile. "You *have* heard of changelings, haven't you? Not quite the same thing, but close enough for this example."

I blink. "Are all the stories true?"

"Hardly."

"What—what would change?" I ask.

The thing about this sort of bargain is that there is always a catch, right? That's the whole reason the Sìthichean are feared. Or used to be, before they got Mickey Moused.

"Others," she says. "We generally just go by the Others. And yes, there is always a catch. You will, if you choose to, see your family every day and never be able to tell them what you are. You may fall into danger—magic is powerful, beautiful, just as the sea is powerful and beautiful and will still drag you under to drown.

"You will never grow frail with age, but you will grow old. You will grow old and watch the world you know age and die. You will be bound by our geas, and you could one day find yourself in my shoes, staring down a frightened mortal you may be forced to kill."

Maybe this would be an easy choice for someone. She's right that humans do dream of immortality—the Holy Grail, the fountain of youth, Tìr nan Òg. Vampires and alchemy and everything in between.

But I don't want to live forever.

I don't want to be forced to kill anyone, not ever.

"Have you had to do this before?" I ask, my voice almost a rasp.

"Yes," she says simply.

I don't want to live forever, but I don't want my blood on Deirdre's hands.

I just met her. I don't know anything about her. But if she's right, if she and Daibhidh are right that they snatched me away from certain death at the hands of those other strangers—those other . . . Others, I guess—she's already saved my life once tonight.

And, of course, I think of Paul.

Paul was so excited to live.

I think of his blond hair, long enough that his very Texan family couldn't stop making remarks about it, but he kept growing it because fuck gender norms, right? He had long COVID and was one of those kids who seemed to have mild symptoms until he developed asthma in the later days of the pandemic. The vaccine helped, but he still got wheezy whenever he exerted himself.

But he was alive.

Strange to survive the pandemic and a mass shooter in Texas only to die of pandemic complications, because that's exactly what happened.

Years of thinking he was out of the woods, but turns out the stress response of an active shooter can trigger asthma symptoms. I didn't even see him go under the water of the lake. I was too busy swimming for the small cove of rock where I thought we'd be protected from the gunshots.

Shooter never even came close, really. Not to us, anyway.

The mums lost their shit. Dad didn't even fight them on it when they insisted on hauling my ping-pong-ball arse back over the Atlantic for me to finish high school here.

Paul wanted to live.

The entire reason I'm standing here right now is because he died instead.

I have a feeling Deirdre is watching this entire thought process play out. I can read nothing in her face, glowing more quietly now, but impassive, blank, like the surface of a lochan at dawn.

The sky is already lightening.

I know the mums feel guilty. Dad does too. And as angry as I get with them, I know they just want to keep me alive.

It's that thought that pushes me over the edge of the choice.

That fight, those words, that rage—that would be the last moment I had with them. Forever.

I'm shaking my head before I can manage any other kind of response.

I don't want to die.

"Okay," I say to Deirdre. "I want to live."

The relief on her face is recognisable even to me. Her entire impressive stature sags with it, just for an instant, and then she's standing before me again like Cruachan Beann, unmovable as the very mountain in the distance beyond the loch.

I feel woozy, like I might fall over. In those few short moments of making my decision, it's gotten even lighter. Birds are happily singing up the sun already somehow. But the stars, which had been fading with the oncoming dawn, are somehow more numerous and brighter. I blink at them, but the impression stays. They are no longer just white, but colours glimmer across the sky in pinpricks of light.

I shake myself and look back to Deirdre. "What now?"

"It's done," she says. Something flickers in her eyes like the shifting of the stars. "There will be more to speak of, but for now, go home."

"That's . . . it?" I gape at her. "No rules or warnings or—"

"You know the one rule, and it's one that is exceedingly difficult to break on purpose." Deirdre flashes her teeth at me, a smile that is more of a grimace, and as curious as I am, I don't dare ask how she knows. "The change is sudden . . . and gradual. Like the turning of the tide, in a way. Creeping by inches and then shifts out of reach, slipping away into the deep."

"What's going to happen to me?" I ask. I hate not knowing what to expect. Just like that, I'm about to tip over the not-okay line all over again.

"I wish I could tell you. It's different for everyone. That is the beauty of it—and the curse." Deirdre gives me a real smile, and it is brighter than the coming sun. "But there will be time for questions, and however afraid you are, this is one thing you need not fear. This choice is a terrible one, but the one gift with no barb is that your magic is *yours* and yours alone. It will shape itself to you. That is the truth of it. I won't lie and tell you this life you have chosen will not be dangerous. But remember there is always, always a choice. The true power is remembering that you are never powerless."

She grows even taller in that moment, her dark waves haloed by the lightening sky.

"We'll meet again, Cam." Deirdre meets my eyes, holding them longer than is comfortable for me—which isn't long at all.

Then, as suddenly as Daibhidh himself, she is gone, and I am alone on a familiar, muddy path, my bare feet in a puddle and my house visible through the trees.

My socks and wellies are nowhere to be seen.

FIVE

Everyone is in the kitchen when I walk through the back door, muddy bare feet scraped against the mat to the best of my ability.

The mums look exhausted, but Granaidh doesn't. She is contentedly sipping her tea, her shiny metal teapot within easy reach for only her, since she'll smack anyone's hand if they try to pour some for themselves.

"Madainn mhath, a ghràidh," she greets me as if I didn't just waltz in from the woods at arse-crack-of-dawn in the morning.

"Madainn mhath, a seanmhair," I say to her. "Mums."

"Nach do dh'innse mi dhuibh gum biodh i air ais?" Granaidh flaps the hinged metal lid on her teapot as she says it, closing it with a tinny *tink* and picking up the pot to pour herself some more tea.

Mum harrumphs—*didn't I tell yous she'd be back*—and though I know she understands, she glares at me and speaks in English. "Do you know what time it is?"

I glance at the microwave. "Ten past four."

Mam, sitting with both her hands flat on the vinyl tablecloth as if she doesn't trust herself to move them, opens her mouth, and I brace myself for getting told to mind my cheek the way I usually get when I answer something literally that's just supposed to hang there to scold me.

But it doesn't come. Instead, Mam looks over at Mum, and the two of them exchange a glance I can't interpret.

"We're staying here," Mam says after a long moment where all I hear is the clink of Granaidh's teaspoon as she stirs a mountain of sugar into her favourite cup. "I just want to say that straight away. We're no leaving."

I look at Granaidh, who pointedly pours milk into her teacup, where it swirls with the vestigial movement from her stirring.

"Really?" I ask.

"Tha sinn really staying," Mum says, rubbing one temple with the pad of her finger. She must be out of it if she's speaking like that.

"Good," I say. "Good. That's—good."

"Tha sin really math." Granaidh says it with no irony whatsoever, but I know she hates it when people sprinkle "really" into their Gaelic, whether they're saying something's really good or not.

Mum glares at Granaidh the way I tend to glare at Mum, and the burst of laughter that breaks past my lips makes three pairs of eyes turn their focus on me.

It's Mam who joins me laughing next, a chuckle at first, and then almost a bark, and she snorts the way she sometimes does when she laughs. And Granaidh loves that, so she's next—eighty years old and giggling into her tea at four in the morning.

"You want to stay here," Mum says, ignoring her wife and her mother alike. "You're sure?"

Her dark eyes are so unlike mine—mine meshed with Dad's to be hazel—and I hold her gaze only for a moment before I have to look away, nodding in answer to the question I can't respond to with words.

I could have never made it home. A wave of emotion hits me, near panic at the unknown sprawling out before us. I remember telling them I was queer, then telling them I was agender, and then all of us finding out I'm also autistic. Now I am something else altogether, and I can never tell them.

But never seeing them again would be worse.

I'm not a hugger. I have to choose when to be touched, and I know my mums both hate that, because when they tried to hug me as a kid, I'd turn into a brick wall under their palms until they stopped.

But I go to Mum where she sits next to Granaidh, and I lean down just enough to put my arms around her.

For once, it's she who goes rigid, but it's only for a split second, only for the amount of time it takes her to suck in a short gasp, and then she hugs me back fiercely.

It doesn't last very long, and I pull away before going to Mam and doing the same thing.

When I look at Granaidh, she just winks at me and shoos me away. "Thalla led chasan ruisgte. Mach à seo."

Mum immediately looks at my bare feet and stares. They're in a state—all mud and blisters.

She mutters something that sounds like she's just repeating what Granaidh said in English—*shoo with your bare feet, get out*—and points upstairs.

"We'll talk later," Mum says to me. "Go clean your feet."

I give them a tight-lipped smile and shuffle out of the kitchen, but not before I hear Mam ask, "Where are my wellies?"

I take the stairs two at a time.

The sight of my mums and grandmother clustered at the table at this hour chases away any remaining hope that last night was a dream. I mean, we live in a world where the terms "milkshake duck" and "thirty to fifty feral hogs" exist in the vernacular as completely comprehensible references, and if there's anything my generation has, it's a sense of whimsy in the face of existential dread.

Most of the events of the night, when viewed alone, could be perfectly explicable if a bit odd. I'm the one who stuck my hand through a door in the middle of the woods. If it had been the other way around, it *would* have been tempting to reach back and shake. I don't think I would have actually done it, though.

Strange lights in the forest, not being able to see faces in the twilight—there are rational explanations for those things. Fainting, even. Vertigo? Any number of things could have caused that, and two strangers trolling me in person about the Others—the Sìthichean, the fair folk—isn't out of the realm of possibility.

Disconcerted, I shower as quickly I can, which will probably give Mam a heart attack. She hates that I take long showers, and she'll probably see my in-and-out as one of the horsemen of the apocalypse.

My feet make muddy rivulets that stream into the drain. If Deirdre and Daibhidh were a rare instance of an in-person trolling event, I can be sure at least that I didn't imagine losing my shoes.

When I'm out of the hot water, I bundle my hair into a microfibre towel and the rest of me into my favourite royal-blue bath sheet.

My room is the only inhabited one on this side of the cottage, and that's a relief.

It's quiet here, almost silent. My room in Austin was in Dad's condo in the city centre, a three-bedroom loft that looks like every eighties hair band barfed leather and chrome everywhere, and it was never quiet. Ever. I got so little sleep there I almost started hallucinating. Even with my sensory-deprivation cocoon, the music from the bars and the club right across the street were murder. Dad says he doesn't even hear it. I made him get his ears checked.

My first night back here in Ballinacollie, I slept fourteen hours straight.

I sit down on the edge of my bed, which is neatly made, just like I left it. It gives under my weight, and despite my still being damp from the shower, the wave of exhaustion that washes over me almost convinces me to crawl under the duvet and fall asleep.

Granaidh doesn't like prints, and she has waged a decades-long blood feud against the clothes moths that exist to devour wool and silk and feathers alike, so my bedroom is almost austere. Pale-green duvet cover and pillow shams, white wood wardrobe, drawers, vanity, everything. When we got back here from Glasgow, Mam said this place looked like a B&B, and I think if Granaidh had been any younger, she would have sprung right out of her chair and boxed Mam's ears for that. For the next week, all any of us heard about was the state of housing in the Gàidhealtachd and how the corporations facilitating short-term rentals have made the second round of Highland Clearances almost total.

Not sure Mam's recovered yet, but Granaidh's not wrong.

Since I'm under the eaves, I've got big, rectangular dormer windows that most in the US would call skylights. They face north, toward Ben

Cruachan and Taynuilt, and when I look up, for a second I think it's started to mist, because there are little pricks of light refracting back at me. The sky is clear and blue again, which doesn't really mean it can't rain, because this *is* still Scotland, but either my depth perception is off or I'm tired enough to be hallucinating now.

Despite my protesting feet, I push myself off the bed again and pad over to stand under the slanted glass of the window. The light pinpricks are still there. They're definitely not on the glass.

To be extra sure, I tug on the handles to push the window open, and it accedes with a small *pompf* as its insulation breaks free of the frame. A gust of chilly air immediately washes me in many regrets, but now that I'm looking out, my goose bumps are forgotten in an instant.

The tiny lights don't show up over land.

No, they're limited to the sky, and because the sun is somewhere behind me, I don't think that can account for what I'm seeing.

Some of the lights are brighter than the others.

My dad used to take me out into the desert sometimes to look at the stars where there was little light pollution. He didn't know what was up there, but he knew I liked looking at them, so he downloaded an app on his phone so he could tell what we were looking at exactly. I've seen Venus and Jupiter near dawn and dusk—that's never a surprise.

But I've never seen Ursa Major—the Big Dipper—in the morning sky when the sun is above the horizon.

It's there, right in front of me, like the great bear might touch down on Ben Cruachan itself.

I push the window open farther, the chill forgotten.

If I crane my head around to look northeast, I can see Perseus, too. And the tip of Leo about to dip below the hills.

A door opens below me, and I jump back, knocking my head against the windowsill. Mam's probably running into Oban or something, though this is early even for her. The last thing I need is for her to see me dangling half naked out the window with a towel on my head. They were kind enough not to flay me for going out all night, but I shouldn't press my luck.

I want to stare at the sky forever.

Deirdre's words trigger my near-perfect audio memory. It might take me a minute to process things I hear, but once it's in here, I can replay it and replay it and replay it—which my anxious brain likes to use for evil.

But right now, I just hear her voice in the pre-dawn hush.

However afraid you are, this is one thing you need not fear. This choice is a terrible one, but the one gift with no barb is that your magic is yours and yours alone. It will shape itself to you.

Something hot runs down my cheek and drips off my chin. It's cold by the time it lands on my boob, and I pull the bath sheet around me a little tighter.

I'm alive, and whatever else is about to come of last night's adventure, I can't feel any regret in this moment for my choice.

Not if it gave me the stars even in the brazen light of day.

SIX

I tear my eyes away from the sky long enough to catch a couple hours of sleep and drag myself back out of bed at ten, feeling groggier than I was before I slept at all.

So far I feel normal. Cam-normal, anyway. My brain feels like mine, I still seem to need rest like a human being, and aside from my eyesight having dramatically improved—I can also read the small text on the bookshelf on the other side of the room with crystalline clarity—I can't see any other immediate changes.

I try something else my therapist taught me and do a body scan, which is a meditation technique I usually can't get through without wandering off into thought, but today I'm curious enough that I manage to think my way through from head to toe. My therapist always tells me to concentrate on how emotions feel in the body, but I am rubbish at that. It's hard to know if my skin is tingling because I've been fundamentally altered or if I'm just bloody knackered. My Fitbit will never know how long I trudged through the woods last night, alas.

I wander downstairs to get something to eat, where it is quiet except for Granaidh's humming as she knits. I think she's making an Eriskay jumper, and despite my familiarity with hyperfocus—my autistic "superpower"—it always amazes me that she can keep track of which stitches go where with one eye on the iPad she reads from and the other on her needles.

With my new eyesight, I can see the text on the iPad a little too clearly and turn away, blushing, the words "luscious breasts" burned into my brain.

Gaun yersel, a seanmhair.

"Dè tha dol, a ghràidh?" she asks me without looking up. "An do chaidil thu?"

"I slept a little," I answer her, as usual with the Gaelic affirmative hovering self-consciously on my tongue, unable to find its way past my lips. *Chaidil.*

She sniffs and jabs one elbow toward the kitchen, where a sweet smell lingers. She holds one hand up to her lips, cupped conspiratorially at the side of her mouth. "Rinn mi cèic. Chan innis mi dhad mhàthraichean. Siuthad."

For some reason, being told to go eat cake for breakfast settles me, chasing away some of the fog. Granaidh knows I've a terrible sweet tooth. If left to my own devices, my fail of an impulse control system takes over, and I will keep eating whatever sweet thing is in front of me. The mums swear all my teeth are going to rot out. I, thankfully, inherited my father's perfect dental health. I've never had so much as the hint of a cavity.

The cake Granaidh's made is even my favourite. A Madeira cake with extra glacé cherries in the cake itself and even more in a small dish covered with cheesecloth to the side. I think sugar is Granaidh's love language.

It's probably why we get on so well.

Cutting a large piece and putting the kettle on to make my tea, I zone out as it comes to a boil.

I don't think I stand a chance of finding Mam's wellies, but I should give it a go anyway.

I barely make it to the table with my tea—two heaping sugars, milk—and the cake before I hold the plate up to my mouth to nibble a cherry off before even setting it on the table.

The cake is so good it takes all my willpower not to just grab the rest of it and down it. I don't even think glacé cherries are technically fruit anymore after they finish the first part of their life cycle getting infused with sugar, but they are so delicious.

I guzzle down my tea despite it being just this side of scalding, my feet doing what Mam calls my "happy food dance" under the table. I can't help it—it's a stim, apparently, and I've always done it. If standing, I bounce. If sitting, my feet tap-dance. It's weird to me that other people don't let good things get them this excited.

It might not be just the cake, though. Once I've tucked my plate and teacup into the dishwasher—and snagged a couple extra cherries from the bowl—I hurry upstairs to get dressed to go outside.

I hear some movement on the other end of the cottage's upstairs where the mums sleep (Granaidh's room is downstairs in what used to be the dining room since we couldn't get a lift installed), and as relieved as I am that Mum didn't seem to be too furious about my unscheduled outing last night, I am not sure I have it in me to deal with her right now. I quickly throw on some fleece-lined leggings and an oversized jumper my favourite colour of teal and pull on a pair of thick, soft lambswool socks Granaidh knitted for me.

This time I strap my Fitbit on and tuck my mobile into the jumper's right pocket.

My hillwalking boots are in the foyer at the front door with everyone else's, and I lace them up despite my feet protesting having to wear shoes at all after last night's abuse.

"Going for a walk!" I call back into the house.

"'Eil brògan ort?" Granaidh calls back in answer with an undisguised chuckle.

I snort in the direction of my appropriately covered feet and answer her shoe question in the affirmative. "Tha!"

"Thalla, ma-tà," she says loudly from the living room, and I obey and scurry out the door.

Immediately, I am greeted with a clear blue sky full of stars. It brings me to a skidding halt before I've taken three steps off the front stoop of the cottage. It's disconcerting and awesome in the truest sense of the word.

I could just stand here all day and stare at it, but Mam'll be back from Oban at some point, and if I've any hope of finding her wellies in the woods—and my poor, likely sodden socks—I'd like to give it a go before she gets back.

I make my way around the side of the cottage to the back garden. Granaidh's roses are still doing their thing. She's got a bush I love that has roses that start out a sunset pink-orange and mutate into rhubarb custard-coloured blooms as they unfurl. It's been there since I was a bairn, and every summer we came up to visit, I would take pictures of every rose it produced in all their stages.

That thought gives me a pang. I've not done it since Austin, and though it'll likely keep blooming into the autumn, I've already missed most of this year's.

Before I exit the garden onto the still-muddy path into the woods, I stop and pull out my phone. There are three buds in varying stages of development, one about to bloom imminently. One rose has just opened, and it is so vibrant it's like someone poured the setting sun into its petals. I snap a picture of it, then of the other remaining rose, which is about to lose the remainder of its own petals, its blossom wide open to the breeze, all pale yellow and wispy pink.

Something wrong inches toward righting itself, and straightening, I tuck my phone away again and make my way past the ancient, moss-covered rock wall at the garden's edge and onto the path.

A thrill goes through me as the trees enfold me and I leave the cottage behind.

The forest is alive before me, its green somehow more intense, more vibrant, than it was even yesterday. Perhaps it's the sun that turns everything to gold, but I seeing through these new eyes feels like drinking in water from the fountain of youth. My step quickens on the path, following a pull I can't explain into the hills.

This time, I easily spot the turnoff toward the falls, which makes my heart stutter from one beat to the next. I'm certain now that last night I didn't come anywhere near it.

That certainty slows my feet on the packed dirt and gravel, and I scuff one boot into a small hummock of grass that has grown up in the middle of the trail.

If last night I somehow wandered into some otherworldly path, how would I even find it again? The thought of wandering the well-trodden ways of forestry-maintained trails all afternoon feels futile. Is futile, I guess. Why on Earth would I be able to find Mam's wellies if I'm looking in the wrong . . . plane of existence?

As if to reassure myself that something really did happen last night, I look up through the canopy of branches above me, where stars still glitter in the sunlit sky.

Deirdre said we'd meet again, but she didn't say how.

Just like that, my stomach gives a flop, and I realise my shoulders have crept up toward my ears. I try another meditation exercise and relax my shoulder muscles, also peeling my tongue from the roof of my mouth where it's practically glued.

This is ridiculous.

I hover on the path in indecision. If I have really become one of these Others, what am I supposed to even do now? Will I know the Others if I encounter any of them? Are there more rules beyond that one they taught me that I'm supposed to know? I hate not knowing the rules. It's part of what got my English teacher in Austin to refer me for autism assessment, my incessant need to ask a billion questions to make sure I do something correctly the first time.

My shoulders are creeping back up again. I give them a shake and shove one foot in front of the other, pressing on despite my sudden wave of doubt.

If I don't find the wellies, I don't find them. Is this the "going with the flow" Mam is always trying to impress on me?

Maybe she'd be proud that I tried to adapt to circumstances, enough to forgive me for the boots.

The air is just a bit warmer than cool, the sun filtering through the leaves warming the dark teal of my jumper enough to keep me comfortable without overheating. I make my way along the path, continuing on ahead instead of following another fork that leads off toward the waterfall. I think the way I'm going only leads to an old logging road, but either way, it feels good to be moving. My feet are surprisingly okay despite the blisters, but that is likely a product of wearing shoes that are the right size for my feet.

I have the sudden urge to *run*.

Some people have flying dreams where they just soar above the ground, but in mine, any flying is always tied to running. When I'm dreaming, there is fierce joy in running. I don't get winded, I don't get wheezy, and I don't get tired. I can just let *go*.

I'm tempted to try it, but these boots are made for walking, not running, and my spatial awareness is not great for judging whether my foot is going to go over a rock or plough into it and send me sprawling. I'm not clumsy; my brain just can't tell where stuff is in relation to my extremities.

I do pick up the pace, though, and the trail widens into a track that still has ruts where vehicles must still travel now and then. The trees fall away on either side, and there, perched cross-legged on a large rock that backs up against a hillock of grass-covered peat, is Ezra.

SEVEN

They visibly start when they see me coming. "Shiud thu," they say in Gaelic, which gives my already-nervous tummy a wee flutter of additional oomph.

"Shiud thu fhèin," I reply before I lose my nerve. "You must stay around here."

"You too," Ezra says as I approach.

"Guilty. My mums and I stay with my gran in Ballinacollie." I gesture vaguely in the direction I came from.

Ezra nods but doesn't say anything in response.

In the light, I can see them much more clearly. Their face is interesting, smooth with an almost sharp jaw and eyes that looked dark brown last night but are in actuality a strange dark grey with some green in them. Ezra's skin is darker than mine by a few shades, olive, and their hair somehow still has that raven's wing sheen of iridescence. Like an oil slick. I've seen that effect done with hair colours, but Ezra's doesn't seem to be coloured. Their waves come to about their cheekbones, which are, frankly, gorgeous. Their lips are full, but a bit thinned by pressing them together as Ezra returns my scrutiny.

I'm staring; I shouldn't do that. My masking script—my learned behaviours that hide my autistic traits—kicks in, and I look away, swallowing in anticipation of being called out for it.

But Ezra doesn't call me out for it, only cocks their head to the side as if seeing something *they* didn't expect.

The movement pulls my gaze back to their face, and I force myself to make eye contact for one agonising moment just in time to see Ezra's strange grey eyes widen.

I must have done something wrong. I shove my hands deep into the jumper pockets, fingers seeking out the stim toy that I now remember I took out when the jumper got cleaned. My fingertips instead wedge into the seam of the pocket, and I take a deep breath and launch into words.

"I'm sorry. You probably came out here to be alone. I'll go."

I turn on one heel before they can do the neurotypical thing of saying it's fine when it's not, but just as I take a single halting step, Ezra says, "Fuirich ort. I mean *wait*."

I stop. "I did understand the 'fuirich ort,'" I say, then realise that might be rude.

Pressing my own lips together to keep from wedging my foot in my mouth any further, I obediently wait.

"You don't have to leave." Ezra lets out an explosive breath and mutters something I can't make out. "It's just—phew, okay. Last night when we ran into each other, I didn't know—I mean, I thought you were mortal."

My head swivels on my neck as I turn to look at them, my gaze fixed on one of those perfect cheekbones.

My mouth opens and closes twice before I can make any words happen.

"You're . . . not?" I ask. That's not at all what I wanted to say. "I mean. When we ran into each other, I was."

Deirdre and Daibhidh's warnings about the Others' one (or two) unbreakable laws clamour for my attention, and my hands leap up to chest height with a small flail.

"Shit," I say. "I'm mortal. Of course I'm mortal. I'm autistic, but so far we don't live forever. Our life expectancy is actually worse—never mind."

Ezra is now staring at *me*, and the urge to run is now almost overpowering. And this time, it's not about wanting to feel the freedom of the wind in my face or whatever. I want to run until I find a volcano and then dive into it forever. I might have to run to Iceland, but maybe my newfound magic includes walking on water. Iceland is vaguely west of here, right? That way.

"Cam," Ezra says, and I cannot for the life of me tell what emotion is on their face.

They get to their feet on the rock, which makes them approximately twice my height, but before I can adjust to craning my neck up to look at them, they step off the rock and somehow float down to the ground rather than dropping with the normal force of gravity.

Ezra closes about half the distance between us in two steps and looks at me. "You were mortal when we met for the first time, but you aren't now. You're . . . one of us."

They're still peering at me in disbelief, and though I wish I could tell what they're thinking, I can see the myriad changes that flit across their face, rippling like the surface of a pond after a fish jumps.

Ezra is one of the Others.

Their intensity last night when they told me to go—my tongue is glued to the top of my mouth again, and I pry it off, unclenching my jaw.

They seem to take my silence as acquiescence, and Ezra takes half a step back.

"That means—shit. *Shit.* What happened? Are you okay?" Ezra's hands twitch at their sides, almost as if they're itching to do something. "Did someone try to hurt you? Who—who did this?"

I can't make words again, and I'm so flustered I can barely manage to raise my hand to hold up one finger to ask them to hold on a minute. I fumble in my pocket for my mobile again and quickly unlock it and open my quick app for moments like this where a screen pops up that just reads *Give me a moment to respond. I am autistic.*

I hold it up, and Ezra reads it, their face softening. They nod.

It's the first time I've actually used this thing, but the relief of it working precisely as it's supposed to floods over me.

For a moment, we both just stand there, and I stare at the rock behind Ezra that they just vacated.

All I need to do is recount what happened. It wasn't traumatic, just confusing. But I can at least tell them what transpired.

So I do. I tell them I ran when they told me to go, wondering if they used some sort of magic to make me go, and I go through hearing the voices to being suddenly rendered unconscious and finish with Deirdre giving me the choice.

I don't know what I expected Ezra to do or say to any of this, but their face is unreadable, and their full lips grow thinner and thinner, and they keep adjusting their shoulders as if following the same sort of relaxation exercise I do to dispel tension.

When I'm finished, I do not expect Ezra's words at all.

"This is my fault," they say. "I should have made sure you got home."

That sparks a flare of what Mum calls my inherited highland stubbornness, to which Granaidh always snorts and asks, "Cò leis a tha thusa?" to pointedly remind Mum that anything I inherited from Granaidh had to come to me through Mum's own genes.

I shake my head at Ezra. "Cha tus' as coireach," I say, hearing the Gaelic a moment before hurriedly switching to English. "Not your fault."

"I did understand that," they say dryly.

Touché.

"I don't know how I wound up where I did, but it wasn't your fault," I insist after a moment. I remember what Deirdre and Daibhidh said about those people I was accidentally spying on. "If Deirdre's right and you sent me away to avoid anyone else seeing me, you probably saved my life."

Not one but maybe two brushes with death.

Or perhaps three, if the day Paul died counts, which I guess it must.

Ezra blows out a breath again. "Deirdre is seldom wrong, so if she thinks you were in danger, you were. Did she tell you anything else? She didn't just . . . turn you loose after that, did she?"

It's clear Ezra knows her, which is somehow comforting. "She kind of did. Told me she would see me again and sent me home."

"She must have had a reason," Ezra mutters. Then they look at me. "But I'm sorry. She and Daibhidh shouldn't have just sent you on your way like that. You must have so many questions, and from the way you reacted to me, they did at least tell you the rules."

"Rule," I correct them. "Can't tell my mums or gran, et cetera. They mentioned a second rule, but Daibhidh didn't think it was important."

"Aye, he's got a point," Ezra says with a wry smile. "It's important, though. Just irrelevant."

Now I'm curious. "What's the rule?"

Ezra winces. If it's so irrelevant, why won't someone just tell me?

But a heartbeat later, Ezra tenses all at once, seeming to listen to something far away.

"I promise I'll tell you," they say, "but right now I have to go. Meet me here tomorrow, same time?"

"I—sure," I say, baffled.

"Do me a favour," Ezra says. "Don't tell anyone you saw me. Not even Deirdre."

I manage a nod, and there is a burst of warmth and air, and Ezra vanishes, a flurry of small black feathers ghosting through the air as a large raven wings skyward from the space where Ezra was just standing.

All I can do is stare after the bird. Both Daibhidh and Deirdre could disappear, but I didn't see them become an *animal*. Granaidh has told me stories of the each-uisge, the water horse that can appear as a gleaming white horse at the shore or as a handsome young man. Gaeldom is full of stories like this, mostly ones that end in tragedy for the mortals who encounter such creatures, though occasionally it's the supernatural beings left lovesick and lonely.

My eyes seek out the stars again, and yearning nearly overtakes me. What if I could see them from the *sky*?

The walk back home is more like a trudge. Nothing else unusual happens, though I'm not sure my brain's processing power could take it if it did. There's no sign of the strange, flatrock-paved path with its mossy banks anywhere, just the usual trodden trails I've roamed since childhood.

The sunlight is going to take some getting used to. I can't tell if things are still changing in my vision or if I'm still tired enough that I missed things when I was leaving. Motes of dust float in the air, which is still with little breeze—the midgies will be out in force soon if there aren't already clouds of the bloodthirsty things lying in wait.

I stop just in view of the house, looking into the woods. It should unsettle me that Ezra doesn't want anyone to know about their presence here, but considering what I can put together from the threat of my own death at the hands of unknown Others, which both Ezra and Deirdre seem to think was far from a nonzero probability, I think I can guess that Ezra doesn't feel safe.

Which likely means I shouldn't feel safe. Since no one has told me how this works, I think I have to assume that immortals can still die.

The idea of seeing Ezra tomorrow intrigues me. I like them, despite the awkwardness of our first two encounters. I haven't had many friends over the years, not with the many times we've moved, but suddenly Mum's pronouncement from this morning sticks. She said we're not leaving.

A certain precipitousness comes with this. I'm so used to being unable to settle in, unable to put down roots that were just going to get ripped from the earth all over again. But maybe for once I can stay.

The thought is too big for my tired brain to really parse. The air is quiet on my skin, warm within the jumper where it makes gaps between the wool and my body. My feet throb a little now that I've stopped moving.

But something else is tickling at me about Ezra. I tug on the thread of it. I'm used to being seen as American in Scotland and Scottish in America—when I was younger, my accent was a mishmash that reflected wherever I was, but the more time I spent with my mums, the more it landed on this side of the Atlantic, but between Mum's Argyll accent and Mam's Glaswegian Scots, I still don't sound right to anyone, even here.

Usually, it's one of the first things people remark on. But Ezra didn't. That is a relief the way my diagnosis was a relief, something I needed without realising I needed it until it happened.

Two short conversations aren't much, but I hope there are more to come.

A telltale cloud appears in the air in the direction I've just come from, and I immediately move toward the house as quickly as I can make my feet move. I do not want to be eaten alive by a hurricane of tiny, biting flies.

I'm almost to the garden when I see it: Mam's wellies, arranged in perfect alignment, their heels up against the stone wall. My socks are clean, dry, and draped over the top of each boot.

When I pick them up, something crinkles in one of the socks. Without looking at it, I fold the socks carefully once, shove them in my pocket, and pick up the boots to take them inside.

EIGHT

Granaidh is down for her afternoon nap when I come in through the front door. She can get around a bit without her chair, but I don't like seeing her chair empty when she does get up. She usually can't be arsed to manoeuvre up to her bed with it, so she abandons it in the living room most of the time and uses a walker that lives either by her bedroom doors (French doors with glass panes and curtains because, and I quote, "I'll live my twilight years in luxury") or by the telly.

Mum's in the kitchen, and I'm ravenous, so I go in and open the fridge to see if there's anything to eat.

"Mam's wellies are in the foyer," I say to Mum, who looks up from the Thursday *Oban Times* from last week. Today's also Thursday, and I guess Mam's not back yet, or the new paper would be here.

"How did you manage to lose them in the first place?" Mum asks curiously. "Never mind finding them again."

I hate lying, so I choose my words carefully. "They're too big and gave me blisters, and I took them off to look at the stars and then forgot about them."

"Did ye aye?" she says and shakes her head. Mum's eyes close, and her lips disappear like the emoji that just has lines for eyes and mouth. That is her "Cam, why" face, but after a moment, she chuckles, which is new.

She doesn't say anything else while I rummage in the fridge and, finding nothing appealing, settle for making a big bowl of porridge, into which I dump my habitual pile of wheat berries, flax seeds, and bulgur wheat because I like the texture to have some crunch.

When I sit down, my mind is on both Ezra and Deirdre apparently having some Gaelic. It makes me wonder what their connection is to the language, since a hundred years ago almost everyone in Argyll spoke it as a first language, but now that number is down to maybe one in ten, if not lower.

"Why do you only speak English to Granaidh?" I ask Mum suddenly.

She blinks at me. Mum is one of those strange people who looks smaller than she is. She's as tall as me—a couple inches shy of six feet—but the way she carries herself makes her look very petite despite her curves. She wears her curly hair usually back from her face with silver combs that were Granaidh's, and the combs increasingly blend with the silver hair that has been spreading out from Mum's temples. Her eyes are dark, and right now they study me as if I've asked the last question she expected.

"Why do you?" Mum counters.

Right. That's fair. I dump a heap of dark-brown sugar onto my porridge and top it with milk still in the pitcher from everyone's tea.

When I don't say anything, Mum sighs. "You have to understand that when I was growing up, it was seen very differently. Mum—my mum—is a bit of an outlier among her peers. When she was at school, weans got the strap for using the Gaelic instead of English. A lot of her generation took that on forever. Most of my friends whose parents were native speakers didn't speak a lick of it themselves because their parents didn't want them to experience what they had."

That hits me in a way I can't quantify. My words are gone again, and I try to process what Mum's said as I blow on my porridge and still manage to burn my tongue on my first bite.

I didn't really expect an honest answer from Mum, and when I spare a glance at her face, she is chewing on one lip and not looking at me.

"But Granaidh spoke Gaelic to you," I say after a long pause when I can gather my thoughts. "In spite of all that."

"Aye, she did," Mum says, but then she goes quiet again.

Tonight's Thursday, so the mums will drive Granaidh to Oban for choir rehearsal, where she helps the choristers with their Gaelic. In the pandemic, Granaidh learned how to use Zoom in order to keep giving Gaelic lessons to her choir folks—and anyone else who wanted to join.

That feeling I get when Granaidh speaks swells like a wave in my mind. Mum's offered me this honesty, so I decide I can offer her some in return.

"When she speaks Gaelic to me, sometimes I get this feeling I don't know how to describe," I say. Even now, I'm not sure I'm going to get it right if I label it. "I think I've always thought it was embarrassment because mine's not good enough, but . . ."

I stop to think, and Mum opens her mouth to prod me like she always does, but the prodding never comes. Instead, she closes her mouth again and simply waits for me to be ready to speak.

That is another feeling I'm not prepared to describe.

"I don't think it's embarrassment about speaking," I say finally. I swallow, one uneaten bite of porridge hovering in my spoon between my bowl and my mouth, probably cold now considering how long I've held it in front of my face. I put the spoon back in the bowl, disturbing a tendril of steam. "I think it's shame. That I am not competent in my own—in my own language. Gaelic feels like it should be mine, but I'm an outsider instead. Like I lost something I never had, even though it's right there."

Mum stares at me, her mouth slightly open. I hurriedly take a bite of my porridge.

I hear and feel the movement of air from her sudden exhale at the same time.

"Yes," Mum says, and I wonder if she's thinking about putting me in Gaelic medium education on and off throughout my schooling.

She looks like she is about to say something else, but I hear the crunch of tyres in the drive, which means Mam's home from Oban. Everything Mum was about to say is gone in an instant, and she gets to her feet.

"Come make a trip in from the car with me?" she asks, and just as I feel a cresting swell of resistance rising to fight the interruption of my meal, she glances at my still-full bowl and closes her eyes for a moment. "Never mind. Eat your food. Mam and I've got it."

She leaves me staring after her, wondering what just happened.

The rest of the afternoon is spent helping Mam in the garden, which is one of my favourite things to do because we don't have to talk. She has the green thumb, not me, and when there's a task, she explains exactly what I'm meant to do and turns me loose to do it.

Part of my job today is gathering the remaining blackberries from the bramble mass at the northwest side of the garden where they are wild and unkempt, and I like it that way, though I know as soon as the first frost hits, Mam'll be at them with the pruning shears so they don't completely annex the rest of the garden next spring. The berries are huge and luscious, sweeter than I remember them being last time I was here.

Mam says the same thing when she snags one out of the mixing bowl I've filled almost to the top.

"Huh," she says. "Best year we've had in ages, I reckon."

When we're done, I can smell dinner beckoning, and as always on Thursdays, it's cock-a-leekie soup and toasties because the mums don't feature driving and singing for a few hours whilst nursing a food coma.

"You're sure you don't want to come?" Mam says before she heads out the door. Over her shoulder, I can see Mum helping Granaidh into the car. "Choir's looking forward to meeting you."

I shake my head, cheeks warming. Too many people all at once.

"Suit yersel," says Mam. "Make sure you're home when we get back and not rambling off in the hills."

I give her a salute, and she chuckles and heads out the door. I watch the car pull away and vanish down the hill before letting out a breath. Much as I love my family, solitude is always a balm. I love Thursday nights.

I've pushed that crinkle in my socks out of my mind until this moment, and now that I'm alone, I mosey into the living room and perch on the edge of the chaise-longue end of the sectional settee, pulling the socks from my pocket.

At first, it seems like maybe someone is taking the piss out of me, because when I peer inside the sock with the crinkling noise, all I see is an innocuous piece of paper that looks like it was ripped from a sheet of A4 and folded a couple times.

When I unfold it, it is completely blank.

I turn it over in my hands. Feels like normal paper.

When I flip it back over, though, I almost drop it. Script appears in a flowing hand I immediately match to Deirdre even without evidence.

Outside, is all it says.

Nonplussed, I turn it over and back a couple of more times, but when no other words appear, I glance toward the kitchen. *Outside* is a vague instruction, but the tingle in my fingertips suggests I ought to obey it.

I go for a pair of slip-on, fleece-lined clogs since I don't plan to go far, and I make my way around the house to the back garden again.

Deirdre is standing at the bramble bush, touching one serrated leaf with a long, pale finger.

"Took you long enough," she says without looking at me.

"I didn't expect an appointment," I tell her.

"You still waited for hours to even look at it." Deirdre looks away from the brambles.

She's just as impressive in daylight. Standing, she's got at least three or four inches on me, and her curves are emphasised by another version of what I saw her in the first time: perfectly tailored tweed, this time olive green with an ivory shirt and gold collar pins joining the corners of a box collar with a delicate chain that sparkles in the evening light. She wouldn't be out of place on the cover of a magazine, and I think if she were to walk into a courtroom, whatever she wanted as the verdict would tumble into place without question.

I would ask how she knows when I looked at the piece of paper, but I expect the answer will simply be "magic."

"No one told me what to do," I say bluntly. "If you want me to do something, you'll probably have to tell me explicitly. I always get in trouble with the mums for that, too. Something about not being able to intuit that someone wants me to also clean the worktops and faucets when I'm just told to clean the sink."

To my surprise, Deirdre grins at that, and a warm chuckle follows. "I thought you'd be a good one for this life. You'll do just fine."

"What do you mean?" I've never really encountered someone who thought my intense autistic literalism was anything but an unfortunate—if sometimes funny—personality flaw.

"Let's just say fulfilling bargains has a lot to do with doing what is stated and not a single step more," says Deirdre. "But that's not why I wanted to see you, fond as I already am of you."

Somehow I think I have maybe just gotten a third mother.

"Okay," I say. "Then what's the craic?"

"It's customary to give new folks a bit of time to settle, and I think since you're starting school on Monday"—she doesn't wait for confirmation, but I blink at her assertive statement of my schedule—"that it would be best to give you a week or so before you get pulled into the Otherworld again."

"Again?" I ask faintly.

She doesn't answer that, only gives me a level look I can't quite hold eye contact with, and then she laughs.

"What's going to happen?" I say after a beat.

"There's meant to be a bit of a cèilidh," she says, and I feel myself go rigid.

The problem with getting bounced from school system to school system is that I missed most of the Scottish social dancing, and just about every pupil in Scotland knows how to do the Gay Gordons or an Orcadian strip the willow or a dashing white sergeant, but I don't. I mean, I can manage a strip the willow since it's mostly just getting passed off by the elbow to spin in circles, but the rest?

At my panicked silence, Deirdre gives me a mischievous smile. "Don't you worry about that. Everyone will be there, but they won't be looking at you. You can even hide in a corner and watch all night. I'll be there, and so will Daibhidh, and between us we'll make sure you're not left to fend for yourself."

I don't know what to make of that, but if Granaidh's choir was a terrifying thought, an Otherworld cèilidh "everyone" will be present for just sounds like my personal version of socialising hell.

Deirdre frowns then, peering at me more closely. "You're getting harder to hear, which means your magic is gathering. But I don't have to read your mind when you otherwise turn to stone—try to trust me when I say they really won't be paying attention to you. It's the best night for you to turn up if you don't want attention. I can't say more than that, but this is the closest I can do to a promise: all eyes will be on other things."

I don't know how to take that or what she means by any of that. "Is there a . . . handbook or something?"

Her peal of laughter cuts through the air, and I jump.

"Sadly, no." Deirdre plucks a berry from somewhere in the brambles and pops it in her mouth. Guess I missed some. "But you don't have much to worry about. I know you must have a lot of questions, but the biggest help I can tell you at this stage is to try and relax. You've got all the time in the world to learn."

"That is not going to be easy for me," I say slowly. "Can you at least start by telling me the second rule?"

I think I've managed to startle her, but the impression I get is chased away in a moment like it was never there at all. "Ah. Yes. The second rule is, very simply, never to break an unbreakable bond."

"What does that even mean?" I ask. "Which bonds are unbreakable?"

"Only one," Deirdre says. Her eyes seem to look past me or through me when I venture a glance at her face. "For most people, it's moot. But some of us find someone—a friend, a lover, a companion—and that bond is sacred. Most of us never do, and many don't even believe anyone does."

"Do you mean like . . ." My voice trails off dubiously. "Are you talking about soulmates?"

My heart gives a small pang at the thought.

Deirdre makes a face. "I suppose that's as good a word as any, yes. But it's not what your world thinks. It's an opportunity, nothing more. Some believe we all get the opportunity at least once, maybe more than once."

"So the second rule is what, exactly?" I ask, more confused than I was a minute ago. "If that bond is unbreakable, how does it break?"

"More easily than you might think," Deirdre says, her voice soft. She plucks another blackberry, but this time she doesn't eat it, only presses it lightly between one long forefinger and her thumb.

It doesn't take much. Deep, purple-red juice spills out over the pad of her thumb, dripping onto the grass.

"The Others' bonds are inviolate," she says, watching the juice run down her finger and hover until its own weight pulls it free into the air. "To harm someone's companion is anathema."

"But if people don't even believe in them," I begin, but Deirdre shakes her head once, and I shut up.

"It's too frightening to believe," she says, then glances up at the sky. "It's time for me to go again, but I'll be back next week. For now, you're safe."

Her words sound more threatening than I think she means them, and I don't want her to go yet.

Deirdre pops the squished blackberry into her mouth and licks away the juice in a flash.

"You're leaving?" I ask.

"Places to go, people to see," she says with a wink, then sobers again, quiet for the space of a breath. "It's too frightening to believe because forever is a long time to be alone."

With that, she's gone.

The bramble, picked thoroughly clean just hours ago, is heavy with berries once more.

NINE

I spend most of the rest of the evening gathering more blackberries until my fingers are stained purple and I honestly don't know what we're going to do with them all. We have an extra chest freezer that is usually half full of venison—Granaidh has friends who always give her some—but by the time I've filled an entire basin with the things, I'm half full of certainty that we're going to be eating blackberries for the rest of time.

Mam's just done the big weekly shop, and I say a mental apology as I use every single one of the freezer bags she's just bought to get this second load of berries bundled into the freezer so they don't all go off. Maybe next week she can pass them out like party favours at choir practice and will forgive me for leaving us without freezer bags.

Perhaps prudently, I send her a text warning her. She'll have questions, but maybe something in Oban will still be open to get some more when they leave practice. I follow up a minute later with a text saying I'm still knackered and might lie down early.

I go to my bed and do exactly that so if anyone asks, I didn't make a liar of myself, and for a while I just lie in bed, staring out the window at the sky. My weather app says the clouds are going to be rolling in from Mull by morning, and as much as I want to stay up long enough to see it get full dark and really look at the stars then, exhaustion wins the battle.

❧

When I wake up, it's with a jolt in the darkness. I'm still on top of the duvet, curled up with half of it folded over and bunched between my knees like the body pillow I could be using instead, since it's shoved halfway off the other side of the bed.

A glance at my wrist tells me it's two in the morning, and I lie there for a long minute, afraid I'm not going to be able to sleep again.

The room is strangely bright despite it being full dark for this time of year, and it takes a minute of sleepily looking around for me to realise my vision must have improved that much.

I push the window open to look outside.

My first look at the night sky makes me understand what people mean when they say something takes your breath away.

The land is lit by starlight, and my first impression is that the universe is lit by a multitude of rainbow fairy lights. I'm straining on my tiptoes, my hands grasped against the windowsill at the height of my ribcage as if my eyes are desperate to drink in the sight of the multitude of worlds visible as I've only ever imagined possible through the James Webb telescope.

It's not like I can see the Horsehead Nebula the size of an actual horse, but I can see its shape, its colours, infinitesimal but infinite, precious in the magic of my newfound sight.

My wrists are getting sore from gripping the windowsill so tensely, and I immediately drop down to my flat feet and grab the stool that sits in front of the vanity, considering my actions for only a second before I step on it and, ducking my head to avoid hitting it on the open windowpane, wriggle out onto the roof.

The edge isn't far from the window, and I have to work myself at an angle to not dangle over the side—if Granaidh were to wake up and see my feet out her window, I'd never hear the end of it. It's chilly out in the middle of the night, and I can indeed see the forecasted clouds blotting the western horizon where they've already made landfall in Mull and Ardnamurchan.

But the rest of the sky is mine.

I lie back on the roof, staring into the depths of the Milky Way, and I lose myself naming every celestial body I can think of.

I don't even realise I've drifted off until I hear the telltale *gù-gù* of the cuckoo—cuthag, in Gaelic, which always feels more fitting—and jolt back awake.

I scramble back inside with a pounding heart as I drop onto the floor more loudly than I want and fumble in the bedside table drawer for the packet of oat cakes I keep there, jamming one into my mouth even though it's stale and poking my head back out the window. The cuthag is still going, and I cough a weak laugh of relief, which makes me cough for real when I inhale a crumble of stale oats.

I don't even know why I've done it as if the house would burn down if I didn't—it's just what I was taught to do. Break your fast before the cuthag finishes her call.

Despite waking up on the roof after an interrupted night of strange sleep, I feel rejuvenated. Awake. I can hear Granaidh stirring downstairs already, which makes sense, since she's always up around five.

Mum's and my conversation from yesterday intrudes into my mind. The idea of bringing it up to Granaidh feels so big and overwhelming that I push it to the back of my mind. Maybe someday.

I make my way downstairs anyway. Granaidh and I don't get all that much time without the mums, and with school starting Monday, my days of lie-ins and summer rambles are about to come to an abrupt halt.

When I get to the kitchen, Granaidh is already ensconced in her morning routine. I hang back to watch her before she notices me. Her movements from the sink to the kettle to the fridge are all almost choreographed, so familiar I could probably take her place, down to the way she spoons three heaping teaspoons of tea leaves into her own personal teapot and taps the spoon's handle on the metal rim of the pot three times. *Clink, clink, clink.*

"Thig a-steach, m' eudail," Granaidh says fondly without so much as looking up at me.

Sheepish, I skid into the kitchen in my socks, obeying her, and when she shoos me to the table, I sit and watch as she gathers the other teapot for me and refills the kettle after she's filled her own.

"How was choir, a seanmhair?" I ask her.

"Och, math gu leòr, tapadh leat," she says, waving one hand. "Tha sinn ag ionnsachadh puirt ùr 'son a' Mhòid."

"Which puirt is it?" I ask. I know the Mòd has a puirt competition every year, but it's coming up in a couple months. "Isn't it a bit late to be learning a new song?"

Granaidh gives me a sly half smile and a wink, and I realise she was joking with me about the choir learning a new puirt. "Uill, tha. Ach tha sinn ag ionnsachadh fhathast."

I crack a smile in return. "Ah. So everyone's been a bit lazy."

"Sin e, sin e," she affirms, then starts humming the puirt I remember hearing a couple nights ago, the one she was singing when I left in the middle of the row.

I listen to her for a while as she tells me it's a familiar puirt with a new arrangement and that the problem is everyone assumed they knew it only to have a rude awakening at the choir's last big practice. I think I can relate to that.

It's nice to sit and drink tea with her, and she's happy to talk to me even if she knows I don't understand every single thing she's saying. The kitchen brightens as the sun climbs in the sky, and after an hour or so, I hear the mums stirring.

Granaidh looks toward the direction of the mums' room briefly, then asks me, "Dè mun smeuraig, ma-tà?"

My brain takes a moment to process the subject change and that she's asked me about the blackberries. She must have peeked in the chest freezer.

"Erm," I say, unsure of how to explain the glut of them without lying. "I . . . found more."

She looks unimpressed by my stating the obvious, but Mam comes in a moment later and rescues me from further questioning.

Mam's big blue eyes get wider at the sight of me, clearly settled and caffeinated, but she recovers quickly and goes to kiss Granaidh on the cheek.

"Morning," Mam says, giving Granaidh's shoulder a squeeze.

"Madainn mhath," Granaidh says pointedly.

"Madainn mhath," Mam echoes.

Mam's not awake enough to ask me about the freezer bags, so I quickly escape back to my room.

I think both of the mums have to work today, so I'm able to stay in my room without intrusion until I need to leave to meet Ezra. I pass the time scouring the internet for information on the Others, but aside from a book called *The Gaelic Otherworld,* which looks promising, I don't find a lot that seems helpful. I have a little money that Dad wired to my Scottish bank account when I left the US, and I order the book before I can talk myself out of it.

The patter of a drizzle on the window tells me to heed Granaidh's "proper clothes" advice, and I grumble myself into a pair of jeans and a less bulky jumper I can wear my mac over.

Granaidh's dozing in her chair in front of the telly and lightly snoring when I get downstairs, so I send my mums a "off on a ramble" text and bundle myself out the door before anyone can stop me.

My hillwalking boots are waterproof at least, so despite the drizzle and the scud of clouds obscuring the daytime stars—including the big one—I'm no feart. I hate having wet feet, but Scotland's been wet for a long time, so folk know how to make a boot that keeps you dry.

I've always actually loved the weather here. Everyone likes to complain about it, but I'll take a brisk breeze and mist over the August Texan oven any day. I was never sure in Texas if I was on the verge of a meltdown or just actually melting down into a great big gob of greasy, grimy gopher guts.

Maybe not gopher. Probably just human. At least until a couple of days ago, I guess.

As I make my way up the trail, my maybe-human guts do their familiar churn of social anxiety. What if I misunderstood? What if I've just imagined *all* of this? Up until a couple of days ago, people didn't just vanish or turn into birds and fly away. I have always had an active imagination—contrary to misconceptions about autism, some of us are very good at imagining things vividly—but imagining up a bunch of magical Sìthichean is something else.

The thought is chased away by the figure I see leaning against the same rock as yesterday. Ezra. Here and as real as Granaidh's snoring.

"You're here," I blurt out when I get close.

"Aye, seems that way," they say with a half-smile.

Today I'm Cam "States-the-Obvious" Smith, I guess.

"I'm still not convinced any of this is real," I say. "I fell asleep on the roof last night looking at the stars and counting nebulae I could name by sight without a telescope. But I'm afraid I, I don't know, ate some hallucinogenic blackberries or something."

I wish I could pinpoint the expression on Ezra's face. Their mouth hangs slightly open with their eyes slightly narrowed—not in disbelief, I don't think.

"You can see the stars like that?" they ask after a moment.

"You can't?" I gape at them.

Wistfulness—maybe that's what it was on their face.

"Everyone's different," they say. "I know that's true in general, but about us, it's *really* true."

"You can fly," I say, unsure if my envy creeps into my voice or not.

"Aye, that doesn't suck," Ezra agrees.

"Why did you have to leave yesterday?" I ask.

Ezra's face shifts almost imperceptibly. I can almost feel their walls go up.

"You don't have to tell me," I tell them.

"There are things it wouldn't be right to dump on you when you're this new," they say, waving one hand in a gesture I take to mean I didn't say anything wrong. "It's nothing that would affect you anyway. Just . . . complications. For me."

"Okay," I say because I don't know what else would be appropriate. "Deirdre came by last night. She wants to bring me to something next week after I've had a few days at my new school."

Ezra looks up sharply at that, then nods. "That's reasonable."

A thought strikes me. "Do you go to the high school?"

They give a short, sharp head shake, which makes their raindrop-dotted hair fall in front of their left eye, and they smile a dangerous smile that makes my heart falter with a startled *thub*.

"I'm a dropout," Ezra says with aplomb. "School's tricky for me. Some of us like to go, but mostly out of boredom, and their means of dealing with that boredom are not always fun for mortals."

They say that last with sharp consonants, and I have to bite back the urge to ask more questions about that.

I settle for a more obvious question. "If you're immortal, are you—I don't know how to ask this. Were you born among the Others? Is anyone?"

Ezra laughs, and their laugh sounds like the way sunlight on amethyst looks. Facets and crystalline fractals.

"I'm eighteen," they say. "I'm as much of a bairn as you are to the Others."

That sets my curiosity aflame, but when I open my mouth to ask another question, Ezra winces as if a loud alarm has just gone off by their ear.

I'm starting to figure out the drill. "You have to go?"

"Yep," they say. "But I'll see you at the cèilidh."

"You'll be there?" The thought is definitely a pleasant one. If Ezra is there in addition to Deirdre and Daibhidh, maybe it won't be so bad.

"Oh, I'll be there," they say, then wince again. "Shit. I've really got to go. But Cam—save me a dance on the night?"

Before I have time to respond to that, they're gone again in a flurry of black feathers.

One long pinion falls to the ground, and I snatch it up before the rain can get it too wet, tucking it carefully into the pocket of my mac.

TEN

Monday arrives with an almost palpable dread.

You'd think I'd get used to starting new schools, having done it six times already, but I never have. Because of the mess I'm in with my curriculum, I'm going from being a US high school rising senior to being a sixth year at Oban High School, where I'm probably among the oldest of my peers since I turned eighteen last month. And where most of the others in secondary six will be doing their advanced Highers, I'm probably going to have a hodgepodge, depending on whatever the head teacher tells Mum.

The school building is huge and blocky, all beige and square glass windows. I half-listen to Mum talk about the clan system in the car on the way into Oban. Not the clan system like families, but like school houses. Very-American Paul, when learning Scottish schools really do have clans kids are put into, laughed hard enough I thought I'd broken him. He finally gasped out something that sounded like an insincere apology for his ignorance and settled down when he realised I was just staring at him.

If I could go back, I'd maybe laugh with him. He had a great laugh, deep belly chuckles and breathless gasps when he really got going.

Mum seems to have noticed I'm not really listening, because there's suddenly silence in the car.

"It's only one year," she says when I look over at her. "You can manage one more year."

I give her the closest thing to a smile I have, which is more akin to an awkward lip grimace than an actual smile. Mum returns it with one of her own. She's probably hearing the neuropsych doctor on the Zoom call telling the parents all over again that all the schools have given me complex post-traumatic stress disorder because so many changes for an autistic kid are traumatic. I mean, seven schools would be a lot for any kid, don't get me wrong. But a kid who desperately needs routine and some semblance of predictability ain't gonna thrive. Doc said I'm an innie instead of an outie autie, which is a cutesy way of saying that instead of projecting my overwhelm outward like a volcano, I suck it in like a black hole.

Except I'm not a black hole; I'm a person, so eventually I collapse.

This is not what I want to be thinking about on my first day at a new school.

One year. Maybe my new magic will make me invisible.

But as soon as we pull up and find a place to park the Subaru—my mums are Subaru lesbians, aye—from the looks we get from the already-clustered gathering students, no such luck.

I'm in half a uniform, since we didn't know what clan I'm going to be in, so while all the other students have jackets that are trimmed with red or blue or green or yellow, I just have a plain black blazer. I refuse to wear skirts, and I'm thankful the times have changed enough that trousers are an option, but already wearing a button-down is going to be a sensory nightmare—thirty minutes in, and I already want to burn it.

Mum knows where she's going, so I just follow her past the other pupils and into the school, which smells somehow like every school ever, though today a bit more like cleaner than it will once it's steeped in eau d' adolescent for a few days.

We're early and have an appointment, and I'm still already overwhelmed by newness. Mum leads the way to the office, and then I just stand there while she sorts everything. In the US I had to go to IEP meetings after my autism diagnosis, but I have no idea what will happen with that here. Because Oban High School has kids from the islands as well as the surrounding mainland villages outside Oban proper, there's a hostel in Oban that accommodates a decent number of students who stay in Oban all week. One of Dad's hard lines for me coming back to live with my mums was them promising not to put me in the hostel.

So Mum and Mam have rented a small office in Oban for them to work out of during the week, though Mam's still working from home today. We'll all come in together, they'll work while I'm at school, and we'll all go home.

When we talk about accommodations for my disability, I don't think literal accommodations is something people think of very often.

I'm doing the thing again where I zone out when something stressful is going on, and I try to focus on Mum going over my schedule with the teacher—maybe the headteacher?—who has come to meet us in the office.

"Does she talk?" I hear the teacher say, and I *really* wish for invisibility.

"She talks," I manage to get out, but that's it for my words for now.

Mum gives me a tight smile and turns back to the teacher. "She talks, Mrs MacDonald, but the more uncomfortable she is, the less likely she is to have words to spare."

Something passes between the two of them, and Mrs MacDonald's pale cheeks flush with blood. I'm not entirely sure, but I think Mum just flung a barb.

This is not going well.

Mum hands me my schedule, for which I am grateful. This part we've talked about at least. We agreed that since I need four Highers to go to university and passed the AP English test as a junior, I'll take the English Advanced Higher (the school and appropriate authorities agreed despite being a bit flustered, since the AP test grants university credit), and I'll take biology, history, and Gaelic—the fluent course—for regular Highers.

I'm exhausted just looking at this schedule, but at least Gaelic's at the end of the day, when I will likely be able to speak exactly zero languages. Bully for me.

One year.

Maybe my newfound magic will help me somehow. Like allowing me to self-yeet to the Isle of Mull if things get too bad.

By the time Mum's about to head out, I think she is realising how hard I've dissociated, and she looks like she wants to hug me, but the fact that she doesn't is honestly the bigger comfort.

"Ceart gu leòr?" she asks softly in Gaelic.

Mum just asked if I'm all right in Gaelic. Maybe *that's* magic in action.

"Tha," I tell her. "No bidh, co-dhiù."

It's not a lie—if I'm not all right this second, I will eventually be again.

Her shoulders sink a bit with her exhale, which reminds me to loosen mine.

"Can you find your first class? Mrs MacDonald said she'd make sure to try and head off any of the ritual public humiliation." Mum is unconvinced, I think. And I think she means the whole get-up-in-front-of-the-class, introduce-yourself thing.

"Aye, I'll be fine, Mum," I say.

We visited once during the summer, and at least that gave me a chance to see where everything is, though as soon as there are students everywhere, my navigation might go out the window.

"Okay," Mum says.

"Okay," I say.

"See you at half three." With that, Mum turns and hurries away without looking back.

I almost feel bad for her.

I do find my first class easily enough, and I'm thankful it's not English but biology, which I'm comfortable enough to do in my sleep. A plus for someone who is not usually a morning lark or anything resembling human before noon.

And Mrs MacDonald, perhaps in an attempt to make up for talking about me like I couldn't hear her, has at least indeed come through on the public humiliation avoidance. My biology teacher, a tiny woman called Dr Campbell who looks like she'd break in half if a pigeon landed on her, simply announces in a quiet voice that I exist, that my name is Cam, and that I'm from Texas, and I can forgive that misrepresentation for the fact that I have to say exactly nothing.

It does cause some murmurs, though, and my ears latch onto the word *gun*, though I can't pinpoint who said it. Yep, America. Where kids dying at school is acceptable collateral damage for "freedom," et cetera.

Thanks, I hate it too.

There is a luxurious fifteen minutes between classes, and I bolt before anyone can talk to me, which is maybe not the social pirouette the mums are hoping for in my final year at high school, but I don't want to deal with anyone else asking if I can talk. Maybe tomorrow.

I find the loo and hide there for most of ten minutes, and then it is English time (also no public humiliation) and then lunch, for which I was supposed to be prepared. I watched a video online and everything and had grand plans of preordering my food in the morning from a touchscreen kiosk so I could grab it and go.

I'm hovering outside the canteen, weight shifting awkwardly from foot to foot in the indecision of whether to skip eating and risk ending the day hangry (unwise) or braving the sea of new classmates and trying to navigate the queue and the storm of loud voices in an enclosed space (unappealing).

"You're the new person from Texas, right?" a timid voice says beside me, and I jump.

I nod, swallowing. My stomach gives an unhelpful gurgle, which this new person kindly ignores or didn't hear.

"I'm Grace." To my surprise, this girl has a school bag that has an enamel pronoun pin on it that says she/her.

"Cam," I say.

"I heard," she says. "Hungry? It's a bit much in there."

"Aye, it is," I say after a beat. "And yeah, definitely hungry. My old school was bigger—a lot bigger—but I don't really like crowds at all."

"Big mood," Grace says, blinking at me. She smiles and motions at the door. "I can help if you want. I'm used to the trenches."

"Cheers." I'm glad I'm able to make some words. My social script kicks in. Small talk, right? I should do that. "I like your pronoun badge. Mine are she/her too, but I'm agender."

To my surprise, Grace beams at me before leading me through the door into the canteen. "Thanks. My sister's trans. People are shite, yeah? So I think it's something small I can do at least."

"Does your sister go here?" I ask.

Already it's too loud in here, and it's like I can feel the input systems in my ears straining to separate out important noise from not-important noise. A loud guffaw, silverware scraping, the clatter of a tray, talking, talking, talking.

Grace's mouth is moving, but I have no idea what she's just said.

"Sorry?" I get out. "Loud."

This time, I understand her. "Aye, she's a fourth year. I'm in S6 and try to look out for her. Mostly it's fine, but there are occasional arseholes."

Grace almost squeaks on the last word as an adult person walks by, but thankfully it seems the din drowned out the curse.

I'm thankful that she seems content to simply show me what to do, so I follow and gather my food, and we pay with the cash-free, snazzy system they've got here, which I like.

Just as we're manoeuvring with our food to a somewhat open table, I hear a loud voice proclaim, "Oh, *there* you are, darling" and everyone in a ten-yard radius turns to look.

The voice sounds vaguely familiar, but I'm distracted from the momentary pause in the loudness by Grace muttering, "Speaking of occasional arseholes."

I think I might have just discovered Oban High School's resident Mean Girl, and I don't mean Grace.

The girl who stopped half a canteen of chatter with one sentence is as tall as me and has dark hair in perfect ringlets my goldy-blonde ones only wish they could accomplish. I hurriedly look away, following Grace toward a different table than the one she'd been aiming at. The new one is in a corner closest to a wall, and I like it better.

"Who's that?" I ask.

"Lisbeth, also known as Satan, and not the sexy, Lil Nas X kind," Grace says under her breath. Then she pushes a breath out through her nose. "Okay, she's not *that* bad, but she's just—I don't know. She tends to be around when other people get hurt or bullied, and she always looks weirdly smug about it."

"Sounds like my least favourite type of person," I say honestly.

I'm not sure if Grace has any other friends—no one else joins us while we eat, and she doesn't seem bothered by me doing mostly eating and less talking.

She shyly offers her mobile number to me as we leave and tells me to text her if I need help or anything, which is nice. I decide I like Grace.

I'm nursing a headache by the end of lunch, though, and my last two classes go by in a blur, culminating in the fulfilment of my prophetic vision that by the time I got to Gaelic I would have zero languages available, but thankfully, the Gaelic teacher takes pity on me when I hold up my mobile-autism-yikes sign a la Wile E. Coyote, and all I have to do is listen and read. I'm even good at those things when I'm not expected to respond. She gives me a strange look when she sees I've written Mac a' Ghobhainn on the paper I hand in at the end of class instead of Nic a' Ghobhainn (the masculine patronymic instead of the feminine) for the Gaelic translation of my surname Smith, but she doesn't push.

It's not until I'm bundled into the Subaru with Mum kindly not demanding to hear about my day when I realise two very strange things at once.

One, for once, absolutely no one has called me girl or lass or any variation thereof. No "new girl," no "that girl from Texas," nothing.

And two, I know where I heard that familiar voice. Lisbeth, a variation on Elizabeth. The Gaelic for Elizabeth is Ealasaid, and that is the voice I heard in the clearing. That is one of the Others Deirdre and Daibhidh said would have killed me on sight.

ELEVEN

By the time I'm back in my room, safely ensconced away from the mums (Mam looked like she had to muzzle herself when we got home to keep from badgering me), I flop onto the bed, exhausted.

One year. I should be able to manage that, right?

There's been too much in the past few days, too much for my brain to cope with, and there'll be more to come.

First and most pressing, I've been changed. Not only that, the change happened with no warning and less fanfare, and now I am even more different than I was before. Beyond the stars and the brambles, I don't know what else will happen in my company. The brambles could have been Deirdre, of course, but I'm afraid to go to the back garden to see if they've again regenerated.

Second, which would maybe be first if I could really wrap my brain around it, I've been made part of a group of preternatural beings that harbour an unknown quantity of people who apparently kill mortals on a whim. I don't know how to tell those ones from the more friendly variety.

I've been on the outside looking in my whole life, and this is not how I imagined becoming an insider.

Third, I've got to keep it together enough to get through another school year, and one of the Others I *know* is dangerous has decided to go to high school, for some reason.

As my therapist would say, that's a lot.

I miss Paul.

He wouldn't have a clue what to do, but he'd at least distract me.

Oh, and fourth, there's an Otherworldly cèilidh I'm supposed to go to and make my own magical debut. I don't even know what day it's supposed to be, though Deirdre said she'd be in touch.

I hate not knowing what to expect.

I open my meditation app and poke at it until I find a short, guided meditation for anxiety and put it on, lying back on my bed.

I'm rubbish at meditating without guidance, but if I have one thing I can focus on, sometimes I can at least slow my heart rate to something resembling normal.

I let the gentle voice talk me through breathing in and out, my mind lighting on every sensation at once—the movement of air over my top lip, the smooth, cool texture of the duvet cover under my fingertips, the light patter of drizzle against the window.

Even though I've been a mess for the past few months, the exercises my therapist has taught me help. It's like establishing and coding processes in my brain.

When the meditation ends, I feel slightly better. I stay where I am, though, lying on the bed and staring at the blank, slanted ceiling above my face. I reach out and touch it. Maybe Granaidh would let me put posters up.

Okay. Process the first: identify the problem.

It's hard to quantify my current problem, but I think it boils down to having choices made for me. I technically don't have to finish this year of school; Scottish education is only compulsory to age sixteen. But the mums would kill me if I dropped out, and Dad would possibly learn to teleport on the spot to get here and tell me off.

Still, the knowledge that there's an out, even an unpleasant one, is sort of helpful.

So the issue is that I don't have much control right now. My schedule is decided Monday through Friday between eight and four, I have to ease into an entire new world at some point in the next week, and while at least we're for sure staying in Ballinacollie, that row with the mums—a century ago, it feels—was just another example of how little control I actually have over where I am.

I'm proud of myself for figuring all of this out. There's enough stuff I leave locked in a compartment deep in my mind, like Paul's death, but having at least articulated something to myself, I feel a little better.

The next process is, by extension, to establish what I can control.

My mums are giving me more space now that I have my diagnosis. They have a biweekly Zoom appointment with an autism specialist here in Argyll who is helping them process so they don't put it on me, and she's also helping establish their own new processes to make our home more Cam-friendly. They used to get so frustrated with me when I wouldn't talk and when I would get distressed that they didn't like me to spend a lot of time alone in my room, but since my diagnosis, they've backed off a lot, and I think our relationship has improved because of it.

I can control giving myself space. I can probably control my room if I ask Granaidh how she feels about me making it mine. That's a start.

I can control what I do with my schoolwork. I might not be able to control my teachers or my fellow students—and I don't want to—but I can control my studying, and maybe if I do well, I'll be able to have more options next year.

That doesn't seem like much. Now that I'm home and have some space, I can barely remember my school day. I've never done well with changes in routine, and this is a big one. But we will settle into a new routine, and I can make parts of that mine.

It's small and sort of silly, but I pull out a notebook from my schoolbag and scribble down a rough schedule for my days. Up at seven, leave for school at eight, school until half three, home by half four. It's almost five now, and I know Mum and Granaidh will be wanting to have tea soon. I draw in a block from half four to quarter past five that is Cam Time. Decompression. Good.

I block out some more time after tea where I can go for a ramble, then add in homework, running, shower. That takes up pretty much the whole evening, but seeing it all listed out like that loosens some of the tightness in my chest.

I don't have the brainspace to deal with anything Otherworldly tonight, and I should probably go relieve the mums of their anxiety about my first day of school. I can do that.

Though as I change out of my school uniform and into leggings and a sweatshirt, I feel a flutter in my stomach as Ezra's half-smile intrudes in my mind.

❧

I say a quick hello to Granaidh, but she's cooking and getting stuff ready for tea. So when she gestures at the back door and says "a-muigh" to tell me my mums are outside, I head for the foyer to grab my shoes and my mac and go around the house to find them in the back garden.

"Never seen anything like it," Mam's saying, staring at the brambles with Mum leaning one arm on her shoulder.

They're veritably bursting with berries, and I come to a stop a few yards away. Oh, god.

Did I do this? Did Deirdre?

"Cam, do you see this? We just cleaned these off a couple days ago." Mam looks over her shoulder at me, and I can't tell if that's wonder or dismay on her face.

"Aye, that's a lot of berries," I say carefully.

"Gies a hand then, love," Mam says, and Mum removes her arm from Mam's shoulder to bend down and hand me a large, clean plastic flowerpot.

I obey, thankful for the physical distraction as I quickly tell them about my day and about Grace helping me in the canteen. I also tell them about my schedule and what I want to do to make sure I have decompression time, and they exchange a look when I glance at them over my now-heaping flowerpot full of blackberries.

"What?" I ask.

"Proud of you," Mam says. Her short, dark curls are a mop on the top of her head, and she beams at me. "That's a good plan."

Mum nods her agreement, and we go back to work.

Fifteen minutes later, we've filled up five flowerpots and a mixing bowl, and we take them inside through the foyer to leave our muddy shoes where they won't track dirt on Granaidh's floors.

When we parade into the kitchen with the spoils, Granaidh stops in the middle of mashing some boiled tatties in a stainless-steel bowl on her lap, the potato masher dropping a gob of mashed tatties into the bowl with a wet *thwack*.

"Mo chreach-sa thàinig," she says. "Às a' phreas againne?"

"From the bushes out back, aye," Mum answers at the same time Mam says, "'S ann," to confirm, and Granaidh bursts out laughing.

"Uill, uill, nach cuir sibh air a' bhòrd iad is nì mi rudeigin dhiubh. Dè fon ghrèin . . ." Granaidh trails off, going back to the tatties as she gestures with one elbow at us to put the berries on the worktop like she said. She shakes her head, her sleek, silver bob of hair swaying like a curtain at her jawline.

"Crumble?" I say hopefully.

"Pie," Mam says with a stern glare I think is a joke.

"Scones." Mum sets down her two pots with a thunk. "Though at this rate, we'll have Mother baking till Hogmanay."

It feels different eating with them when there's almost no tension. Mam tells me about an app she heard about designed for and by autistic people and folks with ADHD for scheduling, and that fills me with a warmth that isn't coming from my cuppa or from the salmon cakes and mashers Granaidh made for us.

I tell them about the short story I read in Gaelic class, "Na Solais" by Iain Mac Dhòmhaill, and that piques Granaidh's interest, so I promise to read it out to her later.

None of us hear the car pull into the drive, but we do see it leave—an old, battered pickup that belongs to one of the neighbouring crofters in Inverinan. Mum starts to get up, but I wave a hand at her and go to the front door myself, hearing their conversation resume behind me as I leave the kitchen.

When we used to visit Granaidh in my childhood, I never thought much of the older folks who would occasionally drop by with things for her. I just thought it was neighbours being neighbourly, but once we moved in, I realised it seems like it's a bit more than that.

They don't really ever stop to chat, for one thing. For another, the things they bring are all things we couldn't just buy at the shops.

The air in the foyer is chilly, and I pop open the front door to see a large cardboard box on the stoop, wrapped loosely in clear plastic to keep the rain off.

I pull it inside and hear a small scratch and a "meep" from within.

I freeze.

My first thought is someone's given us some chicks. We have a coop, but Granaidh had the remaining hens butchered last year after a weasel or something attacked and injured them.

I carefully move the box the rest of the way in the door and shut the door behind it, taking hold of the plastic to peel it back from the edge where whoever that was took care not to make it airtight. I can see blurred movement inside the box, and aside from that one little sound, there's no peeping.

When I pull the plastic all the way back, a small pair of dark, baby blue eyes stare back at me from what looks like a gathered shadow.

And then the "meep" comes again as the tiny kitten opens their mouth and reveals wee, needle-sharp teeth with the small cry.

TWELVE

After a moment of staring dumbstruck at the kitten in the box, I look at the other half of the box, which is loaded with tins of kitten food, a few toys, and, somewhat incongruously and dangerously, what has to be a large, butcher-paper-wrapped parcel of hot smoked salmon, from the smell. That's probably driving the wee feline out of their tiny mind, despite the creature looking barely old enough to handle solid food.

"Hiya," I say to the kitten, reaching into the box to pluck the kitten out.

At first glance, the kitten's sex is female, and while I think gendering pets is ridiculous (okay, so my agender arse is biased), I figure the kitten and I can both use she/her pronouns. She's jet black and has tufts of fluff that indicate she will likely grow into a long-haired void panther one day. She is soft and squirmy until I hold her up to my chest, where she settles, and I hear a breathtaking tiny rattle of a purr.

"Oh, no, m' eudail," I say. "Gaol agam ort a cheana."

Love at first sight, this.

I stroke the kitten's head, giving her a wee scritch behind the ears, and I will fight the mums if they don't want to let me keep her. I've always wanted a cat, but Dad's allergic, and the mums always said we moved too much for it to be fair to pets, who wouldn't understand getting uprooted.

I kind of wish they'd taken that attitude with me.

That said, they're going to wonder what's taking me so long out here.

"Here goes nothing," I say under my breath, getting to my feet and dragging myself back to the kitchen.

Mum's already started on the washing-up, though Mam and Granaidh are eating some chocolate digestives with fresh cups of tea, and before I can say anything, the wee void in my hands announces herself with a loud mew.

"Erm," I say as every head in the room turns toward me. "Someone left a gift."

Mum's hands are dripping soapy water onto the clean dishes in the drying rack. She hurriedly moves them back over the basin and rinses them, grabbing a tea towel.

But Granaidh's already on her way to me, cooing as she wheels her chair across the couple yards between us and comes to a stop at my feet.

"Ò, seall air a' phiseig!" she says, holding her hands out, where I deposit the tiny floof after a moment of selfish hesitation.

"A kitten," Mum says, coming to peer at the creature. "Someone dropped a *kitten* on the doorstep."

"They also left her some food. And us some food. Salmon, I think," I say as if that makes much difference.

Mam joins us, brushing biscuit crumbs onto her plate before she does. "That's a first," she says.

Though I have learnt long ago that the expression on Mum's face is her exasperated face, she looks down at her mother's lap, where the kitten is stretched out on her back in the dip between Granaidh's legs, little pot belly up.

After a moment, though, the kitten scrambles over onto her knee and takes a couple tottery steps in my direction, so Granaidh holds her up to me to take.

"'S ann leatsa a tha i," Granaidh says definitively to me, establishing my ownership of the kitten.

"Mother," Mum says, then stops and heaves a huge sigh when she sees the kitten burrowing into my chest between my boobs. "Theagamh gur ann."

Excitement leaps in my chest at Mum's agreement, and I let out a gleeful squeak, to which the kitten replies with another mew through her rattly purr.

"Dè an t-ainm a th' oirre?" Granaidh asks.

Hm. A good question. What *is* her name?

I shrug. I've never named an animal before. Mam goes back to the table and pulls out her phone—doubtless already looking up the vets in Oban or one-clicking a litter tray and some litter—and Granaidh grins up at me and gives my bum a light thwack before rolling her chair back to the table to finish her tea.

"Ceapag an Fhànais," I say suddenly. "Fànas for short."

"You want to name a cat 'Lump of Space'?" Mum asks from the sink.

"She's a little lump of *void*," I say, prickling with sudden defensiveness. Fànas can mean both *void* and *space*, and I like the diminutive ceapag. It sounds cute.

Granaidh's peal of laughter sounds through the kitchen, and Mam jumps, almost dropping her phone.

"Fànas a' phiseag," Granaidh says, chuckling. "Sin agad e, m' eudail."

With Granaidh's approval, it's settled. Fànas herself has snuggled into my hand and fallen asleep.

It's almost as if the universe knew I'd just figured out a schedule and wanted to punish me for it. The rest of the evening is spent sorting out a makeshift litter tray using the box Fànas arrived in and the plastic that was serving as her umbrella. Turns out Granaidh actually has some litter in the shed to sprinkle on the drive when it gets icy in winter since she doesn't like using salt and says it upsets her perennials that grow downhill where all the salt water would run off.

I put the litter tray in the bathroom next to my room and put out a piece of cardboard and water and food dishes against the wall by my bed. Not sure if the kitten will be able to manage the stairs yet, but I guess we'll find out.

When I put her in the litter tray and gently guide her paw to scratching, I'm amazed that she knows what to do immediately and digs about with aplomb, doing her business without delay. So much easier than dogs. Paul had a puppy, so I heard all the potty-training nightmare stories.

So. Much. Pee.

If I wanted a distraction, though, I've now got one. I haven't any homework from my first day, so I lie in bed with Fànas pouncing around me on the duvet, reading about kitten care on my mobile screen.

I'm not sure how to tell what changes are my magic and what are just random chance. Though the brambles seem like a likely candidate for magic. I wish someone had told me how it *works* aside from the mysterious assertion that it would mould itself to me.

The sky is still covered in clouds, so I can't see the stars now, but a smile pulls at my lips when I look over at Fànas. My own personal space floof.

Belatedly, I remember the feather I tucked in the pocket of my jacket when I last saw Ezra. After a moment of deliberation, I leave Fànas on the bed and hurry downstairs as quick as I can, skating down the hardwood corridor to the foyer on my stockinged feet.

The feather is right where I left it in my pocket, which gives me a small jolt of surprise. Not that I didn't expect it, but I think some part of me expected it to disappear, like fair folk gold is supposed to. I guess a feather isn't really gold. I brush it against my palm. It's pure black in the dimness of the corridor without any hint of the iridescent shimmer of purples and blues and greens. I wish I'd have a chance to talk to them before this cèilidh.

I hurry back up the stairs, feeling like I'm ascending into my own world.

I don't want to close the door to my room if there's a chance the kitten will need to toilet, but she just went, so I close the door for now, my heart racing for a reason I can't explain.

I put the feather on the bedside table, my instinct telling me that Fànas will be all too interested in it, and besides, one of the toys the neighbour provided was a fishing pole with a feather toy at the end of it.

She goes absolutely berserk the second I pick up the pole and dangle the feather toy in front of her, scrabbling all over the duvet with her wee claws catching in the fabric. I wince at that, but Granaidh will likely forgive her.

Fànas makes clumsy pounces and leaps, tumbling this way and that with kitten awkwardness, and if I wasn't already in love with this tiny black being, I would be a goner by now.

There's a light tapping on the window that makes me jump, and at my sudden movement, Fànas bounces into the air with all four paws, tail poofed in an instant.

Ezra's face is framed in the dormer glass.

How did they get *up* there? I scramble sheepishly to my feet a split second later, foolish as I remember Ezra can fly.

I motion at them to back away from the glass, and they do while I open it. It seems to have stopped raining, but some beaded water drips down onto me anyway.

"Hi," I say as if they didn't just turn up at my bedroom window. "Erm . . . what are you doing here?"

I keep my voice low enough that I hope no one else in the cottage will hear me. With my door closed and the rest of them likely downstairs, it's probably safe.

Ezra peers through the open window and points at the feather. "You have something of mine. I'm able to find them wherever they are no matter what, but I usually don't bother unless it's clearly in the possession of someone who wants to see me."

Oh. *Oh.* "Are you saying I *summoned* you?"

They give me a wry smile. "In a manner of speaking, yes. May I come in?"

I glance over my shoulder at the closed door. "Aye, come in. I think everyone's downstairs."

"They are. I saw them through the window when I landed."

I move over to the door and turn the lock anyway. At least Ezra can literally fly away if they turn up at the door and wonder why I'm talking to myself.

There's a light thump as Ezra hops down from the window, and I turn back to them just in time to see their face absolutely light up at the sight of Fànas on the bed, who has recovered from the shock of me startling and is now padding gingerly across the duvet in Ezra's direction.

"Seo Ceapag an Fhànais," I say, introducing the kitten. "Fànas for short."

Ezra grins, perching on the edge of the bed and holding out one hand for Fànas to sniff, which she does, her wee whiskers forward and curious and her stubby little kitten tail straight up in the air.

"I love the name," Ezra says. "Wee void lump, aye, that's you. Abair piseag!"

Fànas sets about pouncing on Ezra's long fingers as they scratch their fingertips across the duvet.

"You had school today," Ezra says. "Survived, it seems."

I appreciate that they're not asking how it went. "Yep, though I was a bit fried by the end."

It's so easy to chat to Ezra, like I can relax into my own skin. I move over to sit on the corner of the bed a few feet away from where they're playing with Fànas, and as the kitten feels my weight depress the mattress, she abandons Ezra and waddles on over to me again.

"Someone just left her on the doorstep tonight," I say. "Granaidh gets strange deliveries fairly often, but this is the first time to my knowledge anyone's left something alive."

"Strange deliveries?" Ezra asks.

"I never used to think anything of it, but since we moved in, I've kind of realised it happens all the time. People drop off fresh food from their gardens, eggs from their chickens, sometimes a fleece or two for her to spin. Occasionally a bottle of whisky, unlabelled—I think a few people around these parts still distil their own. Tonight was the kitten and two entire hot smoked salmons, which I cannot wait to eat." Listed out like that, it sounds a bit ridiculous.

"Interesting," says Ezra.

"Is it?" I pick up Fànas, edging myself onto the bed fully so I can cross my legs, and I set the kitten in the crook of my knee, where she sits down, blinking slowly.

"People tend to take care of each other in these parts, or they did," Ezra says. "My mum was from Taigh an Uillt, and when Dad fell ill, people made sure she didn't have to cook."

"I'm sorry," I say, because I think that's what I'm supposed to say.

Ezra looks up, then bites their lip as if they said more than they meant to. "It's fine. Wasn't that what killed him."

There's a long silence that stretches out between us, punctuated only by the kitten purring. She's wobbling where she sits, half asleep sitting up.

"Why did you want to see me?" Ezra asks.

I have learned a subject change like that means people don't want to talk about the previous topic anymore, but I'm not sure I want to talk about *this* one.

"Erm," I say, stalling. "I don't really know?"

"If you don't want to save me a dance, I won't be offended," Ezra says with a wink, and I think they are telling the truth.

"I'm a terrible dancer," I blurt out, then realise that might sound like I don't want to dance with them, and I barrel onward, and my words come out all in a rush. "I'd love to dance with you as long as you don't mind me not knowing any of the cèilidh dances except maybe a strip the willow. I never learned but always wanted to—it's just that we always moved before they came round in my Scottish schools, and in the US it's all weird square dancing if they do social dancing at all, and—"

I break off and venture a look at Ezra's face, and they've got one corner of their mouth turned up, and their cheeks have a sudden rosy glow. Are they blushing?

"Want to know a secret about Otherworld cèilidhean?" Ezra asks, and at my nod, they continue. "Magic. You don't have to know any of the dances. The Others exist on every continent on this planet, in every culture, in every land. We're different everywhere you go, and on nights like this, anyone could turn up from anywhere and join in. We're the outsiders, the forgotten. Separate from the mortal world but lingering at its edges. I don't know who decided it, but a long time ago, the Others figured when it's just us, when we're in our corner of this universe together, no one should be left out because they don't know where to put their feet—and those who don't have use of their feet can dance however they see fit."

I stare at them through this short speech, my brain processing what they're saying, drinking it in. That last sentence—some of the Others are disabled? The moment the thought passes through my brain, I feel foolish. I'm still autistic. *I'm* a disabled Other.

"All of your thoughts just scroll across your face sometimes," Ezra murmurs. “Other times it’s like you’re on the other side of a wall.”

“I was just thinking about there being disabled Others,” I say quietly. “About getting access to magic without being erased or rewritten.”

Ezra’s face softens. “Everyone’s magic and needs are different. Some people do change, but others don’t. Our magic changes with us, lets us be who we are and how we think we should be in our deepest and most sacred mind.”

They hesitate, and for a moment I think they’re about to leave again.

When they don’t, I hesitantly ask, “What about your magic?”

Ezra cocks their head, gaze seeking out the feather that still sits on my bedside table.

“My magic,” they say, their eyes seeking out mine, the contact burning but unbreakable, “is about fluidity.”

Before my eyes, Ezra’s shortish, black waves lengthen. Their face doesn’t change, not hugely—smooth cheeks are still smooth, full lips still full—but their jaw softens almost imperceptibly. Their shoulders stay the same, but their flat chest is suddenly not flat, and where their waist was straight and angular, it is suddenly curved.

It’s the slight coolness of air on my tongue that tells me my mouth is hanging open.

When Ezra speaks again, their voice is the same but not, from saltwater and smoke to honey and ink, the change at once ineffable and infinitesimal and vast.

“My magic allows me to be seen as all I am,” they say softly.

I think until this moment, I haven’t *really* believed. The stars in the daytime sky, the brambles, the feather, the note from Deirdre—all of it could perhaps have a logical, if improbable, explanation that isn’t magic. I only thought people disappeared, hallucinated, blinked, something.

But I cannot deny this, not now. “You’re—stunning,” I hear myself say. “All of you.”

The tremor in my hands and the quivering inhale of my breath makes me aware that I’ve said that out loud.

I snap my mouth shut, and my teeth click together audibly. Oh, my god. I said that out loud.

But Ezra just smiles at me, a dazzling smile, and in the lamplight from my bedside table, that hair shimmers back its raven iridescence.

"No, you," they say, and one hand raises to cheek height an inch from my face where I can feel the heat of their palm.

Just as I try to nod my assent to their touch, though, their hand falls away as Ezra tenses.

I hear it at the same time—footsteps on the stairs.

"Save me that dance?" Ezra asks, and all I can do is nod helplessly as they rise in one fluid motion and nudge the window open. "If you need me before then, though, you have my feather. Don't let the kitten eat it."

They glance back once over their shoulder and wink, and I see my own reflection in their eyes as if I'm looking in a mirror.

And then they're out the window, the flap of wings in the wind fading in an instant just as Mam's voice calls out, "Cam? We need your opinion on a cat tree."

Fànas stirs on my lap. For once, my words have fled for an entirely new reason.

I carefully cup the sleepy kitten in one hand and get up, going to the door.

Cat trees. My mums are such softies.

THIRTEEN

I realise on the way to school Tuesday morning that I forgot to tell Ezra about Lisbeth—or Ealasaid—and I think that is important. I can't remember the last time my brain went completely smooth in the presence of an attractive person, and I'm not sure how I feel about it.

It *is* nice to feel something, however.

I don't see Lisbeth again over the rest of the week except for one glimpse in the canteen. Grace tells me that she usually doesn't eat lunch with the plebes. I don't know what that means.

I do meet Grace's sister Eilidh, though, and she's a slight, shy girl who hides behind a curtain of medium brown hair and peeks out at me with pretty brown eyes in a rosy-cheeked round face. I've been assigned to the Fingal clan, like Eilidh, and she seems pleased to have something in common with me. Grace is in Diarmid.

I'm able to coast through the week partly because of Fànas, whose pictures provide me with everything I need to keep attention off me personally. Despite being made of void, she's been surprisingly easy for me to photograph with the camera in my mobile, and my camera roll is now almost entirely her little sooty, floofy face. She's enough of a distraction for me that whenever I start getting overwhelmed at school, I just sneak open her pictures and look at her until I calm down. So far, I haven't been caught.

When Friday rolls around, Grace and her sister ask me if I have any plans for the weekend, and I tell them I'm meant to go to a cèilidh, which is true, though I still don't know any of the details. Both Grace and Eilidh seem disappointed by this, but I don't really know why. I leave them after school with a promise to see them next week, and I'm afraid that I'm a little too abrupt leaving because the anxiety is making little effervescent bubbles in my stomach, and I keep swallowing like I might throw up.

Mum and Mam fill the drive home with chatter at each other, which is too much for my brain, so I put in headphones and listen to Sigur Rós as loud as my ears can manage, which calms me. That it's their sleep album helps, though by the time we get home, I'm drowsy, head nodding against the headrest in the back seat.

I sit in the car a minute or so after the mums get out, and though they pause at the bonnet before moving toward the house, I hear Mam tell Mum to come on.

The clouds outside scud across the sky, so quickly I can watch them moving. In between them, the patches of blue are filled with stars.

The door is too loud when I open it. Stepping out into the afternoon, the late August air feels like it has decided to be done with summer. There's a bite to it that I don't remember being there this morning. Then again, Oban is on the coast—the sea changes everything.

My routine works. I don't get any complaints when I go straight to my room when I get home, and Fànas is there waiting for me. She hasn't managed to go down the stairs yet, but she can get up them, so in the mornings I bring her down to see Granaidh, and when it's time for me to get home and Granaidh's enjoying her afternoon norrag—nap—Fànas goes upstairs and climbs the duvet to get onto the bed.

Seeing her there every day is one of the best parts of my new routine. Already she's starting to floof out—her cheeks are getting tufty and, to my delight, so are her ears. If those are any judge, her tail is going to be *magnificent.*

Today, after I drop my schoolbag next to my bedside table and refill Fànas's water bowl, I notice she's batting at something on the bed.

Sliding my phone onto the bedside table and plugging it in to charge, I sit on the bed, and almost before I'm settled, Fànas climbs onto my lap.

The thing she was batting at is a cream-coloured envelope. I pick it up. The paper feels deliciously smooth on my fingertips, like touching five-hundred-thread-count Egyptian cotton after only ever touching burlap.

Only my name is on it in a handwritten swirl of ink that shimmers in the light. It doesn't seem to be sealed, but when I turn it over, the flap parts from the body of the envelope and reveals the edge of something I don't know if I can even call paper.

If someone made lace out of gold filigree, it might look something like this. I'm afraid to touch it.

It's cold like metal when I slide it out with careful fingers, and while Fànas snags a claw in a dangling curl of my hair, I hold the thing up to the light, where it looks like the inscription is written in sunshine. It reflects onto my shirt, and Fànas makes a curious chirping sound and pounces my left boob.

I should have changed out of my uniform before sitting down. With my free hand, I undo the top two buttons on my shirt.

Grimacing at the possible puncture holes in my new uniform shirt, I read the Gaelic on the invitation.

Bidh fàilte bhlàth ort a-nochd aig cèilidh shònraichte.

Nuair thig gairm nan clagan aig meadhan-oidhche, le grèim air a' chuireadh is deòin nad chridhe, thig agus tu fèin nar measg.

My hand is shaking slightly on the delicate swirls of gold—a warm welcome, it says, to a special cèilidh. Is this truly all I need to do to go? Hold this in my hand when the clock hits midnight and as long as I'm willing, I'll just . . . go?

No one's told me what to wear to an Otherworld cèilidh, and I highly doubt my prom dress from Austin would be appropriate. Paul and I went together, him in a white tux and me in a sparkly teal sheath dress that hid the fact I was wearing what was basically soft ballet slippers on my feet since dress shoes and me do not mix.

I shake my head, gingerly placing the invitation on the bedside table next to my phone.

Deirdre just wants me to turn up there? In the middle of all these Others I've never met? No way. Nope.

I scoot down on the bed and cuddle Fànas to my chest, where she immediately leaves little black kitten hairs all over the white button-down.

No sooner have I gotten her little rattly purr going than I hear a knock at the door downstairs.

I know without checking that it's Deirdre. I couldn't explain how—I just do. I deposit Fànas on the duvet and get up to change, quickly doffing my uniform and tossing it on the stool at the vanity to replace it with leggings and a long, soft knit shirt that has thumb holes.

Deirdre's voice filters up the stairs, and the sound of coats and shoes removed mixes with Mam's voice as well. Granaidh's norrag may be cut short.

Fànas and I trot downstairs just as Mam and Deirdre round the corner.

"Hiya," Deirdre says brightly.

"Cam, you didn't mention you had a friend coming by." Mam sounds way too excited to be cross with me.

"Erm, sorry. Was that today?" I say.

Deirdre laughs. I'm struck by the way she looks here. She looks like a teenager—skin dewy and clearer than most of us—and despite her still-imposing stature, her waves of dark hair are pulled back in a loose plait over one shoulder, and she's wearing a fashionable black jacket that wouldn't be out of place in an H&M. She fiddles with a charm bracelet on her right wrist.

"Yes, *today*," Deirdre says as if I've made the best joke. "Or were you secretly hoping I'd abandon you to stand me up?"

That's a little too *Deirdre*, considering that's exactly what was going through my head upstairs.

"Pffft, if you abandoned me, I wouldn't be the one standing you up," I say, surprised at myself for the banter.

Mam laughs, a burst that fills the room and ends in her characteristic snort, which makes Deirdre grin.

"You couldn't pay that kid to go to a cèilidh full of new people alone," Mam says. "She'd sooner try to jump Loch Awe in a single bound."

"Might succeed, too," Deirdre says, giving me a sly grin.

It wouldn't occur to me to *try* such a thing, but now I'm wondering if I could.

"You promised to show me the kitten," Deirdre says.

"I'll leave you two to that," Mam says. "I've got a late Zoom meeting, but you better pop in to say goodbye before yous are off."

I nod at Mam and then motion at Deirdre to follow me up the stairs. No idea where Mum's gotten off to, but I hear Granaidh stirring in her room. Mam's laugh probably woke her up.

When we get to my room, I gesture at Fànas with an awkward flourish as Deirdre closes the door behind her.

"Ceapag an Fhànais," I say. "Fànas for short."

"Oh, I know," Deirdre says, making a beeline for the kitten. Already she is different, as if she shrugged out of her teenager suit when she passed over the threshold of my room. "Fànas and I go way back."

"What? You do?" Did Deirdre leave the kitten?

She perches on the edge of the bed, reaching out to pick up the still-clumsy kitten. "Oh, aye. She and I had a fun game of pounce when I dropped off your invitation."

Oh.

"How'd you get in here?" I ask. The window's latched.

Deirdre gives me a long-suffering look. "Do you really need to ask that question?"

"I . . . guess not. Wait, can anyone just turn up in here?" I hate that idea a lot. I'm not even thrilled that Deirdre popped into my room, invitation or not.

She returns her gaze to the kitten, who is batting at a lock of Deirdre's hair.

"Yes, which is also why I'm here." Deirdre frowns, placing Fànas on the duvet again. "It would be better if you ward your own home, but I've taken care of it for now."

"Will you teach me?" I ask. "I wouldn't know where to start."

"Yes, but not tonight." At that, the woman's face bursts into a blazing grin. "Tonight I get to show you a whole new world."

"I cannot think of anything more terrifying than that," I say bluntly. "This one is bad enough."

"Cam," Deirdre says, leaning forward with her elbows on her knees,

Fànas trying to climb her right leg. "Imagine being able to literally disappear when you want to. Just—*poof*. Gone. Don't want to be perceived? Don't be. Be a fly on the wall. A very beautifully dressed fly."

The sudden thought of a fly in tulle and sequins and a tiara is so ridiculous that I crack a smile.

"Okay, fine," I say. "That sounds, at the very least, better than school."

"I would *hope* so," Deirdre says, holding one hand to her chest in a display of being affronted so cartoonish even I can tell that's what she's doing.

"The mums will murder me if I don't at least say goodbye," I say. "If we're going to, you know, *poof*, it should be after that."

"Of course. By the way, how's the bramble out back?"

At Deirdre's wide grin, I can't even respond other than shaking one hand in the air for a moment before managing to get out a "That was *you*?"

"Couldn't resist. Your Granaidh makes the best crumble, and if I am not mistaken, she's got one in the oven just now." Deirdre plucks Fànas from her leg and places the tiny kitten on her shoulder, where Fànas wobbles precariously, needle-small claws digging in and finding purchase. Deirdre doesn't seem to notice or care. "You wouldn't expect me to poof on an empty stomach, now, would you?"

My own stomach gives an unhelpful gurgle as I lead Fànas and her noble steed down the stairs.

FOURTEEN

The crumble interlude is over far too quickly, and almost before I've wiped the bit of blackberry and custard from my face—I'm rubbish at leaving a meal without wearing some of it—Deirdre bustles me out the door, invitation in hand.

"How did you tell them we were getting to this cèilidh?" I ask when I don't see a car—not that Scottish teenagers have them.

Deirdre gestures vaguely in the direction of Inverinan. "We are walking to my house, and my older brother will meet us."

I hate lying.

"It's not a lie," Deirdre says. "We don't lie. Start walking."

I obey, dubiously following her down to the end of the lane where, between one step and another, the world shifts around us, and I trip. Deirdre catches me by the arm and keeps me on my feet.

"Oops, sorry. It's been a wee while since I travelled with a first timer." She peers at me. "Do you feel sick or anything?"

I shake my head, blinking away the change in light from late afternoon outdoors to indeterminate indoor . . . candlelight?

"This *is* my home," Deirdre says, apparently satisfied that I'm not going to vomit on her feet. "And Daibhidh is my brother, whether we share blood or not. We'll meet him at some point."

I look around at Deirdre's home. We're just over the threshold in an immaculate cottage not so very different to Granaidh's, except it's about three times as large. Closer to "cottage as in where the Dashwoods end up in *Sense and Sensibility*" than it is to "cottage as in Highland." There is a wide staircase that leads to the first floor, and despite the airy openness of the place, it gleams with dark, polished wood. I can't quite tell where the light is coming from.

"It's beautiful," I tell her honestly. "Though I haven't seen all of it yet."

Deirdre laughs at that. "Someday I'll give you the full tour, but not today. We only have a few hours to get ready for the cèilidh."

"I hope I wasn't supposed to bring anything to wear," I say. "Because I didn't."

"Cam. A luaidh. I'm not letting you make your Otherworld debut looking like you were swimming in Loch Ness in search of Niseag."

"Is Niseag real?" I ask.

"If you really want to know, you're more than welcome to visit Loch Ness and try to find her yourself," Deirdre says dryly. "Though there are far more fun things you could do with your time and magic."

Touché.

Maybe. I am not sure I'm brave enough to go diving in an enormous geological trench loch so peaty you can barely see a meter in front of your face. *Anything* could be down there.

"Ceart, ma-tà. I don't like that look," Deirdre says, and she steers me toward the stairs. "Come into my bower, for I shall make a marvel of you."

"Is that supposed to scare me or encourage me?" I ask as I climb the stairs, glancing back at Deirdre.

"Yes."

Oh.

Deirdre points me at the first door we come to, and when I open it, I step over the threshold into . . . a bower.

I assumed she meant the sort of lady's bower one might expect in a regency-era period piece; all lace and—I don't know—powder or something. For noses.

Instead, this is—I have to look back over the threshold to make sure there's still a house there, because on this side of the door, we're in a forest thicket.

I look up, seeking the ceiling, but there is nothing but twisted, interwoven branches that seem to have grown into a dome-like roof. Sunlight filters through them, dappling the mossy floor where I stand. It's soft beneath my feet, like real moss.

"It is real," Deirdre says. "Not many of us can do this kind of magic, but I've always had a way with it. I'm lost if I'm away from the woods for too long."

She doesn't look at me while she speaks, only gazes fondly up at the branches, which move ever-so-slightly inward as if giving the bower a gentle hug.

"It's glorious," I say, the word not quite suited to the awe I feel.

What would it be like to have a door into a pocket of forest?

"You have clothes in here?" I ask after a moment because I don't see any.

"In a manner of speaking," Deirdre says. "But first, I need you to tell me what would make you feel comfortable. Physically. I'm not going to truss you up in something if it's going to make you miserable, aye?"

My mouth falls open, and I fail to make words long enough that Deirdre gives me a small, sad smile.

"You didn't really think I was going to force you into something that would make you hate tonight, did you? I don't actually want to torture you—I'm not that cruel."

Deirdre's lip quirks, and I get the distinct feeling she's just made a dig at others who are.

"I don't know what to expect at all," I say. "Which is . . . a lot for me."

"Ceart, ma-tà," Deirdre says thoughtfully. "Right. Well, in that case, perhaps we should start there."

Something tight loosens in my chest, and I give her a grateful nod.

"Tonight is a big night for many reasons, which is why I thought it would be a good night for you to turn up. All eyes will be on some special personages who are to be there, dignitaries and whatnot, and as everyone is expecting them, they will be much less likely to notice a new baby sìtheag who has been thrown into their world."

Deirdre pauses, then waves a hand, and two puffy ottomans appear, looking as if they are made from moss themselves. She sits on one and gestures to me to sit on the other. I obey, and she continues.

"For the most part, there's almost no ceremony. As a group, we don't much like formality and prefer fun. There will be introductions of the dignitaries, but that will happen straightaway at midnight, and I fully intend to be fashionably late." Deirdre winks. "I'll clue you in on who everyone is where necessary. The tolman is large and can be intimidating, but the cèilidh will mostly be in the talla mòr, and there are enough places in there you can escape to that I think you'll be fine. I'll show you some nooks and crannies to hide in."

"Thank you," I say. I hesitate for a moment before asking, "Why are you trying to make me so comfortable?"

Deirdre pushes her full lips together. She's quiet for so long that I'm not sure if she's going to answer me or not.

"Because others will not," she says finally. "I don't want to lie to you. You have become part of a dangerous world. Many of the Others"—I hear the emphasis on the word—"are capricious, changeable, and decidedly lack compassion. But we are not all like that. There is joy here without malice. I want to make sure you are rooted in that before anything else."

All I can do is nod, my mind spinning. It occurs to me that I have been extremely fortunate to have encountered Deirdre before anyone else in this world—or technically, Ezra, so twice fortunate—and not just for the fact that many would have killed me outright.

"Okay," I say, sitting up straighter on my ottoman. "How—what choices in clothes do I have?"

Deirdre's gaze falls on me with an unreadable expression, assessing me. "Is tu tha dana," she murmurs. Brave? Me? "The answer to that question is whatever you want. Skirts, suits, silk, starlight—you name it. What is it *you* have always wanted to wear but never thought it existed?"

My eyes widen. It's too many possibilities, but then I see a glint in Deirdre's dark eyes, and I realise she knows damn well it's too many possibilities, so she included . . . bait.

"Starlight?" It comes out in almost a whisper, and I look up involuntarily at the canopy of branches over our heads, where even through the tiny patches of blue sky, I can see the stars.

Her eyes gleam. "Yes, a ghràidh."

As long as I can remember, there has been a hollow inside me, a longing I cannot fill. Cianalas is the Gaelic word I reach for, a sweet yearning, a bitter denial. I keep it carefully locked away.

But right now, tonight, I want to *believe*.

Deirdre takes my hand and stands me in the middle of the bower, and as I tell her about my sensory limitations, she listens attentively, and she weaves me a marvel of a gown without me having to do a thing.

I can feel the strands of her magic in the air. It's like a sixth sense has awakened, some new part of me that perceives tiny currents that ply themselves together like Granaidh's spinning. When she's done, I'm afraid to see myself.

Looking down, though, I almost want to cry.

The gown comes to my feet with no train to impede me, though I think even if I were to run, I wouldn't so much as feel these skirts. She has crafted the underskirt from the twilit sky itself, it seems, the deepest blue at my feet gradually lightening to that perfect cerulean at the bodice, and over it ghosts . . . stars. So thin and fine it couldn't even be called gossamer, the outer layer of the gown ripples with every movement, tiny lights suspended that shift and move and shimmer.

She's made me a cape of it as well, and though I barely felt her touch my hair, it's lightly waving back from my face, no strands to brush against my cheeks, and when I turn to stare at Deirdre, there is a soft, pulsing sound that resonates through me like the binaural beats I use to fall asleep.

"Are you sure you're not a fa-fairy godmother?" I blurt out.

Deirdre bursts out laughing. "M' eudail, no. And I wouldn't use the F-word with anyone else you meet." She beams at me, though, a fond grin stretching her lips and bringing out a dimple in one cheek. "You won't turn into a pumpkin in the middle of the ball. But that *is* the nicest thing anyone's ever said about this very simple magic."

"Simple?" I ask.

"Wait until you learn how to do it," she says, amusement dripping from her words. "Mortals are so delightfully easy to impress."

"Have you seen how we live?" I mutter, and she laughs again.

While she readies herself, I stare into the mirror she left me. When I went to prom with Paul, I felt off. Not like me.

But now—I am draped in delicate, subtle stars. There is a light haze around me, almost a glow, almost a mist, and Deirdre said it will help me fade into the background if I want to. For all I know, it could be like Dumbo's magic feather—a gentle trick to get me to do something myself—but it comforts me anyway.

My hair is in perfect waves, its usual ashy blonde threaded through with moonlight and infinitesimal sparkles.

I'm not sure if a glamour counts as makeup, but my skin is dewy and shimmery, and my eyelashes are darker and smokey, and my lips are full and soft.

The best thing is that despite the gown and everything it connotes in the Earth world, for me in this moment it feels the farthest thing from gender. It makes me think of Ezra, their freedom to just *be*. I feel free. I cannot wait to see them tonight.

I pull myself away from the mirror, reeling at the thought of feeling this effervescent, bubbly sensation rising. When was the last time I felt excited for anything?

When I turn around, Deirdre is ready. I don't know what I expected, but whatever I expected, it's not what I see.

She's wearing a suit, for one, or something like a suit. Her trousers are snug, high-waisted, made of some sort of buttery fabric I can't identify. They're a dusty rose colour, and her shirt is sleeveless and shimmery and clings to her like a second skin. Her dark hair hangs in perfect loose curls to her waist, held back from her face with delicate combs of twisted silver and pale pink opals in the shape of teardrops of different sizes.

A silver fob watch hangs from a chain at her waist, and she casually flips it open, then holds it up to show me.

The time is half past midnight—the evening has slipped through my fingers already.

"Ready?" Deidre asks with a mysterious half-smile.

I swallow, stepping forward on feet clad only in near-invisible slippers I can barely feel. The moss is soft beneath me, and I reach into my gown's hidden pocket and retrieve my invitation at Deirdre's gesture.

Ready and willing, I guess.

"Deiseil is deònach," I say out loud.

The bower vanishes.

FIFTEEN

I am not prepared.

That much is obvious—there is no possible way in heaven or on Earth that I, a confused teenager who struggles to cope with a podcast, could be prepared for the instantaneous transportation into another world.

The stories are full of tales of fairy mounds, of the tolmain where the Sìthichean dwell. Stories of people vanishing into them only to return with honeyed tales upon their tongues or fear in their hearts or both. The Others, in the Gaelic world, have never been pixies in bluebells.

It's only Deirdre's hand on my arm that keeps me steady when we appear in a—thankfully quiet—chamber, alone and with me trying to wrangle my breath into something slower than hyperventilation.

"It's okay to be afraid," Deirdre says. "Take whatever time you need."

She could have told me not to be afraid, that there's no need to be afraid, that it's silly to be afraid. In a way, I appreciate her honesty. She and I both know it would be a lie.

But for whatever reason, her permission to be fearful grounds me.

The chamber we've arrived in is cool, cream-coloured marble. It feels good on my bare feet, smooth and without a hint of grit.

I cannot see what is lighting it; there is only a soft and golden glow.

"I'm ready," I say to Deirdre.

I think I've surprised her. Her hand freezes on my arm for the barest moment, and then she gives it a squeeze and lets go, nudging the air with her nose to indicate where we're going.

There are a couple other passageways I see to our right and left, but they are smaller arches, like a doorway in Granaidh's house rather than the larger arch ahead that meets at the top in a sharp, curving point from which carved swirls descend to the floor.

I can hear music in the distance.

"Why is this room empty?" I ask quietly.

My voice doesn't seem to carry, which strikes me as strange.

"There are many like it, and time works differently here," is all Deirdre says in answer.

We walk through the archway.

While some of my fear has settled, there was enough to begin with that I'm still jittery as we move into a wide corridor and the sound of music filters toward us from farther along. My knees feel a bit wobbly, and when Deirdre gives me a look with her head tilted to the side, questioning, I take a deep breath and doggedly continue.

The sound of voices comes on the heels of the music, and not long after that, the smell of food—anxiety or no, the intoxicating scents that reach my nose immediately set my mouth to watering. There is the tantalising, herbaceous scent of rosemary and thyme and caramelised meat, a sweet and earthy scent of honey and hazelnuts, a tang of berries, a hint of woodsmoke.

The air grows warmer by degrees, but within that, cooler swirls of breezes eddy, keeping it comfortable.

And then the corridor curves to the right, and Deirdre and I are no longer alone.

My first sight of the Others steals my breath.

No doubt this is an extravagant affair—obviously, if Deirdre dressed me like this—but in comparison to the prismatic rainbow that unfolds before us, my gown of stars and twilight is almost demure.

The first person I see is a tall, broad-shouldered Black man in a box-collared, sleeveless jacket of molten gold. His skin is dark brown and glows with the light reflected from his jacket, the gold of which is beaten, not gleaming. If it is fabric, I cannot imagine how it looks like it was poured from a crucible. If it is metal, my mind cannot understand how it moves with him.

Before I've even managed to process what I'm seeing, a woman sweeps past him into my line of sight in a cloud of shimmering, peacock-blue feathers that, like the gold, ignore the laws of physics. Her pale skin has a silvery cast to it, and her hair is every inch as silvery as the man's coat is gold, plaited in two thick fishtails down the back of her head that are each home to a crest of the same blue feathers that fan out into a semicircle like a peacock's tail, and those two plaits splay into uncountable tiny braids that form delicate knots to frame the plumage.

Gowns of pure flame, bodies near-nude except for crusts of jewels, suits of draping shadows—I am certain my eyes are wider than full moons. Deirdre is murmuring to me, but she stops when she realises I'm not understanding a word.

No one looks at me, and I don't know if that's my magic or Deirdre's or if I'm just that unremarkable, but no matter the reason, it's a relief.

As my eyes grow used to the cacophony of colour, I can see where we're going, and my heart stops.

The corridor we're in is the same cream-coloured stone as the entry chamber, but as we walk, the ceiling reaches higher and higher, the walls leaning apart wider and wider as other corridors intersect, and ahead of us, beyond the throng of Others who glimmer like jewels poured onto cream velvet, the walls form an arch so grand it makes the first one look like McDonald's.

Where the first had swirls and carvings spilling out from its apex, this one has gold and silver running in moving rivulets that reflect the light. They form webs and whorls and designs so intricate, they would put the stained glass in Notre Dame to shame. But instead of coloured panes, they hold something finer than crystal. It throws back the light in glittering rainbows that fall upon the cèilidh-goers like diamond rain.

Deirdre's voice manages to crack through my awe. "Our timing is bang on," she says. "The dignitaries have been introduced, and now the party's begun."

"Is Daibhidh here?" I ask.

Deirdre nods. "Somewhere. He promised to keep an eye out for you."

I want to ask why he isn't here with us, but Deirdre gives one sharp nod of her head, and I don't.

Our next steps take us through that enormous archway, and the prismatic light pours over the starshine of my gown. It makes me tremble with the sensation, and not in an uncomfortable way. I want to stay here in this cascade of colour and watch it dance upon my skin, but I daren't.

We're not two steps out of the river of Others in the grand hall when her hand catches my wrist and jerks me to a stop.

"Shit," she says, her teeth clicking as she bites off the T.

"What?" I ask.

I can't see anything alarming—or anything more alarming than a massive room full of Sìthichean—but Deirdre doesn't seem to be looking at anything in particular. Her eyes have gone distant, and she stares almost vacantly out over the mass of people.

Music swirls around us with small waves of conversations, snatches of words that whisper on the wind. And there *is* wind. A breeze that smells like sweet grass and moss circles the hall, washing away the heat of gathered bodies with the scent of petrichor.

But Deirdre is not the only one who has frozen.

From one breath to another, the hall has gone silent except for the music, even the dancers—barely visible over the heads of the crowd from here—coming to a halt.

Far from where we stand, almost exactly opposite the entrance we've just come through, there is another.

It is clear at a glance that *that* is the entry of note, because it is elevated several yards above the main floor of the ballroom, encircled with wide stairs that wear branching carpets of deep blue with gold trim down each side and the centre.

"This was not supposed to happen," Deirdre mutters beside me, so low I almost don't hear her.

I am not brave enough to ask what could possibly bring an entire hall full of Others to silence.

After a moment, even the music ebbs.

And there, on the dais over the sea of people, someone emerges from beyond.

It's Ezra.

Time slips out from beneath me. My heartbeat sounds far away, like I'm experiencing it from the other side of a cavern. All the myriad people, all the tumbling colours and shimmering sparkles, all the aromas of promised feasts and succour fade, and all I can see is Ezra.

They stand with a straight back and set shoulders. They are as I first saw them in the woods after they grabbed my hand through the hole in the door, short hair and flat chest, but also they could not be more different.

Ezra wears a simple collarless black shirt joined at the front by swirls of delicate, beaten gold. But when they move, their shirt catches the light, and instead of absorbing it like plain black would, like Ezra's hair, their shirt reflects back shimmers of purple, emerald, sapphire—almost too subtle to detect. The shirt fits their form snugly, liquid and supple.

Their skin is soft gold, almost glimmering, and even from here, I can see their dark eyes are lined in black and gold as well, the waves of their hair defined and gleaming.

Ezra's lips are full, almost pouting, and they do not smile. Ezra holds themself with a bearing I have never seen in real life until now—despite a room full of magic, it is this that tips me off-balance into a foreign land.

My fingers curl, minutely, into the ethereal folds of my gown.

"Fàilt' oirbh uile," Ezra says, and their voice booms through the room. I am not the only one who jumps. "Welcome to all present. I thank you for your hospitality, and I look forward to sharing tonight with you all."

Their eyes seek out the musicians, and after a pause almost too slight to be called hesitation, a trickle of clàrsach strings pours into the hall, and a flute follows in its wake.

Slowly, the hall recovers. Shocked silence dissolves into murmurs, then into laughter even I can identify as nervous, and then the clusters of dancers' heads begin to swirl and eddy once more, and I slowly let out the breath that has been hiding in my lungs like a balloon about to pop.

Before I can ask Deirdre what wasn't supposed to happen, she gives a short, whip-crack of a laugh and says, "Well, now we *really* don't have to worry about anyone being too interested in you, a ghràidh."

It takes me a moment to find my voice. I swallow. "Why—why's that?"

"Because the prince is here," she says simply, and with that, she takes my hand and pulls me in the opposite direction, toward a glittering fountain that seems to pour forth water the colour of honey.

My mind somersaults along with my stomach at her words.

Because the prince is here.

Prince.

Ezra.

I remember their urgent request for me not to tell anyone of their presence here, but they clearly just announced said presence to what feels like everyone. That suggests, I think, that they wanted their presence here to be a surprise.

To everyone but me.

The thought is a strange one, and it doesn't fit inside my skull.

We've reached the fountain, and Deirdre has procured a pair of delicate goblets, which she fills from the fountain itself. She passes me one, and I sniff at it. It could be mead or cider—the scent is sweet, almost too sweet.

At my questioning look, Deirdre just smiles. "Dew nectar," she says. "For those less inclined to end up blootered. Slàinte."

"Slàinte," I echo, clinking my glass with hers.

I take an experimental sip.

The flavour is lighter than I expected, so light it may as well be water, though it carries with it a honey-like sweetness and a touch of fruit that may not be alcoholic but is nonetheless intoxicating.

This dew nectar refreshes me, and it feels more aerated than carbonated, the sensation at once bizarre and delightful.

A small shiver goes through me like dew has beaded on my shoulders and trickled down my back, and out of the corner of my eye as I take another sip, I see Deirdre's head snap up.

"Cam," says Ezra's voice from behind me. "Still willing to share that dance?"

SIXTEEN

I turn, slowly, not sure if I trust my tongue to make words. The dew nectar in my goblet trembles in the crystal, shining like amber in the light. Every eye is on me.

So much for no one noticing the new kid.

I glance at Deirdre, whose wide eyes are as shocked as I feel, and she mouths "Your choice" before taking a step back, reaching out to relieve me of my goblet before ducking out of arms' reach.

"Of course," I say softly, too softly.

But Ezra's heard me anyway, and their face when I finally force my eyes up to meet theirs is alive in a way it was not when they first arrived.

They still stand every inch as straight and dignified, and they hold out a hand to me.

This time it is I who reaches for their hand, not knowing what lies on the other side of this door.

I don't think I could refuse if I tried.

My fingers touch theirs with a rush of warmth that races up my arm where it seems to meet the bubbly freshness of the dew nectar and sing.

Ezra leads me through the crowd of watching Others to the dance floor, and they part with ease to let us pass.

I cannot decipher the expressions on their faces, even the faces I can see. Many are masked, simply or elaborately, but they all flow out of our way like oil away from water.

"You're a prince," I whisper, hardly a breath as they turn me to face them.

The music that shifts then becomes a waltz, and a set of uillean pipes starts up, their eerie resonance capturing the hall.

"In a manner of speaking," Ezra says.

Their hand finds my waist, and that sends another shock through me. My gown is so thin, so misty, that I forgot what it might be like for someone to touch me through it. My arms cascade into gooseflesh, and before I can think, the music swoops, and we swoop with it, my body following it with every step, just as Ezra promised.

Ezra's voice softens. They pull me closer, just close enough to murmur in my ear. "You can speak freely. No one outside the circle of our arms will hear you."

My heart thumps against my ribs. I swallow, still tasting the dew nectar, and I wet my lips, which immediately cool in the rush of moving air as our feet one-two-three, one-two-three across the dance floor.

"What do you mean 'in a manner of speaking'?" I ask.

Ezra is still spear-straight and contained, but I see their throat bob as we spin once. "It means I am their prince, our prince. There is power and privilege that comes with that name, but power and privilege is not something sacred. Mostly, they wanted to see what I would do with it."

With every turn, I see flashes of the crowd around us. We are the only ones dancing, which strikes my stomach like a hot poker to the gut. My hand holds a little tighter to Ezra's shoulder.

"They just . . . made you a prince?" I ask.

"Yes," Ezra says. "One week after I became one of them."

For once in my life, I am glad my face tends to underreact. The thought of being suddenly catapulted to such a precarious position a week into leaving mortality behind is something I don't think I can dwell on without descending into panic.

"Are you safe?" I say softly.

"Safer now than I was yesterday," Ezra answers. We spin once more, and again their cheek is pressed almost next to mine. "There are those here who planned to use tonight to make that more difficult. My presence thwarted that plan, if only temporarily."

I swallow again. Despite not needing to think of how to move my feet, my mind can't quite process the scope of this new life I've landed in.

I don't have time to force it. Somehow, the song is already ending, the music fading, and whatever spell kept us moving fades with it, pulling me into a deep bow even as Ezra mirrors the same.

"One more dance?" I manage to gasp out.

My mind is clearly muddled, but something glints in Ezra's eyes, and as the music shifts to something slower, something sweet and melancholy, so does Ezra shift into their other human form.

They remain in the same clothing, but the fabric expands at the chest, and when they pull me close to them again, their body is softer—but their commanding hold on mine is every bit as firm.

Their hair is now held back from their face with two raven-wing combs studded with emeralds and whorls of gold.

"I was going to ask if you didn't," their voice says, richer than velvet.

The waltz was quick, regimented. This new air is smooth and flowing, and the heat of Ezra's body captures mine and then slips away as we each step to opposite sides, my left hand meeting the palm of theirs.

"What does being a prince mean here?" I ask.

My heart is fluttering wildly at their words, but I've no idea what to say in response, so the question that does come out feels daft.

Ezra's lip quirks, and they deftly turn with me, their eyes holding mine in a contact that feels at once intimate and safe and unbearable.

The eye contact breaks as we change hands to circle back the other way.

"It means they listen to me until they get bored," Ezra says.

In this form, their lips are every bit as full but somehow different, and my brain tries to both process what Ezra's just said and the increasing desire to kiss them in both their forms.

"What happens if they get bored?" I don't intend to whisper, but it comes out that way, a low-pitched, husky tone I am not sure I've ever heard out of my own mouth.

"I am hoping I am allowed to abdicate," says Ezra dryly. "I'm mostly trying not to get too far on anyone's bad side, but it might be too late for that."

I wonder why they're telling me all this. It also doesn't escape me that if Ezra's in danger in any way, my back probably just grew a target, and I was too enraptured to think that through before dancing two dances in a row with the prince who seems to think they have a shelf life of dubious length.

But as our slow revolution shifts and we are drawn close again by the dance, the warmth of their cheek palpable on my own, I am already certain those calculations would not have made a difference. Heat cycles between Ezra and me, and for a time we don't talk, not a word.

The rest of this strange new world recedes into a dreamlike mist. I cannot remember the last time I was so aware of my own body and it didn't make me want to scream. Right now, my skin sings along with the music, an almost audible hum as the lilting melody runs up and down my arms, tracks up my spine to the base of my scalp, sends tingles coursing from my hands where they meet Ezra's shoulder and chest.

I swallow as I realise I'm half a palm's width from my hand resting somewhere not really suitable to touch in public, and a moment later, it follows that their own hand is similarly placed on me. I can feel the flutter of Ezra's heart.

I'm certain they can feel mine.

Too soon, the tune begins to fade, and Ezra pulls me closer, only millimetres. "I'll need to make the rounds," they say. "If we get a chance, will you dance with me again?"

"Yes," I tell them, then, too quickly, another sentence tumbles out of my mouth. "Do you have to go?"

Ezra nods, but their hand on my waist tightens. After a moment, they wince. "I've been careless. I will try to make sure my interest hasn't put you in danger."

"I would have made the same choice either way," I say.

I don't know how I seem to just say these things to them. I've never been bold, never been assertive. But when Ezra looks at me, my self-consciousness simply fades away. I'm so used to people simply looking past me that I've forgotten how to be seen.

I'm not sure I ever knew.

Too late, I process Ezra's words more fully.

"Interest?" I say, and their troubled expression turns to a smile.

"Let's just say I usually don't dance much at these cèilidhean," they say.

As the song ends and we turn once more, Ezra lowers me into a dip, and thanks to the magic of the Others, my muscles know what to do. The strength of their arms holding me up almost makes said muscles give out anyway, and when they swoop me back up onto my feet, the magic releases us, and I actually stumble.

"I hope we get many more dances," Ezra says to me. "You're the most resplendent star in the sky tonight."

As they speak, their face changes. The guarded intensity is gone, replaced by something soft and open, almost surprised if I had to guess, and the sight shocks me into raising my own hand to their face.

The moment my fingers touch their cheek, the crowd bursts out into cheers, and both Ezra and I jump.

Then the look is gone, that vulnerability passed like a wave retreating into the sea, and Ezra's eyes take in the crowd, their shoulders straightening once more. The sight of them is . . . commanding. I don't want to say royal; the word smacks of staid hierarchies that don't apply here. But Ezra is powerful.

Before I can say anything else, Ezra takes my hand and plants a single kiss on my knuckles, and in a flutter of warm wings and a brush of feathers against my skin, they are a raven, winging into the air.

I am left in a sea of strangers, and to my horror, they part for me like they did for Ezra.

But then Deirdre is there, gliding toward me with a warm smile that disperses the Others like they fear her. Maybe they do.

"You," she says in a low voice, "seem to have been keeping secrets."

SEVENTEEN

Deirdre leads me to what I expect is one of the out-of-the-way corners she told me existed, an alcove at the far end of the ballroom that I suspect is like the magic in her house, because the moment we step into it, we enter a private garden lush with flowers I can neither identify nor count, all impossible shades of blue.

"I didn't know they were a prince," I say as soon as she peers behind me and gives me a nod a second later.

Deirdre frowns at that. "Of course they didn't tell you."

"They asked me not to tell anyone they were here." I figure at this point, Ezra won't mind me saying that much. "I'm sorry."

But Deirdre just waves one hand and keeps frowning, staring at a bush as if she's looking through it instead.

"Your house," she says after a beat. "When I went to ward it, there was something already there, but I couldn't place it. Subtle. I should have known it was Ezra. When did you meet them? *How* did you meet them?"

I tell her the gist of it, leaving out the bedroom visit and the door in the woods, but I do tell her they asked for a dance.

"Reckless," she mutters. "But a sword that cuts both ways sometimes cuts the way you want it to."

"I don't know what that means," I say.

I'm not sure if she means Ezra was reckless or if I was. Or both. Maybe both.

"It means that Ezra taking such a public interest in someone literally no one else knows of but Daibhidh and me will have everyone talking. Everyone. Talking." Deirdre still isn't looking at me, and I have the strangest impression that she's running the computations for a thousand different risk scenarios at once in her mind. She does glance at me then and continues. "There are things you will need to know, but I was hoping we'd get at least one night before—"

She breaks off with a frustrated sigh.

"You think they're in danger," I say. "How can I help?"

Deirdre just blinks at me. "Yes, they're in danger, but they're clever despite their youth. They proved that tonight, if it was in any doubt. Not a soul in that room expected the prince to turn up . . . except you."

It feels like a century since I had that glass of dew nectar, and my mouth is suddenly very dry.

"As for helping, I think you have done that simply by existing and dancing with them. You went from an unremarkable newcomer to a curiosity, and if there's anything the Others like, it's new toys." Deirdre bares her teeth.

"I'm not a toy," I say quietly.

"I know that. They don't. Let me think."

I fall silent, looking around the garden. After that dance, I was ready to swoon. Now I feel like I just want to sit down. There is a marble bench a few steps away, and I go to it and sit. My gown spreads around me like a pool of stars.

I reach into the pocket of it and pull out my fidget cube, quickly depressing the roller ball button several times.

When Deirdre starts talking again, she does it slowly, almost as if she's talking to herself and not me, despite addressing me.

"They'll see that you came out of nowhere, and they'll also see that you arrived here with me. That provides you a strong level of protection." Deirdre pauses, chewing on her lip for an instant that ends as soon as it begins. "So they'll know you're new, guess correctly that it's my doing, and know you've turned the head of the prince, who most of them won't want to anger."

"What about those who want to anger Ezra?" I ask, a tendril of anxiety unfurling in my belly.

"I suspect that wherever Ezra flew off to after your dance, it had something to do with mitigating that possibility." Deirdre looks at me—really looks at me—for the first time in a while. I can feel her eyes on me even with my own gaze trained on the ground in front of me. "Speaking of that dance, you two don't waste any time, do you?"

"I don't know what that means either," I say.

Deirdre snorts. "It means watching you was electric—and everyone in that room noticed."

That sends sparks through me.

I don't have time to think of anything to say in response, though, because a shadow moves in the direction of the ballroom entrance, and Deirdre lifts a hand to me. I stand.

"It's a sin to let you go any longer without tasting the feast," she says brightly, and I would have thought she'd been talking about food for the past fifteen minutes if I hadn't been here all this time.

"I could eat," I agree.

The shadow in the corner materialises into the woman in blue feathers from earlier, but she stops when she gets a few steps into the garden.

"Forgive me, Deirdre. I didn't realise it was you out here," she says.

"We were just leaving," Deirdre says with a mock bow.

"Of course." The woman steps away from the path to let us pass, and her eyes linger on me. "Your wee rionnag here has caused quite a stir."

While I love the diminutive for Ceapag an Fhànais, I don't love it used on me by a stranger. Particularly because she's called me a star. I don't want to be a star—I want to be among them.

Deirdre doesn't answer, only gives the woman a mysterious smile and takes my arm in hers as we pass.

I don't look back until we are in the ballroom again. The aromas of food remind me that though it's likely the wee hours of the morning, the last thing I ate was Granaidh's crumble, which is hardly dinner.

"People may want to talk to you," Deirdre says to me through a smile as we circumnavigate the ballroom toward a long table laden with food. "If you can, it could be good to talk back."

"You want me to socialise." That thought makes me almost forget about the entire haunch of venison I can see crusted in pepper and herbs.

"No one will be offended if you keep to yourself, but if someone's friendly . . ." Deirdre trails off pointedly.

"I can do friendly," I mutter. "What if they're unfriendly?"

"Any of that Southern charm make it into you?" she asks. "Even something like 'kill them with kindness'?"

She's got a point. If there's one thing I can usually do, it's earnest. Not that it's always interpreted as such, but I am pretty much devoid of guile.

"Who makes the food?" I ask suddenly.

"We don't enslave beings as cooks, if that's what you're asking," says Deirdre. "The lovely thing about everyone's magic being specific to them is that some of us really like to eat. Those someones are usually quite happy to share—any excuse for a feast is an excuse to show off."

I can't help the smile that tugs at my lips at that. This world might not be any safer than my other one, but amid the fear and uncertainty, there's something wholesome about a bunch of immortals who just really enjoy feeding themselves and others.

This is ready to be an "eyes far bigger than stomach" situation, but I can't help filling my plate with succulent roasted boar falling off the bone and dripping heather honey, a cut of venison, perfect pearl potatoes that are precisely bite-sized and buttery, steaming mussels, a warm bannock with butter and rowanberry jam—all of it looks and smells divine.

At first, I half expect Deirdre to just smile indulgently and roll her eyes, but to my surprise, she fills a plate as full as I do and leads me to a table in a dining room that branches off the ballroom of the talla mòr. Here, the ceiling hangs lower, buttressed by the same creamy stone and golden light that glows a touch warmer, more orange like firelight.

There has been no sign of Daibhidh for some reason, but when Deirdre and I settle at the table, I get distracted by the centrepiece of living moss and a tiny tree twinkling with fireflies that remind me of that first night when Deirdre and Daibhidh knocked me unconscious and saved my life.

I'm so fixated on the small tree in its perfect splendour, branches barely longer than my fingers, that I miss the soft clearing of a throat until a nearby movement startles me.

I look up to see a middle-aged Other with a gentle face and a small half-smile looking down at me.

"May I join the two of you?" he asks.

His voice is as gentle as his face, and he has no hair. His eyes are blue and bright, and while he waits for Deirdre to answer, his smile grows warmer. His lips are thin without being severe, and he stands with his hands folded carefully in front of him.

"Faodaidh, gu dearbha," says Deirdre after a beat, gesturing with a hunk of bannock in her hand.

The stranger sits, but he doesn't introduce himself, only places his hand on the table in front of him, and a plate modestly full of bramble-glazed salmon and pearl potatoes appears in the empty space.

"You've made quite a stir for one so young," he says to me.

I've a forkful of boar halfway to my mouth, and the meat totters and tumbles off the utensil, landing with a small splat.

"It wasn't intentional," I say honestly.

Deirdre and the newcomer exchange a long look, one I cannot begin to read. With careful hands, he cuts his salmon with knife and fork despite the fish being so soft it could be easily pulled apart with fingers.

I manage to get my bite of boar into my mouth, and my tongue immediately lights with the burst of flavour so tender and rich that I have to put my fork down before I use it to shovel the rest of my plate down my gob at once.

Something of it must show on my face, because the stranger gives me another small smile. He swallows before he says, "I'm afraid one thing we've always done well is food, for better or for worse."

The sentiment tingles my awareness—stories of mortals stumbling into a tolman to feast with the fair folk, returning to find their oats and fish are little better than ash in their mouths. It's a petty kind of caprice, I suppose, to give someone a taste of magic you know they will never taste again.

I swallow my next bite, unsure of what to say.

For a time, there is only silence while we eat. I wish I could say that my knowledge of the unsteady footing of this world, its clashes with my own—I wish I could say it dulls the flavour and the joy, but it does not. Each bite is somehow better than the last, from the caramelised, buttery garlic cloves to the tart, fragrant rowanberries.

"You honour us by sitting with us," Deirdre says quietly when the stranger meticulously clears the last flake of salmon from his plate.

That makes me sit up straighter. Who is this man? I notice for the first time that his right hand's pinky is always curled inward, a tiny thing, and when he replaces his fork upon the table and flexes his hands lightly, the pinky does not straighten with the rest of his fingers.

"There is little joy in watching the machinations of the bored," he says in answer to Deirdre's question. "And I like this little one. She belongs here."

I still cannot find my words, but there is no malice, no condescension in his. Before I can say anything else, he pushes himself back from his chair and stands.

He looks at me kindly, I think, with something passing over his face that slumps his shoulders for a half second before restoring him to straight-backed dignity. Just before he turns and walks away, he says, "Welcome home."

EIGHTEEN

Deirdre simply watches his retreating back. He is dressed simply in a long, pale blue shirt that, while tailored, wouldn't be out of place on a yacht or on a picnic blanket in a park.

"Who was that?" I ask.

"An Smeòrach," Deirdre murmurs.

I don't have time to ask anything else, because across the room, I see a familiar face.

It's neither Daibhidh nor Ezra, and my now-full belly turns over with the sight of someone I can't believe I ever even *considered* thinking fit into a school with teenagers.

Her hair is in black ringlets every inch as perfect as they were in the Oban High School canteen. She wears a gown like a sheath of amethyst, as if she is a weapon and the dress simply keeping her danger contained. The gown itself looks like what someone imagined when they invented sequins, but it is to sequins as diamonds are to rock salt.

And she is looking right at me.

Even from here, I can see her eyes match the smokey purple of her gown, and making eye contact burns as if I'm looking into the sun.

Ealasaid looks past me, and it is as if a cord snaps taut when her eye contact switches to Deirdre. It resonates across the room, discordant and painful like two notes played too close together on an out-of-tune fiddle.

The purest voice I've ever heard snaps that grating string.

Deirdre exhales in a sigh of pure relief, and Ealasaid turns toward the voice as if she never so much as laid eyes on either of us.

"I think it's time to go," Deirdre says.

"Wait," I say, my ears straining toward that voice.

At that, Deirdre's frown softens, and she glances once in Ealasaid's direction and nods at me, leading me the opposite way around to the side of the ballroom where Ezra made their entrance.

An Smeòrach is the one singing.

He stands on the dais, as demure as Ezra was proud, and like the silence that greeted Ezra, so too is the hush that has descended upon the room.

I know the song; Granaidh has sung it. "Cumha na Cloinneadh"—a lament for children long dead. It is a simple song, only a few lines, but it is in those few lines its power lies.

It's a pìobaireachd, sung like the pipes are sung, and An Smeòrach's voice raises goose bumps along the flesh of my arms.

The arching rise to the vaulted ceiling, the stone of the walls—the talla mòr is built like a cathedral to draw the seeds of sound into itself and let them bloom.

The song repeats, and as An Smeòrach begins again, he is no longer singing solo.

Throughout the hall, other voices raise with his in harmony, in unison, the low rumble of basses and the honey of contralto with his tenor, the soaring lift of sopranos all blending into a tapestry finer than cloth-of-gold, more delicate than the myriad marvels of jewels and magic that surround us, more smooth than the dream of my dress that cloaks me in stars.

When it is done, when the last notes dance into sparks like the embers of a banked fire, on the opposite side of the dais, there is Ezra.

They are watching me as if they know I'm about to be stolen away, and with a look I cannot interpret, they nod once and turn, vanishing into the murmuring crowd once more.

"Come," Deirdre says to me. "An Smeòrach will sing for you again—do not fear."

I follow, though my gaze is still glued to the room, to An Smeòrach himself upon the dais, his shoulders sagging again as if the song placed the weight of the hall itself upon them.

When we pass him, he seems to know we are leaving. He holds his hands out to me, and without knowing why, I take them. He kisses my cheek.

"Keep safe, a chuachain," he says, and he squeezes both my hands gently, and then he is gone.

Gone the way the Others simply vanish—not slipping into the gathered people in their finery, not turning into a bird, just gone, the squeeze of his hands a ghost in mine.

I take two steps after Deirdre, and we are in my bedroom.

Ceapag an Fhànais is on the duvet, curled into a tiny, tiny ball of black.

"Shin thu," I greet her, and she doesn't budge.

Alarmed, I go to the bed and gently place one finger in the furry hollow under her chin at her chest, and to my relief, she makes that wee kitten *prrow* sound and unfurls, blinking blearily and stretching her small paws and extending their even smaller needle-claws.

"Why did we need to leave?" I ask Deirdre, keeping my voice low.

"You remember the night I found you," she says.

I nod.

"You weren't the only one spying, accidentally or not." Deirdre perches on the edge of my bed, suddenly looking exhausted.

I'd assumed she'd pulled me out of there because of some sort of danger to me, but it occurs to me as I watch a slowly waking Fànas that perhaps it wasn't me in danger.

At some point in the next short while, my mind will finally process the reality of the precariousness of my situation. I'm not ignorant of the fact that I perhaps evaded death three times in as many months only to land, fresh from the frying pan, in a white-hot fire.

But right now, I'm not able to feel it. Not yet. It's not that I have a death wish—far from it.

I think of what An Smeòrach said to me before he left the table. He said welcome home.

“Ezra was here,” Deirdre says suddenly. “I think they’re protecting you, which is both a kindness and recklessness, though that is Ezra in a nutshell.”

Fànas has a bit of white fluff on her chest, and I lean down to pluck it from her.

“It would be good if I could protect myself,” I say without thinking.

“Yes,” Deirdre agrees. “That isn’t just good—it’s necessary.”

The fluff isn’t fluff. Mystified, I pick the kitten up and peer at her. “She didn’t have a white spot before, did she?”

“You’re asking about the kitten?” Deirdre says.

I hold Fànas up to her. “She was all black when we left.”

Deirdre opens her mouth and then closes it again, and after a couple seconds, she laughs. “Cat-sìthe,” she says. “You’re not hopeless if you manage to waken an elfin cat by accident.”

“I did what?”

Fànas, bless her, seems oblivious to whatever I did or didn’t do. I put her back down on the bed, where she immediately sets about pouncing the tiny glimmering lights on the duvet that reflect off my gown.

“She’ll protect you and yours,” says Deirdre. “You gave her a wee bit of your magic, which should be interesting in a kitten.”

The kitten is about the size of one of my feet and, as evidenced by her falling on her face mid-pounce, doesn’t look capable of protecting anything. I’m not sure she wouldn’t come out second best in a tussle with a minuscule Highland midge.

“I’ll take your word for it,” I tell Deirdre.

A wave of fatigue catches me, and I dig in my gown’s pocket for my mobile, which says it’s somehow after three. It doesn’t feel like we were there for three hours.

“More like eight,” Deirdre says. “Time is different there.”

I forget she can hear me thinking.

“Less now.” Deirdre gets to her feet, and with a gesture, the clothes I wore to her house appear neatly folded on the corner where she was sitting. “I need to think—I’ll talk to you tomorrow and we can figure out a plan to keep An Smeòrach happy. I think he’ll be very put out with me if I don’t keep you safe.”

"Who *is* he?" I ask again.

"One of the oldest of us and the one perhaps the Others are least likely to cross. He showed us both a very great honour by sitting with us, and he favoured you in particular before he left, which is far less of a two-edged sword than the attention of the prince."

"I didn't do anything worth favouring," I say.

"No, you didn't." Deirdre's bluntness is both unnerving and refreshing. I'm not sure which wins. "But some of us have a soft spot for foundlings, and he's one of them. As am I, if you haven't guessed."

Foundlings. I take it that's the word for someone like me who trips and lands in the Otherworld permanently.

Just before Deirdre is about to disappear, she hesitates and then walks over to my chest of drawers on the other side of the room. She unhooks the fob watch from her trousers and sets it there.

"If something happens—anything at all—simply open the watch. I can't guarantee I'll be able to come immediately, but you're not alone in this new world."

That's all she says.

I'm left alone with Fànas, my dress casting shimmers of light across my room in Granaidh's cottage.

NINETEEN

Granaidh is the only one awake when I get up in the morning, and at first I think she doesn't even hear me approach, but when I cross into the kitchen from the salon, she turns and looks straight at me, a strange look in her eyes. There's a cookery book in her lap, though she's not cooking anything just now. It's open to a promising page: Yorkshire puddings.

She gestures at me. "Thig a-nall, thig a-nall."

I go over to her obediently, and she tugs me down to look at her closely, not forcing eye contact but scrutinising my face.

"A sheanmhair?" I ask, my voice still groggy from sleep.

She releases me, but there's a heavy crease between her eyes in the midst of her other wrinkles. She shakes her head and goes back to the cookery book in her lap.

"Dè mar a bha a' chèilidh?" She asks how the cèilidh went as I put the kettle on for my tea.

"Math gu leòr," I answer, which is the truth. Good enough.

The cèilidh may have been more of a ball than a cèilidh, but despite my floundering several fathoms out of my depth, it's the first time in ages I've gone to an event of any kind without being overwhelmed with panic.

Which probably is a mark against my own instincts of self-preservation, but at this point, I guess I'm on borrowed time.

"'Math gu leòr,' thuirt i," Granaidh mutters. "Uill, m' eudail, an do dhanns thu?"

"Dhanns." When I answer her question of whether I danced at this cèilidh in the affirmative, she closes the cookery book with a sharp report and barks a laugh every bit as sharp.

"Math sin a chluinntinn, math sin a chluinntinn," she says with an approving nod.

And that's all she has to say on the matter, though as I make my tea, I catch her peeking at me sidelong again.

"What?" I ask in English, and Granaidh just shakes her head.

She starts humming, though, and even though her back is to me now, the tune sends a shiver up my spine.

"Cumha na Cloinneadh." The same song An Smeòrach sang last night.

"An tig mi a chòisir còmhla ribh?" I blurt out before I can stop myself.

After everything last night, *this* is somehow the thing that pushes me beyond the edge of strangeness?

I hear my own words a beat after, which is even stranger that I said them and still have to wait to process them.

Shall I go to choir with you?

Granaidh stops humming.

Now she spins her chair to look at me again, and I squirm on the inside under the intensity of her gaze.

"Thig, a ghràidh, mas e do thoil e." With that, she rolls her chair out of the kitchen and leaves me to my tea.

It'll be a few days before the choir meets—enough time for me to well and truly panic—but I think I've surprised Granaidh. Mas e do thoil e—usually people translate that to the English "please," but it's more precisely akin to the French *s'il vous plaît*—if it pleases you, if it is your pleasure.

I wonder how she meant it. I don't think it was as simple as a "Yes, love, please," and now I'm certain I have to go.

I'm not sure what made me say it. That's probably more Gaelic than I've spoken to her in one sentence, maybe ever. Maybe it's the song. Maybe it's the way I felt hearing all those Otherworldly voices last night. Maybe it's the sense of being under threat without having actually been threatened yet. I don't know.

I spend the rest of the day in my room, ostensibly working on homework but mostly getting distracted by the kitten, who I keep watching for any signs of magical ability. There is no sign of any cat magic or Deirdre whatsoever.

By the time teatime rolls around, I'm half convinced Deirdre was taking the piss.

It's unsettling that she hasn't turned up—she didn't tell me a time, but she did say we'd talk tomorrow, and unless she meant that in a very literal "it's after midnight and therefore Saturday, so I will talk to you Sunday" way, she's late. I hate not knowing when someone's going to appear.

I'm just about to go downstairs for tea when I hear footsteps coming up.

Mum's already halfway down the hall toward my room when I open the door, and she startles. "Someone left you a note in the back garden."

She holds out a purple envelope, peering at me.

I take it. Nonplussed, I turn it over, but there's no name on it.

"How do you know it's for me?" I ask.

"What?"

I waggle the envelope at her. "You said someone left this for me, but there's no name on it."

Mum blinks twice and frowns. "It's teatime," she says, and she turns and goes back downstairs.

I may be pretty rubbish at deciphering neurotypical social cues, but even I know that was weird.

Holding the envelope more gingerly, I walk back into my room and shut the door. They might get cross with me for stalling, but I'm not opening this in front of them.

The envelope is sealed—or appears that way—but the moment I touch the flap, it springs open.

There's a single, unfolded piece of lavender paper inside it, and I pull it out.

What a fascinating new addition to Oban High School, it reads. *I'll look forward to getting to know you. I'm sure we'll be the best of friends.*

It's signed Lisbeth.

Ealasaid.

I don't know why she goes by Lisbeth in the mortal world and Ealasaid in the Otherworld, but a slimy sense of foreboding seems to eke off the paper and up through my fingertips. I take a few steps toward the bed, and no sooner do I perch on the edge of it when wee Fànas, who has been sleeping peacefully in the precise centre of the bed, springs to her tiny feet and hisses, tail in full bottle brush.

"Obh, obh, a ghràidh," I say, trying to sound comforting. "You're okay, love. Tha thu ceart gu leòr."

But she launches herself at me with a growl that would be funny if she didn't seem like she was about to leave me full of pinpricks.

Fànas, however, despite her kittenish clumsiness, has perfect aim all of a sudden.

A sooty comet hits the paper and envelope still in my hands, and just as quickly, Fànas lands on the floor with both of them, which makes me yelp—she's never jumped off the bed, let alone in a flying leap.

Her growl sounds like a very large bee with more rattle. I scramble to my feet, but before I can move more than half a step in her direction, Fànas attacks the paper with claws bared, and where they pierce it, blue smoke rises from the punctures. The paper shrivels as if it's been placed on top of live coals, slowly collapsing in on itself until it vanishes without so much as a hint of ash, and Fànas yowls.

"Math thu," I say when I can draw a breath. "That's a good piseag."

I scoop her up, and her growl turns to a purr.

I feel like Deirdre would want to know about this, but I'm about to be late for dinner, so I put Fànas on my shoulder and hurry down the stairs as quickly as I dare.

I make it through dinner with little conversation except for Mum's "Mother says you want to join us for choir?" which she says as if I've announced I'm swimming to Tobermory and not that I'm just going to sing in Gaelic with my family.

At least I've got one full day to faceplant before I have to face school and Ealasaid.

Back upstairs in my room, though, I try to work through what happened. Mum found an envelope in the garden and somehow knew it was for me, which means either just touching it somehow communicated that—or Ealasaid was here.

Both of those options are unnerving, but the latter more so.

If the house is somewhat protected (I no longer doubt that my wee cat-sìthe is indeed capable of helping), maybe Ealasaid couldn't get any closer than the garden, but regardless, she just very pointedly displayed that she can get close to us, get close to my mum, and also get something into my house . . . all whilst the mortals in the house are none the wiser.

I get up, going over to where Deirdre left her watch. Part of me is afraid it isn't there, but it is, behind the clothes I was too lazy to put away last night.

I open it, not sure of what to expect. It's a lovely watch, so silver it's almost milky, gleaming like it's lit from within. The face is perfect crystal, and each of the hands is so delicate they look like thread. The minute hand has a tiny crescent moon at the end of it, and the hour hand a sun, both engraved with actual details that would make a machinist weep.

"Deirdre?" I say out loud, feeling daft. "You said to let you know if something happened, and something happened."

I wait for a heartbeat or two, but Deirdre doesn't appear. She *did* say she might not be able to drop everything and turn up at a moment's notice.

My skin feels like it's made of aluminium and someone just stuck a buzzing tuning fork against it.

Fànas is still downstairs, so I'm alone.

I didn't even get to say goodbye to Ezra last night—I just ran off with Deirdre without a word. I hope they understand I wasn't trying to be rude. My entire memory of last night feels surreal, too big for my brain.

I need to do something to calm myself, so I close the door and open the window.

The air is brisk and cool, but it's dry, so I pull over the stool from the vanity and climb out onto the roof. I hope to every lucky star I might have that the mums don't venture out to the car for anything and happen to look up, but they're probably downstairs chatting to Granaidh still.

For a while I just lie back on the roof and stare at the stars. The sky has some clouds, but there is enough break between them for me to see, even in still-bright evening light. It's easy to let them mesmerise me, the shimmers of starfire I would need the James Webb telescope to see before now. It feels like falling up, and my fingertips drum on the roof like rain.

So when Daibhidh appears directly next to me, I almost fall off the side of the house.

He catches my arm and hauls me back to stability, and I splutter a gasp.

I've not even seen him since that first time.

"Sorry, love," he says. "Deirdre couldn't make it, but she said you needed her."

I nod, struggling to find my words.

"Take your time," he says and scoots over a wee bit to give me some space.

Slowly, my breathing returns to normal, but there's a lump in my throat that tightens it, and that makes the words stay stuck for a bit longer.

"Ealasaid left something in the garden for me. Mum brought it in but seemed to forget it existed the moment it left her hands," I tell him. "And then Fànas destroyed it."

Daibhidh looks at me sideways. "Fànas?"

"My kitten," I say, which doesn't seem to help his confusion. "Deirdre said I gave her some of my magic."

At that, he snorts, leaning back on his elbows.

He doesn't seem overly alarmed, which plants a seed of dread that I've misconstrued "if anything happens" to something more literal than Deirdre meant by it.

"Sorry to bother you with it," I mutter.

Daibhidh looks up. "I'm just thinking," he says. "Like you."

"Oh."

I let him think, feeling squirmy and embarrassed that I didn't extend him the same courtesy he gave me. I want to apologise again, but the mums (and Therapist Lindy and Paul and Granaidh and Dad) say I apologise too much.

When he finally speaks, he gives me the impression he is choosing each word very deliberately.

"Ealasaid is dangerous, but she is not the most dangerous—she will try to scare you before she does anything that could harm you. Her usual way is to make people paranoid to the point that they snap first—and she then gets to pretend her retaliation is justified."

"That is absolutely fucked," I say without thinking, and then follow it up with a "Sorry."

Daibhidh chuckles. "Aye, well, no one's ever accused a sìtheach of being level-headed."

"You seem pretty level-headed," I say, and he chuckles again. Then I remember what I keep meaning to tell Deirdre. "That night in the woods. Did you and Deirdre hear what Ealasaid and the others were saying before you—before you knocked me out?"

The man looks at me sharply. "You heard them? You actually heard words they were saying?"

"Yes?" I shift my weight and slide a little on the roof. "They said they were waiting for a sign of something or someone but hadn't seen it, and then they said, 'It takes three, and we've got three. If there's no sign, we've got time,' and then more people showed up, and they seemed to not want the others to hear what they were saying."

Daibhidh sits up straight. "You are absolutely certain of what you heard."

"As certain as I can be," I say.

His reaction has made my shoulders tense up, and I scramble backward toward the windowsill.

"You're safe enough here. I've got to go—one of us will send word tomorrow. Whatever you do, keep close to the house." With no further explanation, Daibhidh disappears, again leaving me with more questions than answers.

My favourite thing.

TWENTY

If time moves differently in the tolman, I think I've altered the space-time continuum in my own home merely by existing.

Sunday drags on like March 2020. I haven't heard from Deirdre or Daibhidh by the time I wake up in the morning, which isn't that much of a surprise, and naturally, because Daibhidh told me to keep close to the house, the only thing I want to do is go for a long walk in the forest.

The mums are in cleaning mode, Granaidh is in bed with a headache, and I did all my homework yesterday, so I've absolutely nothing to do while I wait for someone to tell me what's happening.

I'm supposed to be on the verge of adulthood, but I've somehow managed to punt myself back into being a wean in a whole new world.

Even Fànas seems out of sorts today—maybe she senses that I'm on edge.

I need to do *something*. No one's given me any sort of instruction aside from my magic moulding itself to me and my nature. Helpful.

Since I don't think I can call down starfire to raze my enemies to the ground, I'm going to settle for picking brambles. Daibhidh said close to the house, not in the house, so I figure the back garden qualifies.

I prudently bring three big tubs with me, since there are so many of these berries still. Granaidh's having trouble giving them away.

Not only am I apparently a baby sìth, but I feel like I may as well be a fake one. The only magic I'm capable of is accidental, though I suppose Ceapag an Fhànais is special. I won't look that gift cat-sìthe in the mouth except to boop her snoot.

The brambles are heavy with berries yet again. I wonder if Deirdre's magic has an off switch. They're lovely berries, but the chest freezer in the foyer is officially chock-a-block full.

At this rate, bags of frozen berries are going to be party favours at all the Gaelic choir practices in the West Highlands.

My fingers are stained purple almost immediately, and I snack on some of the berries as I go—after a careful inspection for any local wildlife.

"Hey," says a familiar voice not far away.

I look up to see Ezra on the other side of the stone wall.

"Hi," I say, immediately with a flutter in my chest.

They're in femme mode today. Their waves are plaited in a thick French braid over one shoulder, and they're wearing a dark-grey jumper with an open neckline that leaves one shoulder bare except for the strap of an olive-green vest. Boot-cut dark-rinse jeans, black shoes.

"I didn't get to say goodbye on Friday," they say. "Sorry we didn't get another dance."

"Me too," I say. I put the almost-full basin of berries down and go over to them. "Deirdre wanted to leave pretty quickly."

"Not an unwise decision," Ezra murmurs. "I should have told you I'm the—prince."

"It's your business," I say truthfully.

"Even so. I was reckless. It's one of my many flaws." They say that with a quirk of their full lips, tilting their head to the side, which makes the light brighten their cheekbone like highlighter. "When I first came to the Otherworld, I had no one, and the few people I knew didn't exactly come with the best associations. And then they made me their prince, and I've been fumbling along ever since, just trying not to die."

"I think I can relate to that on some level," I say.

Ezra stands on the other side of the wall, only a pile of stone and moss between us, but I don't think it's *that* holding them back.

"That's likely why it's so easy to talk to you," they murmur.

“Is it?” I ask.

I feel lightheaded this close to them, and I steady myself on the stone wall.

The moment stretches out, rolling over the garden like morning mist. It reveals as much, leaving me with my toes at the edge of a cliff where just a minute ago there was solid ground.

“I don’t know what I’m doing,” Ezra confesses, and I don’t know if they mean in general or here, right now. With me.

“That makes two of us.” My voice cracks on the sentence, and I clear my throat.

Ezra is quiet again for another long stretch, and I study the moss on the wall, eyes following its tiny fronds, its spongey texture, the almost luminous green.

“Part of me wants to turn and run right now,” Ezra says suddenly. “There’s a voice screaming in my head that just talking to you puts you in danger, and it might not be wrong.”

It’s as if my spine jerks taut at those words, and my fingers turn to claws on the wall in panic—panic I don’t quite understand.

But Ezra is going on. “But I don’t think anyone’s told you anything about what’s been happening in the Otherworld.” They wait for my confirmation, and after a beat, I nod. “If Deirdre is the reason you’re one of us and An Smeòrach showed you public favour, those are both good things—they are two of the kindest of the Others. But Cam, that doesn’t mean they’re kind.”

I swallow at that. “What do you mean?”

“It means that none of the Others—myself included—do anything without a reason. Call it ulterior motives, call it caprice, call it whatever you want.” Ezra’s smile turns flinty, the skin around their eyes unlined where the smile goes no further. “And right now even the oldest and most powerful of them are hedging all their bets.”

“I think I—” I break off, thinking of my impression of Deirdre dragging us from the cèilidh after that staring match with Ealasaid. I think of someone like Deirdre afraid. “What are they so afraid of?”

“Each other,” Ezra says softly. “Some of them don’t like how things are now. They don't like that the mortals mostly no longer fear them. They don't like this new world where everything is real so nothing is. And they don't like the idea that they should keep to the fringes. Not anymore."

"Thank you," I say without thinking.

"For what?"

"No one has told me any of this. I've just been—I have to go to school tomorrow with Ealasaid, and I think I should be afraid of her, but I have no way of protecting myself, and I'm not good at people, least of all people who don't like me, and . . ." I take a deep breath, trying not to ramble. "What if she hurts someone? What if she hurts my family? She was here yesterday and gave something to my mum. It's taken care of, and Deirdre and Daibhidh know, but . . . I'm just standing here picking infinity blackberries."

Ezra's gaze shifts to the brambles. Their eyes are thoughtful, and they fiddle with the end of their plait before dropping it again.

They reach out one long-fingered hand and touch a leaf.

A dangerous half-smile spreads across their face. "Case in point," they say. "Deirdre's magic here isn't harmful—to the contrary, in fact. But she is using it. All these berries are enchanted, and I can't tell what they do."

My head swivels to look at the still-pendulous branches of blackberry vines. "What? We've been eating them—Granaidh's been giving them to people!"

"They're not harmful. That much I can tell, but she has enchanted them to do *something*."

"Ezra," I say urgently, then stop. "How am I supposed to—I can't even *human* well! How am I supposed to know who to trust or how to stay alive and how to keep my family alive?"

At that, Ezra stops staring at the plant, glancing over my shoulder at the house with an unreadable expression.

"Can I trust you?" I ask, my voice almost a whisper.

Ezra steps closer to the stone wall, and despite the coolness of rock against my legs, I can feel the heat of Ezra's body. They place their hands over mine, very gently.

"You can," they say. "But you shouldn't. Just like I shouldn't trust you."

I swallow, unconsciously arching my hands upward to increase the contact with Ezra's palms.

"What do I do?" I ask.

"Find out what your magic does," they say.

"How do I even do that?" I wouldn't even know where to start.

"Seek out what makes you come alive—seek out what makes you fear death. And then pay very close attention to what happens next."

This close, I somehow can't tell if they smell like blackberries or I'm just smelling the bushes or my own purple fingers.

"Okay," I say. My voice hitches as I go on. "When—when will I see you again?"

They're so close now it's like we're dancing again, alone in a sea of strangers.

"If you're sure you want to, you have my feather. You know what to do from there." Ezra's hands leave mine, and mine rise up off the wall, the void of their warmth instantaneous.

"I'm sure," I say.

Ezra swallows, and I pull my gaze up to meet their eyes. It feels like looking up into my stars, like falling up.

"Good," they say, and their hand reaches up to my cheek the way they almost did that night in my room.

Instinctively, I lean into the sensation. Their hand is so soft, so gentle.

"I'll see you soon," they say.

The soft touch of their hand becomes the flutter of wingtips as Ezra flies away.

I have to hold myself up on the wall of the garden, eyes tracking the raven until the trees shroud my view.

I look at my Fitbit. It's early afternoon.

My gaze rises to the woods beyond the garden.

I gather my one full basin of blackberries and stack it on the other two, bringing it inside, where I hurriedly fill it with water to rinse off as many bugs as possible.

I don't want to answer any questions from Mam or Mum or Granaidh, and I can hear the Hoover running somewhere on the other side of the house, far enough away that it isn't torture but close enough that it cements my decision.

Pulling a blank sheet of paper from the pad on the fridge where we make our shopping list, I scribble a short note. *Air cuairt x*

On a walk.

I stick it to the fridge with a magnet where it'll hang over the handle. Someone will see it when they go to get milk for their tea.

Before I can lose my nerve, I switch from my trainers into Mam's wellies and scurry back out the door.

Seek out what makes you come alive—seek out what makes you fear death, Ezra said.

That first night I stormed out of the house in the middle of a row, I remember how I felt in the green, surrounded by moss and trees and the smell of home. Life. And I remember how close I came to death.

I don't know much, but I do know that both of those things await me in the woods.

TWENTY-ONE

Everything is different this time. It's not like that first night where it was late and twilit.

And it is like that first time, because in the first bend in the path, I find myself back on that strange, mossy trail that I am now certain does not exist in the mortal realm.

I want to know how that happened the first time—if I was mortal then, how did I stumble into the Otherworld? There are myriad possible explanations; it's not like I would have been the first. Gaelic tradition and lore is full of stories of people doing exactly that. Some return. Some don't.

I wonder how many returned like I did, forever changed.

I follow the trail through the woods, relaxing in the presence of the trees.

There might be an explanation for this feeling, too. It could be as simple as the quiet. I'm pretty sure there have been studies done on nature and the human psyche. But for me it feels like something more.

It's damp, of course. Western Scotland is always damp, but I find a stone to sit on amid the moss and shamrocks growing, and I bend down to pluck a small handful of the shamrocks to eat. They're tart and lemony. Every time I eat one, I always have the urge to gather enough for a salad.

There's little breeze here, but I don't see any midgies. It's unnerving, though if part of my magic is otherworldly beastie repellent, I won't say no.

I figure the rock is a decent place to sit. One of the things I've been trying to learn is how to be present in my body. Between the PTSD and the autism, my body can be an uncomfortable place to be. But I pull up on the rock and sit cross-legged, which is awkward in wellies.

If my magic moulds itself to me, it would help to know what that means—it would help to know who I even am.

I asked if I can trust Ezra, but can I even trust myself? I don't know.

I try to concentrate on the way my chest seems to expand here, an airy lightness that I don't think I've felt anywhere else except maybe on a ferry headed into the islands.

For a long time, all I feel is the cool air on my face and my bum growing damp through my trousers.

My imposter syndrome feelings come flooding back the longer I sit. I thought I at least had an idea of something I could do, but instead I'm just sitting on a rock like a lump.

Is this learned helplessness? The thought is sardonic as it ricochets around my skull.

With an irritated grumble, I hop back off the stone. If looking for the good feelings isn't helping anything, maybe . . . maybe what I need to do is the opposite.

I don't think Ezra was suggesting I go try to get myself killed. I also think Daibhidh and Deirdre would skip me like a stone across the Sound of Mull if they could hear what I'm thinking, but even if Deirdre can read my mind when she's right next to me, I don't think she can do it long distance.

I close my eyes where I stand, trying to remember the path I took before. There's no real reason to expect that the Otherworld's paths remain the same, but maybe that will work to my advantage.

On a whim—or maybe a hunch—I try to picture the clearing where I accidentally spied on Ealasaid and her compatriots. It was little more than an oasis, a small treeless space surrounded by rowans.

A fairy ring.

I open my eyes, deciding to follow my instinct. That instinct pulls me to my left like a magnet.

I start walking.

My first steps take me from the path and into hummocks of soft, dew-covered moss. The ground is like a sponge, able to soak up the generous gift of Scotland's rain. The wellies sink into it up to the ankle.

But before too long, I emerge onto a wider path, this one just as moss-covered and lined with rounded stones—it's as if the green reaches out to claim everything it can touch. On either side of me, the path is lined with oaks, old growth.

The familiarity is undeniable.

I follow the path forward, my feet growing more reluctant with every step. If Ealasaid awaits there in the clearing—if anyone does—I could be in major trouble. I never saw the faces of the Others Ealasaid was meeting with, and if there's someone else there when I arrive, I'll have no way of knowing if they are one of them.

Despite that, I force my legs to keep going, taking step after step.

Sunlight filters through the branches of the trees. It lends itself to mysticism; nowhere else on Earth have I seen the golden green of the sun's caress on a Scottish forest. It's all the more beautiful for its brevity and, perched upon the mosses and shamrocks and sparse bracken beyond the trail, where it lights on beads of dew, it sends back trails of sparkles.

Even if I didn't believe in magic, this sight might convince me.

But the feeling of wonder is juxtaposed with the growing pit of dread that fills my stomach. I've also forgotten to eat, which my belly helpfully reminds me a few steps later with a gurgle that sounds far too loud in this near-silent wood.

To my right, a hillock rises, and without following it upward, I know without any doubt that my hiding place was at the top of it. Which means I'm getting closer.

The path opens up even more ahead, fanning out before the next hill, and if I follow it, it will take me into that clearing. Even from here, I can see the tops of the rowan trees, lit with gold at their highest branches from the slanting sun.

I swallow. My tongue sticks to the roof of my mouth, and I consciously unclench my jaw, trying to relax. It's not very helpful, but it feels at least like something within my power.

The closer I get to the clearing, the louder my heart begins to pound. For every step I take, it beats two to three times, like my footsteps are the kick drum and my heart is the snare.

It's ridiculous; there's not going to be anyone even there. It's the middle of the day on a Sunday. I'm sure the Sìthichean have plenty of better things to do than go for a walk. They're not all eighteen-year-old babies trying to find their own feet.

I reach the opening of the clearing, and squinting my eyes shut for a moment to prepare myself, I take a deep breath and turn.

In my mind's eye, I see the fireflies from that night dancing through the clearing. They're not there now; only the golden sun and tiny tendrils of mist haunt the air. It's so green, lush and verdant and bright.

I almost manage to reassure myself as I walk down the forested trail to the wide, open space surrounded by rowans.

It's bigger than it looked from up on the top of the hill, and when I glance up to where I must have been lurking, the sight immediately shakes me. From here, the top of the ridge is easily visible. That they didn't see me before Deirdre found me is a miracle.

At first, I think the clearing is empty. There's only a small hummock of moss in the centre that I don't remember, but it was shrouded in the dim light of the late summer gloaming. But as I step closer to that hummock, dread tickles at the back of my neck.

It's hardly half a foot high, but it's a shape that's been burned into my memory since spring.

My feet keep moving, slow, slow, despite the counter-rhythm of my heart and breath that urge each other faster, shallow and tight like fingers drummed around the rim of a bodhrán.

From one step to the next, I'm not in Ballinacollie—I'm at the lake in a blistering Texas spring, the water hardly enough to cool air and people alike. There is sobbing and screaming, but in my mind there is nothing but silence, frozen, stock-still as I see the body.

Paul.

I can see him again, stretched out straight on the beach, someone continuing chest compressions despite the last of the water long since having spurted from between his dead lips.

He was grey. Lifeless.

Which is how I know what I'm seeing now.

Closer to the hummock, I can make out the lift of feet pointed upward, the dip to the legs, the way the greenery makes a canyon between them. There is the shadow of an arm, covered in shamrocks and moss, and it's only when I'm close enough to look down on the corpse that I can see the green has not yet swallowed it whole.

Only a sìtheach could look so lifelike even in death.

Unlike Paul, this man—I think it's a man—is simply pale, pale like any people whose ancestors put down roots in places the sun abjures. His face is perfect, carved of alabaster and touched with gold from the sun that highlights the honeyed locks of hair that spill back from his cheeks and twine in rivulets of sunshine throughout the shamrocks.

I've not yet had the courage to ask Deirdre if the Sìthichean can die, but I've been given an answer nonetheless.

I don't know this man. I've never seen him. He looks young, which means nothing. All I can tell is that he's not mortal.

And then, in the midst of this place devouring the dead, something of my last experience here repeats.

Voices.

TWENTY-TWO

Without further thought, I turn and run for the hill. If they're moving for the clearing—it would be daft of me to assume they're not—I'll be trapped in this bowl. Even as it is, my chances of escaping are close to nowt.

My wellies sink into the spongey ground as I climb. Faster. I need to be faster.

I'm not fast enough.

The barrier of land between me and the voices vanishes. They must have rounded the corner, and there is no way—none—that I'm not still in plain sight.

I sink into the bracken, trying not to think of ticks when I've got much, much bigger things to fret about.

But whoever it is doesn't see me.

I freeze where I sit half-crouched, easing myself onto my bum, which also sinks into the dense moss carpet of the forest floor.

There's a breeze on my tongue as I take shallow breaths through my parted lips, trying in vain to deepen them.

When the people come into view, it's only the still-fresh image of the dead man's face that keeps me silent.

It's Deirdre and Daibhidh.

Any thought of their involvement in this death is immediately shattered by the sound of pure anguish that wrenches itself from Daibhidh's throat. The stolid, stoic man has not shown such emotion in my presence, and it immediately makes all the hairs on the backs of my arms stand straight up.

He falls to his knees beside the man, his hand going to caress the pale skin of the stranger's cheeks. Deirdre's breath hisses inward a split second later, and she goes to stand beside Daibhidh. Her shoulders slump as she reaches out to place a hand on the man's shaking back, and even from where I'm sitting, I can see her close her eyes and swallow.

The two of them usually pop in and out of existence like they can tesser, but they walked here. Maybe they can't simply appear here? Why would this place be different?

Daibhidh makes a high, keening sound that I know because I've made it. My fingers make fists in the moss, tight, holding on to it as if it's only that keeping me where I sit.

I'm too frozen to reveal myself, and though I feel like my intrusion on this moment of grief is a violation, I can too easily remember Ezra's instruction to pay attention to what happens in moments of fear.

In any other circumstances, I would rejoice that perhaps I've gained the power of not being perceived when I don't want to be, but right now, watching two people who have been kind to me grieve, it feels like a sick joke.

"He didn't do anything," Daibhidh says. "He wasn't part of this."

Deirdre sighs, a weary sound that I half expect to disturb the bracken on the opposite side of the clearing with its force.

"That's just it, my love," she replies. "We are all part of this now."

Part of what, I want to ask, but in a way, Ezra has already answered that. The human world has been cloven down the middle in recent years—us versus them, factions feeding on their own, certain groups that only want to watch the world burn so long as they can shoot rockets into space with impunity—perhaps I should be surprised that the Others are the same. But maybe they're more human than even they think they are.

I can offer no other explanation—if they are fighting each other, then what Deirdre has just said affects me. If this is my world, I am part of this too.

Whatever *this* is.

"And the wean?" Daibhidh asks.

As I watch, he visibly pulls himself together. His shoulders stop shaking, and he lets his hand fall from the dead man's face. He gets to his feet with the help of Deirdre's hand, but his face is still pinched. The way his gaze bores into Deirdre would I think make even the most eye-contact-comfortable person flinch.

Deirdre herself looks away as if to prove me right.

"We protect her as long as we can," she says. "She didn't ask for this."

A cold spike goes through me. I'm suddenly certain they're talking about me.

"Someone's gonnae need tae tell her, teach her how tae defend herself. You're no doing her any favours keeping her ignorant." Daibhidh's voice goes softer with the Scots words, some of his gruffness smoothed away so much that I'm comforted by the sound of it, despite the content of what he's saying being harsh.

Mam's voice is like that for me too.

"I know," Deirdre says, almost inaudibly. "I wanted her to get to experience some of the fantastic before shoving fear in her face."

Daibhidh's face softens even more. "And that's good. But it's—"

He breaks off, all softness turned jagged in an instant.

A moment later, two mourning doves wing out of the clearing, and Daibhidh and Deirdre are gone again, leaving me alone with their friend's corpse.

I don't wait around to find out what spooked them. I shove myself to my feet and hurry up the rest of the hill, almost diving over it when I reach the top of it.

Stopping there would be stupid. I keep running, aiming vaguely southeast, hoping that whatever allowed me to find the borders between these two worlds will be kind to me and not evade me now.

The mums are going to wonder where I've been, and I've still got school tomorrow. Part of me wonders if I can feign illness and stay in bed with Fànas. I think, though, that would just be postponing the inevitable.

Eventually, my hurried pace slows, and through the trees in the distance, I catch a glimpse of Loch Awe, a familiar one.

I continue on in that direction, and before too long, I indeed find the path home.

I'm absolutely covered in bits of moss and bracken and leaves, and I'm already itching at the thought of any less welcome hitchhikers crawling on me. I despise ticks.

All I want to do is get inside, strip off my clothes, throw them in the washing machine, and hide in the shower so I can try to process my little excursion.

But someone is waiting for me at the back gate, and despite the dark hair, my gut knows straight away that it's not Ezra this time.

It's Ealasaid.

I skid ungracefully to a halt several yards away, and when she turns to look at me, I feel like a herring facing down an eagle.

Whatever kept me from being seen in the woods has clearly evaporated. I don't have time to wonder why.

"There you are," she says, her voice deceptively breezy. "I thought I was going to have to wait around all night, and it's a school night."

"I got your note," I say, for once glad at my tendency to go monotone when I'm in distress.

"Oh, good," she says. "I'm surprised it took as much effort as it did to get your mother to take it. You and Deirdre and the little princeling have this place wrapped up quite tidily. One might call it overkill."

"I don't know what you mean," I say bluntly. "Besides, if you wanted to talk to me at school, why didn't you just wait until then?"

"Impatience is one of my favourite vices," says Ealasaid. "Besides, I ought to welcome a new neighbour properly. It's the polite thing to do."

"Neighbour?" I don't like the idea of her living nearby.

"I actually came to warn you." Ealasaid goes on as if I've not said anything. "You're new, and you're Deirdre's, and you don't know what that even means. More importantly, you don't *matter*, but you must have a certain sense of self-preservation if you're here at all."

I clench my toes in my wellies—Mam's wellies—and wish I could teleport inside.

"Especially considering those three mortal women in there"—Ealasaid gestures at the house—"who haven't the foggiest idea that they've got a foundling in their midst. You want them to stay safe, yes?"

Not trusting my voice, I nod.

"Good." Ealasaid walks toward me, and it takes every inch of strength I have not to flinch out of her way. When she passes by me, close enough to touch, close enough I can smell a soft lavender scent clinging to her, she cocks her head. "Then do yourself a favour. Stay out of my way, or I'll kill them all."

She doesn't disappear, doesn't turn into a bird. Ealasaid simply walks on past me as if she forgets my existence the moment her back is to me. I wait until the path takes her out of view, and then I sprint to the gate and fumble it open, running up the three steps in one leap.

Granaidh is in the kitchen when I burst through the door, and she takes in my dishevelled appearance with one long, unblinking stare.

"Air cuairt, eh?" is all she says, and I nod, hurriedly closing the door behind me.

I doff the wellies and put them back in their crate.

Granaidh gives a small chuckle when I pass her in her chair—hard for her to miss my soaking wet bum when she's at eye level with it—but she doesn't say anything else.

I'm halfway to the stairs when I suddenly stop, turning around again to skate over the laminate flooring to her again.

Without speaking, I bend down and kiss her on the cheek, and she makes a soft "oh!" of surprise and then clucks at me, shooing me away with her hands as if I've gone and embarrassed her.

But when I turn away again to go upstairs for real, she catches me by the wrist.

"An tè ud," she says after a brief pause. "Na leig a-steach i."

For a second or two, my brain doesn't make sense of the words, but when it clicks, I nod, swallowing hard.

I head upstairs on teetery legs.

That woman. Don't let her inside.

TWENTY-THREE

Undressing in the bathroom reveals not one, not two, not three, but *four* ticks on my clothes, which I immediately catch in balled-up toilet roll and flush, shuddering.

I guess one of my natural magical talents will not be pest control.

The mums always roll their eyes at how long I take in the shower, but as a kid it was one of the few places I could be alone and undisturbed—for the most part, at least until someone started telling me off for hogging the hot water.

I give myself a thorough tick check in the shower as well before scrubbing until I'm satisfied my shower loofah won't scrape off an embedded tick and leave any chunks in me to get infected. I may sound obsessive, but ticks get under my skin both figuratively and literally.

Even though I'm under the hot water for what feels like an age, by the time I get out, I'm still not sure what to do. I think that heavy, oil-slick feeling in my stomach is guilt for eavesdropping. I should tell Deidre and Daibhidh that I was there and saw them, but the idea is overwhelming.

Once I'm out and clothed, I decide I'd rather tell Ezra first.

I leave the door to my room cracked so Fànas can come in since I've not seen her since I got back, and I pull the feather out of the drawer in the bedside table where I stashed it.

It still looks pristine.

I hold the quill end between my thumb and forefinger, fighting the urge to trail the feather down my cheek where Ezra's hand was just a few hours ago. They said they can tell where the feather is; I don't know if that also means they can sense anything the feather touches. My face heats at the thought.

I twirl it a bit, unsure of what I'm supposed to do other than simply wish for Ezra's presence. Part of me is afraid they won't show up and I'll just be sitting here until teatime with a feather in my hand.

The wait isn't long, however.

Even though I'm expecting it, the tap at the window gives me a start. I hop up, going to unlatch it.

Ezra has changed yet again, tonight in a thin, long-sleeved henley shirt that's a shade or two too dark to be called blood red. When I open the window, they move out of the way, but then they lower themself through it, and I don't react quickly enough to move backward in time, so their body brushes against mine as they land, and I almost lose my balance.

"Sorry," I gasp.

"Don't be," says Ezra. "Though I didn't expect to see you so soon."

I don't know what to say to that, so I say nothing, moving a few feet away to sit on my bed to give myself a bit of room to think.

"Did something happen?" Ezra asks.

They come to sit beside me, but I notice they don't sit as close as they did last time.

I nod, unable to answer.

As if summoned by Ezra's presence, I hear a light pawing at the door, and a tiny black muzzle nudges it open and scoots through.

"Ò, shin thu, a charaid!" Ezra greets Fànas, and a smile wipes away some of my nerves.

The kitten trundles across the floor with her little stubby tail straight up, and when she gets in range, she launches herself at the duvet and claws her way up onto the bed with studied expertise, depositing herself in front of Ezra.

"I found a dead man," I say, my gaze focused on the kitten.

Ezra freezes with his hand halfway to Fànas's head. "Tell me."

I tell them everything, describing what I found from the way the moss and shamrocks seemed to be closing over the corpse like a wave to the arrival of Daibhidh and Deirdre to the unwelcome appearance of Ealasaid.

When I'm done, Ezra sits in stunned silence—or I think it's stunned silence. I'm not really sure. It goes on long enough that I start to get worried.

"She threatened your family," Ezra says through their teeth.

I nod hesitantly, drumming my left hand's fingers against the duvet, which draws Fànas's attention.

It takes a beat or two for me to recognise what I'm seeing in Ezra.

Anger.

Or maybe something stronger than anger. Fury.

If I don't always trust my voice, right now it seems like Ezra doesn't trust their own. Their olive skin is paler than usual, but there are ruddy blooms upon their cheeks, and their jaw moves, revealing tight tendons in their neck.

"Ezra?" I say their name quietly. "Are you okay?"

They seem to shake themself, and it's almost as if I can see them returning to their body from somewhere far away. Just like with Daibhidh's grief, this is something I recognise too.

"I will not let her do that," Ezra says. "Not to you."

It's the emphasis they place on the last word that hits me. Too late, I remember what they said about their father when I said I was sorry he'd gotten sick. *It wasn't that what killed him.*

I can't bring myself to ask.

At my silence, though, Ezra looks down at the floor and sighs.

"The Others killed my entire family," Ezra says. "In front of me."

Even though I'd guessed it was something like that, their sudden confession still sends me reeling.

"It doesn't happen often, but sometimes someone—or someones—gets too bored with simply causing the usual chaos." Ezra's voice is as monotone as mine gets. I want to reach out and take their hand, but I don't know if they want that. "There are punishments for it, and I got to see that firsthand as well. They were going to kill me too, but An Smeòrach and a few of the older Others had gotten wind of it, and they arrived just in time."

Ezra's tone is clipped, dispassionate, but my heart wrenches with it. I know what it's like—I know what that's like, to survive when you think you shouldn't have.

"You know how it goes. Join them or die." They look at me, and I think they see my hand inching toward them, because they hold out their own until I reach out and take it. "Until very recently, I had a lot of regrets about my choice."

I suck a breath in through my nose and let it out slowly. It quivers, and Ezra twines our fingers together almost absently, like they don't notice they're doing it.

I can't assume they mean anything by the hand holding. I've learned the hard way that just because I'm feeling something doesn't mean someone else is, no matter how kind they are. Paul used to tell me I lived in my own world so much I forgot other people weren't there with me. Paul was right.

I don't pull my hand back, but I try to rein in my emotion here. I *think* I understand what Ezra is feeling—it echoes in me like the same bone-deep, hungry loneliness I've felt since Paul died—but I can't know that, and there is no way I can ask. Not now.

"I'm sorry," I say.

It's asinine and hollow; it's like offering someone a single strawberry when they're starving to death.

"You didn't do it." Ezra smiles mirthlessly. They let out a breath, almost the same way I did, a forceful burst of air. "I haven't actually talked to anyone about it in a while. Sorry if that was too heavy—I guess I'm just so used to being around the oldest of the Others that finding someone who isn't a thousand years old and who had to make the same choice I did is a relief."

"I don't think my choice was as hard as yours," I murmur.

What would I have done if I'd had to make it the day Paul died? I don't know if I want the answer to that.

"I think your family would have wanted you to live," I say finally, more because it's easier to say to someone else than because I can believe it for myself.

Paul would have wanted me to live—he'd have kicked me in the shins if I so much as joked about doing otherwise—but . . . I don't let myself finish that train of thought.

One of Paul's other favourite things was a saying he learned on Tumblr: don't mistake shared trauma for compatibility. Paul was right about a lot of things.

Ezra is very quiet for a time, and we sit there with Fànas eventually growing bored of trying to pounce our joined hands and curling up between us on the bed.

"What do I do at school tomorrow?" I ask when I become sure Ezra's not going to respond to my previous statement.

That seems to snap them out of wherever they went, and they immediately become more alert.

"As terrible as it was to find someone's body, you learned something you're capable of," Ezra says slowly. "I noticed you could do it at the cèilidh to an extent—despite other distractions, no one who looked like you did that night should have been able to walk two steps through that ballroom without attention."

They wince almost as soon as they're finished speaking, and when I open my mouth to say something, they barrel on.

"I don't mean that in the sense of like—oh, God—I don't mean it in the skeezy—I sound like a regrettable swipe on Tinder, don't I? I just mean you looked stunning, and the Others don't usually let stunning pass them by," Ezra finishes, and now their face is bright red.

"I—thank you," I say.

From the warmth in my own cheeks, I think the both of us are going to look like stoplights before too long.

Ezra laughs nervously. "Just stating the obvious, not that you don't look stunning always. You're just . . . impressive."

I am not entirely sure what to say to that, so I steal one of Ezra's own lines and just say, "No, you."

"Now you're just flattering me," they say.

My phone on the bedside table lights up, and I wish I didn't immediately read Mam's name and know what she wants.

"Teatime," I say, though the last thing I want to do right now is eat.

"Ah," says Ezra. After squeezing my hand once, they pull theirs away. "I probably should wait to have a proper invitation before turning up to tea, or they might have questions."

"They—would definitely have questions," I say.

Ezra looks at me sideways for a moment, then they just chuckle.

Their expression changes to thoughtful. "Would you feel safer if I perhaps was near Oban tomorrow? In case of emergency."

I wouldn't have thought to ask, but the second they say it, something in me relaxes. "Yes," I answer without hesitation. "That would be—thank you."

"No need to thank me. I prefer you alive."

"Likewise," I say, which makes Ezra chuckle again for some reason.

My phone buzzes again, and Ezra gets up, but they hesitate for a moment before leaning one hand on the windowsill. I wait for them to say something.

"I hope I *don't* see you tomorrow," they say, winking at me. "But not because I don't want to see you."

Yet again, I try to answer, but by the time I get my vocal cords moving, Ezra has flown away.

TWENTY-FOUR

Even with my meditation, my rain sounds, my ocean waves, my binaural beats, Fànas purring, and my eye mask, I can't sleep for most of the night.

I end up tossing and turning and going over every interaction Ezra and I have ever had. It *seems* like they care about me, but they might just get lonely. They literally fly away before anything goes too far, though I have no clue what "too far" even means in this situation.

They said I shouldn't trust them, but who I really don't trust is myself. The last time I liked someone—really liked someone—it didn't go well. Which is to say it went worse than "not well." My therapist says I make understatements because I'm afraid to say the truth when the truth is bad, so here's the truth: I fell in love with a boy called Jason who said he loved me back, he said he'd never felt like that with anyone before, and then he started hooking up with Casey Sorens right after we made it official, and I had no idea for months.

Then Paul died, and now I am pretty sure I am just . . . broken.

So I spent most of Sunday night wide awake in bed, worrying about whether I'm—again—misinterpreting absolutely everything under the sun instead of worrying about possibly dying, because my priorities are well-structured and logical.

My therapist also says I have resorted to self-deprecating sarcasm as a defence mechanism.

I'm so silent on the way in to Oban in the morning that both Mum and Mam keep looking at each other until I say, "I'm fine. Just didn't sleep well."

"Right, ma-thà," says Mam, and Mum shoots her a baffled look that I don't understand beyond it being odd for Mam to be the one to randomly speak any Gaelic, since of the two of them, she's the one who started learning from absolute zero.

I close my eyes and lean my head against the windowpane. Not even the scenery sparks any feeling.

Walking into the high school sure does, though.

Just the sight of the crowds of students is enough to make me want to emulate Ealasaid's note and quietly implode, crumpling inward until I dissolve into nothingness.

The lights are too loud today, buzzing and bright, and the students seem to all have either forgotten to bathe or bathed in body sprays.

But no one seems to notice me.

I even walk right by Grace, and before I register that her face is one I actually know, I'm past her, and she doesn't even react.

When the same continues all through the day, it occurs to me that I might be doing it. It seems—maybe, just a guess—that whatever my magic is, the thing that triggers it is fear.

I don't know if I like that, but it makes sense. Fear is one of the most primal emotions we have and one of the few I recognise with any ease. I take some comfort in the glimpses of blue sky I see through the classroom windows throughout the day, because they remind me that the stars are there and that the very first thing that my magic gave me was the wonder of space.

Just when school gets out and I think I've managed to escape Ealasaid, though, I hear a singsong voice that sends a chill through me.

It's not a far walk from the high school to the mums' new office space, but it takes me past the Aldi and the Lidl on Soroba Road, and there is a crowd of high school kids in the Lidl carpark.

I think everyone who has been bullied knows the stab of wariness that comes with seeing a group of peers who may or may not be hostile.

Though my last couple of years in Texas were quieter, I've never forgotten how it feels to wonder what will happen when all those sets of eyes turn on me.

But right now, they're not focused on me.

It isn't hard for me to spot the target—she's a wee girl, definitely high school age, but much younger than the rest of the crowd. I've never seen her at school. She's got brown hair so straight it looks like it's been steam-rolled, and her shoulders hunch in on herself like she's a turtle trying to climb inside a shell—but the shell is gone.

Ealasaid is there, at the fringes, simply watching with a half-smile on her perfect face.

It amazes me that she can blend so easily into this group. Ezra is a shape-changer, but Ealasaid—she's a chameleon.

Gone is the statuesque beauty from the ball who could be cast in marble and not look out of place in the Parthenon. In her place is a kid, still beautiful but only in the intimidating way of the miraculous few who escape the pustules and pains of puberty, not an ancient god ready to call down smiting lightning.

Except Ealasaid is the latter.

I don't know what they're saying to the girl in the middle of that crowd, but what is evident is that they're not letting her go. If a teacher or someone were to walk by right now, Ealasaid would have plausible deniability. She's not a participant; she's merely present.

There is nothing I can do to help.

I pause a short distance away, in clear sight but—I hope—hidden.

Can Ealasaid see me? I'm not sure I have any way of knowing that. She knows where I live, so it would be stupid of me to assume she doesn't know that my mums have an office in Oban and that she isn't able to chart the most logical walking route between the high school and the office.

Ezra and Grace both said her modus operandi is to be present for things like this, that she likes to goad people.

And after what she said to me yesterday about not getting in her way, I feel confident in saying that this display is a test. For me.

I shift my weight from one foot to the other. It's not at all like what happened to Paul—that was guns and screaming and chaos.

But I feel like I did then, my reactions too slow, unable to think fast enough to do anything that could make a difference. I am frozen to the spot where I stand on the footpath, cars whizzing by behind me on the road.

Whoever that kid is, she doesn't deserve being used as bait to goad me into—what, exactly? My shoulders are so bunched up, they're practically brushing my earlobes. It's the same posture as the kid, like I'm mirroring her out of sympathy and my own futility.

I *hate* bullies.

Just as I think it, a wave of *something passes* through me, and the streetlight over the edge of the carpark explodes in a shower of glass and fizzing electricity.

The gathered high schoolers yelp and scatter, and the moment the circle breaks, the wee girl turns tail and runs. Everyone else is too busy darting out of the way of falling glass to stop her or go after her.

Ealasaid looks around, eyes assessing, not even bothering to move.

She said she would kill my family if I got in her way. What have I just done?

I take my cue from the girl and run.

I don't stop until I get to the office.

If the mums notice anything amiss with my arrival, they don't say anything, but outside the window, a dormer that overlooks the CalMac terminal from the top floor of this building, a raven lights atop the mast of a sailboat at its moorings. The sky is dotted with fast-moving clouds just now, but the blue between them fights a losing battle. In the west, a bank of deep purple-grey storm clouds lurks upon the horizon, the slanting blur of rain already visible in the distance.

The water in the harbour is so blue-green, teal like the waters in the Caribbean. I have the sudden urge to run right back out the door and dive in and swim and not stop until I hit Craignure in Mull. Until I catch the coming rain.

Instead, I leave Mum to finish her emails while Mam washes up their teacups in the office's tiny kitchen, and I go back downstairs to get some fresh air.

Ezra is waiting for me.

They are dressed all in black today, black jeans and a black jumper that wouldn't be out of place in the pages of *Vogue*, all angles and straight lines. Their waves are brushed a bit back from their face, but one errant lock that is almost a curl falls down over their forehead.

"I saw the streetlight from the sky and saw you running, but she didn't follow. I don't think she even saw you—well done," they say without preamble.

I give them a tight smile, glancing up at the office window. "I think I have to be afraid to use that magic. Which is fine when I'm actually scared, but if I don't know to be scared yet, it could backfire."

"It won't always be like that," Ezra says with confidence. Their hand rises a little from their side, but it drops back down again. "You're just learning. One day it'll be as easy as breathing."

My own breath hitches at that thought, and again the longing hits me to swim out of Oban and into the sea.

"I hope you're right," I say, thinking of the dead man's peaceful face. "Otherwise I'll probably end up not breathing at all. I had wondered if the Others could die or be killed. Guess I have my answer."

"Only if three agree," Ezra says so smoothly it sounds almost like a reflex. "And it takes a lot of doing to get three of us to agree on anything, let alone ending an immortal's life."

Relief is slow in answer to those words, and I nod, mulling them over.

Belatedly, something hits me, and I take a full step back from Ezra.

"What?" they say, hands twitching again.

"It's just—shit." I can feel the blood draining from my face, and I wobble on my feet, turning instinctively to look back in the direction I left Ealasaid. "Can I say it out loud?"

Ezra's eyes flash jewel-green, and a ripple of warmth emanates outward from their body. The sounds of the waves and cars grow dimmer, distant.

"You can now," Ezra tells me.

Nodding shakily, I clear my throat. "That first night I met you—I just remembered what I heard Ealasaid and the others say. They said something took three and they had three. I had no idea what that meant then. They could have been moving a piano, for all I knew, but now . . ."

Ezra's face darkens like the clouds coming in from the west. Just then, though, the door behind me opens, and Mum and Mam come out with their bags, Mam dangling her travel mug from her pinky.

"Oh!" Mam exclaims, seeing me with Ezra.

The warmth cloaking us dissipates from one heartbeat to the next, and Ezra's face shifts away from danger to a smile.

Mum sees them an instant later, and the key ring in her hand jingles in surprise.

"Are you going to introduce your friend?" Mam prompts me, and I want to kick myself.

"Erm, aye. Mam, Mum, this is Ezra. Their pronouns are they/them," I add, then want to kick myself again since I'm not sure if Ezra wants me to tell them that.

"Ezra," Mam says warmly, wedging her travel mug in her bag precariously to reach out and clasp Ezra's proffered hand in both of her own. "What a lovely name. I'm Roberta, and this is my wife Catrìona."

Mum is more guarded as usual, but when Ezra extends their hand to her, she shakes it just as warmly. "Pleased to meet you, Ezra," she says. "How did you two meet?"

"Ezra stays near us," I blurt out just as Ezra says, "We actually met in the forest," and we both look at each other with the kind of panic only a parental introduction can account for.

"Is that why you keep running off into the woods?" Mam asks with a wink. "Well, ah'll no complain so long as you're safe."

"Mam!" My strangled yelp earns a wide-eyed handwave from Mam.

"Lily Cameron Smith, I just meant *hillwalking*, though yes, also that other thing." Mam, to my surprise, is turning beet red.

"So far no casualties between the two of us," Ezra says smoothly, though their cheeks are also tinged with pink.

"Please keep it that way," Mum says, giving Mam's shoulder a wee pat. "Perhaps if you stay nearby, you would like to join us for dinner some night? We've met Cam's lovely friend Deirdre, but she's so far been stingy about yourself, it seems."

Impulse to swim to Mull intensifying.

It's not *that* far, is it? The ferry takes forty minutes, so probably I could be there in a couple hours if I yeet myself into the harbour right now.

But Ezra just laughs. "I'd love that, if it's all right with Cam."

My gaze snaps to their face, and I hurriedly say, "Yes, of course!"

"Magic," says Mam. "How about tomorrow?"

"I'm free tomorrow," Ezra says immediately, looking at me.

"That'd be brilliant." My voice comes out a bit faint.

"I should let yous go," Ezra says then. "What time tomorrow?"

"We usually eat around six," says Mum. "My mother will swoon if we push it much later than that."

Ezra grins. "I don't blame her. I'll see you then."

"See you then," I echo, and Ezra gives me what I think is a reassuring smile before waving and turning away.

The mums don't stop gushing until we get home.

TWENTY-FIVE

I don't know if I should be alarmed that I've not seen Deirdre or Daibhidh yet when they said they would come by yesterday.

Granaidh's got tea cooking when we get home, so I retreat to my bedroom, hoping for some sort of sign. The longer time stretches on without me telling them I saw them, the worse I am going to feel. Even if the most likely explanation for their absence is that they're grieving, I can't help the swirl of bile that keeps creeping up my throat thinking of their faces almost covered in moss, subsumed.

Mam peppers me with questions at dinner about Ezra, and Granaidh is shockingly silent, only watching me quietly from her place at the table and sipping at her tea.

The problem is, I don't know much about Ezra at all, and what I do know, I can't exactly tell them. What am I going to say, that they're sometimes a bird? That they slip between genders like Loki? That they're a reluctant prince who was set on that path by the very people who stole everything from them? I give enough half-truths that it seems to satisfy Mam, but by the time I'm done picking at my food like a bird myself, I'm exhausted.

I wonder what Ezra will think of my calling them a "budding ornithologist with a passion for rock climbing"—I never actually saw them climb that big rock they were sitting on, though I suppose if you squint, reaching the top of a rock by unconventional means could qualify as climbing.

It's impossible not to be aware that Ezra told very careful truths to the mums when they all met. *So far no casualties between the two of us.*

It feels like such a . . . such a *sìtheach* sort of thing to say. Technically the truth but also hints at there being casualties, which is true.

There's a text from Grace on my mobile when I finally escape back upstairs.

Didn't see you at school today—hope you're okay x

Seeing the message gives me a pang. I don't know where Fànas is, but I wish she were here to comfort me. I like Grace and her sister Eilidh. I wouldn't mind having them for friends.

But won't my being close to them put them in danger? The thought of either Grace or Eilidh in a circle of hostile bullies under Ealasaid's watchful gaze makes my stomach churn. I shove my mobile away and flop back onto my bed, scrunching my eyes closed and pounding my fists against the duvet.

I hate this.

I can't tell the mums or Granaidh about what happened—what *is* happening—to me, and the idea of floating through school like an imperceptible ghost for the entire term makes me nearly as sick as thinking of Ealasaid taking out her frustrations on that lovely wee pair of sisters.

A small poking sound and scrabbling claws makes me smile and open my eyes. Fànas's tiny black face appears over the edge of the bed, and she immediately starts purring, crawling up onto my chest and sitting down, eyes slow blinking. She sits so primly, her two paws pressed snugly against each other and her wee stubby tail wrapped around her legs.

"Ceud mìle taing," I thank her profusely, and she purrs louder.

Stroking her at least helps me calm down.

"We've got to go this alone," I say to the kitten. "No use getting anyone else hurt or killed."

I can't tell if the piseag agrees. I am not entirely sure what a cat-sìthe even is. But the distraction is welcome. I budge up enough to snatch my phone from the bedside table, hurriedly closing the message from Grace and glad I keep read receipts off as a personal principle.

Reading the Wikipedia page on the cat-sìthe does not take enough time, however. It's short, describing a large black cat with a white patch on its chest that is given a wide berth by the Gaels of old and is said to perhaps be a witch who can transform into a cat nine times, the ninth time remaining forever in cat form. Since Fànas is a kitten, I'm not sure that is the case in this particular instance.

"An e bana-bhuidseach a th' annad?" I ask, and her sole response to my asking if she's a witch is to cush down into a loaf on my chest, which only serves to make her into possibly the cutest witch who has ever existed.

There's also a legend of the King of the Cats, cait-shìth stealing souls, and a Samhain tradition of leaving a saucer of cream out for the cat-sìthe, but nothing about accidentally awakening one from the average wee black piseag.

"Guess you'll remain a mystery, m' eudail," I say to her, and she peers out at me through slitted eyelids, but she springs off my chest when a tap sounds at the window.

My heart lurches, and I give Fànas a pat before sliding off the bed, hoping to see Ezra framed in the dormer, but it's not Ezra. Deirdre gives me a tight-lipped smile and backs up while I open the window for her.

"Can't you just—" I waggle my hand at her as she lowers herself over the windowsill, and she shakes her head.

"Not anymore," she says. Her gaze falls on Fànas, whose bottle-brush tail is slowly returning to normal. "Either that cat is more effective than she should be or you yourself are making it harder to get in here."

I hope it's the latter. "Are you okay?"

Deirdre grimaces. "I'm sorry I didn't come by yesterday," she says. "I'm afraid something . . . came up."

Now is the time for me to come clean, but before I can, Deirdre is going on.

"Daibhidh and I found a very dear friend dead yesterday afternoon. An immortal who should have lived another thousand years at least. Daibhidh and I argued for hours about how much we should involve you in this, but . . . he told me it's not going to help you to keep you ignorant."

"I know," I say softly.

Deirdre looks at me sideways. "What?"

Not making eye contact, I stare at the chest of drawers on the other side of the room and tell her what happened, my body going rigid as I brace myself for her reaction.

But Deirdre doesn't react, not at first. When I'm finished and risk a glance at her face, she isn't looking at me, just staring into space.

"Daibhidh was right." She does meet my eyes then, and for a moment, her face, though unlined, exudes a weariness that reads much, much older—old enough to make Granaidh look young.

I have a feeling I wasn't present for whatever he was right about.

Thunder rumbles through the air, startlingly loud, and Deirdre's head snaps almost audibly to look westward, though the window on that side of the house has the shades drawn.

But when it happens again, it feels like the thunder booms *through* me.

"Mo chreach-sa thàinig," Deirdre murmurs. "I'm sorry, Cam. I have to go. Now."

"Everyone needs to stop fucking disappearing!" I say, too loudly, but Deirdre doesn't look back.

She takes one step, leaving me staring after her, and before I can stop myself, I feel a surge within me and follow, stepping into a near-imperceptible shimmer in the air she's just vacated.

Rain buffets my face, wind whipping my curls across my cheek so hard it stings. Pressure blooms in my ears, and I pop them immediately. The relief is immediate and palpable.

Something seizes my arm and yanks me to the side. I tumble to the ground before I can even see where I am, and Deirdre throws up her hand with a shockwave that slams outward from her palm.

She says nothing, but in the brief moment her face is near mine, her eyes are hard as jasper and hold the fury of a volcano.

Sprawled on my side on rocky ground, I look up to see a handful of people I don't recognise, and the air crackles with electricity I am certain has nothing to do with the storm.

We're high up—for all I know, we could be at the summit of Ben Cruachan. I can't see through the mist and rain that pummels me in sheets.

"Don't move," is all Deirdre says before she launches herself at the Others.

I scramble backward, finding a boulder with my back before I go more than a few inches. Missing it with my head was a narrow thing—I'm lucky Deirdre didn't body slam me a little to the right or I'd be concussed.

With the torrent of rain falling at a slant over the hilltop, I can barely make out the Others, but it's obvious they're fighting. Two long-haired Others grapple with one another ten yards away, their movements almost too fast for my eyes to track.

A howl begins on the wind, rising in pitch and volume until I have to cover my ears. At first I think it's just my sound sensitivity—even the Hoover is agonising to me—but even as I curl inward on myself, the Others do the same, throwing their hands up over their ears and flinching away from the noise.

A woman advances on the hilltop out of the mist, her mouth open impossibly wide as she screams.

In the rain, her dark hair is plastered to her neck and shoulders, and it clings to her. She's wearing only a thin white shift, translucent and soaking wet against her flat chest and diminutive frame. Nothing else about her is in any way small. Her arms stick out at acute angles from her shoulders, all her fingers splayed and quivering.

Her scream cuts the air like a red-hot knife in butter, and the Others reel, stumbling away from her regardless of who they were fighting only moments ago.

I can't stop staring at her, and the instant her eyes make contact with mine, I wish I could shove myself all the way into this rock.

I am terrified, but she can see me.

Her scream does not stop.

She advances on me, ignoring all the others, and my back presses hard against the boulder, a sharp edge digging into my shoulder blades through the long-sleeved T-shirt that is the only thing standing between me and this hurricane-force weather.

All of a sudden, a gust of hot wind pours over the top of my head in the opposite direction from the rest of the wind, and the woman's scream cuts off abruptly.

In the wind, shapes fly over the boulder above me, mere blurs that leave trails of scents of peat and heather and warmth.

I cannot see Deirdre. Shapes in the mist scramble and scatter, and when I blink, almost all the figures are gone.

Only An Smeòrach remains directly in view, and two others I don't recognise.

Deirdre rises to her feet on the other side of another large, lichen-covered rock twenty yards away. She winces, catching herself on the stone. Her shoulders heave, and she grimaces when she takes a step toward An Smeòrach, but he spins and looks directly at me.

"You brought the child," he says incredulously.

"I didn't bring her." Deirdre's voice is hoarse as if she were the one screaming. "She simply followed."

An Smeòrach's head swivels toward Deirdre. "Either you were clumsy, or she is more precocious than I expected."

"The latter," Deirdre says. She raises her hand to her lip, dabbing at it.

It comes away red, and the rain immediately turns it pink, dripping onto the rocky ground.

An Smeòrach comes to me, and like he did in the ballroom, he holds out both his hands. I take them and let him pull me to my feet.

"It is good to see you again, a chuachain," he says, "but this is not the place for you."

"Tha mi duilich," I apologise, barely able to get the words out. My own voice is as hoarse as Deirdre's, and I can hardly hear it over the wind and rain. "I didn't mean to—I was just so frustrated that everyone keeps disappearing."

He gives me a sharp look, not unkindly, and he lets go of my right hand to reach up to my cheek, where I feel a trickle of water.

Not water. Blood.

When he pulls his hand back, my blood wets his finger.

Even in this downpour on the top of a mountain, he smells like peat and sweet tobacco.

I wipe rainwater from my face when he drops my other hand and turns to Deirdre.

"Before the week is out, bring her to me," he says. "Daibhidh as well. There is little time."

Deirdre nods, her face blank. The other shapes come closer. One is the Black man I remember seeing in gold at the cèilidh, and he exchanges a glance with An Smeòrach before vanishing in a shimmer of fog. The other is a tiny woman with short hair in a pixie cut, and though she looks like Tinkerbell and barely comes up to An Smeòrach's shoulder, she could have been chiselled from the boulder behind me. Without a word, she disappears as well.

"Forgive us our rudeness," An Smeòrach says to me. "We are accustomed to simply coming and going as we please, and we forget that the newer ones among us lack our context."

His manners are so polite despite the fight, despite the fact that the rain is washing my blood from his finger.

"I was stupid," I say.

"This is your world now, and you deserve to know it," he says. "The mortal world will fall away for you as it did for all of us, and it is cruel to leave you to flounder in it."

Acid rises in my throat at those words, and I don't know what to say—does he mean I can't go home?

But a moment later, he answers my question. "Take her home, Deirdre. She is your responsibility—and mine. By the end of the week." An Smeòrach takes my hands once more, and, again like he did at the cèilidh, gives me a kiss on the cheek. "Not all of us are cruel all the time. Take heart. I am going to leave now, a chuachain. I will see you soon."

With a small bow, he lets go of my hands and does just that.

I'm left alone on the top of a mountain with Deirdre.

TWENTY-SIX

Deirdre has to help me get home, because my chaotic magic apparently only works when it feels like it, and we leave a wet puddle in the middle of the floor of my bedroom before she sighs, reaches out with a finger, and with one tap, has me dry, though still shivering.

We can't have been gone more than a few minutes, but it feels like an age.

"Sorry," I say finally.

"It's not any more your fault than if you were toddler running out in front of a car," she says, which is less than helpful. "But you should understand that if I just 'disappear,' as you say, it's always for a good reason and likely for your own safety. Though it seems I am increasingly overruled."

She sounds defeated but not angry, and it's such a familiar . . . *mother-y* feeling that I am immediately awash in a child's shame.

A petulant mew sounds from the bed, and I wince. "Gabh mo leisgeul," I say to the kitten apologetically. "Sorry we just left."

"An Smeòrach said before week's end," Deirdre says, though her eyes have brightened at the sight of the kitten, who she reaches over to scratch behind the ears. "We should set a day so you can tell your family—might want to make it an all-nighter."

"Friday sounds best, then," I say, uncertain. "Is that too late?"

"It's cutting it closer than I'd like." Deirdre snorts. "It's been a while since I had to contend with parents."

"What if we say I'm staying at yours Wednesday night to work on a project?" I offer. It's not entirely a lie. "It would be more convincing if they didn't think you stayed just down the road, but—"

"We can work with that," she interrupts me. "Think you can stay alive and relatively unscathed for two days?"

"I think so. Ezra will be here tomorrow for tea anyway, so I'll have . . . backup."

Deirdre does a double take and then closes her eyes, tilting her head to the side before sighing and opening them again.

"The prince is coming round for tea with the family, she says, as if this is nothing. Gasta. Sgoinneil. I'm sure this is fine."

I half-expect her to vanish on the spot, but she doesn't.

"Is that bad?" I ask.

Fànas mews again, so I sit and pull her into my lap.

"If I told you to keep your distance from them for your own safety—and Ezra's—would you listen?" Deirdre asks. She sighs again. "Don't answer that. I saw you two at the cèilidh."

"It's not like that," I say.

"Mo chreach," she says for the second time today. "You *are* a child."

With that, she really does vanish.

She almost immediately appears again, looking none too happy about it.

"Sorry," she says. "I should have said goodbye. I'm not bowing."

"I don't expect you to?" I say, mystified. "But thank you."

"Two days," she mutters. "Two days."

Then she's gone again.

I hold the piseag until I can work up the courage to go downstairs and ask the mums for a school-night sleepover.

Mam is the easy one to convince; she's delighted I'm *making friends*, which is, I suppose, true. I think she'd let me kayak to St. Kilda if she thought I'd come back with a pal.

Mum is less convinced. I find her in the study, which is another spare room that's been converted since Granaidh no longer makes it up either of the house's two staircases. She's perched on the chair at her desk and massaging her temples like she doesn't know what to do with me. That is also a very familiar mother-y feeling, and it's one of my least favourites.

"Cam, what's gotten into you?" she asks. "You're off in the woods all the time after randomly meeting some—some person, you're going to parties, and half the time I look at you, you look so spooked I think you're developing the second sight."

I guess when she puts it like that, it is weird.

"It's been a weird year," I say truthfully. Another understatement. Sorry, Lindy.

Mum looks up, rolling her chair back from her desk, her gaze falling to my legs.

"Why on Earth are you covered in gravel?" she says.

Oops.

My leggings have heaps of tiny, jagged pebbles stuck to them, all bone-dry but definitely present.

"I went outside in the storm and tripped," I say, recognising a very Ezra-like half-truth with a wince.

Realising I could have blood on my face, I shake my hair so it falls down in front of my ears, which tickles my jaw, but I'll endure.

At my pronouncement, Mum just gives a rueful laugh. "At least that is a very Cam thing to do."

I shrug, both at her words and in hopes it'll move the hair away from my jaw. It doesn't.

"Okay," Mum says after a beat. "Wednesday night. But Ezra is coming over tomorrow, yes?"

At my nod, she nods as well.

"And Deirdre is a very nice girl." Mum runs her fingers through her hair, shaking it loose from its bun as if it's giving her a headache, which it probably is. "And Thursday you're coming to choir with us, yes? Mother will be heartbroken if you change your mind."

"Guilt trip," I say automatically, and this time it's my mother who winces. "But yes. I said I'd be there, and I will be. Also, if I'm with Deirdre Wednesday night, yous can work here during the day and just drive in with Granaidh. I can go to the office after school and do homework until choir practice starts."

"Not a bad idea," Mum agrees. "I'll get you a key cut tomorrow—you should have one anyway."

I turn to leave.

"Cam," says Mum. "When was the last time you talked to your father?"

Oof. "Erm . . . I don't know."

"Fix that," she says pointedly. "He didn't expect to lose you for your senior year."

I give her a tight nod and retreat from her office, avoiding Granaidh and Mam where they sit in the kitchen, but I skate to a halt at the foot of the stairs, out of their line of sight.

". . . an do dhèan thu e?" It's *Mam* speaking Gaelic. *Did you done it?*

"An do *rinn* thu e," Granaidh corrects her. *Did you do it.* "Ged a tha cuid de dhaoine ga ràdh an dòigh eile."

A gentle fix, an explanation that some do say it the first way.

My eyes prickle with a sensation I am not familiar with, and I open and close my mouth a couple of times like a goldfish, trying to dispel the tears before they can form.

"An do rinn," repeats Mam.

For a moment, I imagine Gaelic being the language of this house. The thought freezes me where I stand, and I hear Mum's footsteps coming through the living room and push myself into motion up the stairs.

"You two are thick as thieves in here," she says when she goes into the kitchen, breaking the spell.

Of the three of us in the younger generations, Mum's the only one who got the Gaelic from her own mother's knee. But she's quickly becoming the least likely to use it—I wish I knew why.

My feet feel extra heavy as I climb the stairs, and it takes most of the way to my room for me to decipher that what I'm feeling is loss. I envy Mum what she had. I envy the ease with which she understands Granaidh. I envy feeling at home in any language. Even in English, I share my tongue with no one.

My room feels too big. The sight of Fànas curled up in a tiny ball in the centre of the duvet only strengthens that feeling, and I curl up around her in the foetal position. She stirs as my weight depresses the mattress, stretching out her little paws and flexing those wee claws.

Her purr kicks up immediately, and I reach out and scratch her cheeks, which she leans into so much she almost tips over even from lying down.

For a while I just lie there with her. Her fur is so soft, and the wee white patch on her chest is the only bit of her that isn't pitch-black aside from her eyes, which are still a deep blue-grey. I wonder what colour they will turn as she gets older.

Eventually, I grab my phone and pull up an email to Dad.

Dad and I are a lot alike. Neither of us are the type to text every day or even every week. We both like our space, and of my parents, he's least likely to get cross with me for gaps in communication. He knows it doesn't mean I don't love him. And vice versa, I guess. We both hate small talk.

I type out an email just telling him that I've made some new friends and that school is fine, that we got a kitten—I attach a bunch of pictures, several thousand words' worth—and that his tick protocols saved me from at least four of the little buggers.

I do feel a bit better once I send that off.

But too much is still nagging at me, worrying at the edges of my heart like the way I used to chew on my nails.

I want to talk to Ezra, but when I think of them, I feel like I'm falling, or like I've just stepped from my bedroom onto a mountaintop with one slight move of my feet. I've felt this before, and I don't think I can trust it.

Have you, though? A tiny voice in my mind whispers the question almost too quietly to be heard over Fànas's purr.

I don't have an answer to that.

I somehow have to get through tomorrow at school before I even see Ezra, and that thought reminds me of Grace's text.

"What would you do?" I ask Fànas, who of course does not answer.

After almost a half hour of deliberation, I write back.

I was there—just wasn't feeling very well and kept to myself. Hope you had a good weekend!

It's a ridiculous message to have taken that long to write out, but I feel even more ridiculous sending it. I fight the urge to hurl my phone across the room.

When I close my eyes, all I can see is that terrifying, open-mouthed scream. I think everyone's heard "scream like a banshee" before, but she was the real thing. And since no one else on that hilltop so much as glanced my way until An Smeòrach arrived, the fact that she was moving directly at me is disturbing.

I've no proof, but I am certain she saw straight through whatever shroud my magic uses to hide me.

"Ban-sìthe" just means one of the Sìthichean who is a woman, but in English it's become synonymous with that sort of scream. Even the memory of it hurts my ears.

Reluctantly, I open up the camera app on my mobile and look at my face. There is indeed a trickle of blood—now dry—coming from each of my ears. Pure dumb luck that Mum didn't see it, though I forgot to clean off my leggings, and now there's smudges of dirt and tiny pebbles all over the duvet.

That one woman, one ban-sìthe, was able to incapacitate everyone in that fight regardless of which side they were on. I don't even know what sides exist.

As I pry myself off the bed to tidy up, I understand Deirdre's urgency a bit better.

It drops a lead anchor into my gut and stays there.

If the Sìthichean are scared, that does not bode well for me.

TWENTY-SEVEN

I spend Tuesday practically vibrating.

It's so bad that both Mam and Mum ask me if I want to cancel dinner with Ezra in the car on the way home from school, and I have to tell them I don't actually have the means to do that, which is true—it's not like I'm carting their feather around with me wherever I go, and if I wait until we get home, it'll be too rude to consider.

The mums weren't there in Texas for what happened with Jason. I'm pretty sure they heard about it from Dad, but it also got overtaken by Paul's death. Even now, I can hardly think of one without the other, and each pain twists in a different part of my core.

Mum and Mam weren't there the nights I waited and waited for Jason to text. They weren't there for the nights he was supposed to come by and then just didn't show, and they weren't there for the way I lost a stone—literally fourteen pounds—in a month because I felt *something* was wrong, but he denied every question I asked.

The memory of it is slimy, slithery. It curls through me, burning like acid in my middle. It's tied up with anger I can't disentangle. That was my last month with Paul, the last one I ever got to spend with him, and I was a wreck for most of it. I was a weepy, jumpy, obsessive bin fire of a human being, and Paul, through all of it, didn't get upset at me once.

I know Ezra isn't Jason. Obviously, I know that. But some part of me is certain that when six o'clock rolls around, Ezra will just . . . not be here.

I wait in the salon with Fànas, who has picked up on my jangled nerves and has morphed into a tiny soot demon, bent on destruction. She's usually not an ankle biter, but every time I move my feet, she pounces, and I'm pretty sure any minute now, there will be tiny pin-pricks of blood showing through my beige wool socks.

"Sgur dheth!" I exclaim when ten acupuncture-sized needles pierce my feet again.

To my utter shock, she does stop, sitting back on her rump so hard, it comes with a wee thud.

I didn't think a kitten could look abashed, but at her wide-eyed stare, my own face crumples, and I scoop her up, holding her to my chest.

"I know you don't *mean* to, but ow," I tell her seriously.

She starts purring.

A knock sounds at the door.

I hop to my feet, scooting across the floor on my stocking feet, past Mam, who looks disappointed that I'm going to intercept Ezra before she can embarrass me.

She rolls her eyes and turns back to the kitchen, where Granaidh is doing a quick release on the Instant Pot, from which a mouth-watering smell of pot roast wafts.

Holding Fànas against me, I make it to the door, and my Fitbit lights up when I move my arm to open it. Bang on at six.

Ezra is on the other side of it.

"Feels sacrilegious to use the door," they say with a wink. "Hi."

"Hi," I say.

"Thoughtful of both of you to greet me." Ezra steps inside as I pull the door open.

"Fànas was waging war against my feet, but I think we've reached a ceasefire," I say.

Ezra is dressed similar to how they were yesterday, but today their jumper is forest green. Cashmere, I think. I suppose they wouldn't turn up in any of their other forms, though the momentary vision of me bringing a raven and a kitten to the dinner table is so absurd and surreal that I have to bite back a nervous laugh.

It's not fair that they look so good in so many different colours.

"Granaidh made pot roast," I say. "I should have asked if you eat meat."

"I do, don't worry," Ezra assures me.

They take off their shoes and place them in a tidy queue with mine and the mums', which fills me with a sudden warmth.

"This way," I say, leading them down the hall. "They're all in the kitchen."

If I thought it would be any less stressful the second time, I'm instantly proven wrong when we round the corner to three pairs of eyes watching very intently.

"Ò, nach 'ad a tha innealta," exclaims Granaidh, and Ezra says, "Taing mhòr dhuibh" very politely just as Mum says "*English*, Mother," and then everyone falls silent at once.

"Chì thusa—deagh Ghàidhlig aca," says Granaidh, swatting at Mum with a tea towel before hanging it back daintily on the handle of the silverware drawer.

"Even so," Mum says, and she bustles past Granaidh's wheelchair to get the stack of plates sitting on the worktop. Granaidh looks away, and I feel a sharp pang. "Sorry we haven't set the table yet, Ezra—been a bit mad today."

"No worries at all. Can I help?"

"Absolutely not," says Mam. "Won't be but five minutes."

"Where are you from?" Granaidh asks, and I almost drop Fànas.

I can't remember the last time I heard English from her, and the sheer wave of wrongness almost knocks me off my feet.

Ezra looks momentarily at a loss, but after a moment, they swallow and say, also in English, "Ballachulish. But I stay near here now."

Granaidh nods. "Your parents?"

"Passed away, I'm afraid."

That sends another wee shock through the kitchen, and Granaidh clucks to herself.

"I'm very sorry, a ghràidh. Here, why don't you sit down, and I'll get you some of my bramble cordial I've made up for tonight. Bramble out back has gone wild this year."

Granaidh glances at me as she says it, shooing Ezra toward the table with the wooden spoon she's just picked up, and at first I think she wants me to get the cordial, but then she pokes me in the hip with the spoon to get me to sit as well.

The table is a bit cramped set for five, which pushes me and Ezra back into the corner—the hole, as Mam and I call it—and the warmth of their shoulder so close to mine makes it hard for me to concentrate on the conversation Mam's trying to make. Granaidh comes over with two large tumblers full of purple, fizzy juice on a tray balanced atop her wheelchair, each topped with sprigs of mint from the garden. Both Ezra and I thank her, and she beams, which soothes my heart a little after seeing that hurt look on her face at Mum's words.

". . . Cam says you're interested in ornithology," Mam's in the middle of saying to Ezra, who has just taken a sip of their cordial and almost spits it right back out again.

Ezra coughs, clearing their throat. "Aye, you could say that. I quite like corvids."

I have made the unfortunate mistake of taking a drink while they're answering, and I barely avoid a spit-take myself.

Thankfully, Mam is whipping the mashers in an enormous bowl and has her back to us, but Mum gives me a strange look.

After that, dinner goes mostly smoothly, though the abundance of blackberries is enough to make all of us laugh—Granaidh's made a sauce out of them for the pot roast (surprisingly tart and tasty with the savoury beef) in addition to the cordial (also delicious) and blackberry squares for afters with warm custard.

I'm going to have a word with Deirdre.

"I was going to go to Sabhal Mòr Ostaig before my parents passed," Ezra says when Mum asks them about uni plans. "Now I'm taking a couple of years to decide."

"Did you grow up with Gaelic, then?" Mum asks, though for once it's she who isn't making eye contact.

"My grandfather was from Lismore," Ezra says. "On my mother's side. My father came from Syria. Both of them learned Gaelic, but not until I was in school. So yes and no?"

"You have beautiful Gaelic," Granaidh says, and in my head I hear it as she ought to have said it. *Gàidhlig bhrèagha a th' agad.*

"Ceud taing," Ezra thanks her, and she reaches out over the table and pats their hand.

Before too long, though, it's obvious Granaidh is getting tired, so she goes off to bed. It doesn't feel right to hear "good night" instead of her usual "oidhche mhath leibh," and it shakes me even farther into my unsettled state. She takes Fànas with her.

Ezra insists on helping with the washing up, and Mum seems too distracted to refuse. They leave us drying the dishes with a stern "Don't stay up too late—yous have school tomorrow" from Mam, which only adds to the strangeness since stern is usually Mum's job.

"Pretty sure they love you," I say as soon as they're gone. "Sorry Mum was a bit of a git."

"Families can be complicated," Ezra says, picking up one of the last plates. "Did you tell your gran my pronouns?"

I blink. "No, I didn't. Maybe the mums did."

I've just realised she indeed used the Gaelic iad for *they*, which I know is an English carry-over.

"It's weirdly comforting to hear anyway," Ezra says softly. "Cam—"

They break off without saying anything else, and I wait, but they don't go on.

I finish with the teacup I'm drying and put it in the cupboard. My hands are shaking.

"I wanted to ask you something," Ezra says, "but I don't know how."

"Okay," I say. "What did you want to ask?"

"Are you sure it's okay that I came over tonight?"

I start at that. I don't know what I was expecting, but that wasn't it.

Ezra goes on in a hurry. "I just mean—you've seemed a bit out of sorts, and I would understand if like—if it seemed like I was fishing for an invitation the other night and then kind of turned up and got one and if you just felt like you had to go along with it."

I'm shaking my head hard despite not being able to form words, and I hope my vehement denial is clear enough. Ezra waits for me to speak.

"It's not that," I say finally.

Granaidh's door is closed, but they're French doors and mostly glass, so I'm certain she can hear everything we say in here. Plus, she's trying to go to bed.

"Come on." I brush my fingers over Ezra's shoulder, hesitant to touch without an invitation, and I slide past them to go upstairs.

"Will the mums approve of me going upstairs?" Ezra asks. "I don't want to upset them."

"They won't care," I say.

At least I'm pretty sure they won't. I'm eighteen, and it's not like we're going to dive into bed or anything.

The thought makes me squirm. Confusing.

When we're safely ensconced in my room with the door shut, I let out a breath.

"You were saying?" Ezra says.

Once again, their face is guarded, like they've built Hadrian's Wall up in front of them and are merely peeking over it. I sit on my bed. Looking up at Ezra standing feels wrong, imbalanced, and they seem to feel it too, because after an uncomfortable shudder of my heartbeat, they come and sit too, but not close.

I haven't told anyone but therapists and family about what happened last year.

"I'm—I'm not great with feelings," I say after a long beat. "Or people. I . . . Last year, some bad things happened, and I lost"—*Everyone*—"people I cared about. Not like what happened to you. It wasn't like that, but I don't know which way is up half the time, and even less so now, and then I met you, and you grabbed my hand through a hole in a door in the middle of the woods, which makes no sense, and now everything is fucking *terrifying*."

Ezra is completely still. Not a movement, not a ripple.

"Deirdre asked me to stay away from you," I say all in a rush. "Or she asked if it would be worth asking and then decided it wouldn't, and I don't know why—"

"You want to stay away from me?" Ezra asks, their expression completely unreadable.

My heart wrenches in half.

"*No*," I say so forcefully I even startle myself. I am processing my feelings as I say them out loud, and my fingers are shaking like a hummingbird's wings. "I'm saying I can't stay away from you. I couldn't bear it if she made me."

My words hang in the air like wind chimes with no wind.

TWENTY-EIGHT

I think my words are just going to hang there forever.

Time stretches into infinity, and my insides start to collapse into themselves, shrivelling up like all of my vitality has been sucked dry.

But then Ezra is closer, so close, and I didn't even see them move. Their warmth blossoms by my side, and they raise their hand to my face the way we have both done instinctively so many times, and they wait for my nod before they make contact.

Contact.

My pulse flutters against my skin, racing along my veins like it's trying desperately to get closer to—

Ezra's lips touch mine.

The gasp of breath sends cool air flooding through our combined heat, but all it does is fan the flames. Their full lips are soft, so soft, and nothing could have prepared me for the way my skin lights up at every touch.

Ezra's hand slides back from my jaw, their fingers twining in my curls, and I reach for them, too, seeking purchase on the flat planes of their shoulders, their chest. My touch is light but not hesitant—just being allowed to touch them at all feels like looking at the sun.

My senses teeter on the edge of overwhelm, and all I can think is *more*.

Imagination teases me, showing me what it could be like to explore the changing shapes of Ezra's landscape, and then, just as suddenly as it began, they're pulling away.

"Don't stay away," they murmur. "But your mum is coming."

In a flash, we're both at the window, Ezra nudging it open, one hand tightly at my waist.

"I don't want you to leave," I whisper.

"I won't," they say. "I promise."

Their lips brush mine just as I hear footsteps in the corridor outside my room, and Ezra dissolves into feathers and wings, stirring the air even as they soar into the night.

I go to the door and open it before Mum can knock.

She peers past me into my room. "Ezra go home already?"

"Aye," I say. "They just left."

I'm gambling on the mums having been in their own part of the house, and Mum nods. "Well, make sure you tell them they're welcome back any time. Lovely, lovely person."

"I will," I say with a surge of hope that melds with relief in my chest. I pause, then ask, "Did you or Mam tell Granaidh Ezra's pronouns?"

Mum blinks at me. "I thought you did—we both forgot. Mam even brought it up when we went upstairs and was relieved."

I glance downward as if I can see through the floor to Granaidh's room. That hope turns warmer, more tender, despite the question that hovers in my mind.

"I just came up to say goodnight," Mum says. "And to make sure Ezra got home."

She adds the last bit pointedly, and I wince.

"I know you're eighteen, Cam," she says, seeing it. "It's just—I don't want to see you hurt again."

"I know." I do, really.

I don't know how much the mums know about Jason, and I don't really fancy asking. But her worry isn't unwarranted.

"Ezra's different," I say finally.

"I think you may be right," Mum says. She gives me a small smile. "You're still both so young."

I don't know what to say to that.

Mum's about to turn away, but one thing has been bothering me for a while, and not just tonight.

"Mum?" I almost trip over the words. "How come you made Granaidh speak English? Ezra has lovely Gaelic, and not many people speak it these days. I think it hurt Granaidh's feelings."

Mum freezes, one hand on the door jamb as if to steady herself.

"Well, your mam doesn't speak it fluently, and it would be rude to have dinner in a language not everyone is comfortable speaking. You should know that, Cam." With that, she turns and heads back down the hall, calling a "Goodnight" over her shoulder.

I'm left standing in the doorway to my bedroom. All I can hear is Mam's tentative *An do dhèan thu* and Granaidh's gentle correction to *An do rinn*, and Mam giving it another go.

I don't think it's Mam who isn't comfortable with the Gaelic. She's trying, and it's been generations since anyone in Mam's Glaswegian family had any of the language at home.

There's a clashing discomfort lodged in my sternum. It feels like someone trying to force puzzle pieces to fit when they don't.

I close my door and lock it, turning to see Ezra—the raven—perched on the windowsill, watching me with black eyes that reflect back the light from the lamp.

"You can come back in," I tell them.

When they shift back to human form, it's not how they left. Ezra's now in a tight-fitting, raspberry-coloured knit T-shirt and black yoga bottoms, all of which puts the very noticeable changes in their body on display. From angles and planes to—whew, curves.

I realise I'm staring, and I give a short, helpless laugh.

"No fair," I say. "You get to knock me speechless every time I turn around, and I'm just—"

"*You* are just nothing, Cam," Ezra says. "No 'just' about it."

I turn away briefly to get my bearings, and in the mirror of the vanity across the room, I catch a glimpse of myself. My skin is practically a mood ring—any indication of my feelings paints itself across my neck, my chest, my face. I may have had to work on my facial expressions and making those match neurotypical expectations, but everyone's always been able to see when I'm flustered.

"Maybe it's magic. Maybe it's Maybelline," I say in a shaky voice.

"Cam," Ezra says, and I turn back to them. "The moment I saw you—you were still mortal, but you were like pure starshine."

"That was just my hand," I say, and they laugh.

They close the distance to me.

"No," they say. "It wasn't."

Our lips touch once more, and my entire body trembles. Ezra pulls me close to them, their long, black waves framing both our faces, and this form is so soft, so different to the Ezra I kissed only a few short minutes ago, but this is still Ezra, every inch as Ezra, every touch telling me that I am only touching new facets of the same person.

When we finally break away again, both of us are breathing heavily, and even Ezra's chest is flushed above the neckline of their shirt.

I'd forgotten what it was like to *want* like this.

"I'm sorry," they say after a beat. "I'm . . . impulsive and impatient. I don't want to rush you."

"You're not," I say.

My own voice sounds alien to my ears, husky and low in a way I've not heard it before, even with Jason.

"But I might be rushing myself." I close my eyes and take a deep breath, reaching out a hand to Ezra that I hope they'll take. They do. "I don't want to rush you either."

"You're not," they assure me, "but I don't want to rush in general. Not with you."

"Okay," I say.

"Okay," they say.

"I want you to stay." It's true. But then Deirdre's face intrudes, and I remember what I'm doing tomorrow. "Shit."

"What?" Ezra says.

"I forgot to tell you what happened. Maybe we should sit down."

I lead them over to the bed, the flood of warmth from our kisses cooling with the memory of sheets of rain and wind and the scream of the ban-sìthe.

As quickly as I can, I tell Ezra the story, of following Deirdre to the mountaintop—I still have no idea where we even were—the fight, the blood, the endless shriek. And I tell them of An Smeòrach's arrival and that he charged Deirdre to bring me to him.

Talk about a mood killer. Ezra's face is a master class in subtle shifts of emotion that I wish I could read fluently. They flicker across Ezra's visage like lightning in the sky.

When I'm done, Ezra gets up from the bed and paces, otherwise seemingly unruffled but for the jerky movement of their feet.

"You're certain she saw you," Ezra says. "The ban-sìthe."

I nod. "No one else but Deirdre did, I think. But she looked right at me and was coming for me. Do you—do you know her?"

"Yes," Ezra says. "And no."

They tuck their hair behind their ears, stopping halfway across my bedroom but with their gaze somewhere on the other side of the world. With their hair tucked back like that, they look almost vulnerable.

"What does that mean?" I ask.

"It means I know of her. I don't need to tell you she's dangerous. I think you've figured that out yourself. But she's old—older than An Smeòrach, older than Deirdre, maybe even older than An Càrn Òir, who is the oldest of us I know of." Ezra hesitates before going on. "An Smeòrach told me she has slumbered since the Middle Ages. Apparently she woke up on the wrong side of the bed."

A sardonic smile accompanies that last, but I don't think Ezra really thinks it's funny.

"Has Deirdre explained the Sionnachain?" Ezra's smile fades as soon as it began.

"Sionnachain?" I know the word, but not the significance. "Doesn't that just mean will-o'-the-wisps?"

"Yes, usually. But now it's becoming something more."

Unbidden, I see the clearing again, Ealasaid and the shrouded Others and the dancing fireflies-that-were-not-fireflies.

"Does it have something to do with the fight?" I ask, already knowing the answer.

"I think it has to," says Ezra. "I've been trying to track them, which is a fool's errand. Like their namesake, the Others using that name as their banner are elusive. There one minute and gone the next."

"What do they want?" I take a deep breath but hold it until my lungs are about to burst, letting it out slowly. It does nothing to calm me.

"There are some among the Others who want things to go back to how they were, when mortals believed in magic—and feared it. Plenty still have their fun, the petty kind. We've always been petty, so that's nothing new. But for some, that's not enough." Ezra's eyes cloud again.

"What do they want?" I ask again, almost a whisper.

"We have the power of gods," Ezra says. "Once, mortals believed in gods that laid no claim to benevolence except when it suited them. The Sionnachain want to go back to that time, put the fear of God back into the people who once made offerings to them, pilgrimages to their sacred places even when supplanted by new religions. But they don't want harmony—they want subjugation."

I think of Ealasaid and her silent satisfaction as she watched a group of teenagers surround someone they perceived as weak.

"I think I should go," Ezra says. "I need to see An Smeòrach and An Càrn Òir myself. I may be a puppet of a prince, but this is my world too."

I want to go with them, but I don't ask. Their words hang heavy in my mind. It seems even the Otherworld is choked with the vines of the same poison that is seeping into the mortal world.

"I'll be with Deirdre tomorrow night," I say.

"I'll find you," says Ezra.

They come to me and take my hands, kissing me softly on my still-tender lips. Ezra presses something into my hand.

"Here," they say. "If you want to make it easier for me to find you."

I look up and meet their eyes and nod without understanding. The brush of their wings melds with the breeze through the open window.

The thing they put into my hands is a small parcel of folded cloth-of-gold. I unfold it with a delicate touch. At its centre is a pair of perfect, iridescent black feathers on twisted hooks of beaten gold.

TWENTY-NINE

Grace corners me in the hallway at school the next morning.

"Hey," she says. "I don't want to be weird or anything, but if you don't want to be friends, you can just say so."

Bollocks.

"It's not that I don't want to be friends," I say.

The hallway is too loud for this kind of conversation, but now I don't think I have a choice.

"I'm not great with people," I say, which is the same thing I said to Ezra. I cringe and decide to go with a bit of truth. "And Ealasaid has—you warned me about her, and you were right. She doesn't like me, and I don't want her to hurt you to hurt me."

Grace rocks back on her heels. "So what, you're just going to hide every day? I've known her for years. I can handle myself."

"I know." I fight the urge to disagree, because against Ealasaid, Grace absolutely cannot handle herself.

Especially after what Ezra told me about the Sionnachain—there is no chance Ealasaid isn't one of them.

"Then forget her," Grace says with a dismissive wave of her hand. She hesitates. "I know I'm being pushy. I meant it when I said you don't have to be my friend, but I like you, and Eilidh likes you, and it would be nice to . . ."

She trails off, looking away and fiddling with the strap on her schoolbag.

I'm going to regret this. But I don't think I can deal with an entire school year with no one at this school I can talk to, even if I can't talk to them about anything I'm going through.

"Okay," I say. "I'm sorry I was blowing you off. I wasn't trying to be rude. I just . . . I've been bullied my whole life, and I don't want to see other people deal with it."

"Safety in numbers," Grace says, though her smile is so radiant it clashes with her words. "We've got your back if you've got ours."

The movement in the hall turns like a tide of urgency as class encroaches, and Grace stands up straighter.

"See you at lunch?" she says.

"See you at lunch." I nod at her and scurry off to class, hoping I haven't done something unbearably stupid.

By the time lunch rolls around, though, I've seen no sign of Ealasaid at all. Her absence is almost more nerve-racking than her presence, and when I meet Grace and Eilidh in the canteen at what I think is their usual table, my neck hurts from tensing up all day in anticipation of a strike.

Eilidh's face lights up to see me, and she asks how my weekend was and how the cèilidh went. It's a bit of a shock to realise it's only been a couple of days since then, and at least I'm able to tell the truth about some of it.

"Cèilidh was good," I tell her. "The food was amazing."

I remember to ask about their weekend as well, and they both chatter on for a wee while about the fanfic Eilidh's writing and bicker about a show I've never seen because I was in Texas when it started.

"The first series is on Netflix," Grace says. "You *have* to watch it, oh my God."

When I blink, all I can see is an alternate timeline splaying out in front of my eyes, some world where I hadn't stumbled into the Others, some world where my biggest worry was a high school bully, some world where I could just hang out and watch Netflix with Eilidh and Grace.

Eilidh has chimed in and is animatedly telling me about the show's magic system, and I try to look interested.

I feel awful that I have to *try*—this would usually be right up my street, but regardless of how I feel about that alternate timeline, even if I existed in it, the danger would still be here. Ealasaid would seem like a high school bully, but she'd still be a dangerous sìtheach. Whatever the Sionnachain are planning would still be weaving itself into existence, threading the loom and readying the pattern.

"What sort of stuff do you usually watch?" Grace asks, interrupting Eilidh's monologue.

Eilidh looks like she wants to protest, but after a moment, she grins sheepishly.

"Erm," I say. "I watch a lot of *Cosmos*. I like astronomy."

Grace's eyes light up. "Have you seen—"

Just then, the electricity in the canteen flickers, fizzes, and goes out with a loud *pop*.

I throw myself to the floor without thinking, hands up over the back of my neck.

A few kids nearby burst out laughing, and that sound jolts me almost as much as the pop did.

In the dim light of the powerless canteen, no one else seems afraid, just startled.

I slowly get to my feet and sit back down.

"Jeezo," someone says at the next table. "You all right there?"

I'm so used to being mocked that I'm not sure if it's an earnest question.

"Imagine that sound in an American school," I say and turn back to Grace and Eilidh.

One of the teachers calls out to stay where we are—just a power cut and someone's looking into it.

"Are you okay?" Even in shadow, Eilidh looks concerned.

"Don't like loud noises," I say, which is the truth.

Minutes tick by, and the power doesn't come back on, but just as I'm numbly managing to finish my lunch, another pair of teachers come into the room, murmuring to each other.

My ears pick it up.

"Not a clue what cut the power, but you should see the football pitch. Sinkhole, right in the middle of it—bang on in the centre of the pitch like someone carved it in there on the chalk line." I don't know most of the teachers' names still, and this one isn't familiar to me. "They're getting the council out to look at it."

"Bloody hell," mutters the woman next to him.

"Cam," Grace is saying. "Earth to Cam."

I look up. The teachers are halfway across the canteen—how did I hear that?

I shake myself. "Sorry. What were you saying?"

"Nothing—you just look spooked."

Eilidh pokes at her phone, lighting up her face in the pale green of her lock screen. "Time to go if they let us."

The teachers instruct us to go to class, and in the hall on the way there, the news of the sinkhole is spreading, to exclamations of dismay since I guess that means any sport on the pitch is cancelled indefinitely.

I can see it from the window of my next class, and I'm not the only one who clusters by the window, peering out over the pristine grass sliced open in a perfect circle by a gaping maw that descends into darkness.

Concentration escapes me for the rest of the day.

It could just be a sinkhole. Those happen. And as unlikely as it is for the earth to drop away in a perfect circle in the centre of a football pitch, it *could* be a coincidence.

But I think I'd be stupid to assume it isn't something even more dangerous.

I keep stealing glances out the windows whenever I'm close enough to see it, and while nothing seems to be crawling out of it, I can't shake the idea that if I were to jump in that hole, I would land in another world.

I'm not going to test that theory.

Deirdre is waiting for me the moment school gets out, her face grim.

"Did you hear?" I ask her.

"I saw," is her only answer.

She puts her hand on my shoulder, and just as we leave Oban behind, I hear Grace call my name.

Once again, my ears pop, but instead of the sense of going up to a mountaintop, there's a strange pressure above me that tells me wherever Deirdre just led us, it took us *down*.

"Shit." She glances behind us as if she expects Grace to come through after us like I did.

"We just disappeared right in front of the school!" Either Deirdre has forgotten mortals don't usually do that or—

Deirdre waves a hand in the air like the thought is an annoying fly. "Doesn't matter, except your friend might be a bit confused for a couple hours."

"What? Confused how?"

"It's usually not a problem, but you have the worst luck—she was focused on you when you travelled, and she might be a little cheesed off thinking you dodged her."

I grimace. "Brilliant."

"You're the one who wants to be in high school."

"If it takes three to kill me, my mums and gran will do exactly that if I up and drop school," I say.

"Cute that you think mortals could kill you," she says.

I'm not sure if I should be offended—Deirdre's mood is so sour it could pickle cucumbers.

"Where are we?" I ask, more to change the subject than anything.

All I've got is "cave," and I'm not sure that's helpful.

The walls around us are striated, ages far beyond ancient pressed into each other with the force of time itself. The tunnel arcs naturally to the right, and water trickles down the centre of it past our feet.

"Under the football pitch," says Deirdre. "I didn't want you venturing down here alone."

"I wasn't planning on it." Now I think I am offended. "I may be young, but I'm not quite *that* stupid."

"You followed me into a battle that almost killed you," she snaps. "So I beg to differ."

"That was an *accident*!"

"You shouldn't have even tried to follow me." Deirdre rounds on me. "You should have stayed where it was safe."

"How am I supposed to even know what I'm doing if you won't bloody well teach me?"

I usually hate confrontation, but I hate being treated like a toddler more. "You can't just snap your fingers and make me like you and then treat me like I'm a ball and chain around your ankle! And you just go and enchant my family's brambles without telling me what you did to them, so they've been eating them for days and spreading them all over the sodding west of Scotland, and you expect me to just trust—"

"I'm trying to protect you." Five short words, so quiet.

They stop me in my tracks.

"I'm a person, not a Fabergé egg." I claw and extend my fingers as if I can calm myself with the action. It doesn't work. "Are you going to be there to protect me and my family every minute of every day?"

Deirdre's mouth hangs open, just a little, just enough to see a glint of white teeth, and then she snaps it shut, her lips twitching.

"No," she says. "I won't be. Maybe I should have killed you on sight."

The words freeze me to the floor. She says it so nonchalantly, like she's saying she should have picked up more eggs at the Co-op.

"Well, now you'll need help," I say after a long beat. "Missed your chance to do it easy. Did you have something you wanted to see down here in this hole or are we going to see An Smeòrach?"

Her hand claps down over my lips so fast I've barely realised she moved before I'm jerked backward into nothingness.

THIRTY

The first thing I hear is a litany of curses that would make my father blush—he can swear like a shipful of sailors and would be impressed if he could hear Deirdre as she displays her competence in both English and Gaelic swearing. I don't even catch the context of half the Gaelic, but then profanity's something they don't exactly teach us to fluency in Gaelic Medium Education.

She's moved us again, and this time we're somewhere in the tolman, by the walls, which are a familiar creamy stone. With a curt gesture, she motions for me to follow her.

Just before she yanked us out of the sinkhole, I remember a whiff of something sour that wasn't Deirdre's snitty mood.

We walk for what feels like an aeon in silence, the only sound that of our feet on the floor and the small thuds of my schoolbag against my leg. Nothing to make me feel like an adult person among the Others like being in my school uniform and carrying a bag with my clan name embroidered on the outside of it. If this is Deirdre's way of putting me in my place, I might change my mind about liking her.

We finally reach a branching corridor that ends in a large wooden door. Most of the doors and entries here arch similarly, and this is no exception. It's the one aspect of the Otherworld that seems like it belongs in a Tolkien novel.

Deirdre knocks three times on the enormous door, and it swings open on the third boom. Huge as it is—it's at least twice as thick as the doors in Granaidh's house, too—it moves silently and smoothly like a spectre.

It opens into a large room. Instead of stone, the walls appear to be plaster or stucco, their colour a rich ochre that glows with the light of small golden bulbs in half-spheres that dot the walls at whimsical intervals, all of different sizes ranging from a marble to a large apple. Wooden shelving of dark walnut protrudes from the walls, built in but giving the impression that they grew that way. No seams meet the eye; no nails or pegs or even mortise-and-tenon give so much of a hint that the shelves were ever anything but one piece.

The floor is smooth stone but richly carpeted, and I've a feeling no moth would dare lay its eggs in those plush fibres. Deep green and gold and brown in leaf patterns, it's so soft-looking that I resist the urge to kick off my shoes and sink my toes into the carpet.

Deirdre, as usual, is unimpressed and already moving. She strides in farther as the door whooshes shut behind us, and I've no choice but to follow.

We pass rooms that branch off to the sides, but she doesn't stop until we reach what must be the back of the home, where a doorless arch reveals a glimpse of enough books in one glance it would make the Library of Alexandria weep.

As Deirdre leads me in, I barely make it past the threshold before stopping, awestruck.

Like the ornate ballroom where they held the cèilidh, the ceiling here vaults skyward. My neck cranes backward to look up, and it just keeps going far enough into the upper reaches of the room that it almost gives me vertigo. Every wall is covered in books from ceiling to floor, and just the ones I can see are everything from current fiction—is that Angie Thomas's name on that spine?—to what looks like a hand-bound manuscript so ancient it very well could have been written by Homer.

"You asked, I brought. I'll come get her when you're done," says Deirdre perfunctorily, and then she spins on her heel and leaves with a rush of air.

I drag my gaze back down to Earth and turn to see An Smeòrach watching me with a soft smile.

"I think she's sorry she changed me," I blurt out. "I mean . . . hi."

An Smeòrach chuckles, a light laugh that makes his blue eyes sparkle.

"I believe you're very wrong, a chuachain," he says in that gentle voice of his. "I think she is angry that she brought you into a world more dangerous than the one you left."

It's so similar to what I was thinking in the canteen that I have to collect my thoughts before I can respond.

"I was just thinking about that today, and I don't think it's correct," I tell him, aware I've just disagreed with one of the oldest and most powerful of the Others.

"How so?"

"This world's danger is about to spill out into the other one," I say. "How would I have any chance of protecting myself or my family if she hadn't changed me?"

An Smeòrach gives me a sharp look, keen and as bright as his eyes. "You agree with the prince, then."

"It depends on what Ezra said," I venture. "But likely yes."

"Come," says An Smeòrach.

He gestures toward a table farther into the library. This particular library isn't nearly as long or wide as it is tall, but it's at least as big as the one at Trinity College in Dublin, where my mums once took me to see the *Book of Kells*. When I say as much as I sit down in a cushioned chair at the table, An Smeòrach chuckles again.

"I modelled it after that library," he says. "I've always been fond of it. Though it lacks in verticality."

The corner of his mouth twitches, and I smile back at him, though it feels wobbly.

"Why did you want to see me?" I ask.

"Because you stumbled into something you ought to have been shielded from, and it has put you at extreme risk," he says simply. He takes a chair opposite me and sits, his back straight and his hands folded lightly on the edge of the table in front of him. "When I said you agree with the prince, what I was referring to was that Ezra believes a small faction of the Others, the Sionnachain, essentially want to violate the first law of our people."

"I thought they couldn't even do that." Apparently I didn't know enough to be in proper agreement with Ezra, which makes me feel foolish.

"Even our strictest rules have certain loopholes," he says. "And in that case, we owe it to you to prepare you more completely for . . . certain eventualities."

Light blooms between us on the table, a swirling galaxy of starlight that circles toward a bright centre. I try not to jump, but An Smeòrach still notices my movement.

"An Càrn Òir tells me you can see the stars at midday, and Deirdre that you can remain unseen when afraid—that much I surmised myself the night of the cèilidh, as even I had to fight through your magic to catch a glimpse of you until you relaxed at the table." He twitches a finger, and the galaxy vanishes, leaving afterimages floating when I blink. "If I had to guess, I would say also that you have not been misgendered by mortals since you became one of us."

That catches my attention almost more than the rest. He's . . . right. No one's called me girl or hen or any variation of gendered pet name. My pronouns are she/her anyway, but I'm used to being peppered with other little microaggressions from people who think they're giving a friendly pat on the back rather than a careless poke to a bruise.

"That's true," I say, pronouncing each word with deliberate slowness. Despite wracking my brain, I can't think of any evidence to the contrary. "And there's Fànas. Ceapag an Fhànais."

An Smeòrach's brow furrows.

"My kitten," I explain hurriedly. "She's . . . erm. A cat-sìthe. But she didn't start out that way."

"Where did you get this kitten?" he asks, nonplussed.

"Someone left her in a box on the stoop," I tell him. "People are always leaving random things for Granaidh, but not usually alive things."

"I imagine not," he agrees. "What a wee puzzle you are."

I shrug, uncomfortable.

"Some of what you can do is quite common for us, like being perceived as you wish to be perceived—and moving unnoticed where you prefer to be unnoticed. Other things are less so. Few can see the night sky when our closest star hogs the day; fewer still can follow a sìtheach when they travel if they do not wish to be followed. And perhaps most unique, I've never heard of a cat-sìthe who wasn't born as such." An Smeòrach pauses. "I wish we had more time, a chuachain. There is much of our world I think you would love to explore."

That sounds dire. I wet my lips, unsure of how to respond.

"How exactly did you meet our young prince?" An Smeòrach asks, freeing me from needing to figure out an answer to my apparent doom. "Ezra seemed to imply that you met when you were still mortal."

"I ran out of the house after a row with my mums," I say with a sheepish, tight-lipped smile. "I wandered into the woods and saw a door with a hole in it, and . . . I put my hand through the door. Ezra grabbed my hand."

An Smeòrach stares at me, unblinking. The silence stretches out until I realise I've somehow shocked him.

"What?" I ask.

"Curiouser and curiouser," he says, quoting Lewis Carroll, which does nothing to assuage my down-the-rabbit-hole feeling.

"What is?" I bounce my foot, not liking the suspense.

"That door leads to the tolman," he says, "which means not only did you stumble into the Otherworld as a mortal, but you very nearly tripped into the very heart of our home without an invitation."

The way he says it makes me take a shuddering breath as if I can feel a death sentence hanging over my head.

"And you say Ezra grabbed your hand," An Smeòrach says. "What a strange thing for the prince to do. When exactly was this?"

I pull out my mobile, which earns me an amused smile from the ancient sìtheach as I flip through my diary to find the date.

"First of August," I say. "Late evening, just after sunset."

An Smeòrach smiles in satisfaction, a glint in his blue eyes. "Lùnastal in the gloaming. Even so."

"What do you mean?"

"Even the mortals still celebrate Lughnasadh's older traditions," he says. "Do you truly not know what day that is?"

Oh. *Oh.* "You think that's why I was able to wander in?"

"It helped, I'm sure, though you must have already been sensitive, and I hardly think you were seeking a prince's hand in marriage on purpose." An Smeòrach looks like he's trying not to laugh now.

My brain makes sense of his words a moment too late. "I'm sorry, what?"

"What a delightful thing. Such a whimsical accident that could have been much more tragedy than whimsy."

"*Marriage*?" It's the only word I can force past my lips, and finally, it dawns on this man that I have no idea what he's talking about.

He bursts out laughing like the songbird he's named for.

"Wee lamb," An Smeòrach says, "you and Ezra joined hands through the door—it's only binding for a year and a day, but most have enough sense to see who's on the other side first. At least you two seem to fancy each other. There have been many-a more unfortunate pairing."

The mums are going to kill me.

THIRTY-ONE

I guess to an immortal being who lives in a skyscraper-sized library, a year and a day is like a minibreak, but to someone who's only been alive for eighteen years so far, signing away one nineteenth of my life to a relationship that isn't even technically official without knowing it is a far larger issue.

By the time An Smeòrach stops chuckling, I'm still thousand-yard-staring into a shelf that somehow contains both *The Da Vinci Code* and the complete works of William Shakespeare, which almost manages to distract me for the pure fact that his book cataloguing strategy is as bewildering as anything else I've encountered in the Otherworld.

"Does Ezra know?" I ask finally, which sets An Smeòrach off again.

"I would say the poor thing's forgotten the significance themself, but to be fair, they've had a lot on their mind, much of it my fault." An Smeòrach sobers a bit.

Something occurs to me, later than it should.

"Erm, if I've married Ezra, does that make me . . . I mean, they're a prince." I leave out what Ezra's said about the less-than-flattering status of their position, but I'm certain An Smeòrach knows.

Then again, from the way he cocks his head to one side as if I've just spoken fluent Klingon, maybe this didn't cross his mind either.

"Technically, yes," he says. "Though it's been long enough since we entertained the idea of any royalty whatsoever that I'd forgotten that quaint tradition. Do you have a preference on title?"

My eyes might bulge all the way out of my head, and I actually back up in my chair. "No title? I didn't even mean to get married, and—"

I can't tell if he's taking the piss out of me or not. He simply watches me flail until I break off and slump back into my chair. Sure, why not?

"My dear child, I think we can table this particular discussion for a later date. We have more pressing things to worry about, and while it's amusing that you find the idea of a title more distressing than the prospect of your own death, I would like to prioritise the latter if you don't mind."

Ooft. "Of course," I say.

My voice sounds very far away.

The whole "you're married" thing could be a prank. It would be a very sìtheach thing to allow me to believe something distressing that could technically be true, but I guess I'll have to find out later.

"Come with me," says An Smeòrach.

I get up from my chair and follow him out of the library, which gives me a pang because I think I could stay in there forever and not read everything on those massive shelves. I'm not even sure how he gets to the things on the upper shelves, though the obvious answer is magic.

He leads me through what I presume is his house, which is cloaked in comfortable opulence, if such a thing exists. Everything is exquisitely made without screaming ostentatious. Unlike the ballroom where the cèilidh was held, An Smeòrach lives simply, without prismatic crystals or much that could be considered luxury aside from the library.

It is big, though. The path we take winds through corridors and around bigger chambers, some of which are easy to identify as a dining room or a sitting room, others more ambiguous, such as a room that seems empty except for a series of nine plinths, none of which hold anything but air.

We arrive at another room that is completely empty. It looks almost like a dance studio; the walls are lined with mirrors. But unlike the typical dance studio, the mirrors have no joins—it is one contiguous mirror somehow. Even at the corners, the image is undisturbed, undistorted, an impossibility to anyone who's ever been in a carnival funhouse.

"What are we doing?" I ask him. I don't think he's brought me here to teach me how to do the Gay Gordons.

"Thus far, your magic has all happened based on pure instinct. Left unchecked, it will continue to do that, and you will learn organically how it works."

An Smeòrach stands in the centre of the room, surrounded by a dizzying number of reflections of the both of us that splay out into infinity.

"I've brought you here," he says, "to speed up that process. In normal circumstances, it's fine to let the younger of us take their time. Time is something we possess in large quantities in the Otherworld."

I'm not able to do anything but nod.

"But right now, it is becoming increasingly evident that you may be forced into the position where you have to defend yourself or someone you love against Others much older, much more powerful, and much more experienced than yourself." An Smeòrach raises both his hands, and flames spring into being over his palms. In an instant, they pour away from him, forming a roaring maelstrom of fire. "Time is not a luxury you have, a chuachain."

The heat from the inferno reaches me even ten yards away, halfway across the room from him. It lights the entirety of the space, the mirror bouncing it back at us until it feels like we're standing in the centre of the sun.

An Smeòrach claps his hands, and the orange glow turns blue. It's like turning off a light; the change is so total, so complete, that I blink as my eyes adjust, my skin tightening with the sudden cold before I can process that whatever he's holding now feels like pure ice.

Just as quickly, a trickling sound begins, and water pours from his hands, swirling into a whirlpool around his feet, though An Smeòrach remains untouched. Like Corryvreckan between Jura and Scarba, the waters rage, splashing me even where I stand. With every drop that lands upon me, something pulls at me, as if the whirlpool wants to drag me into its maw.

I reach out a hand to it, a reflex, an instinct. The spray in the air coalesces around my fingers, swirling at their tips, and I sway on my feet like kelp beneath the ocean's waves.

The sensation vanishes as suddenly as it began, and with a splash, the room is empty and dry again.

"Is math a rinn thu," An Smeòrach praises me. "That was very good indeed."

"What was?" I ask.

I don't even know what I did or if I could separate his magic from mine.

"Most Sìthichean demonstrate an affinity for certain types of magic. I simply ran through a few to see if you would respond, and you did. Very quickly, too." An Smeòrach's expression holds approval, I think. "Now. With more awareness this time, listen. Not just with your ears—listen with all of you and see what happens."

"What if I hurt something?" I say uncertainly.

"I am not an easy person to hurt. Nor is this room. Do not worry."

Asking me not to worry is a bit like asking the Corryvreckan whirlpool not to whirl, but I'll give it a go.

I've no idea what to expect from An Smeòrach next, but the moment the wind rises in the room, whipping my hair against my cheeks, that same sense within me responds, shoving my hair out of my face with enough force that I slide several inches backward in my stocking feet on the smooth floor.

"Good," he says, snapping his fingers.

There is a sound like falling rock tumbling over a cliff, and the ground shakes under me. I scramble to keep my footing, twisting to dive out of the way of a boulder that comes rolling directly at me.

"Also good," says An Smeòrach. "Even if you can't grab hold of something, dodging it is the next best thing."

The rock vanishes, and the air lights up with electricity.

Every inch of my body comes to life.

Energy whips out from An Smeòrach, and both my hands snap outward, snatching at it like grabbing the loose ends of a pair of jump ropes.

His eyes flash with approbation, and this time, instead of dropping the lightning, he holds on to the other end of the current stretched between us. It crackles purple even as green vines shoot up from the ground beneath our feet.

All I can think is *They look like power lines.*

I drop to a crouch and slam both hands into the floor, connecting the lightning in my palms to the tendrils reaching back for me, and it's as if I've plugged in an entire house strung with fairy lights. Every vine in the room tightens and sparks, sending a shower of purple fizzing into the air.

And then An Smeòrach is gone and something heavy snaps around my neck from behind, jerking me up to my feet and backward off the ground. My legs dangle, and my hands grab for the vine, encountering the ancient sìtheach's arms holding it tight.

It's cutting off my air.

The vine digs into my neck, and my mind is a whirlwind of panic. I shouldn't have trusted him. I should have known they'd just decide to kill me. I shouldn't have—

The world explodes in light.

Like a supernova contained in one room, time stretches out as pure white engulfs everything I can see. It's not white, not really. White light is every colour, and so it is in what I see, echoes of rainbows contained in the harsh burning brightness.

When it fades, my back is against a wall, and I'm half-sprawled on the floor. The vine has disappeared from my neck.

And An Smeòrach . . .

An Smeòrach is on his feet halfway across the room, brushing himself off as if he simply slipped, but he wears a smile like Fànas the day she hopped up on Granaidh's tray with the dish of clotted cream.

"I'm never one to hesitate about saying I told you so," he says, and at first I think he's talking to me until I slump onto my side to see Deirdre in the narrow doorway. "I told you so."

"Yes, you're very clever," says Deirdre, but I think she doesn't sound angry.

In fact, that might be relief.

I push myself to a more upright sitting position. "Will someone explain what just happened or are you just planning to strangle me again?"

"You, my dear child, are an absolute cracker of interesting wee gifts," says An Smeòrach. He looks at Deirdre, though I think he's still speaking to me. "Water, definitely. Wind and lightning without any doubt. Debatable whether the stunt with the vines was actual affinity with flora or lightning alone, but that last . . ."

An Smeòrach gives a contented sigh.

"Please go on," Deirdre says flatly. "I'm burning with curiosity."

Despite her tone and general posture of boredom—it's so obvious even I can identify that; she's actually examining her fingernails—I think she truly is burning with curiosity.

"Starfire," says An Smeòrach. "I've not seen that in some time."

"Promising, then." This time, Deirdre's gaze finds me where I sit, and the smile that curves her lips is far from mocking.

"Very. With a little more time, Cam, I think you will be able to do these things consciously. We will see—"

But I don't get a chance to hear what he thinks I will see, because something moves deep within the mirror, and just as I recognise the shape, that mouth open so wide to scream, the mirrored room makes a sound like a glacier calving.

Cracks spiderweb through the silvered glass.

"Take her and run!" bellows An Smeòrach, and Deirdre scoops me off my feet before I can react, sprinting out the door as if I weigh less than nothing.

THIRTY-TWO

"What's happening?" I say, trying to find purchase on Deidre's shoulder, but she's running so fast all I can see is a blur.

My body jerks as she comes to a sudden halt. "A Chàirn Òir," she says as the tall Black man from the cèilidh and the mountaintop appears to my right.

Deirdre drops me to my feet, holding me up with one arm. He is wearing similarly unassuming clothing, like An Smeòrach, a simple, mustard-yellow shirt over white trousers and bare feet. The cuffs of the long-sleeved shirt are embroidered with gold thread, swirls, and dizzying waves.

"Where is he?" the man asks.

"The arena. She's here."

"I know. I heard her." The man, who I assume is An Càrn Òir, glances in the direction we came from. "Alone?"

"He is alone. It would be foolish to assume she is." Deirdre catches him by his upper arm, which is to say she practically pats it, because it's far too muscular for her to get a grip. "I can help."

"You must keep the child safe," he says. "This is now twice. We neither of us believe in coincidences, Deirdre."

Without another word, An Càrn Òir blurs and sprints back in the direction from which we came, and I am again scooped up into Deidre's arms.

Even if I knew the tolman, I could not have traced our path. Deirdre's route is dizzying, and it doesn't help that I get motion sick even in cars, let alone being carted around by a sprinting sìtheach.

When she finally puts me down what feels like hours later, it's in a cold, empty hall of grey stone that looks more like the sinkhole under the football pitch than the rest of the tolman.

She's not even breathing hard, but I have to sit down on the floor to get my head to stop spinning.

"It gets better. Your magic will compensate for your mortal body's lack of efficiency, but it takes time." Deirdre doesn't look at me, her eyes scanning the room as if expecting something else to jump out at us any second.

"What is happening?" I ask. "Will he be okay?"

"An Smeòrach and An Càrn Òir are more than capable of taking care of themselves," Deirdre says, though she bites off the last word as if it has a bitter taste. "As for your first question, I don't know."

"Shouldn't we help them?" I say.

Just a few minutes ago, I was terrified An Smeòrach had decided to kill me. Now I'm ready to throw myself off a cliff against that ban-sìthe again, for all the good it would do.

Deirdre voices that exact thought. "Even if you could consciously use your magic, all you would do is make them divide their efforts between keeping you alive and fighting her. Safest for everyone if you and I simply run."

I don't think she particularly likes the idea.

"Deirdre?" I venture, unsure if I'll get another chance to say it. "I'm sorry you're stuck with me."

At that, she laughs quietly, though she's still alert, slowly turning to look around the room.

"There is no need to be sorry," she says. "I'm not used to feeling protective of anyone. One could say I'm a bit rusty."

"Where are we?" I ask.

"We're still in the tolman, but this part of it is older still than the rest." Deirdre gestures to the deep carvings in the stone walls, barely visible in the dim light. "Even a thousand years ago, this place was barren and empty. It is said the Valkyries used to visit here, once upon a time."

I remember what Ezra said about the Others being everywhere, in every culture—just under different names and traditions.

"Have you ever met them?" I ask, trying to imagine Norse gods walking these halls and not even sure what I *should* imagine.

"Once," Deirdre says, and her eyes go distant. "I would not care to meet them again."

She is silent for a moment as if listening to something I can't pick up, like a radio frequency she's tuned to but I'm not.

"You asked about the brambles," she says abruptly. "I did enchant them."

"I know." I peer at her, but I cannot read her expression.

"That night you were spying on Ealasaid, Daibhidh and I were trying to do the same, but they were prepared for that. They are paranoid enough to assume that others among the Sìthichean will attempt to ferret out their machinations and plots." Deirdre gives me a sharp, feral smile. "They are also, however, far too arrogant to imagine that a sensitive, bumbling mortal could trip over them by pure chance."

I shift my shoulder blades uncomfortably. "If I have any real magic, it's the power to be in the wrong place at the wrong time."

"There are worse curses," she murmurs. "Believe me."

My arms tingle at her words. I only nod.

"Daibhidh and I have suspected that the Sionnachain mean to do . . . something. It is nearly impossible to discover what. They make foxes look like fresh-hatched chickens. But that night, Lughnasadh, Lùnastal—they sacrificed one of our own." Deirdre scrubs her hand across her face. It's such a human gesture that I blink at it, but she's going on. "Of all I expected from them, that was not on the list."

There is no breeze in this room, but somehow my earrings are tickling at my neck. I shake my head, and they keep moving.

Ezra.

"Deirdre," I say urgently. "Can people travel in and out of this room? Not like we did—the way—"

She interrupts me. "Yes. Why?"

I unleash my wish to see Ezra, focusing on the feathered earrings in my ears.

Within a breath, they stumble out of a shimmer in the air, collapsing on their knees in front of us.

When they look up at me, blood runs from their nose and mine freezes like my heart has turned to ice.

I'm at their side in an instant. I don't think my feet have so much as moved, but I am on my knees next to them, my arm around their waist, propping them up.

"Cam," they say, and bloody froth dribbles from the corner of their mouth.

Deirdre appears in front of them on her knees, hands cupped to either side of Ezra's face.

Her hands glow gold, warmth exuding from her flesh, and Ezra coughs, their core tightening against me with the spasm.

"What happened?" Deirdre asks.

"Someone shot at me," Ezra says. "In raven form. I managed to pull the arrow out, but it shouldn't have even pierced me."

I don't know enough about sìtheach immortality to explain that, but from the grim set to Deirdre's jaw, it's not good.

I remember what An Càrn Òir said about coincidence. "This happened at the same time someone attacked us," I say, and Deirdre's gaze snaps to me, as does Ezra's.

"Someone attacked you?" they say.

Their arm is a little stronger around my shoulders now, and it gives me a flare of warmth.

"An Smeòrach was helping me with my magic," I tell them. "The ban-sìthe appeared."

"We think," Deirdre says. "It could have been an illusion."

"Or a distraction," Ezra agrees.

"The mirror shattering didn't seem like an illusion," I say.

I could be wrong, but that silhouette, that sound—I don't think I'm wrong.

"So they've decided to kill the prince." Deirdre's pronouncement is flat and unemotional, but it sends a barbed spike into my gut.

"What would they gain from that?" I ask. "Ezra said their title is . . ."

I struggle to think of a way to say it that isn't too blunt.

"A joke," Ezra supplies.

Deirdre gets to her feet, apparently satisfied that Ezra's wound is tended for now. "It's not a joke. We just don't particularly worship our royalty the way the mortals do. Or used to."

"Then really, what would they gain?" I press her, helping Ezra to their feet as well.

"What did they gain from killing my entire family?" Ezra says.

Even Deirdre flinches at that. Ezra gives me a tight-lipped smile, but I can feel their pain even if they are being blasé. Of the two of us, it's the non-autistic one who's going for blunt today, I guess.

"You know that was several steps too far, even for us," says Deirdre.

At first, I think she's talking about Ezra's bluntness, but she goes on.

"And if killing mortals for sport is several steps too far, how much more is killing one of our own? We are not so numerous that any of us are expendable." Deirdre holds up a hand as if anticipating a rebuttal. "I'm not saying mortals are expendable. They're not. But if you and An Smeòrach and An Càrn Òir are correct and the Sionnachain have more ambitious goals than simple mischief, Cam's question is a good one, and it's one I don't have an answer to."

"Who decided Ezra should be prince?" I ask slowly. "An Smeòrach?"

Ezra shakes their head. "No. He guided me through it, but it wasn't his idea. I'm not sure anyone's ever told me whose idea it was. Everyone just seemed to think it was a fine idea—make the orphan wean a prince, that'll help with the rage and grief."

Deirdre winces. "No one's ever accused us of being particularly forward-thinking. And even our best intentions tend to cut both ways."

A thought germinates from the seed of something else, unrelated on the surface but maybe worth following to see what it grows into.

I think Deirdre rubbing her face—what a human gesture that was. And I think of the petty caprice of the Sìthichean, the thing they—we—are most known for, despite the romantic pixies-in-bluebells, Thomas Kinkade shine the modern world has cast upon the Otherworld. But I also can see Ealasaid in my mind's eye, watching other mortals bully a mortal girl.

They're not Others. They're just pupils from the high school. Humans have petty caprice down to an art.

So why wouldn't the Others be susceptible to the very poison trickling through the currents of mortal waters? All over the world, people are ready to cast blame, close borders, inspect children's genitals before footy practice, all things prepared to decide whose freedoms actually matter at the end of the day.

"What if—" I accidentally interrupt Deirdre, whose sentence I haven't even picked up on. "Sorry."

"What if what?" she asks, unfazed.

"What if they resent that someone who was mortal until very recently became a prince?" I say slowly. "People get upset over stupid shite like that every day. People tend to resent those who have never had power getting any of it."

"That sounds like exactly the level of petty that would make a bunch of wannabe gods resort to murder," Ezra says.

At that moment, my mobile rings.

I push aside any existential crises about getting reception in the Otherworld and pull it out, because the only people who will cause my phone to ring through my "do not disturb" function are my mums and Granaidh, and they never call unless it's an emergency.

It's Mam.

Ezra and Deirdre are staring at me as I answer.

"Mam?" I ask. "Yous all right?"

"Tell me you're not in Oban, Cam," she says without answering.

"I'm not in Oban," I say slowly. "I'm with Deirdre."

Her gust of a sigh is loud enough through the speaker that I wince and hold the phone away from my ear as Mam says, likely to Mum, "She's not in Oban."

"Mam, what's going on?" I know how I feel every time I hear of a shooting in the US anywhere near where Dad lives, and that feeling is creeping up my spine.

"There's some sort of disturbance—hostages, I think. We just needed to make sure you made it back out of town." Mam's voice sounds too tight for that to be all.

"Yous are at home, right? You and Mum and Granaidh are all in Ballinacollie?" I hate the tinny sound to my voice. It sounds too flat and wrong and calm for the slithering sensation in my midsection.

"Don't worry, love," Mam says. "Granaidh's at home."

"Granaidh's at home," I repeat. "That means you're not. Is Mum there? Where are you?"

"We'll ring as soon as we're home—don't worry. We're okay. I've got to go, all right? We'll ring soon."

She hangs up on me.

Ezra and Deirdre are staring at each other.

"You're not leaving us behind," Ezra says, stealing her mind-reading trick or perhaps just anticipating the obvious.

"Then you do exactly what I say when I say it, do you hear me?" Deirdre fixes me with a stare that could turn me into part of this stone floor, and I nod. "Ezra?"

They nod as well.

"Don't make me regret this," she says, and then she grabs us each by a shoulder and shoves.

THIRTY-THREE

Eerie quiet blankets Oban Harbour.

Part of me relaxes some tension that at least there is no screaming to make anyone's ears bleed, but the rest of me knows too well the type of storm that could follow this calm.

The teal waters are still. It's low tide, and the *Isle of Mull* ferry is moored, ready to sail back to the island in one of the last sailings of the day.

Usually at this time of year, there are tourists at Ee-usk eating seafood, folk wandering about by the pier, buskers singing for their supper. It's still light, but none of that is true right now.

"Deirdre," I say. "What's happening?"

"I don't know. Wheesht."

Mam said a hostage situation, but there's no police, no sirens, nothing that I can see. It's as if the sinkhole at the high school sucked up all the people of our sleepy harbour town at the gateway to the Western Isles.

The islands themselves spill out before me on the sea. Lismore, so close, as is Kerrera. Mull is not much farther. For an incongruous moment, I am overwhelmed by the connectivity of this place—despite declining infrastructure, the water has always been the true bridge to our islands, and Oban feels like the heart pumping lifeblood into everything we're fighting to keep alive.

"There should be people here," Ezra murmurs. "Where is everyone?"

"Where were you attacked?" I ask them.

This is somehow the moment I remember we are apparently married. I have to physically hold my arms at my sides, so I don't wave them about to deal with the emotion of it, and I'm relieved when Ezra points out over the sea and says, "Near Craignure. I like to fly to Mull. Between the campground and Duart Castle, only a little inland from the coast."

I can't stand this silence. Normally I love silence, thrive on silence. Silence is just about one of my favourite things on this loud, overwhelming rock hurtling through space. But here, in a normally busy town at a touristy time of year, the wrongness seeps into me like poison injected into an artery, spreading through my body with every pump of my heart.

My phone is still in my hand, and the screen lights up with a text from Mum.

Hiya, love, hope you're having a good night with Deirdre! Check in when you have a wee moment? Also, your gran told me to tell you that Fànas managed to come down the stairs on her own. X

That takes the wrong-feeling and pours it down the back of my neck like a cracked egg.

"Something's—"

An enormous force slams into my back, and I go flying forward on the pier. My phone sails from my hand, hitting the restaurant wall with a crack only an instant before the same wall makes contact with my face.

The shock of the impact rings through me. Though my head feels like the time I knocked it on the ceiling in Dad's crawlspace at his old house, I fold over at the waist at the intense pinch in my side.

My arm hits something cold and hard, and the movement wrenches a scream from my throat.

A . . . knife. There's a knife in my side. Or a spike.

It's made of iron.

Mum's voice in my head is the only thing that keeps me from yanking it out to get it out of me. That's how you bleed to death.

I'm still in my school uniform, and the breeze sends a chill through me as it hits the rapidly expanding bloodstain.

I can't see Ezra or Deirdre. They were right over there—a voice in the back of my mind screams that I flew almost fifteen yards through the air—but there is nothing there now. Only the silent, empty wharf.

A burst of wings flutters to the floor beside me, and Ezra is here.

"Ezra," I choke out, reaching for their hand.

They grab it, their face white at the sight of the bright red colouring my entire left side, but they don't make a move to pull out the iron.

"Deirdre's coming. Hold on," they say.

"Did they get you?" I ask.

"Don't worry about me." This time it's Ezra supporting me, though the wall is doing a decent amount of the work.

"No, worry about the little princeling," says a vaguely familiar voice.

But the face attached is unfamiliar at first.

The woman is tall, blonde. Her face is somehow more birdlike than even Ezra's raven form, and the thought helps me place her.

Feathers.

She's the woman who spoke to Deirdre and me at the cèilidh, the one in the blue dress.

And she's not alone.

The others with her are Ealasaid and a man I would bet was in the clearing that night. Ealasaid, though, wears an expression too flat for the way her eyes keep darting around the harbour.

A rush of wind stirs the air, and Deirdre lands in front of me and Ezra like a superhero dropping out of orbit. Her impact cracks the tarmac, and she gets to her feet without so much as flinching.

"I thought better of you," she says to the woman.

The pain in my side is growing worse, and I bite my cheek on the moan of agony that tries to escape past my lips.

"I thought you would have enough pride not to die for a couple of near-mortal weans, so it seems we're both disappointed today." The woman flicks her hands at Ealasaid and the man, and they advance, though I think Ealasaid hesitates.

"You're here ready to break the first law," Deirdre says, "and I guess you've stopped caring about the second."

The man keeps moving toward us slowly, but Ealasaid stops in her tracks, shooting an uncertain glance at the woman.

All *she* does is laugh.

"You expect me to believe one of these weans is your soulmate, Deirdre? I thought you were against cradle robbing."

That line hits different from supernatural beings long accused of doing literally that.

"Not me, òinseach," says Deirdre. "*They* are."

For a bare moment, everything disappears as those words sink into my skin. I can feel Ezra's hand tighten on mine, the heat of their shoulder against my own, the stickiness of my blood soaking through their shirt too.

For that barest moment, I think it might stop her from doing whatever she's about to do.

This woman disabuses me of the thought a heartbeat later. "They can die together. Since there's hardly enough of a sìtheach between them to count as one, I think we'll give that law a rest."

Deirdre's body goes still and set, and despite the cold, wet shirt that makes me shiver and the way every breath sends stabbing pain through my body, I try to listen to the air, the ground, everything near us that could help.

Her head turns minutely, and I can almost see her trying to calculate whether she can travel with us without hurting me more, weighing the risk of my maybe-still-mortalish body with the risk of staying where we are, staring in the face of certain death.

"Is it true?" Ealasaid's voice breaks the silence.

It's hard to make my eyes find her face. The world feels fuzzy and strangely magnetic. But she's staring down at Ezra and me with naked longing in her eyes.

"It's true," Deirdre says.

"I didn't ask you," Ealasaid retorts at the same time the blonde woman snaps, "It doesn't matter if it's true," and the man mutters something I can't hear, and everything jumbles together in my ears.

"It's true," Ezra whispers.

The world falls away.

I'm leaning against their chest, and it almost doesn't matter that we're about to die. Tension dissolves, weightless. I can smell the salt in the air.

"Ezra?" I say.

"It's true," they say again.

"Yes" is all I can manage.

My head tilts back against their shoulder, and I can see the stars through the break in the clouds, just a sliver, a slice.

"No!" It's the blonde woman's voice, but I can't tell what she's reacting to.

My body tingles. I think if Ezra weren't holding on to me, I would fly across the pier into the iron pillars where they moor the ferries and stick tight.

I don't know what makes me do it. It's maybe the worst idea I've ever had, but the iron is like a railroad spike in my gut, and in or out, it's killing me.

I grab it with my right hand and yank.

My vision goes speckled and grey, and I hear Ezra shout, but I reach for that magnetic feeling and fling it away from me with the spike.

It goes wide of the woman—and Deirdre, thankfully—and it splashes a line of blood spray across the restaurant wall.

The spike lodges into the man's neck as if I've chucked it at a snowbank and not flesh.

I get one glimpse at the blonde woman's murderous fury as the man screams, and then she vanishes, jerking him with her into nothingness.

The last thing I see is Ezra's face.

THIRTY-FOUR

I wake in an unfamiliar bed.

The ceiling is high, and it's strange waking up to see it so far above me. I'm used to being in a bedroom right under the roof, so I have to be careful not to bash my head.

The thought is accompanied, appropriately, by throbbing in my skull.

That's right. I got stabbed *and* concussed.

I manage to move a little, which sparks movement near me.

Ezra.

They're in a plush, red velvet chair. They've changed since the harbour, which is probably good because of the blood, but their eyes are hooded and dark, and the sharp angles of their shoulders are rigid.

But their face relaxes at the sight of me.

"You're awake," they say.

"Unfortunately." My voice is hoarse. "Whoever told us we were immortal forgot to mention the fact that we can still get stabbed and nearly have our heads broken."

Ezra cracks a smile at that. "Can I come sit by you?"

I must still be a little loopy, because that makes me giggle. I can't remember the last time I giggled. The sound is like soap bubbles.

"Is that a yes?"

"It's a yes," I say, "though I don't think I can move much."

“You really shouldn’t,” they agree.

The bed is far bigger than the double bed I’m used to, and Ezra climbs in on the far side and lies down on my right. I can’t really see them, and turning my head makes me want to throw up. They reach out and take my hand and give it a squeeze.

“How almost dead did we get?” I ask.

“Very,” says Ezra. “Though oddly enough, Ealasaid saved us.”

“What?”

That doesn’t really compute.

“She wasn’t prepared to break both our laws at once, it seems,” says Ezra.

Both our laws.

Right.

“Did you know?” I don’t even know whether I’m asking about the . . . second law or the whole *we’re married* thing.

“No,” Ezra says after a moment where their hand goes still on mine. “Everyone has said it’s a load of shite since I became immortal, so it’s not like I was looking.”

I’m about to ask something else, but Ezra keeps going.

“And yes,” they say, so soft it’s almost a whisper. “It’s like my universe shifted when I met you. But I didn’t trust it—I didn’t even let myself think it until Deirdre said it out loud.”

“It’s rude that she didn’t tell us in advance,” I say. I don’t always make jokes in serious situations, but when I do, it’s the worst possible time to do it. The moment it’s out of my mouth, I blurt, “I’m sorry. I’m—”

“Cam, you have had a *hard* week,” Ezra says, leaning up on one elbow so I can actually see them. They look younger than they ever have, despite us being the same age. “And it’s okay if you’re totally freaked out by all this or don’t believe it or whatever—like, honestly, it’s freaky and unbelievable, and what is it even supposed to *mean*—”

“Well, at least we’re already married,” I say without thinking. “For another three hundred and fifty-odd days, anyway. So we’ve got some time to figure it out.”

Ezra blinks. “What?”

The *what* has the same sound as a *how hard did you hit your head*, and it's the second thing that makes me close my own eyes.

"We're . . . married," I say. "An Smeòrach asked how we met, and I told him, and he kindly informed me of the significance of joining hands through a hole in a door on Lughnasadh night."

Ezra starts to splutter. Actually splutter. I don't think I've ever heard anyone do that for real.

"I'm sorry, what?" they manage to get out finally.

"That's what I said," I say.

It's a struggle, but I fight my way onto my right side, which makes me wince and Ezra make an alarmed noise until I'm settled. They frown at me and grab a spare pillow, folding it in half so my head has more support. It's such a sweet gesture that I feel a little less awkward.

Ezra settles in on their side, facing me, and their slate grey eyes turn serious.

"We're married," they say. "A year and a day?"

"The traditional way," I agree.

"Don't we have to, I don't know, consent?"

"Good question." I pause, a familiar twist of anxiety unfurling to stretch. "We can go yell at An Smeòrach whenever I can get out of this bed."

"Cam," says Ezra. "Will you tell me something?"

"I can try," I say honestly.

"Did *you* know?"

"About the surprise elopement or about—about the other bit?" I can't bring myself to say *soulmates* out loud.

"The latter," says Ezra.

"I . . . don't know. I don't know how it's supposed to feel, but I can tell you what I felt, even if it might not answer how I feel," I say.

I can almost feel myself retreating into a safe shell. There's the hot curl of shame next to the anxiety now, and they feed off each other.

"That's all anyone can do." Ezra brushes their knuckles over my cheekbone and gives me a sad smile as if they have already read my mind and decided I'm going to hurt them.

“I’m always nervous around you,” I begin, which is a horrible start. “I can’t seem to mask the way I’ve done my whole life. I’m so used to having to put up this facade, this version of me at my most socially acceptable, but with you, the mask is out in orbit somewhere.”

Ezra gives a nod but says nothing.

“And then you were one of them. Like me, new. Seeing you was a burst of relief. And when we danced”—my breath hitches, and I have to clear my throat—“nothing else existed. There was just you. Just me. I felt like I’d come home.”

I look into their eyes, searching for something impossible, and my heart is beating so fast I think it might fly out of my chest.

“After last year, I told myself I never wanted to—I told myself I was done,” I say. “But it’s safe with you, isn’t it? It’s safe.”

“The hole in your side would disagree,” Ezra says, and they wince at their own words. Their eyes close for a moment, their chest expanding and contracting as they take and release a breath. “But yes. It’s safe.”

“What do the Others believe about soulmates?” I ask.

“That it’s different for everyone. Some are romantic pairings, some aren’t. The common thread is just that—a thread or a cord. An inexplicable need and a quiet bond. Forever is a long time to be alone.” Someone has said that last before. “And there’s more. That day you first found me on the rock? Right after we met? The first time, not when I asked you to come back.”

I nod. The movement surprisingly doesn’t scramble my brains.

“I wasn’t actually in the area. I just kept flying aimlessly around Loch Awe like there was something I needed in the other room but I couldn’t remember what I’d gotten up for.” Ezra presses their lips together. “I’d barely been sitting there a minute when you showed up. I was trying to figure out what I was looking for. But what I was looking for found me.”

“I meant what I said the other night,” I whisper. “I can’t stay away from you.”

“And I meant what I said when I told you not to.” Ezra swallows, their Adam’s apple bobbing where one doesn’t exist in their other form. “I don’t know what I would have done if they’d killed you.”

"They didn't," I say. "We're both still here."

"For now," says Deirdre's voice from the other side of the room.

I'm facing the opposite way, and I am not going to try and turn fast enough to see her, but Ezra looks like he wants to throw something at her for interrupting.

"Apologies, my twitterpated puppies, but I thought you might appreciate healing our dear Cam before she has to explain a stab wound and a concussion to her mothers and grandmother. While I think I could take the mums, Granaidh would throw me in Loch Awe, I'm sure."

I wish I could see Deirdre's face, but Ezra's too busy helping me roll back onto my back, and I can't say I mind looking at them instead.

"Healing?" I ask.

"Even with iron, there's enough we can do," Deirdre says, and I would hear the smirk in her voice even if she didn't make it over into my line of sight. "I'll be telling the story of how you pulled an iron blade from your side and used it to stab Mìcheal for the next aeon at least. My only complaint is that you missed his carotid artery."

"That wouldn't have killed him, would it?" I ask dubiously. I was hoping to knock the ringleader with it, not stab anyone, but I missed.

"No, but it would have absolutely showered Gretchen in his blood, and if you haven't guessed, she hates getting her hands dirty." Deirdre bares her teeth, and I am grateful not to be the intended recipient of her spite.

I don't recognise the other Sìthichean who come in, and I'd sooner forget the healing itself. Maybe they're used to feeling their insides knit together, but I'm not. The pain is as bad as the stabbing. I don't so much hold Ezra's hand as I cling to it the whole time the room swirls with magic. I dissociate to the point that all I feel is the pressure of Ezra's hand and tension that seems to turn my entire body into a knot.

It ends before I'm even aware they've left. My eyes scrunched shut when they started, and when Ezra says my name softly, I pry them open to an empty room, a still-aching side, and a bed absolutely drenched in sweat.

"If the agony of getting stabbed with iron wasn't enough of a deterrent, healing certainly would be. How come it didn't flatten you when

Deirdre healed the arrow wound?" I say when I can manage human speech again.

"That was just wood," Ezra tells me, planting a kiss on my sweaty brow. "It's the iron they were purging from you. Everything's got its poison."

"They really were trying to kill us." I lie back on the bed, feeling as though my bones have been replaced with gelatine.

"Looks that way," says Ezra.

"Is An Smeòrach okay?" I almost sit bolt upright on the bed and immediately regret it, collapsing backward with a grimace.

"He's fine. Or, more accurately, he's raging. He and the older Others are making plans, I think. You passed out for a while when they were working on you." Ezra rolls onto their side to peer at me. "Do you want to get cleaned up?"

I look down, thinking I'm still in my blood-soaked school uniform, but someone must have magicked me into a nightgown. Or a shift, whatever it's called. It's soft fabric but rumpled and sweaty.

"That would be nice," I say. "I should also probably make sure I get to school on time. Going to need to pretend nothing happened so the mums don't freak out."

They're probably already freaking out. As Ezra helps me sit up, I remember my phone crashing into the wall of the restaurant on the pier.

"My mobile," I say.

"The case you had on it saved it from too much damage," Ezra tells me. "I hope you don't mind that I sent your mum a message just saying you and Deirdre were working away and you'd see them tomorrow."

Relief floods me. "Thank you." I wince. "Though I'm going to need Granaidh's wheelchair at this rate, and they'll know something happened."

"You'll be fine in a few hours." Ezra gets up, stretching. Their eyes are ringed with dark circles—were they that worried? "Think you can stand?"

They offer their hands, and I take them. My legs feel as weak as Fànas's, and I teeter even with Ezra's support.

I let Ezra lead me to a bathroom—a real bathroom with a flushing toilet and everything, though I guess those have existed for hundreds of years—where there's a pool of steaming water inset into the floor.

Ezra hesitates as we stand there, and something lurches in my core at the thought of them leaving, but I also don't have the courage to ask them to stay.

We hover there for a stretch of time I can't quantify, and finally, on still-wobbly legs, I pull them to me and kiss them.

"You'll be here when I'm done?" I ask uncertainly.

"Always," they say.

Ezra kisses my cheekbone, their thumb trailing across my jaw, and they leave me to the bath.

I could float away before I even touch the water.

THIRTY-FIVE

I don't know how I make it through school after leaving the tolman.

Deirdre and Ezra assure me they'll be nearby, but that doesn't make walking into Ealasaid's territory any easier.

Just because she didn't actually murder me when she had the chance doesn't mean she's safe to pass in the halls of Oban High School.

What I don't count on—and maybe should have—is Grace.

The shorter girl accosts me between classes when I'm still on high alert for any sign of Ealasaid.

"Look, I'll just make the decision for you. We don't have to be friends, since it's clear you don't want anything to do with me or my sister," she says.

Too late, I remember what Deirdre said, which feels like a million years ago now. Grace was looking right at us when we travelled away last night.

"If that's what you want," I say because I don't know what else to say.

As usual, I've done something wrong before I even figure out what anyone wants from me. We've had lunch together and texted a couple times, but apparently I was supposed to do something else? I have no idea.

Grace frowns. "That's it? Really?"

"Grace," I say slowly. "I have had a really, really bad couple of days. It has nothing to do with not wanting to be your friend. I moved here because my life is complicated, and it has not gotten less complicated."

She waits, and when she decides I'm not going to elaborate, her frown grows deeper. "So your life is complicated. So is everyone's."

"I know," I say, "but I literally cannot talk about it."

"Seems like you'll talk to other people, just not us," says Grace. "Does that girl you left with yesterday even go here?"

I've barely slept, my side still twinges, and the entire surface area of my skin hums with residual magic from the healing the Sìthichean did, or at least I think that's what's making it hum.

"That girl"—the idea of Deirdre as some random girl is both funny and terrifying—"is a friend and a neighbour, and I'm allowed to talk to her if I want."

"I'm glad you have at least one friend, then," says Grace, her words like stinging nettles.

That, for some reason, is the thing that gets under my skin.

"I used to have another one, but I literally watched him die, so excuse me if I have a little trouble opening up to people I just met last week," I say, louder than I mean to.

We're not alone in the hallway by any stretch of the imagination, and anger is not fear, so my instinctual vanishing act has not kicked in.

"Maybe you should have saved him," says Grace, and she spins on her heel and stalks off down the hall.

A ripple goes through the other kids nearest us, and I'm left standing frozen in an eddy of open space.

I don't know Grace well, but I don't think that was like her. Texting her about it is out of the question, and I'm not sure texting her sister Eilidh would be much better.

The rest of the day is every bit as weird. At lunch, one of the kids in secondary four punches his best friend, which I only know is their connection because someone says it right in front of me. And even though Ezra and Deirdre both told me the healing weirdness would wear off throughout the day, by the time I'm in Gaelic class, my skin feels like someone's hooked it up to a generator. No matter how much I rub my arms, the hairs won't lie down.

There's no sign of Ealasaid or Grace as I leave the school and hurry down to the mums' office. The key Mum had made for me works perfectly, and when I climb the stairs to the top floor, blissfully silent except for the seagulls in the harbour, I drop my school bag and collapse in the middle of the floor, sprawling out on my back.

The carpet is that universal so-low-pile-it's-really-no-pile stuff ubiquitous in offices in every country I've lived in (which is only two, but still), and it smells like old Hoover dust. I don't even care.

I expect Ezra to show up soon, but it feels like a century since I've been alone, and it brings with it the sensation of pure bliss.

After lying there spreadeagle on the floor for a few minutes, I prop myself up on my elbows and pull my shirt up to look at my left side.

Where I was stabbed.

With an iron blade.

I've never paid much attention to what knives are made of—and I'm certain even as a mortal, taking a five-inch dagger to the gut would be pants regardless of the make and model—but I will never forget what it was like to have something lodged in my abdomen.

Even thinking about it makes my hand shake as I run my fingers over the skin.

When I took my bath in the wee hours of the night, the mark was angry and red, but it's faded now to silvery scar tissue. I didn't notice when I yanked it out and flung it, but the blade was star-shaped. It punched into me like a reverse cookie cutter.

Knowing the Sìthichean and their sense of humour, I wouldn't be surprised if a star-shaped weapon was chosen for me on purpose.

I guess Gretchen and her minions didn't expect me to survive with a scar.

I also can't believe Deirdre just wants me to go to choir practice with the family like nothing bizarre is happening in the West Highlands. There's a sinkhole at Oban High School, yesterday everyone in Oban's town centre all left at once but no one actually went missing and, since I got what Deirdre now thinks was a fake phone call from Mam to lure us into Oban to kill me and Ezra, all of these things seem to be about . . . me.

All of it gives me a tornado feeling. Living in Texas and bouncing around the south with Dad when I wasn't in Scotland, I learned about tornadoes early. I know the way the air feels when the clouds hang just right in the sky, that strange unlight that drapes across the land. I know what it's like when you see the clouds start circling, the unreality of watching points form when the funnels begin.

We were only close enough to see actual funnels a few times, but it's not a sight you forget. The sirens were always torture. Deafening and unignorable—for good reason—they were half the reason Dad had to deal with undiagnosed autistic meltdowns without knowing what was happening to me. The other half of the reason was that I'm basically a walking barometer. The pressure changes were painful.

All day, it's felt like that. But without the sirens, without the funnels, without that strange unlight, I have nothing but shadows to jump at.

I pry myself off the floor after a few more minutes, doing some stretches to try and work out some kinks.

Not too long later, I hear a tap at the window.

A large raven sits there, cocking their head at me.

I hurry to open the window for Ezra and let them in, hoping no one in the line of sight sees me purposely let a raven fly into an office building, but the moment the window's closed again, Ezra shifts to human form, and I almost lose my breath.

I honestly have no preference for whether Ezra flows one way or another, but every time I see their other face, I'm shocked by how beautiful they are all over again.

Today they're more femme than I've seen them, looking almost uncertain in olive green skinny jeans and a dark-grey cashmere turtleneck. They're stunning, voluptuous. Yet again, I'm just staring at them instead of doing the expected human thing of saying hello.

"Hi," I manage to get out past my tongue, which is ready to trip over itself.

"Hi yourself," says Ezra, a small smile creeping across their face.

There are a million things we should talk about. We're apparently married. We're soulmates. The Sionnachain want us dead. I'm supposed to go to Granaidh's Gaelic choir practice tonight, which will be full of people and therefore terrifying. The sinkhole. Deirdre. An Smeòrach. My lack of coherent magical abilities. Fànas. Anything. The list goes on.

Instead, we collide like we've fallen into the orbit of a neutron star and its inescapable gravity.

Their lips meet mine, and our bodies are flush up against each other. Ezra's hair is loose waves to their chest today, a similar length to mine, and my fingers tangle in it, get lost in it. Their lips taste like the salt on the wind.

I didn't think it was possible to want to be closer to a person than in a tangled, tight embrace, but as we gasp between kisses, their grip and mine grow tighter still. Their arms loop around under mine, their palms pressed flat to my shoulder blades, using that leverage to pull me closer. I lose myself in the softness of their chest pushed against my own.

The cashmere of Ezra's jumper is deliciously plush against my fingertips when I run my hands over their shoulders, and Ezra shivers under my touch.

When we finally break apart, both of us are dishevelled, shaky breathing and trembling fingers. Ezra smooths my curls back from my face. I might melt into a puddle.

"So," Ezra says, breathless, their gaze heavy with their dilated pupils, "how was school?"

My laugh comes out dreamy and far away. I don't want to break this spell.

We sit down on a dark-green loveseat the mums bought—I think we might be the first to use it—and I tell Ezra about the day.

"I don't like this," I tell them. Now that our fevered greeting has passed, that tornado feeling has returned in full force. "Did you talk to Deirdre or An Smeòrach at all today? Does anyone know why Oban was empty last night?"

Ezra shakes their head, but I don't know whether they're answering my first question or my second one until they say, "No one knows."

"Ealasaid wasn't at school today," I say. "Not that I expected her to try anything there, but there has to be something more happening. I don't think killing us would be their only goal. And there's no way in hell there's only three of them among the Sionnachain. They wouldn't risk this big of a mess without support."

"That's exactly why everyone's so on edge. The one thing you could always trust the Sìthichean to do was keep the two big laws. It's not even supposed to be possible to break them." Ezra slips their hand into mine, interlacing our fingers.

The feeling threatens to pitch me overboard into full-on desire all over again. There are a billion reasons to be upset right now, but the thought of losing Ezra after I just found them makes my very atoms want to spontaneously cleave themselves down the middle.

"But they almost did," I say. "How did we even survive last night?"

"By the skin of every last one of our teeth," murmurs Ezra, turning on the settee so they're facing me, their right knee bent inward and resting on the cushions, shin flush with my thigh. "Deirdre saw the attack coming and tried to throw you out of the way, but she was too late. The blade had already hit. But her movement threw *me* to the side, and Mìcheal missed me with the second dagger—I was able to fly to you just as Deirdre and Gretchen collided. Gretchen literally threw Deirdre into the harbour. If it had just been you and me, we'd be very, very dead."

My whole body goes rigid where I sit, frozen like someone's poured liquid nitrogen down my spine and if I move, it'll shatter.

"What are we going to do?" I ask. "How do we fight an enemy we can't see when we don't even know what they *want*?"

"That's what I'm trying to figure out," Ezra says slowly. "So far, I have nothing."

"I wish I wasn't so utterly useless. I might as well be a stoat for all the magic I can do on command. Which is none. Like a stoat." I give Ezra a tight-lipped smile.

"Oh, I don't know. Stoats might surprise you," they say with a wink, but there's no real mirth.

We're the two newest of the Sìthichean, the two closest to mortality. I don't know where we even begin to compete with people who have been making mischief for thousands of years.

But there's one thing Ezra has that even An Smeòrach may have forgotten: Ezra knows what it's like to start from zero in this world.

"Your gears are turning," they say. "I can almost see them spinning in there."

Ezra reaches up and gently taps my temple.

"I need to learn to control my magic," I say to them. "More than just feeling it out or having An Smeòrach throw vines at me until I retaliate. I don't want to just be a rabbit in the headlights the next time—the next time the Sionnachain come for me. For us."

"Believe me, if I live to be ten thousand and never see you stabbed again, it'll be too soon." Ezra lays a hand gently on my knee. "What can I do to help?"

That's the question, isn't it? They've barely been among the Others longer than I have—in the grand scheme of immortal life, we might as well have been born on the same day.

"I need you to teach me," I say to them. "Everything you know about your magic and magic in general."

They nod, though Ezra bites their lip, looking as if I've just asked them to explain Einstein's law of relativity.

I think of what they said about their narrow escape from the blade meant for them.

"And Ezra," I say, feeling the soft weight of the feathered earrings in my ears, "can you teach me how to fly?"

THIRTY-SIX

Ezra and I make little progress before it's time to meet the mums and Granaidh for choir. Like with An Smeòrach, we spend time with Ezra trying to articulate what they do while they do it, and though they're able to talk me through how they *feel* when they shift shape and even slow down the process so I can feel around the edges of it, by seven o'clock, we're both frustrated and defeated.

Not the best mood when trying to get ready to sing.

The choir gathers in a church not far from the pier, and I manage to find the mums just when they're getting out of the car with Granaidh.

"Feasgar math," I greet them, and Granaidh looks up, holding on to the door while Mam fetches her chair from the boot. Mum is carrying two enormous canvas bags but gives me a smile.

"There you are," Granaidh says, and again, hearing English from her feels . . . unsettling.

Mum doesn't seem to notice that's unusual, but Mam glances at the back of Granaidh's head in consternation.

Usually Granaidh is fine to wheel herself in her chair, but the path from the carpark to the church isn't very accessible for wheelchair users, so Mam has to help. It's one of those things most people don't notice until they are around someone it matters to—so many places might as well be on Mars for all the barriers that wheelchairs either can't get over or can't get through for being too narrow.

The bumps in the pavement and over the kerbs grow under wheels. At least the church itself has made efforts, since many of the older parishioners have mobility issues, and the other groups that hire out the church on weeknights—like the choir—are similar.

A couple other people are heading in before us, but just as we reach the door, an older woman in a bright red coat sees us and lights up.

"Oh, Roberta and Catrìona, is this your kiddo? She's gotten so big!"

"Nach is' a tha mòr," agrees Granaidh, and hearing the Gaelic from her soothes my heart.

I give the newcomer a small smile, not knowing what to say.

"Sìne, you must be so happy to have a grandchild so close," the woman says to Granaidh. She holds the door open for us. "I'm Kate, love. You probably don't remember me, but I met you ages ago when you were just a wee thing."

"Cam," I say, since at that point, she probably knew me as Lily.

Kate starts speaking animatedly to Granaidh and the mums, which I appreciate as it allows me to fade into the background. Being around new people always makes me nervous and half-braced for queerphobia, despite me being fairly certain the mums wouldn't come to any social gatherings that made them feel unwelcome for being gay.

It's not like it's far-fetched, even these days. Especially considering I spent half my life in the American south.

But that tight knot in the centre of my chest slowly softens and unwinds as we come in. The other choir members greet the mums so warmly that I actually have to look away because if I don't, the tears stinging my eyes mean I might start greetin', and *not* in the way that means to say hello.

Despite everything going on outside—both in the Otherworld and the mortal one—this small pocket of warmth feels precious, almost sacred. No one in my family is particularly religious or spiritual even, but "sacred" feels like the right word for a place that welcomes you home.

With a small jolt, I remember An Smeòrach's parting words to me at the cèilidh did exactly that.

Everyone deserves to have such a place.

Mam sings tenor and Mum's a soprano, so they take me to the conductor to see where I'll sit, and while the thought of being separated from both of them *and* Granaidh is a wee bit intimidating, the conductor is so warm and kind and no-nonsense that for once, I again feel like I've gotten myself all worked up for nothing.

The conductor of the Oban Gaelic Choir is a woman called Mairead in her mid-fifties with dark brown hair that has a streak of white at the front and nowhere else. When she smiles, the whole room feels like it might grin back at her. Her blue eyes sparkle, framed by rosy cheeks and expressive natural brows, and I like her at once.

I quietly sing a few notes along with her at the piano until she is satisfied and slaps both her thighs with her palms and says, "Right, that's you with the alto twos, then. Brilliant!"

I turn round to guess where to sit, and a few of the other altos make some space for me in the second row of chairs, a couple of people down from Mam, but with a buffer of altos so the tenors don't confuse me on my first night. It's been ages since I sang outwith my solos in the shower, but I'm surprised at the bubble of giddiness at the prospect of singing with other people.

One of the basses brings me some sheet music, and Kate sits next to me a moment later with her own—I guess she's an alto as well.

"Your Granaidh is truly delighted you've come back to Argyll," Kate says to me in a soft voice, almost conspiratorially. "She'd just get worried sick about every news story out of the States, even if it happened in California, and, well . . ."

I hesitate before meeting Kate's eyes, looking away again right after making contact. For once I know what she's thinking—the reason I'm here is certainly not a shooting that happened as far away from me as California. Far, far closer than that.

"I'm glad to be home too," I say, and the words feel right. "For lots of reasons. I miss Dad, but . . ."

This time it's me who trails off, and Kate gives me a squeeze on the shoulder. "No place like home, is there?"

"There really isn't." I peer at the music the man gave me.

"Taigh an Uillt" is the name of the song, and I'm not sure I know it, though that's the Gaelic name for Taynuilt, which is not far from Ballinacollie.

Thig fo sgàil a' Chruachain

Faigh ann fois is bàigh

Come under the shadow of Cruachan, find here peace and joy.

For days I've been a tense ball of anxiety, but as Mairead leads the choir through some warmups and into the song, something in me takes a breath for what feels like the first time in a year.

I don't know the song, but I can sight-read, and despite the complex arrangement, Kate is a huge help, and I am able to pick it up as we go. It's a love song for a place, full of praise for the people and homeland of one wee corner of Argyll.

It's easy to lose myself in the music, the blending of notes and voices. This late in the year, the choir is preparing for the Royal National Mòd, so the singers have the song down cold. Their voices bring life to the notes on the page, the Gaelic words written upon it. Every so often, Granaidh interjects between run-throughs to correct our pronunciation according to the Gaelic used in Taynuilt, though she explains everything in English since fewer than half of the members are fluent speakers.

The music washes over me, and when we finish with "Taigh an Uillt," we move on to a puirt-a-beul set for the Mòd that is as complex as it is exhilarating. There's no way I'll be performing with the choir, so I'm able to enjoy listening to the Scotch snaps of the Strathspeys and the whirl of the reel in what we call mouth music without succumbing to the pressure of perfection.

Was it really just last night I was almost stabbed to death right outside this place?

We're standing for this song, and those words almost send me off balance.

But they also do something else.

Accompanying the surge of protectiveness I feel for this place comes a wave of warmth and with it a sense of repelling force. Like the strands of wool strung across a loom that are so fragile each alone, the sensation grows stronger with every additional tendril that shuttles across its weft.

I can feel it.

Maybe if I hadn't been so frustrated with Ezra I wouldn't notice, but grasping at frayed edges and finding purchase on nothing has made my magical perception hypersensitive.

If magic is instinct, my instinct is to protect these people. It rises with each quickening syllable of the puirt-a-beul, each six-part harmony, the rapid-fire Gaelic that dances so nimbly from phrase to phrase, spinning poetry and playfulness into sound that feels like a strip the willow, one turn into the next, into the next, into the next.

Instinct . . . and intention.

I still don't know if anything befell the people of Oban yesterday while Gretchen and Micheal and Ealasaid were trying to murder me, but if anything I can do can protect these people now, I have to try. I picture a web of vines, of thorns that can bite. I build an image of a thicket in my mind, burrs and brambles surrounding the people I want to protect.

Brambles.

The image of brambles bursting with berries intrudes in my consciousness as we again spin from Strathspey into the reel, and I remember what Deirdre said about her enchantment.

Was that *her* way of trying to help?

I think it must have been.

It is here, in this church, surrounded by strangers on a Thursday night, that I catch hold of my magic for the first time.

Just like Ezra has tried to tell me from the start, strong emotions serve as a catalyst. But this is the first time it's been an emotion as warm and freeing as this.

I don't want this feeling to fade. It's the same sense of openness, of expansion, that comes with plunging into pitch darkness when overwhelmed by a migraine. Like the heavy restraints of burdens lift away. I can see the humming frequency of song; it fills the air, vibrating filaments of magic that drift like harp strings untethered to a harp.

The clarity that comes with the sight illuminates the inside of my mind like starlight, motes of brilliance suspended where there was void and shadow.

I can see the light and wind I have used to cloak myself from view, feel the minute changes in my pupils, in the muscles of my eyes that allow me to see the heavens. And I can see the weft and the weave of reality that I know will part like a curtain if I want to travel to another place in one step.

The final notes of the song cut off abruptly, a sharp, intentional end, and someone in the soprano section whoops happily.

There is no magic in Gaelic or music, nothing that will transcend time or save a language—but there *is* too.

Though the song has ended, returned to the rustle of movement and the murmur of conversations, I can still see and feel every strand around me. It's not just in me; whatever allows the Others to change reality is not theirs—ours—alone.

It is quieter in the mortals who surround me, but perhaps that is what keeps me so distracted that everyone else is sitting down before I realise I'm the only one standing and almost drop into my seat.

It may be quieter, but it's not gone.

Conscious of it or not, magic flows through them too.

THIRTY-SEVEN

I feel a bit foolish when I see what Mum was hauling in those two big canvas bags. Blackberries. Naturally.

Good-natured chuckles float through the church when practice ends, people milling about and relieving Mum of some of her burden. I hover on the sidelines, but no one seems to think that's too strange. A few people wave to me when they leave, and a few others welcome me to the choir.

I float over to where Granaidh is sitting. She's speaking in Gaelic in a low voice to one of the basses, a man who looks older than she is and walks with an intricately carved wooden cane, his hand on the shoulder of an eagle.

When Granaidh sees me, she smiles. "Shin thu, a ghràidh. Seo m' ogha," she says to her friend, introducing me.

"Is mise Cam," I say.

Folk don't shake hands much these days since the pandemic, but this man doesn't seem to mind.

"Aonghas," he says, but before he can say anything else, I hear Mum's voice.

"Ready to head out, Mother?" she says.

Aonghas nods at me and clasps Granaidh on the shoulder, making his way toward the door.

"Aye, I am now," says Granaidh.

It's like a tiny poison dart to the chest. The barb is impossible to miss—or at least it is to me. I'm not used to being the most socially observant person in the family. Mum, yet again, doesn't seem to notice what she's done.

"Go get your Mam?" Mum says to me, and I look around for her.

She's speaking to Mairead, so I walk toward the piano at the front of the church.

"Is math sin a chluinntinn, a Roberta," Mairead is saying to Mam, which stops me in my tracks. "Abair gu bheil do chuid Ghàidhig air tighinn air adhart!"

Mam looks up at my approach, and I think I see the flush of pink tinge her cheeks—is she embarrassed I just heard the choir conductor tell her how well her Gaelic's come on?

"Sin a tha fìor," I say, giving Mam what I hope is an encouraging smile. It's true indeed.

The pink in Mam's cheeks gets decidedly darker.

"Tha Mum ag iarraidh falbh." My words are an apology even if all I say is that Mum wants to go.

Mam says goodbye to Mairead, and as we follow Granaidh and Mum out to the car, she is bizarrely silent.

The air outside is cool and fresh; it must have rained while we were in the church, and for once, it feels like all is well with the world.

At least until we get into the car.

"Wasn't it nice that Cam came with us tonight, Mother?" Mum says once we're on the A85 heading toward Taynuilt.

"It was," says Granaidh.

"Bha," says Mam.

In the back seat with Mam, I'm at an angle to see the way Mum's hands tighten on the steering wheel.

My sense of rightness shatters. In what world is it Granaidh speaking English while Mam speaks Gaelic and Mum's *cross* about it?

"A sheanmhair," I say to Granaidh. "Dè mar a bha an latha agaibh?"

Such a simple question—the first thing you learn in any language class, pretty much. A "how was your day?" But Mum's shoulders tense up so much they practically hit her ears.

"Och, it was fine, love," says Granaidh. "Fànas and I watched our stories, and I made a wee cake for you to come home to. That's all."

We're barely to Connel Bridge, just passing the bridge itself, and already I wish I could fly home alone.

This time I can't help but look at Mam, and she's frowning, but not at me. Her eyes are trained on the rearview mirror—and Mum is glaring back at her.

I feel the flash of movement before I see it.

"Mum! Deer!" I blurt out.

She slams on the brakes, and not a moment too soon—a yearling doe vaults out from behind a bush on the left side of the road where there is little but shrubbery and Loch Etive.

I'm thrown forward in the car with a flash of panic, my only thought for Granaidh's back and the trauma of such a jostle.

The deer bounds away, missing the bonnet of the car by mere inches, and my back hits the seat behind me. My collarbone pinches with the bite of the seatbelt across my torso. I'm thankful that I'm on the left side of the car so the strap didn't cut into my new scar.

"Well spotted, Cam," Mam says, reaching over and giving my knee a squeeze.

"A bheil sibh ceart gu leòr, a seanmhair?" I ask Granaidh, hoping she's okay and didn't get whipped around too much.

She doesn't answer.

"Mother?" Mum puts the car in neutral and pulls the hand brake. "All right?"

"I'm fine," Granaidh snaps. "I want to go home."

Mum freezes with her hand still on the brake, and without a word, she disengages it and puts the car back in gear.

I usually like silence, but like yesterday at the pier, this silence is awful. It feels rotten, like a bloated corpse left out in the sun that is about to burst.

After the joy of choir practice and finally feeling my magic on a conscious level, everything in me feels jangled and off-key.

The rest of the drive crawls by. I fiddle with one of my earrings, wishing Ezra were here but all too aware they'd appear in a moving vehicle if they tried to travel to me right now.

To pass the time, I try and work through what Gretchen and company want, why they seem so ready to change everything about how the Sìthichean interact with mortals. Why here? Why now? The thought of the Others all over the world descending on the mortal world with all the magic mortals have forgotten how to fear sends a chill through me that the adrenaline from the near-collision with the deer does nothing to assuage.

By the time we turn south along Loch Awe, heading for home, I am nowhere near an answer.

I am, however, relieved to be home.

We pull in the drive, and I practically leap from the car, going immediately to the boot to get Granaidh's chair myself the moment Mum opens it. I bring it around to her. When Granaidh braces herself to get into the wheelchair, though, she won't look at me, and just before she wheels herself toward the house, I catch a glimpse of a wet track along her cheek.

Mum is gathering her things from the car, and Mam is doing the same, and if I don't say something now, I'll lose my nerve.

"Stay here a moment, please," I say to the mums.

They exchange a glance, but I think I've surprised them so much by engaging that they stop what they're doing. Mum puts her now-folded, empty canvas bags on the roof of the car, waiting expectantly for me to explain.

She's not going to like this, I don't think.

When the door to the house closes, I turn to them. "Mum, why the hell are you forcing Granaidh to speak English?"

"Cam, she's a grown woman. I'm hardly forcing her." Mum actually rolls her eyes as if I've said something ridiculous.

"I've been watching Mam work her arse off to learn Gaelic and speak to Granaidh in Gaelic, and every time you walk in the room, you switch to English and you make damn sure the rest of us do too." All the pent-up energy from the drive makes me feel like a microphone held too close to a speaker, and I'm almost shaking in my own feedback.

"Excuse me?" Mum says. "You will not speak to me that way."

"Cam—" Mam raises one hand and then lowers it, frowning.

"We just spent two hours in a room singing in Gaelic but the first time Granaidh got to have a conversation in Gaelic with Aonghas and me, you interrupted us to leave." My hands are turning to claws and flexing over and over again, my nails hitting me in the palms. "Do you have any idea how *precious* Granaidh's Gaelic is? You've thrown me in GME every time you've had a chance since I was a wean, but we live with a native speaker, and you're killing her language right in front of me, and I can't stand to watch it! Do you have any idea how many kids I've known over the years who *wished* they had someone like Granaidh to talk to, let alone someone who loved them the way she loves us? She got hit at school if she spoke her own language. It's a bloody miracle she's tried this hard to give it to us."

I don't think I've ever yelled at Mum before, and I don't like it, but I'm proper raging. As usual, my fuse just burns and burns and burns and burns and burns until finally, after me thinking I'm handling a feeling, it hits the dynamite.

My eyes burn like that now-charred fuse, and I bang my wrists against my hips, and what makes me even angrier is that I don't have Granaidh's Gaelic. I don't know how to be raging in Gaelic. I don't have the words or the idioms or the life in me to have this fight in the language that should have been mine at Mum's knees and wasn't.

But I do know one thing I can say. "'S ann leatha-se a tha an taigh seo, is i a' Ghàidhlig na prìomh-chànan ann."

This house is Granaidh's, and Gaelic is the primary language in it.

I'm still in my school uniform, and I don't even care.

For the second time in a fortnight, I take off running into the woods.

THIRTY-EIGHT

I am dripping magic.

Now that I can see it, as I finally slow along the Otherworld path I found without trying, it pours from me, its threads seeking, searching, slipping between infinitesimal currents in the air.

I don't know if it is my rage or if it's something else. The only thing I do know right now is that I don't want to be found. For the first time in full consciousness, I drape myself in my own magic, wrapping it around me like a cloak.

My school shoes might be toast. Walking through the forest's spongy moss will not be great for them, but I can't be arsed to care.

The past fortnight has run roughshod over everything I know, burned away everything I thought I knew about myself.

When was the last time I looked up at the sky?

I stop under the canopy of a large hazel, moving out from the shadow of its branches just enough to look up. The rain that fell when we were singing washed away the clouds, it seems, because the sky is wide and full of stars.

Standing beneath them with my magic in my hands to use as I will, it feels like I could reach out and touch them.

The urge to leap up into the air, to try and chase that feeling, almost overtakes me.

But I don't. There is a stronger pull right now, and one I think my subconscious was dragging me toward even as I fled the house and whatever part of Mum's anger will fall on my head when I return.

What I need to do, need to see, is the place where all this began.

Not the clearing where I found Deirdre and Daibhidh's dead friend. I need to find the door.

I thought my life had changed when Deirdre dragged me out of my own impending demise, but that's not where my world moved beneath my feet.

That happened with a simple, innocent urge. It happened with one hand stuck through a hole in a door and the unexpected grasp that met it from the other side.

Even as I think it, the path around me shifts.

It's still the same path, the same lush carpet of mosses and shamrocks that blanket the rocks lining its edges with green. But what is new is that those even rocks placed with such care—how could I have ever thought this path organic?—begin to glow.

I follow their green-gold light.

My footsteps are unhurried; tonight, this is a pilgrimage.

The first time I walked this way I had no idea where I was going and certainly no idea where I'd end up.

Even after, I didn't know that door led to the tolman, into the heart of the Otherworld, shrouded within this ever-changing borderland between the old world and the new.

I don't know which is which.

Like last time, the sense of being *home* almost overwhelms me. It is in every leaf and filament of moss, every jagged edge of bark on every tree. This is where I belong.

I felt it even before the door, before Ezra, before Deirdre and An Smeòrach and Ealasaid and Gretchen and the star-shaped silvery scar upon my body that will remain however long I get to live.

I feel it still.

Time passes differently here. They say your life flashes before your eyes before you die, but as I walk down this familiar, unknown path, all I see is a future spread out before me. All I see is two worlds, both of them mine.

Peace steals over me, like fresh drops of Beltane dew upon my cheeks. It soothes the remainder of my anger.

When the door appears in front of me, I smile.

It is as strange as it once was, but now I can truly see it. This door grows between two yews, grown *of* the two yews, their trunks stretching above it and containing it at once. The hole is still in the centre, looking as if it is missing its glass. I never asked An Smeòrach why the hole is there, but now I understand why the path leads directly under this door.

I don't reach through the hole this time. Instead, I simply open the door and walk into the tolman.

Seeing what Ezra must have from the other side feels like looking out of the wrong side of a mirror.

The door opens into a corridor of that familiar, cream-coloured stone, carved in whorls where it meets the wood of the yew. Even this side of the tree trunks are patterned, as if someone whispered to the bark and asked the trees to grow according to their design. Pale light spills through the window. I imagine Ezra here, perhaps leaving, seeing one pale hand appear on this side of an invisible border between worlds.

Without even having seen each other, we reached for one another.

I've no idea where anything in the tolman is from here; the times I've been inside, it's always been Deirdre leading me from one place to the next, and we always arrived by different means.

It's as if something woke my magic, like my anger burned away whatever barriers I had constructed in my own mind. Now that I'm here, now that I can see, it's clear my first visits may as well have been blindfolded.

The stone is not just cream coloured. Like marble but finer, tracks of gossamer thread through it, reflecting back bits of light in shades of gold. Once, I walked outside into the sunlight to see threads of glimmering silver splayed out across the path. They dazzled me until I realised they were slug trails, and the memory of that illusion haunts me as I walk a few steps along the corridor of stone.

What if this beauty is nowt but an illusion? Sunlight on slime, tricking the eye?

I follow the corridor a few steps farther, tugging my magic tighter around me like pulling up the cowl on my cloak. The deeper I walk into the tolman, the more certain I am that something is wrong.

Two steps later, my earrings pulse like someone attached jumper cables to them, and I stumble.

Ezra.

My half-taken breath halts in my throat.

Time stops.

When the pulse comes again, it sends zings of electricity down the sides of my neck. My ears have always been sensitive, and the sensation courses down the tender skin of my neck, pouring over me like glacial runoff that leaves my whole body shivering.

Ezra is in danger.

The corridor stretches out before me, innocuous and beautiful. I have no way of knowing where Ezra is, no way of knowing what's happening to them or how I can possibly help them.

The watch Deirdre gave me is at home, a place I can't travel into even if I knew how to fold time and space the way the Others do.

Think, Cameron.

Ezra said our connection is like a cord. I don't know if that's true—I don't know if this idea of soulmates is even real or if it's just a legend, another trick of the Sìthichean.

But even if it's not, I have something.

If Ezra can find me by the earrings they gave me, that means there is a connection. And if I have to want them to find me, that means that connection *has* to go both ways.

The current pulses again, this time so strong it almost drops me to my knees.

My scar jolts with it, sharp as if that iron blade has only just punched through my skin and into my gut.

No.

I try to feel my earrings, the gold, the feathers. It's not any weirder than a lock of hair as a lover's token, and it's every bit as much a part of Ezra as that would be. I close my eyes, trying to shut out the corridor around me, and for once, I don't try to shut out any of the sensory overwhelm that so often works against me.

The currents of air that I feel in the hairs on my arms and the light peach fuzz on my cheeks. The smell of stone with a touch of peat and smoke. Warmth in the air, the absence of any electronics except the phone in my pocket and the Fitbit on my wrist. My magic is a sixth sense, like swimming at the same time as walking, the paradox of existing between two worlds.

When the pulse comes again, even stronger, sending yet another stab of panic shooting through me, I lean into it, holding on to that pain, the electric crackle, the shock.

The edges of my magic's tapestry are alive. They grab hold of that current and weave it into themselves, and like that old, familiar experiment of two tin cans and a string that become a communication device, at the other end of those new-formed lines is Ezra.

Ezra's mind.

Their mind opens before me, a sea of shadows and waves, of warm updrafts and fierce cries—alive and free. They are not free now, and if I don't do something quickly, they won't be alive, either. Where just a few hours ago, I tried to steep myself in their magic, tried to feel what they feel and failed, now, in this moment, I surrender to the undertow and let it pull me beneath the surface.

THIRTY-NINE

There's nothing like a Texas summer in the age of climate change.

The heat is oppressive and heavy. It coats your skin the second you set foot out the door. With a high enough dew point and humidity, it feels like you're drowning and you'll never be cool again.

Going to the lake with Paul was supposed to be an escape.

Crowds of people are one of my least favourite things, but that day when it was a hundred and ten degrees Fahrenheit in the shade, forty-three Celsius, I let Paul talk me into going swimming.

The Hamilton Pool Preserve is a gorgeous grotto of geology that looks like a hand scooped away the bedrock to form an open-air amphitheatre of jewel-blue-green water ringed with a canopy of lush foliage that drapes like garlands over its edges. Catfish swim lazily about, and natural waterfalls shed droplets like diamonds in the sunlight.

It's one of the most sought-after swimming holes near Austin, and Paul happened to get a reservation.

Even with the air-con blasting in his Jeep, we were sticky and flushed by the time we got to the pool.

He'd promised me it wouldn't be too busy, and he was right. The preserve keeps numbers manageable and requires reservations, and when we arrive, there are only a few handfuls of people on the steep trail that leads from the carpark to the pool.

Despite the suffocating heat, Paul and I were excited to be out. Or Paul was, and I was doing my best. Jason weighed as heavily on me as the humidity, and in my fretting, the distraction of tromping along the trail in the blazing sun at least kept my mind occupied.

When we arrived at the pool, I almost lost my breath.

"See," Paul said, grinning and adjusting the strap on the duffel bag he was carrying with a blanket and beach towels, juggling a cooler in his other hand. "I told you it'd be perfect."

"You're always right," I said in a sing-song voice.

We both moved as fast as we could to get a spot in the shade, spreading out a blanket and dropping everything we came with in a heap. We'd left our phones in the car, bringing only Paul's old thirty-five-millimetre camera he loved to shoot with. I drank some ice water while he photographed the pool. I even let him take a few shots of me, something I hated doing when I couldn't see the pictures straight away.

Then, grinning, we stripped down to our swim costumes and waded into the pool.

Paul was the best friend I ever had. He pushed me but never too far. He was content to let me float on my back in the deeper parts of the pool, my ears under the water. Floating like that is a kind of sensory deprivation for me, in the best sense. It shuts me off from excess stimulus, allows my mind to relax and breathe. The light bobbing of the water, the way my body sinks and floats in rhythm with each inhale and exhale . . . Paul knew and understood what I needed better than anyone else, even Dad. Even the mums.

I couldn't see him when it happened.

There was a loud sound that ricocheted around the pool's grotto, even intruding underwater to the point that I flailed to an upright position. Some rock crumbled away, dropping into the pool, and at first, I thought that was all it was. For a while, no one had been allowed to swim at the pool due to unexplained rockfalls.

I made for the spit of sand that forms the pool's beach, seeing other people doing the same.

But the sound happened again, and then it happened again, a *pop-pop-pop*, bursts of sound.

In the distance, someone started screaming.

Pop-pop. Pop—pop-pop.

Closer now, and the screaming grew louder.

"Paul!" I yelled his name, and he didn't answer.

I'd been floating long enough that he could have had to go to the toilet.

A tall Black woman and her white husband started beckoning at me, urgent.

"Honey, get over here, quick!"

I obeyed as more shots, even louder, broke the air.

The woman and her husband pulled me away from the water, my feet caked with dirt and leaves, and they led me toward some tree cover on the far side of the grotto, pushing me to the rock face with my back against the stone.

"Are those gunshots?" I croaked.

"Yes," said the man. "Stay down."

"It's gonna be okay," the woman said, more to herself than to me. "It's gonna be okay."

"My friend is out there somewhere," I said. My teeth had started chattering. I couldn't tell when.

No more shots.

We waited like that for an interminable amount of time. It could have been ten minutes or ten hours. The sun barely moved across the sky, but with rock digging into my back and my feet in the dirt, arms around my knees and rocking, I felt like I had always been there, locked in that stasis of horror.

Eventually, though, we heard shouting again.

This time it wasn't coming from outside the grotto.

"Get him out!" someone was yelling.

I stood up and walked out from behind the trees in what felt like slow motion.

There, on that wee stroke of a sandbar, two university-aged boys were pulling Paul out of the water.

The current pulls me under, but there was no current that day, just a still Texan pool on a hot summer afternoon and death in the air.

I am lost in the memory, reliving it over and over.

The sound of the shots that didn't take his life. The blue cast to his skin that did.

All of it feels like it could be this moment, but it's not.

Slowly, by inches or by degrees, I feel something that isn't the sticky heat of a Texas summer.

Electricity pulses through my earrings again, jolting me out of a past I can't change into the present.

I don't know where I am. It's as if I stepped into Hamilton Pool and came up in Loch Awe, at the bottom of it in the peat and silt and whatever exists so far beneath the surface.

I claw my way upward, reaching for a lifeline that sparkles like slug trails in the sun.

I am in a house I don't recognise.

It is tidy to the point of being immaculate, like the houses staged by estate agents rather than the ones people live in. The floor plan opens up the living room and dining room, a hearth blazing with warmth against the far wall. The sofa in front of it is burgundy, plush, the kind of thing Fànas would love to use to sink her wee claws into. Not a hint of lint spoils the smooth surface of the upholstery.

A bookshelf laden with books and art pottery sits against the far wall, a large silver bowl taking up half of one of the shelves without so much as a fingerprint to mar the reflective surface.

It's in that surface I see the blood.

I spin to my left, where a pool of red spreads across the hardwood floor.

If I didn't know what it was, it might be beautiful. That deep ruby against the cool tones of the pure oak. This floor is not like the laminate at Granaidh's house—my house—but looks like it was hand cut and polished to perfection. It is almost as reflective as the tacky gloss on that spreading pool of crimson.

There is a corner of a wall blocking off view of the source. It's as if someone opened up this entire floor of the house but wanted to make some distinction between living space and cooking space, and I have to take several steps to get around the blood.

My heart pumps my own blood frantically through my veins, like the reminder all its hard work to keep me alive could be ruined with a puncture in the wrong place.

As I make my way around the white wall, I want to turn and run.

Ezra sits in the middle of the kitchen floor, a man's head in their lap. The head is still attached to the neck, but barely, severed half through just under the jaw. Ezra's face bears a slash of arterial spray in droplets that have dried where they landed.

Beside them is the body of a woman, her neck twisted all the way around. My stomach lurches.

Her face—her face is theirs. Not exactly, not a carbon copy, but Ezra in their femme form leaves no doubt of who gave birth to them. I don't know what gender Ezra was assigned at birth, and I don't care.

Right now they are almost unrecognisable, buried in a bulky sweatshirt and soaked in their parents' blood.

"I couldn't save them," they say. "I couldn't save them. I couldn't save them. I couldn't save them."

As I watch, the air parts, and a trio of Sìthichean appear, grim faced and without a hint of mischief. One of them is Daibhidh.

After a moment, Daibhidh jerks a hand, his muscles tensing, and a fourth trips through the shimmer of magic, landing with his knees in Ezra's father's blood.

Ezra doesn't even look up.

I know that look in their eyes.

I am stock-still and alone, watching as those two university lads perform CPR on my best friend.

Something wails in the distance, and I can't tell if it is a siren or the keening of the bereaved or the endless shriek of the ban-sìthe.

There is a bracing thudding all around me that could be my heart.

Death could come for me right now, and I would welcome it.

Paul's feet flop when one of the lads jostle him.

Pump. Pump. Pump. Breathe.

Pump. Pump. Pump. Breathe.

Pump. Pump. Pump. Breathe.

The lad doesn't stop until the paramedics arrive, a score of SWAT team officers fanning out through the grotto, and I don't move.

I hear the paramedics' explosive exhale.

"There was nothing you could have done, son," says a woman EMT. "He was gone before you pulled him out of the water."

Ezra still isn't looking at the Sìthichean, though one is trying to get their attention.

They stare straight ahead, waiting to join their parents on the floor.

Eventually, one of the Others snaps her fingers in front of Ezra's face.

"We are sorry," she says to them. "This should not have happened. We can be cruel, but we seldom seek to harm for the sake of harm itself."

Ezra doesn't answer.

"This one's punishment is death," the woman goes on. "If you want to watch, you can. And then you will have a choice to make."

At first I think Ezra isn't going to look, but when the two Others holding the murderer pin him against the refrigerator, its stainless steel stained forever with blood spatter, Ezra's head turns as if someone else is turning it.

The woman produces an iron blade. It's not like the dagger that stabbed me, no. It's long and sharp, and it severs the murderer's head from his body in one perfect, deadly strike.

Ezra still does not speak.

"It would have been a mercy if we had been a few moments later," one of the Others murmurs.

"Death is a mercy that should only ever be a choice," says the woman wielding the blade. She wipes it clean on the shirt of the corpse. "That choice is taken only when necessary."

Daibhidh is silent, but I remember how he fled when the choice was given to me.

"And this one shall have that choice," agrees the first voice.

"You may join your family," the woman says gently to Ezra. "We will not judge if that is what you choose. But you cannot remain mortal and live."

Ezra's head swivels on their neck once more, but they do not look at her.

They look at me.

FORTY

My face breaks the surface like I've been underwater my whole life.

I don't know how much time I spent submerged in Ezra's mind, my own, our thoughts and memories melded into a pit of quicksand.

But the moment they make eye contact with me, the air parts before me. I step through on shaking legs.

Ezra lies sprawled before me, covered in blood that this time, I'm certain is their own.

Despite my urge to run to them, I daren't act on it. I hover where I am, tight in the cocoon of my own magic that I hope will keep me hidden.

Ezra, of course, is not alone.

Worse, we're still in the tolman.

I don't know where we are in the tolman, but I'm certain I haven't left it. Whoever has Ezra has them right under An Smeòrach's aquiline nose.

Turning slowly, I survey the room.

The floor and walls are the same cream-coloured rock as the corridor I left behind, but there is no visible door. The room is the size of my bedroom, Ezra near one wall where I've appeared a couple yards away from their feet.

I am not surprised that the first face I see when I move is Ealasaid.

She looks bad. That's the only way I can describe her at first glance. Insofar as an immortal can look haggard, she does. Her skin is sallow, almost yellow-tinged wax. She looks jaundiced, and I don't think it's the light. Her black hair is no longer perfectly defined ringlets but a tangle of curls and frizz that are so dull and matte they barely shine in the light of the glowing bulbs in the walls.

She's got a dagger in her hand, but it's so far clean, unbloodied. I don't know what she used on Ezra, but it wasn't that. Not yet.

Gretchen is here with her, but there is no sign of Mìcheal, for which I think I should be grateful.

Swallowing, I drop into a crouch, afraid to move too quickly in case my magic fails and they see me.

"Stupid," Gretchen is saying harshly. "This wasn't the time, and you've alerted An Càrn Òir now."

"I was trying to right my mistake," Ealasaid says, but her throat bobs when she says it. "I was wrong to abandon you when we were so close."

"You were," says Gretchen. "But there is such thing as overcorrection."

"I'm sorry."

"Let me think."

I place my hands on the floor to steady myself, not trusting my balance to waddle in a crouch, and in a slow bear crawl, I close the distance between myself and Ezra.

Don't move. Please don't move. I form the thought with as much conviction as I can muster, reaching out one hand as soon as I'm close enough to rest on Ezra's calf.

Either they're completely unconscious or they can feel me through their gift, because they don't so much as twitch.

I force myself to take slow, even breaths, calling upon every late-night meditation I've used to try and sleep. It took months to convince myself I had a right to air after Paul drowned.

Now I draw each lungful deliberately, taking care to feel it pass through my nostrils, attentive to the way it is cool in my airways on the way in, warmed by my body on the way out.

I don't know how to heal, and I'm afraid to try anything too big, but one thing that gives me a small amount of confidence is that I can pull my cloak over Ezra's leg where my arm overlaps it.

As the silence draws out in the room, I take a longer, deeper breath and breathe out through my nose.

If magic is intention, I have a chance.

I focus on the contact between my palm and the relaxed muscle of Ezra's calf. They are warm, alive. That thought is enough to embolden me. I draw on the edges of my magic with every breath, taking in cool air and breathing out warmth, care, thoughts of safety and healing.

There is no real way for me to tell if anything is working, but at least I'm trying something. I'm not frozen like I was with Paul. I'm not cowering for my life this time. I'm here.

But I still don't know what to do.

"We can salvage this," Gretchen says softly, breaking me out of my concentration on Ezra. "Wait here. Don't do anything else. I'll be back."

Gretchen steps through the wall.

Or perhaps through the air. I can't tell which, but she leaves Ealasaid behind, and Ealasaid slumps up against the wall with a sigh, staring at Ezra's prone form. Her sigh has a bitter cast to it, almost giving off the same acrid scent that happens if you leave a metal pan on the stove so long that the metal itself starts to burn.

I don't know how much time I have, but I doubt it's much.

I wish I could communicate with Ezra somehow, and I don't trust that the glamour keeping me hidden extends to my voice.

Somehow I managed to travel.

Not just travel but travel to where Ezra was, the way they've done with me.

Think, Cam.

I did two things. I've travelled before, following Deirdre. Each time I've done it, it's been like the magic ball of wool in the labyrinth, using something else, some fragment of someone else's spirit or essence to guide me through the veil.

I don't know if *veil* is even the right word, but it suits as well as anything. I've thought of it like a curtain parting.

Think.

Time moves differently here. The pathway from my house to the tolman is both in the Inverinan forest and not, on the shore of Loch Awe and not.

The Otherworld is both within the mortal world and not. Time flows here; time flows there. It's a river, a current. Step into it on one bank and you might step out of it on another, downstream or upstream, depending on which way you move in the water.

And from one bank to another, the location might change.

Maybe it's not a curtain or a veil that is the right analogy for this.

I close my eyes, ignoring Ealasaid in her silence, even removing my hand from Ezra's leg to help myself concentrate.

When people travel, there's a shimmer to the air. Like a bending of light.

Like a bending of light through . . . water?

I think of the diamond droplets that fell from the grotto at Hamilton Pool, each catching photons and throwing them back more brilliantly than before. The bending of the spectrum of light and colour made with mist and rain and sun that makes a rainbow.

That shimmer, that stream.

It was twilight when I first stumbled into the Otherworld. A between-time, a sacred time. My people mark the turning times, one tide to another, afternoon to evening, shore to sea. Through all of that, rivers flow. Every river is also a bridge between one place and another. They carry silt, peat, water, fish, life, plants, sustenance, everything.

I'm close. I can feel it.

I stare at the wall where Gretchen disappeared, my hand returning to Ezra's leg where a muscle twitches, just a little, just enough to tell me they're alive and that they feel my presence.

It's not Gretchen who steps through the shimmer in the air.

Or not at first.

The face that appears is a man's, cold and calculating.

On his neck is an ugly gash of a scar where I flung an iron blade at his throat.

He walks into the room, and Ealasaid jumps to her feet in one fluid movement, all trace of her exhaustion gone.

Gretchen follows on Mìcheal's heels. Where his face is set like stone, hers is simply resolute. Not a line mars her brow, not a crease crumples the smooth skin of her cheeks.

"What's the plan?" Ealasaid asks.

"We kill the prince, and then you will see to your own scheme. It's earlier than I wanted to set it in motion, but Mìcheal says the Others are uncertain, and if they listen to An Smeòrach, all will be lost, and we will spend another thousand years waiting for an opportunity." Gretchen clasps her hands in front of her for a moment, and then she reaches over and takes the iron dagger from Ealasaid's hand.

My heart misses a beat.

Gretchen goes on. "If she slumbers again, we'll need to wait for one of the other old ones to wake, convince them. It's time."

"Wait," says Mìcheal. He holds up a hand, eyes scanning the room.

I hold my breath in my lungs until I think it will burst.

"What?" asks Gretchen.

When Micheal says nothing, Gretchen begins to walk toward Ezra.

If I don't do something, she is going to kill my soulmate right in front of me. And then they will kill me too. I've no doubt under the stars and sun that they will turn that blade and sink it into my heart.

I draw a shuddering breath as Gretchen advances, almost close enough to feel the heat of her body.

My hand shakes on Ezra's calf, and their muscle tenses beneath my touch. With every desperate fibre of my being, every strand of new-woken magic, I dredge up the memory of An Smeòrach's vine wrapped tight around my throat.

"Gretchen!" Micheal bellows. "We're not alone!"

I yank on my threads as I lunge to my feet, grabbing at the dagger in Gretchen's hand, and the room goes supernova.

This time I don't go flying, every thought in my head of protecting Ezra, but one of me against three of them will not keep us alive.

I can't travel home, not into the house, and there is no way—none—I'm bringing the Sionnachain into Granaidh's home.

I throw myself to the floor, dagger blade in cutting into the palm of my hand, and I fling my arms around Ezra, diving through that veil of water and time, one place fresh in my mind.

We fall into the floor.

FORTY-ONE

Ezra and I land with a gust of air knocked out of us, but the landing is soft and smells of moss.

It worked.

It *worked.*

"Deirdre!" I scream her name into the silence of her bower, feeling a ripple of my magic carry the sound on a shockwave like taking one end of a blanket and giving it a sharp shake.

She doesn't immediately appear, and I collapse onto the floor of the bower, half-flopping over onto my side to see if Ezra is okay.

Their eyelids flutter, and their throat moves as they swallow, no Adam's apple there the now. The entire right side of Ezra's face is bloody, their eye swollen with angry, red-purple bruising in a puffy spread across the arch of their cheekbone.

"Ezra," I say. "Are you okay?"

"You saved me," they murmur, opening their eyes.

They close them again after meeting mine as if vision is too much for them.

I'm still clutching the knife, and the pain breaks through my desperation enough for me to drop it in the moss, my own blood on the iron blade.

"I don't know for how long," I tell them honestly. "They're going to do something—something big, but I didn't hear what. Mìcheal knew I was there."

"Mìcheal is nearly as old as An Smeòrach," Ezra says hoarsely. "That you were able to hide from him at all is a miracle."

The flash of triumph that accompanies those words is short lived, because Ezra's abdomen convulses, and they cough, bloody froth bubbling over their lips.

"What did they do to you?" I ask, alarm stilling my hand.

"Poured rusty water down my throat," Ezra says, coughing again.

Rusty water. Basically a tincture of iron down the throat of a sìtheach—the thought makes my veins themselves want to oxidise.

I look at my palm. In addition to the cuts from the blade, the skin itself is angry, inflamed. Like just holding the thing has burned me in the way a cross burns a vampire in television shows.

"We need Deirdre," I manage to get out.

"Present," says Deirdre from behind me, and I turn in time to see her take three steps and freeze when she sees my bloody hand, the iron knife, and the pink foam at the corners of Ezra's mouth. "Dè fon ghrèin a thachair ribh?"

"Not what happened," Ezra croaks. "Who. Ealasaid caught me—I didn't even see her coming. She got an iron collar around my neck and dragged me into the tolman, into one of the cells."

Deirdre's entire body goes rigid. I guess I shouldn't be surprised the Others have some sort of dungeon, but the thought is unwelcome anyway.

"I think Gretchen didn't have anything to do with that part," I say so Ezra doesn't have to speak more. "When I found Ezra, they were unconscious. Gretchen didn't seem happy with Ealasaid, but I guess she decided now was as good a time as any to make their move."

"You two stay here," she says and vanishes.

"I was planning to run a marathon," Ezra says, closing their eyes again. "That's right out."

"Ha, ha, ha." I pause, reaching out a hand to touch their cheek, trying to find an unbruised place so I don't hurt them. "Are you okay?"

"I've been better." Ezra opens their eyes again. "I don't know if you got

COVID in the pandemic, but this feels like that. Absolutely flattened."

"I didn't get it," I say softly. "Not sure how I avoided it in Texas, but Dad basically locked me in my room. My friend Paul had it and got long COVID. I'm pretty sure that—that's how he died."

Ezra's gaze sharpens. "I'm so sorry."

"When I found you," I say, then hesitate. "I wasn't sure I could find you. I used the earrings—figured if you could reach one way with them, maybe I could reach the other. It worked, but it did something."

To my surprise, Ezra's face softens at that. "It *was* you," they say. "I wasn't sure. But I felt you in my mind."

"I didn't mean to . . . intrude." The thought of someone entering my mind without permission horrifies me, and doing it to someone else—well. "I was just trying to find you."

"I'm glad you did. I was stuck in a loop of just seeing my parents die over and over again. I wondered what broke me out of it." For the first time since I found them in that cell, they smile at me.

Their smile is sweeter than nectar, sweeter than honey. Despite the blood on their face, they are the most beautiful person I've ever seen. I lean forward and gently kiss them on the tip of their nose, where it seems safe and unlikely to cause them pain.

"Let me see if Deirdre has anything I can use to clean you up," I say.

I stand, looking around the bower. This is where we got dressed for the cèilidh, but there's no sign of Deirdre's wardrobe, which probably means anything useful is hidden away with magic. I make an irritated noise. Of course.

"Would it kill her to have a sink?" I mutter.

No sooner are the words out of my mouth than a stone on the other side of the room begins to rise out of the floor, shifting as it does into a basin with a fountain in the middle.

"Did you do that?" I ask Ezra.

"Do what?"

Their eyes are closed again.

I go to the basin, where a folded cloth even rests on the edge of it.

"Thank you," I say to the room.

I wet the cloth, bending over to take a sip from the fountain. The water is as clear and sweet as any highland spring.

When I return to Ezra, the first touch of the cool cloth makes them flinch, so I pull it back.

"Sorry," I tell them. "I should have warned you it was cold."

"It feels good," they say.

Slowly, as if I'm trying to clean paper-thin glass, I dab away the blood on their face and at the corners of their mouth. I have to get up twice to rinse the cloth, which makes me grimace.

Deirdre returns just as I'm wiping away flecks of dried blood from Ezra's arm, where their shirt was ripped halfway from elbow to shoulder.

"An Smeòrach and An Càrn Òir are having the tolman searched for the Sionnachain," she says. "If there's something to find, they'll find it."

"And if whatever they've planned isn't in the tolman?" Ezra asks.

Deirdre is quiet. "Then we hope we get some sort of clue in time to stop it."

"Is there anything we can do for Ezra?" I wave the bloody cloth in the air. "Your bower was kind enough to supply us with water, but . . ."

"There is, in fact," Deirdre says.

With a wave of her hand, she conjures a small apothecary box from the air.

"If we survive this, you're teaching me how you do that," I mutter.

"If we survive this, m' eudail, I'll teach you anything you want to know. I promise." Deirdre kneels beside Ezra and lays out the box on the floor next to them. She picks a vial that swirls in the light with a blue tinge and grimaces. "This won't be fun, Ezra. I'm sorry."

"And here I was worried I'd reached my pain quota for the day," they say weakly.

I go to their other side and sit cross-legged, taking their hand.

Deirdre helps them sit up enough that they can drink the contents of the vial, and Ezra flinches as the liquid touches their tongue. They have to visibly choke it down, and their hand clutches mine tight enough I'm afraid they're going to break my knuckles.

When Deirdre and the Others healed me, it felt like she had given every one of my cells a paper cut and poured lemon juice in each of them. I can too easily imagine how Ezra is feeling with that iron oxide solution in their very bloodstream. Deirdre grabs a pillow for them just as their body seizes and begins to convulse, and I'm not prepared for the sheer terror of seeing Ezra so incapacitated by pain.

All I want is for the pain to stop for them, for this solution to work swiftly and completely to chase the toxin from their veins. But even with magic, nothing is immediate. Nothing is omnipotent, despite the ability to pull apothecary kits from thin air.

It goes on so long I have to lie down next to Ezra, and they curl into foetal position, the pillow already soaked with perspiration. I take on the role of big spoon, wrapping my arm around their waist and pulling them flush up against me. Their skin burns like someone stuffed the Earth's core into their gut, and every breath they take comes with the intensive labour of expanding one's rib cage when the entire body is on fire.

At some point, I start to hum the song "Taigh an Uillt," maybe because the name—House of the Stream—conjures the image of flowing, cool water. Before too long, my skin emanates that coolness to the point that moisture starts to bead on my skin that isn't from Ezra's sweat or my own.

Then there is quiet.

When Ezra finally stirs, it's to tighten their hands against my arm that is still draped over them.

"Thank you," they say to me.

Deirdre left at some point, but I don't remember when. I think she may have popped in and out a few times in the course of Ezra's slow, painful healing, but I can't be sure.

My voice feels hoarse when I ask, "Are you feeling better?"

In answer, Ezra gives my arm one more squeeze and pushes themself to a sitting position, and I mirror their movement.

"I think I could take on a newborn lamb, aye," Ezra says, and I crack a smile.

"I love your smile," they say suddenly.

Even though I feel like I've been in the current of a mountain stream for the past day, something warm melts inside me.

"Yours is pretty great too," I say.

"Where's Deirdre?" Ezra stretches, rotating their shoulders, which makes me wince when there are several resulting pops.

"No idea." The sink is still there, and I get up to go get a drink from the fountain. "Did you hear anything while Ealasaid had you?"

Ezra shakes their head slowly. After a beat, they manage to stand, though they look one unexpected noise away from tipping over.

"She didn't exactly monologue about her plans." They frown, shifting their shoulders uncomfortably as if to settle the remaining kinks. "Actually, she kept apologising."

"What?" That doesn't sound much like Ealasaid.

"She kept saying she was sorry, that she didn't approve of killing Others, that she didn't have a choice. I think I told her there's always a choice, but that could have just been inside my head. I was a little out of it on account of the . . . torture."

Ezra wobbles, and I hurry to them, helping them over to the fountain, where they prop themself up to drink.

It takes me a moment for my brain to accept the word *torture* as the appropriate word, but there is no other word that describes poisoning someone with something horribly painful to incapacitate them and then kill them.

"The sinkhole at the school," I say suddenly, staring at the sink in front of us.

Ezra looks up, wiping water from their cheek. "What about it?"

"What could be the purpose of that?"

"You don't think it's a natural phenomenon?"

I shake my head. "I don't know if you saw it, but it looked like someone traced it smack in the middle of the pitch. It's not impossible, exactly, but—"

"Highly unlikely," Ezra agrees.

They're quiet for a moment, and I listen to the burble of water from the fountain, wishing Deirdre would come back.

"Do you have any idea how the centre of Oban was completely empty the day they attacked us there?" I ask. "I'm sure that phone call from Mam was a trick to lure us there, but they can't have known we would come for sure."

Ezra braces themself on the edge of the stone basin, staring at me. "You're right. We've been running from one thing to another since then, and I don't think anyone's had time to think through all of it."

My brain is whirling through things, looking for patterns, trying to make sense of anything that could help us.

"How does the forest work?" I ask. I hear my own words and wince. "I don't mean, like, biology and ecology. I mean the between-space. There's an area between Argyll and the tolman that is neither really here nor there."

"That," Deirdre says from behind us, "is a very good question."

FORTY-TWO

WWW mortal world or the Otherworld or both?"

"Yes," Deirdre says with a quirk of a smile. "Which is what I came to tell you. You two should stay here while the elders"—she says this with no irony—"take care of our wee Sionnachain problem."

I want to argue, but it wouldn't be logical when Ezra has self-identified as being in the weight class of a newly whelped sheep and at best, I am the firework in a Katy Perry song.

Deirdre gives Ezra a once-over, and her smile vanishes. "I'm not leaving the two of you in here."

She comes over and puts one hand on each of our shoulders, and the air shifts.

We're in her living room, and she points to the sofa. "Sit."

We sit.

There's a table in front of the settee, and in the blink of an eye, she has it full of food.

"No minions, eh?" I say.

"I believe in a well-stocked larder," Deirdre says dismissively. "Besides, I'm one of the ones who likes to cook. You two. Eat. I'll be back."

"What if you don't come back?" I ask and immediately regret it.

"I'll be back," she repeats, sounding more deadly than the Terminator. Deidre points at Ezra. "Protein or I'll not heal you again."

Ezra nods, reaching out for the drumstick of a chicken—still attached to a roasted chicken—and pulls it off.

With that, Deirdre looks satisfied we won't keel over from starvation, and she leaves before either of us can say so much as a good luck.

Ezra puts the drumstick back down. "I don't like this."

"Neither do I," I agree.

"I didn't mean the chicken."

"Neither did I."

I am hungry, but I don't think I could eat if I tried. My stomach feels like a tsunami of acid.

"Why would the Sionnachain open up a sinkhole portal between worlds?" I ask. It unnerves me that one of my first thoughts about that sinkhole was wondering if I jumped into it whether I'd land in another world or not.

"My first thought is that they want to give something an easy route out."

"Something."

"Aye, something." Ezra swallows, looking at the chicken as if it's somehow betrayed them.

"Something like what?" I fight the near-hysterical laughter that wants to bubble out of my mouth, afraid if I do, my stomach acid will come with it. "A Balrog?"

At Ezra's steady look, I stand up.

"I wasn't actually serious about that. Please tell me there's no such thing as a Balrog." Looking at Ezra is too much. All of this is too much.

"There are plenty of ancient fears hidden away in the deep," Ezra says. "Almost every culture has its monsters. We're no exception."

Something about that hits different.

Who needs monsters when we have people? How many Earthlings died in the pandemic, seven million? And there were people protesting vaccines, protesting masks, protesting the idea that they had any responsibility for the health and lives of their neighbours. Right up to the point they died alone and drowning in their own lungs.

People excel at being their own worst fears.

"Deirdre said all the elders are going to the sinkhole to fight . . . whatever is there," I say slowly.

Ezra nods. "I can see those gears turning again. What are you thinking?"

"When you travel, how do you get where you're going? I mean, how do you know where you'll end up?" It sounds like a non sequitur, but it's not.

"I don't follow," Ezra says.

"Please just answer. It's important." I feel like I've got my toes over the edge of a cliff, and I just need to know how deep the water is before I jump.

"There has to be an anchor." Ezra looks dubious about the importance of the theory behind magical teleportation, but they go on. "If you're trying to go to a particular place, you use that place, but most often, there's more to it than that."

They gesture at my earrings.

"It's really difficult to *only* want to go to a place. It's much easier to go to an idea or a person." Ezra stops. "Does that help?"

I can't tell if the lurch in my stomach is excitement or pure terror.

"It helps." I stop pacing, staring at the roast chicken that is missing a leg. "When I found you, I was looking for *you*. When I followed Deirdre, it was frustration at being left behind. And I think when Deirdre took us to that empty facsimile of Oban, the town was an illusion. There was *no one* there. How could anyone, even with magic, just disappear that many people on a whim? If they could, we'd be in deeper shit than the deep shit we're in."

"You might be right." Ezra leans forward with their elbows on their knees. They pick up the drumstick again and take a bite, chewing it as if it's cardboard instead of chicken.

For a second, I really think they've considered the problem and are just planning to eat some chicken about it, but as soon as they've choked down the meat on the drumstick, they drop the bone on the plate and grimace.

"I hate when Deirdre's right," they say. "I do feel a bit better. And I think we need to go."

"I need to do one thing first," I say.

My mind flits to my family at home, hopefully safe. I miss Fànas and hope that whatever magic I bequeathed to her will help her keep my family safe tonight if something is truly going to happen. I have no real choice but to trust that between Ezra, Deirdre, and myself, the house is as safe as anything can be.

I do have my phone with me, and after a moment of thought, I send Granaidh a text since I'm not ready to speak to the mums directly.

Bidh mi aig Deirdre a-nochd. Gaol agam oirbh. x

The moment I send the simple message off, telling Granaidh that I love her and that I'm staying with Deirdre isn't enough. If I don't make it home tonight, the last thing I will have said to the mums is to yell at them.

Or at Mum herself, anyway. But I don't want that to be Mam's last memory of me alive either.

I send Granaidh another message. *An innis sibh dham mhàthraichean gu bheil gaol agam agus orrasan? x*

I don't have it in me to wait to see if she writes back. I turn my mobile off and set it down on Deirdre's table.

It's not much better using Granaidh as a relay to tell my mums I love them, but after that row . . . I don't know what else to do.

"I'm ready," I tell Ezra. "Do you have any idea where we're going?"

"Not a clue," they say. "Which is why you're driving."

The first thing we do is retrieve the iron dagger from Deirdre's bower, where it is still sitting on the moss, looking as innocuous as a piece of slag. My blood still colours the blade. This time, I pick it up by the hilt, which is wrapped in leather.

Ezra just watches me warily. "Are you going to use that?"

"Only in the most literal sense," I say. "It's Ealasaid's dagger."

"You're going to use it to find her." Ezra sucks in a breath. "Are you sure?"

"When you were still unconscious, Gretchen said something about Ealasaid's plan. She didn't specify what it was, but if Gretchen intended to be with the other Sionnachain . . ." I trail off.

"You think Ealasaid is the one to find." Ezra nods and lets the breath out slowly. "Right. Let's do this."

I take their hand because I don't think I will manage to do anything without some reassurance that I'm not alone. Ezra pulls me toward them and kisses me, a short kiss but one so soft and full of passion that even in the heartbeat or two our lips are joined, my heart rate leaps.

Instead of making me terrified to go, the kiss does the opposite. We almost lost each other twice this week. If we don't go now, it's only a matter of time before the Sionnachain try again. I don't want to know if the third time's the charm.

Still holding Ezra's hand, I close my eyes, clutching the dagger in my other hand. Connecting to Ezra was comparatively easy. Maybe because we're soulmates, maybe because they were reaching out for me.

The threads of magic that spool around the dagger feel like they slip every time they come close to grabbing hold of anything tangible.

"It's not working," I mutter.

"Maybe it's not the dagger you need," Ezra says. "What is it you want to do?"

I'm not sure if they mean for me to answer the question, but their words click in my mind like the sensation of the final piece of a puzzle snapping into place and making the entire image make sense.

It's not simply finding Ealasaid I want to do. I want to stop her from doing whatever it is she's trying to accomplish.

I tighten my hold on Ezra's hand, once again trying to listen more than talk in my own head. This time, it's the feeling of need I focus on, the image of Ezra unconscious and bloody on the floor, the girl Ealasaid's bullies had cornered in the carpark, the weight of a star-shaped dagger stabbing me like a hole punch.

There.

With Ezra's heat next to me, it's almost as if my magic is amplified when I find what I'm looking for—those threads suddenly snap into place with double the force, and before I can adjust to the dim hope of actual success, salt spray hits me in the face a split second before Ezra and I plunge into the sea.

The water in the Sound of Mull is seldom warmer than about fifteen degrees Celsius—sixtyish Fahrenheit. Hitting it without warning freezes my lungs, and it was only due to the instinctual reflex of gasping that I got a breath before we plunged past the surface on the way down.

Ezra's hand clings onto mine, but barely, and my other hand slips on the dagger, holding to it only by the grace of my reflexive hand-clenching that I do in moments of distress.

This is not what I expected.

We both kick hard upward, bursting through the water with another gasp from both of us.

There's a ferry not far from us, and someone's pointing at the two people overboard, but even bobbing in the frigid waves, it's obvious no one else is paying attention. Clearly, my magic knows right now that being seen might save our lives. Or I haven't fully mastered my control when plunging into a cold sea.

"Ezra," I say, spitting out saltwater. "We need to get on the ferry."

They're treading water one-handed, and though the swells aren't too big, my stomach twists in fear.

Ezra nods once, shaking their head to get their hair out of their face.

"Here goes nothing," they say, and we collapse in a heap on the deck of the ferry.

I'm not sure I'll ever get used to traveling like this. The shock of moving from one place to another instantaneously is harsh on the body and the brain, but Ezra, thankfully, had the presence of mind to deposit us on the deck where passengers aren't allowed. The wind cuts through my wet school uniform. I look around, trying to orient myself with the world.

We're heading west toward the Sound of Mull's narrowest passage, which means we're either going to Craignure in Mull, Tobermory on the north side of the island, or farther out into the Outer Hebrides. There's a sailing to Barra once a day, and I think sometimes the South Uist ferry leaves from Oban if there's something amok in Mallaig. But this ferry is small, and while I can't see its name, I've been on it enough times to know it's the *Loch Frisa*, the wee poky ferry to Mull and not the larger *Isle of Mull* named for the island itself.

But then I turn eastward.

A maelstrom of magic forms a funnel above Oban.

FORTY-THREE

At first, I think we have made a horrible cock-up.

I'm not sure how no one aboard the *Loch Frisa* has noticed the tornado in Oban, but despite its enormous size and obvious force to me, it is magic. They can't see it.

It's a short ferry ride to Craignure, and as soon as Ezra and I hop over the rail onto the main deck, it's clear that's where we're headed. We must be on the morning's first ferry, which means it's a little before eight.

"Please tell me you see that," I say to Ezra, staring over the water toward Oban Harbour.

"I see it," says Ezra.

"What do we do? Is that where Deirdre is?" I don't know how anyone could stand in a torrent like that and live, immortal or not.

But it's not Ezra who answers.

From the other side of the ship comes a sound I've only heard once before and hoped to never hear again.

The shriek of the ban-sìthe from the mountaintop.

This time of day, the ferry is packed—it's the first sailing, and it's mostly tourists since the locals in Mull will be going the other way on the big ferry leaving Craignure.

The wail that rises over the wind washes out every other sound—the engines of the ferry, the waves, all of it. But it doesn't cover the screams.

“I can’t hide from her,” I yell to Ezra. “I can try, but last time I saw her, she looked right at me when no one else did.”

I don’t care if she hears me now—it’s not us she’s here for, I’m certain. It must be Ezra’s doing, but the horrid wail lessens after a moment, fading just enough that I can think.

“What do you want to do?” Ezra yells back.

My magic can’t make me invisible to her.

I cover my ears with my hands, my body tensing as I try to figure out where she is despite the consuming keening. A strange, floral smell creeps past the brine of the sea.

I can’t hide from her in my usual way . . . but maybe I can do something else.

Thinking back to An Smeòrach’s testing that one day we got a chance before everything went to hell in a hand-woven handbasket, the things that came easiest for me are all things that I have here. Right now.

We are surrounded by water, and even though I feel like a drowned rat in the bitter bite of the wind, on a ferry has always been one of the places I feel most alive.

“You have an idea,” Ezra says. “I’m in, whatever it is.”

For the first time since I looked up at the sky and saw nebulae there, I truly feel like one of the Others.

I give Ezra a wide, desperate grin. “Want to do something reckless?”

The smile that spreads across their face is all the answer I need.

Ezra is good with water but not lightning, wind but not stone, but that’s perfect—wind and water are all I need.

Neither of us have any idea what sort of battle is raging on the mainland, but with the ferry approaching Mull and a literal banshee on board, something tells me the real fight is here.

The Sionnachain miss being feared by the mortals—what better way to do that than put on a show in a place the mortals can’t escape?

The ban-sìthe lurks on the starboard side of the ferry, and as Ezra and I creep around the wall from the cabin, broken glass litters the deck under her feet. She has her back to us—and she has one hand clenched tight around the throat of a man.

The screaming has abated, but I think it's because people have fallen unconscious. Ruptured eardrums, maybe. Even peeking through the window into the cabin of the ship shows tourists collapsed over rucksacks, blood dripping from their ears. The engines of the ship have stalled, but the only reason I know is because the vibrations of the ferry deck are no longer thrumming beneath my feet.

I don't know if this will work, but we have to try.

The threads of magic leap to me, the whole of the sea beneath us. With Ezra's help, I weave mist around the whole of the ferry, so thick it may as well be soup. We drape the deck in it, and breathing it leaves water droplets clinging to the fine hairs inside my nose.

Ezra's magic joins with mine the way plying threads together makes them stronger. Together we build a singing chord of white noise that drowns out everything in sight, muting the ban-sìthe's scream.

We creep closer to her. Even with an iron dagger, I don't think we have any chance of killing her without a third person's agreement. But both Ezra and I have been debilitated by iron this week. We don't have to kill her. We just have to stop her.

A trickle tickles my ear, and I don't have to check to know it's blood.

Getting closer to her, even with mist and magic providing us some cover, means getting closer to her shriek. When we are only a bare couple of yards away, Ezra squeezes my hand, and I raise the dagger, ready to leap.

Something hits me from behind.

There is no stabbing this time, no flying through the air, but I slam into Ezra, and we both impact the corner of the ferry's cabin. I hear something crack and hope it's not a bone.

The ban-sìthe turns, bringing with her the full force of her scream.

Her mouth is still distended, gaping open impossibly far, and her teeth are somehow perfect ivory, set into pallid flesh that looks like she has spent millennia in a cave.

I don't have time to dwell on the *of course she has* that accompanies that thought, because Ealasaid is here, and even as Ezra and I right ourselves, she closes the distance between us. The ban-sìthe hovers where she is, fathomless and ancient and implacable.

The Sionnachain looked at *this* and decided she was goals?

The blade fell when I did, and I shove my foot on top of it half a second before Ealasaid slams her hand against my throat and my head against the one still-unbroken window on this side of the ferry. I hear glass crunch, the sound reverberating through my skull.

"I told you not to get in my way," Ealasaid says.

Ezra is barely upright, still weak from what she did to them, and I feign struggling enough to kick the dagger toward them. Electricity crackles in the air, almost like a real tornado is coming. Maybe one is.

Ealasaid shakes me like I weigh no more than a rag doll, and my head cracks up against the glass again, sending another crunch snaking out from the point of impact.

"I really hate bullies," I manage to force out with the pressure of her hand against my jaw, and I seize the threads of electricity floating around us, focusing all my energy on the contact of her hand on my throat.

The sìtheach flies backward into the starboard rail of the ferry, her back hitting it right in the middle with a force that would kill a mortal on impact.

Ealasaid is back on her feet in an instant, moving faster than should be possible.

"You," she says, "do not get to decide what happens here."

The ban-sìthe grabs Ealasaid by the throat.

Of all the things I expected, this was not among them.

Even Ealasaid cannot take the full force of the ban-sìthe's shriek in her face, and she writhes in the ancient immortal's grasp.

Ezra stumbles to me as the ship rocks in the waves, and they press the dagger into my hand, meeting my eyes.

They don't need to speak. I know exactly what they're thinking.

Ezra explodes into motion, leaping into the air and soaring up, up, up on black wings that vanish into the mist. Almost as soon as they fade from sight, they reappear, plummeting toward the ban-sìthe and Ealasaid with an ear-splitting cry of their own that does exactly what it is meant to do.

It draws the ban-sìthe's attention.

I dive past her the way I used to slide in softball before Dad stopped making me play. The deck abrades my leg all the way up to my thigh, but I scramble to my feet, not caring if it's inelegant, and I raise the dagger at the ban-sìthe's back.

Ealasaid sees me. Her eyes are wide and bloodshot, and I think in that moment, even she forgets that her life is not at stake. Or perhaps she thinks the dagger is meant for her and hopes agreeing with me and Ezra might spare her. I don't know, and right now, I don't care.

I see her mouth move, hear the Gaelic words in my mind.

Dèan e.

Do it.

I slam the dagger into the ban-sìthe's back as hard as I can.

My force is overkill. The dagger plunges into the ancient's back and through her bones as if I just stabbed a piñata, all papier mâché and no real resistance. My ears ring as the shriek is cut off. The sudden silence is the kind of relief that hurts.

For a moment, nothing moves except a flurry of black feathers from Ezra's dive, and then the ban-sìthe's hand crumbles, dropping Ealasaid to the deck, where she lurches to the side, gasping.

I am learning that immortal does not mean impervious.

The ban-sìthe collapses in on herself, and with a start, I see the iron blade rusting where it penetrated her skin. All that remains is a pile of moth-eaten rags and a smattering of rusty flakes and leather chunks, quickly turning muddy with the damp in the air.

I happen to be looking toward the stern of the ferry when the tornado of magic, faint now with the distance, falters and scatters like a dust devil, leaving only a shimmer behind to say it almost swallowed a town.

"There's more," croaks Ealasaid. "There will be more."

Ezra, still a raven, lights on the rail of the ship and changes back, slipping from the rail to the deck as if they've not just nearly died. The shudder in their knees belies their weakness, though, and I'm not unscathed myself. Blood tickles the side of my neck in a steady stream from my ears.

"Perhaps you'll be the one to talk sense into the Sionnachain," Ezra says softly. "If all of your ancient allies are as loyal and stalwart as this one—and stop me if I, a recent mortal and your most recent victim, am out of line—you lot may have bitten off more than you can even fit in your mouth, let alone chew."

I wish I could decipher the expression on her face. As the wind disperses the last of the mist, Ealasaid vanishes.

I take three steps and collapse to the deck. Ezra sinks beside me, leaning their head back in what is almost a lolling motion. I'm amazed they are still somewhat upright.

"What do we do about them?" I say, a vague flop of my foot meant to indicate the people onboard.

There's blood on the frame of one of the broken windows, and I don't see any sign of the man the ban-sìthe had been holding up.

"That is a good question," Ezra says, and then they lean their head forward to look to our left. "Maybe they can help."

Alighting on the stern of the ferry are more Sìthichean than I've ever seen at once except at the cèilidh, and the sight at first sends an icicle through me until I recognise An Smeòrach and Deirdre.

An Smeòrach doesn't even hide his smile, but Deirdre looks like she might pitch us both overboard.

"What part of sit and stay don't you two understand?" she says.

"My dear," says An Smeòrach. "They're not Cù Chulainn."

I have a feeling if the Hound of Culann were here, he'd have some words for the Mavis of the Sìthichean, but as far as I know, he's not. I can ask later if the legendary Irish warrior hero—human, not actually canine at all—lives in the Otherworld with us. I doubt he'd appreciate dog jokes either way.

The Others move in to do their magic, but An Smeòrach and Deirdre come straight to us.

In mere seconds, Ezra and I are bundled into a room in the tolman, clean and dry and clothed in a few seconds more, and we barely even manage a celebratory kiss before we fall asleep.

FORTY-FOUR

I wake to a message from Granaidh on my mobile, which Deirdre must have brought in whilst Ezra and I were sleeping. All she says is that she told the mums I was at Deirdre's and that I'd come home on my own from school. I am most definitely not going to school, but bless her anyway.

Besides, I've an email saying school's cancelled.

Something about a sinkhole.

Never in my mortal or immortal life (so far) did I think my eighty-year-old grandmother would be covering for me, and the feeling is a strange one.

Ezra wakes to find me lying on my back, staring at my phone, and their movement startles me into dropping it onto my face.

"Ow." My nose stings, and I sneeze.

"Sorry," says Ezra.

I roll over to look at them. "We're alive."

"A welcome discovery."

When we went to sleep, they had long hair and curves, but in the night, it seems they sleep-shifted into their other form. Their short, dark waves are tousled, and when they stretch, the flat planes of their chest tighten the snug, dark-grey T-shirt they're in.

I snuggle into their side, which seems to surprise them for the briefest of moments, but then their arms fold around me, and they pull me into their chest.

The sound of their heartbeat is pure music.

"What do you think she meant about there being more?" I ask.

"Nothing good." Ezra's chin presses against my hair, and I can feel the movement of their jaw when they speak.

I mull that over in my mind for a long stretch, just listening to Ezra breathe.

"We're . . . married," I say. "I still can't wrap my brain around that."

"Mood." Ezra's chest bounces as they laugh, a sudden movement that jostles my head.

"What's funny?"

"Thinking about the last fortnight as our honeymoon. That's funny."

I snort, because . . . well, they're not wrong.

"For real, though. Married? We're on year eighteen out of a possibly very large number." The whole *till death do us part* thing is terrifying enough for mortals.

"A year and a day, anyway," says Ezra, and then they reach for me and tilt my face up so I can see them. "But if you let me, I'll spend the next three hundred and change until that year and a day runs out showing you that the Others are capable of love."

Love.

From anyone else, hearing that after a fortnight would send me soaring out the door so fast I wouldn't *need* wings.

But Ezra's not just anybody.

"You've got a deal," I whisper.

With that, I scoot up on the bed and kiss them, and they pull me to them with a strength that seems impossible after yesterday. Just a few hours ago, we were curled up on the floor of Deirdre's bower as some potion burned the iron from Ezra's blood, and they made it through that, and we made it through the night. We made it.

Their kisses are soft, warm, and though it's them who initiated, Ezra pulls back after far too short a time.

"As much as I would like to kiss you for the rest of the day—at the very least—do you need to go home?" Ezra's hand brushes my hair back from my face, and the entire left side of my body breaks into gooseflesh.

"I guess I should," I say reluctantly. "But maybe—maybe you could come for dinner again? It might be awkward because I didn't even tell you about the awful row last night, but the mums love you, and I'd understand if it was a bit much, but—"

"I'd love to." Ezra pulls me to them again and kisses me so thoroughly, any doubts I might have about their sincerity float out of my head.

I'm a little breathless when we break apart again, and we roll out of bed, which is a novel feeling. Jason and I never managed to share a bed for a whole night, and I feel strangely shy about this being the first time I've ever done that. Though then again, I'm not sure if nine in the morning until whatever time it is now counts as "the night."

Someone has left us food, a fresh bannock with suspiciously purple dark berries in it that makes me do a thousand-yard stare for a full five seconds before I give in and slather a chunk of it with soft butter and a drizzle of honey.

"If that bramble doesn't give us a break, I'm depositing the lot of it in her bower," I mutter between bites.

Ezra just laughs.

It seems we're in An Smeòrach's home, which is likely for the best. We find him in his library, where he's actually in a white T-shirt and pyjama bottoms, which makes me wonder if we woke up in Bizarroworld instead of the Otherworld. I didn't notice in the morning that he's sporting a yellowing bruise that spans the whole of his elbow. I don't dare ask, but it looks like someone has already helped its healing along.

"Things ought to be quiet for a time," he says, his own voice soft amid the books. "I hope you will both forgive me for not understanding the scope of the danger until it was altogether too late."

"I think you can blame the Sionnachain and not yourself," I say without thinking, and then my social script kicks in, and I wince, hoping I wasn't too direct.

But An Smeòrach simply laughs that musical laugh of his.

"Yes, I've no hesitation in blaming them for everything they've done."

He looks to Ezra. "You have done very well, my prince. None among even the eldest of us would want that title, and despite the burden we have placed upon your shoulders, you wear it with aplomb. I cannot wait to see what mischief you make when you're *not* fighting for your life."

"I guess we'll see," says Ezra, and while their smile shines a bit hollow, they stand up a little straighter at the praise.

I don't think I've heard anyone address Ezra with their title until now, and from An Smeòrach at least, there seems to be no hint of mockery that I can detect.

"As for you, a chuachain, you have been treated to one of the more tumultuous introductions to immortality even in our very long history," he says to me. "I hope—and I expect—that you will receive a respite from such troubles. An Càrn Òir is already composing a ballad of the sìtheach child who stunned her enemies with starfire and slayed a ban-sìthe side by side with her soulmate prince *and* both of their would-be murderer. Perhaps we'll hear it at Oidhche Shamhna."

Oidhche Shamhna—All Hallow's Eve.

"That sounds terrifying, thank you," I say honestly, and Ezra almost chokes. But then I grin. "At least I know I can disappear in plain sight if it gets *too* terrifying."

Just before we leave, An Smeòrach calls out, "A chuachain—do tell Sìne that Dòmhnall Binn sends his very best."

I spin around on my heel to ask what he means, but An Smeòrach's books on their shelves are the only things left in the room.

Sìthichean.

❧

Though we don't technically need to hoof it, Ezra and I walk from the tolman to my house. It's nice just to see the forest with them, holding hands and pointing out lovely things like the fairy ring of mushrooms near a fallen snag and, to my delight, an enormous owl that swoops across our path. I watch it longingly until it soars out of sight, and Ezra watches me with a look every bit as yearning on their face.

Too soon, we are on familiar ground. I think even Otherworld magic was no match for my wrecked school uniform after what we put it through last night, so I'm wearing brown tweed trousers and a cream-coloured jumper that makes me feel like I'm wearing the tolman walls. The boots they left out for me are the most comfortable things I've ever put on my feet. Their deep brown leather shows itself to be proof against the wet of a West Highland forest walk, and even if they weren't a gift, I'd be tempted to steal them. I'm sure stealing from the Sìthichean would prove much more fun as one of them than as a hapless human.

Ezra walks me to the back garden, hovering out of sight, but I hear a plaintive meow and turn to see Fànas in the windowsill of the kitchen. At least I think it's Fànas.

"We weren't gone for twenty months instead of twenty hours, by any chance, were we?" I ask.

Ezra stares at the cat. "Erm, no. But that cat is definitely bigger than when we left her."

Not sure how we'll explain *that* to the family.

"I'll see you tonight, yeah?" Ezra says. "You're sure the mums won't mind?"

"I'll let you know if they do, and you can just . . . come over after dinner and hide in my room." I grin. "I think I can manage to keep anyone from hearing us now."

"Naughty," says Ezra with a wink, and my face gets hot.

"I meant talking." My voice cracks on the words. "I mean, I think I meant talking."

"We've all the time in the world," Ezra says.

They kiss me, and their lips somehow taste like dewdrops, and when I open my eyes to them flying away into the many-starred light of day, I can't help but smile.

Going inside, however, is another matter.

Fànas is in a right state. She's at least twice as big as she was when I saw her last, which isn't mahoosive—yet—but it is unmissable in a kitten that fit in the palm of my hand just a few days ago.

"Cà' eil Granaidh?" I ask Fànas, because Granaidh's stories aren't on the telly, and the door to her room is open, so she's clearly not in there.

Granaidh's wheelchair is at the foot of the stairs up to my side of the house, and that delivers a clenching tension to my gut.

"Granaidh?" I call out. I hate the tinny tone to my voice.

"Shuas an-seo!" comes the answer from . . . upstairs.

Alarmed, I climb the stairs two at a time, Fànas under foot with every step to the point that I almost fall *up* the stairs and only narrowly avoid stepping on the cat at least once.

Granaidh is lying on her back on my bed, staring at the ceiling. I know she's awake, since she just answered, and she does turn her head to look at me.

"Feasgar math," I venture, greeting her.

She pats the bed next to her. "Trobhad, a ghràidh."

I go to the foot of the bed and crawl onto it, lying down beside her.

Granaidh's quiet for a long moment. "Chuala mi na thuirt thu an-dè. Na biodh dragh ort gum bi do mhàthraichean ro chruaidh ort mu dheidhinn. Tha fhios gu bheil mo nighean danarra gu leòr ach tha agus mise."

I swallow, and I don't know what to say. I'm glad she doesn't reckon the mums will flay me for my tirade yesterday, but I still feel afraid that Mum will end up the one reason the whole house doesn't speak Gaelic at home.

But as Granaidh said, my mum may be stubborn, but she is her mother's daughter—and I'm the next generation of muley Camerons.

"Tapadh leibh, a seanmhair," I say to Granaidh, thanking her after a long pause. Then, haltingly, I confess something that's been on my mind. "Cha d' fhuair mi a' Ghàidhlig bho ghlùin. Tha . . . cianalas orm."

It's close to what I said to Mum—she's the one who got the Gaelic at her own mother's knee, not me. But to Granaidh, it's not anger. Just longing for something that didn't happen and now never will.

Granaidh reaches over and pats my hand. Her hands are always so soft, her skin almost unreal. She doesn't answer, only gets up, slowly but waving off my attempt to help, and she braces herself against the slanted ceiling to make it to the door.

"Theagamh nach d' fhuair, a ghaoil," she says. "Ach gheibh thu bhom ghlùin-sa a-nis."

Perhaps you didn't learn it then, my love. But you'll learn from me now.

When she looks back at me, I'm half propped on my elbow, blinking back tears.

She looks at Fànas, who is sitting primly on the stool at the vanity, watching the both of us.

"Is mòr a' phiseag seo," says Granaidh. "Cat-sìthe a th' innte, gun teagamh."

With that, she turns to go, leaving me gaping at her for naming Fànas precisely what she is.

"Nach fuirich sibh mionaid, a seanmhair?" I say, sitting up so quickly I bonk my head on the ceiling, which I think gets Granaidh's attention more than me asking her to wait a second.

I wince, rubbing at my head. Few too many knocks on the noggin' in the past few days.

"Siuthad, ma-tà. Tha na stoiridhean gu bhith ann." Granaidh taps her watch to emphasise that I'm about to make her miss her stories.

"Deagh dhùrachdan bho Dhòmhnall Binn," I say, remembering what An Smeòrach told me to pass on, warm wishes from Sweet Donald, who I certainly don't know. So I ask. "Cò esan?"

Granaidh starts and barks a laugh that makes Fànas twitch. "Cò esan?" She laughs again, and then she sniffs, shaking her head. "Smeòrach Chloinn Dòmhnaill, Dòmhnall Mac Dhòmhaill, leannan agam latha bha siud. Leannan nach maireann."

My brain tries to parse what she's just said.

The Mavis of Clan MacDonald, one Donald MacDonald.

Granaidh's lover, once upon a time.

Who no longer lives.

I hop off the bed and hurry to the door. Granaidh sits on the top stair, scooting down to the next with as much dignity as anyone can.

"Tha e beò, a seanmhair," I say and then immediately want to shove my fist in my mouth. What if I'm not supposed to tell her An Smeòrach is alive?

She turns, peering up at me. "Och, tha fhios a'm," Granaidh says. She goes back to her task of scooting down the stairs on her bum. "Draoidheachd gu leòr air a' Ghàidhealtachd, a Chamshroin. Mar a b' àbhaist."

With that, she disappears from sight, and after a minute or two, I hear the telly turn on.

I go back to my room and shut the door.

My heart feels ready to burst.

Fànas hops up on the bed when I sit back down, and her purr rumbles through the air.

"You looked out for them, didn't you?" I say to her, to which she mews, a sound that creeps closer to a meow than a mew.

I stay upstairs half-dozing with Fànas until I hear the mums' car in the drive. I'm surprised when almost immediately afterward, I hear footsteps on the stairs.

Mum appears in the doorway, looking like she hasn't slept in days.

"Thank you for texting Granaidh last night," she says softly. "But I wish you wouldn't have run off."

"I'm sorry, Mum."

"May I come in?"

I nod, and she does, but she only ventures as far as the stool at the vanity, where she sits.

"It's hard for me," she says without further preamble. "My Gaelic's not as good as yours, and soon it won't be as good as your mam's either. But you made me realise last night that it's hardly an excuse. Is mar sin, nì mi mo dhìcheall."

Her words soothe me, and Fànas leaps from the bed and goes to Mum, rubbing against her ankles. I don't think I've yet seen the kitten display such affection toward her, and I think it surprises Mum as much as it surprises me.

Mum said she'll do her best, so I can too. "'S e a nì sinn uile—ar dìcheall."

We will all do our best.

Mum comes over and kisses me on the forehead without another word, but then she stands back on her heels. "Thuirt Granaidh gum bi Ezra a' tighinn a-nochd."

"Bithidh," I affirm.

"Math fhèin. Tòisichidh mi dìnnear."

Mum turns to go start dinner, and it's not until she's gone back downstairs that I realise I never told Granaidh Ezra was coming for dinner.

And what's more, there are no windows in my bedroom that overlook the back garden.

But she told Mum they'll be here.

A suspicion grows, but I set it to the side for now. Instead, I take a deep breath alone in my room, and I open the dormer window as wide as it will go.

My phone buzzes with a text. From Eilidh, Grace's sister.

I'm so sorry for what Grace said to you. I don't know what got into her, but she's mortified and she's got the fear about telling you herself. Whole town went mad this week. Let us make it up to you?

I text back a simple *I understand—chocolate shop after school when school's back on?*

Then I put the phone aside and turn it all the way off. Everyone I need right now is right here.

The sky is clear, and the sun is high. Soon, I'll go help Mum with dinner. Ezra will come join us, and we'll start something altogether new. We'll live between two worlds, walking in both of them.

For right now, though, I lean on my windowsill in the bright light of day and lose myself among my millions of stars.

AUTHOR'S NOTE

A chàirdean còire,

Thank you so much for reading All the Stars in the Daylight Sky.

This book has meant so much to me since I wrote it in the summer of 2021, even more so as my life came to parallel Cam's with the loss of my best friend Rekka Jay in the summer of 2023.

Rekka was one of my biggest cheerleaders as I wrote this book. They loved it, loved Cam and Ezra, and believed in my writing in a way that few ever have. Rekka was my stalwart champion. A true love. The type of friend who changes you forever.

The world has changed much in the past four years, and much of that has made things scarier for many of us. It can be easy to forget that we all share this world and that humanity has only survived because we work together with far more regularity than we tear each other apart. The ties that bind us are not so easily broken as some would like us to believe; our truest strength is community, mutual aid, and the commitment to protect one another. We cannot control the actions of the powerful few, but we are, always, rooted in the strength of the many when we remember exactly who we want to be.

Cam's story—and Ezra's—is very personal for me in a way my other YA books haven't quite touched. This book is the first I've set in my homeland, going as far as to place it on the shores of Loch Awe where, generations ago, my own family made their homes and lives in Gaelic Argyll.

Cam isn't me, but she's got a lot of me in her. Like Cam, I'm agender and autistic. Many of the folkloric tales about changelings ring true to me; there are many arguments to be made that people like me (us) were seen as touched by the Otherworld, changelings, different. I remember reading *The Gaelic Otherworld* (John Gregorson Campbell) in sections about changelings and seeing myself reflected back in a strange way that made me feel, perhaps incongruently, even more at home in my own culture.

Also like Cam, I have had an international life and much upheaval. While Cam's dad isn't my dad (Hi, Dad and Jo Ellen!), I did put him in the same city where I was born and where my own father lives. My mums, while not exactly Mum and Mam (Hi, NeeNee and Carrie!), love me with the same ferocity. My other three parents share complexities as well. All seven of the adults who participated in raising me or who chose to be my parents ended up in Cam's family in glimpses.

Much of what I gave Cam was a sense of not-belonging I've had my entire life. Part of having moved forty-five times is that it's very difficult to put down roots. It took me twenty years to earn my right to live in Scotland forever; Cam, thankfully, doesn't have that struggle ahead.

The Gaelic in the book is my language, the language of a fluent speaker but not a native one, with all the messy broken connections and chains that entails. Our language is under extreme threat, despite the passage of the Scottish Languages Bill literally as I write this note. It will take more than words to keep her alive, more than political acts of symbolism, more than official status, more than laws, more than a wish. More than generations working together. But it's a start on a long road of recovery.

If the language calls to you in any way, fàilte. You can find an enormous amount of support and resources that didn't exist twenty years ago when I first moved here. Online: LearnGaelic.scot, Speak Gaelic, Faclair.com. I know many of the humans who worked on the Gaelic Duolingo course, which is a great first blas (taste) of the language—but don't trust online translators to get things right. ;) If you want in-person or distance-learning courses, check out Sabhal Mòr Ostaig, the Gaelic college in Skye, and Ceòlas in South Uist. Both do immersion courses that put our beautiful language in context of its people, our community, and our culture.

ACKNOWLEDGMENTS

Mo cheud mìle taing dham choimhearsnachd Ghàidhlig is càirdean còire a bhios a' seinn còmhla rium, air an àrd-ùrlar còmhla rium, ag ionnsachadh dhomh ar cànan, gam cheartachadh, a' cur taic rim sgrìobhadh is rim cheòl, agus a bhios gam thogail a h-uile latha ann an dòighean fad is farsaing gu crìoch an t-saoghail—chan fhaigh duine craic nas fheàrr na sibhse:

My sincerest thanks to my Gaelic community and loved ones who have sung with me, performed with me, laughed with me, taught me our language, corrected my errors, supported my writing and music, and are generally the best craic on Earth:

Ceòlraidh Ghàidhlig Ghlaschu (The GG), Bùrach, Còisir Alba, Còisir Ghàidhlig Baile Ghobhainn, Còisir Ghàidhlig an Òbain, Còisir Ghàidhlig nan Loch, Còisir Ghàidhlig Sgìr a' Bhac, Comhairle nan Leabhraichean, Coinneach MacThomais, Iseabail Nic an t-Sagairt, Joy Dunlop, Riona is Megan Nic 'IlleBhàin, an Dotair Alasdair Mac 'IlleBhàin, Sìleas Nic na Ceàrdaich, Coinneach MacRàth, Babs NicGriogair, Iseabail Mhoireach, Seumas MacFhionnlaigh agus Zara Rudow, Robbie MacLeòid, Alice Nic a' Bhatair, Fiona Ross, Calum agus Izzy Ros, Calum Rosach, Mairead Rowan, Catrìona NicRàth, Dòmhnall Iain Mac 'IlleDhuinn, Kerrie Cheanadach, Alison NicRàth, Lisa Robertson, Catrìona Lexy Chaimbeul, Seumas MacLeòid, Magnus Greumach, Mairead na h-Òganaich, Daibhidh MacGriogair, Màrtainn agus Fionnghal 'ic a' Bhàillidh, Iain MacCarmaig, Ryan Johnston, Jonathan Fairgrieve, Ronnie Moireach, Angus Mac a' Ghobhainn, Cloudy MacLeòid, Eachann MacEachairne agus Heather Nic 'IlleDhuinn, Effie Rowan, Coinneach MacLeòid agus Pàdruig MacCuibhein, Lana Pheutan, agus Josie Duncan.

To Sìleas, I hope you'll forgive me for borrowing the Oban Gaelic Choir—and the spot of Gaelic reader from Christine!—and that you'll perhaps get a wee bit of joy knowing that I gave "Mairead" your joyous smile and energy nonetheless. I tried to take good care of them even in my alternate Oban. Thank you for being a light in our Gaelic choir world and for being my friend.

To KT and Iseabail, I hope *you'll* forgive me for not transplanting the GG into Argyll! You both have acted with such warmth and kindness in my life, and I'm truly grateful for the welcome and the community that you have shown me in the past eight years in the GG and beyond. I'm honoured to be your friend, and I love you both. Life's too short not to be a mushy wee sap. (Kenny, I can see you blushing from here, ya legend!)

Those who knew our friend Gordon McKeeve will recognise glimmers of him in An Smeòrach. Gordon used to sing "Smeòrach Chloinn Dòmhnaill" at cèilidhs, and I thought it fitting that he live on in my own personal legend, though keen eyes will note some obvious differences to our beloved Gordon too. (He and I both shared that wee wonky pinky!) Gordon is known, among Gaels, as the greatest mòd gold medallist who never was. A tenor with a voice that could stop you in your tracks, he was the very first to welcome me when I joined the GG in 2017. The years spent singing with him right by my side feel formative in a way I find hard to articulate.

The warmest spirit and the fiercest friend, Gordon passed with cancer in 2020. You can hear Còisir Alba, the Alba Choir, singing "Cumha na Cloinneadh" at Eurovision Choir's 2019 competition, with Gordon among us. While Gordon never competed for a gold medal, he won the silver pendant at the Royal National Mòd, and his voice echoes through the memories of our community. I will never forget hearing him precent Psalm 65, which Gaelic choirs know as "French," in the great cathedral in Salzburg, Austria in 2018. You can hear him sing with the GG on a 1993 recording from Lios Mòr Records. His voice sang with purest beauty. It is one of the honours of my life to have known him and sung with him.

I gave An Smeòrach Gordon's kindness, his eyes, his care, his warmth, and his voice. No one truly dies so long as their spirit lives on in us.

Many thanks also to Sara Megibow, Susan Dobinick, Suzy Krogulski, Kerry McManus, Chelsea Abdullah, Paul Eckersley, Suzanne Lander, Nancy Seitz, and the teams at Astra Books for Young Readers and GMC Publications for making this novel happen. Nancy and Suzanne, as someone who's worked as a copy editor myself, I have to especially thank you for your care and excellent work with all my Gaelic and Scots sentences!

All the Stars in the Daylight Sky was the twenty-first novel I wrote, and at the time of writing this note, I've just finished my fortieth. This business has tried my patience and my resolve for half my life in myriad ways, and I would not have kept going were it not for the support of my family (biological and chosen) and friends scattered around this rock:

Rekka Jay, who I miss with every beat of my heart; Bud and Pat and Matt for loving me with open hearts after we lost Rekka; NeeNee and Carrie for choosing to be my mums; Dad and Jo Ellen for finding me after thirty years and loving me a lifetime's worth every day since; my sister Jayne, the bravest woman I've ever known; fellow queers down the pub; KT Hanna, Penny Tanous, Mairead Rowan, Seumas Mac Fhionnlagh, Zara Rudow, Oona Dooley, and Sarah Glenn Marsh for keeping me sane; Larz Yerian for your steadfast friendship through hell and back; the WAWDGISHWHESTFQ crew, ten years on and going strong; Jenney OC for always snapping up my books; Amal El-Mohtar for your light-bringing joy and friendship no matter how infrequently we meet; Tao Wong for being a stalwart comrade; Jess Lunn for the reminder that cities don't have to mean neighbours are strangers; Mark Carver for holding my hand in the darker times; Ryan Johnston, Jonathan Fairgrieve, and Iain Cormack for showing me care when I needed it most; Joy Dunlop for epitomising your name and holding space for me; Sarah Loch and Sara Nordja for always cheering me on.

My love and gratitude to all. Knowing you makes life worth living.